Wings Over the Mountains

Book 1

THE LAST GOOD MAN

JERRY PETERSON

WINDSTAR PRESS

This book is a work of fiction. Names, characters, places and incidents are the products of the author's imagination or are used fictitiously. All characters in this book have no existence outside the imagination of the author and have no relationship to anyone, living or dead, bearing the same name or names. All incidents are pure invention from the author's imagination. Any resemblance to actual events or locales or persons, living or dead, is entirely coincidental.

All Rights Reserved. Except for use in any review, the reproduction or utilization of this work in whole or in part in any form by any electronic, mechanical or other means, now known or hereafter invented, including xerography, photocopying or recording, or in any information or retrieval system, is forbidden without the prior written permission of both the publisher and copyright owner of this book.

Copyright 2014 c Jerry Peterson
Windstar Press

All Rights Reserved.

ISBN-13: 978-1491266823
ISBN-10: 1491266821

Cover Design c Dawn Charles at
bookgraphics.wordpress.com

March 2014

Printed in the U.S.A.

DEDICATION

To Marge, my wife and first reader.

To the members of my writers group, *Tuesdays with Story*, sharp-eyed readers and writers who demand the very best of me in my storytelling and craft of writing.

To a friend and one-time colleague who prefers to remain unnamed.

ACKNOWLEDGMENTS

This is the seventh book I've published as indie author, the second under my Windstar Press imprint.

We indie authors depend on a lot of people to make our stories and books the best that they can be. Tennessean, who now lives in Missouri, Dawn Charles of Book Graphics, cover designer extraordinaire, worked with me on this volume. She provided the cover.

A knock-out cover is vital to grabbing potential readers searching for a good book to buy. Nearly as important are the words on the back cover that say this book is a great read. For those words, I turned to New York Times bestseller Jacquelyn Mitchard. Oprah Winfrey made Jacquelyn a million-seller when she selected Jacquelyn's *Deep End of the Ocean* as her first Oprah Book Club selection.

I always close with a note of appreciation to all librarians around the country. They, like you and your fellow readers who have enjoyed my James Early mysteries, my AJ Garrison crime novels, and my short story collections have been real boosters. Without them and you, there would be no reason to write.

ALSO BY JERRY PETERSON

Early's Fall, a James Early Mystery, book 1. . . . "If James Early were on the screen instead of in a book, no one would leave the room."
– Robert W. Walker, author of *Children of Salem*

Early's Winter, a James Early Mystery, book 2 . . . "Jerry Peterson's *Early's Winter* is a fine tale for any season. A little bit Western, a little bit mystery, all add up to a fast-paced, well-written novel that has as much heart as it does darkness. Peterson is a first-rate storyteller. Give *Early's Winter* a try, and I promise you, you'll be begging for the next James Early novel. Spring can't come too soon."
– Larry D. Sweazy, Spur-award winning author of *The Badger's Revenge*

The Watch, an AJ Garrison Crime Novel, book 1 . . . "Jerry Peterson has written a terrific mystery, rich in atmosphere of place and time. New lawyer A.J. Garrison is a smart, gutsy heroine."
– James Mitchell, author of *Our Lady of the North*

Rage, an AJ Garrison Crime Novel, book 2 . . . "Terrifying. Just–terrifying. Timely and profound and even heartbreaking. Peterson's taut spare style and truly original voice create a high-tension page turner. I really loved this book."
– Hank Phillippi Ryan, Agatha, Anthony and Macavity winning author

"Jerry Peterson's new thriller, *Iced*, is a thrill-a-minute ride down a slippery slope of suspense and shootouts. Engaging characters, spiffy dialogue, and non-stop action make this one a real winner."
– Michael A. Black, author of *Sleeping Dragons*, a Mack Bolan Executioner novel

The Last Good Man

Book One
CHAPTER 1

Big damn place

PAPPY BROWN PORED over the printout of his classes, the classes that were about to take a shark-sized bite out of his bank account.

"Gawd, ya could sure stack a lot of hay in here, couldn't ya?"

The voice came from behind Pappy. He twisted around.

There stood a tall, gawky kid with no chin and an Adam's apple the size of a small boy's fist. The youth gazed up, gape-mouthed, into the superstructure of the University of Tennessee's arena high above the basketball court where several thousand students had cued up to pay their fees, the buzz of their multiple conversations sounding like bees mumbling around a hive.

The kid swiveled his head, as if he were measuring by eye the length of the arena. "This is absolutely one humongous place."

"You from the farm?" Pappy asked.

The youth brought his gaze down to meet Pappy's. "Yeah, James Dempsey, freshman. From Bucksnort."

"First time here, huh?"

"You got that right."

Pappy extended his hand. "Willie Joe Brown, Maryville. I'm a freshman, too, the world's oldest."

Dempsey stared at him, perplexed, as he shook Pappy's hand. "Really?"

"Sixty-five. I could be your grampaw."

"I guess you could."

The lines moved. The two shuffled forward, Pappy in his plumber's twills, Dempsey in cutoffs and a T-shirt that read 'Aggies do it in the cornfield.'

"You got a major picked out, James?"

"Junior. Call me Junior. James is my dad. Agriculture engineering. How about you?"

"Not the damnedest idea."

"Why's that?"

"Well, I'll tell ya, Junior, I did something stupid. I sold my business and then discovered I didn't have nothing to do anymore other than fish and drink beer. And that made my granddaughter mad. She insisted–insisted–I find something better to do."

"Take some classes?"

"'College,' she said, 'Grandpops, you always wanted to do that.' I guess I did, so here I am."

"That's some story."

"Isn't it, though? So you're goin' for ag engineering, I bet that's a load of tough classes."

"Oh, I've got a three point nine-seven through four years of high school. I think I can handle it."

"Hate to remember what I got in high school. Of course that was back when Thomas Edison was still trying to invent the light bulb."

Dempsey's eyes widened.

Pappy winked. "I'm pullin' your leg"

"If you didn't have the grades, how'd you get in?"

"Somebody took pity on an old duffer."

"You're puttin' me on."

"No, they gave me points for my time in the Army."

"My great-uncle was in the Army. My dad was Navy."

"Next, please."

A new voice. Pappy swiveled to it and discovered two things: the voice belonged to a pleasant-looking woman in a blue blazer with a University of Tennessee crest on the breast pocket, and there was a hint of rose water about her, a contrast to the smell of sweat that permeated the arena. Pappy handed his papers on. "William Joseph Brown Junior," he said. He again winked at Dempsey when he said 'Junior.'

The woman read down the printout. "Everything looks to be in order. Are you changing any classes?"

"No, ma'am." Pappy took in her name badge, then added, "Bernice."

"It's Missus Lippmann to you."

"Pardon?"

"My name is Missus Lippmann. I work in the Registrar's Office. If you should have any problems with your classes in the first three weeks, I want you to come see me."

"I guess I can certainly do that."

"How are you paying? Cash, check, credit card? Are you on scholarship?"

"Oh gosh no, no scholarship. A check."

"I should warn you, if your check has the least bit of rubber in it, I will send the campus police to have a chat with you."

Missus Lippmann smiled.

Is she joshing? Pappy took out his checkbook. He opened it on the table and bent down to write. "This sure is a lot of money."

"Yes, and I appreciate every dollar of it. This is my house payment for the next several months."

"You get it?"

"You don't think I give these checks over to the university, do you?"

"Ah-ha. Do I get a money-back guarantee on my classes?"

"You'll have to talk to the president about that."

"Our former governor?"

"Lamar Alexander, that's right."

"I can do that, see, I did the plumbing at his momma's house."

"In Maryville?"

"That's right."

"You're a plumber, then?"

"I was. I sold my business to my son, so now here I am, a spankin'-new student at big UT." Pappy tore out his check. He handed it to the registrar clerk.

She stamped PAID on his class schedule and on the duplicate which she kept. "Your check will be your receipt. If I don't see you sooner, I'll see you back here at the beginning of the spring semester."

He gave a thumbs up, then turned away to find Dempsey waiting on him. "June, my bank account's considerably lighter."

"My dad's, too."

"You been by the bookstore yet?"

"That's my next stop."

"Well, what say we go together?"

"Fine by me."

Pappy and Dempsey hiked up the bleachers toward the exit. Before they got half way, someone called out, "Grandpops!"

He swung back.

A young woman waved to Pappy from below, in the pay-tuition line.

He returned the wave. "I mentioned my granddaughter, that's Caroline. Come on, I'll introduce you."

Pappy trotted back down the bleachers to the floor. There he elbowed his way through a claque of students, his fellow freshman close in his wake. "Hang with me, boy. You're about to meet the greatest twenty-one-year-old gal of your life."

"Hey, watch it, old man," someone barked.

Pappy stopped. He pivoted and stared up into the glowering face of a thick-set student some eight inches taller and one-hundred fifty pounds heavier than he.

Dempsey pushed in. "Sorry," he said to the other student and hustled Pappy on.

Pappy twisted back. "I can hold my own."

"I don't think so. Do you who that is?"

"No and I don't give a dingly damn. He called me an old man."

"You are."

"Well, I'm not that old."

"That's Bo Smith. Mean as they come."

"Right tackle for the Vols?"

"That's him."

"Junior, this time I do give a dingly damn. Thanks."

Pappy and Dempsey continued on until they broke through the last knot of students that separated them from Pappy's granddaughter and the cluster of young women with her.

"Caroline," Pappy called out.

Caroline Brown gave a head jerk in the direction from which Pappy and Dempsey had come. "What was that all about?"

"Guess I stepped on that fella's foot back there. Junior thought he was going to pound me into the floor for it."

She shifted her backpack. "I'm sorry I stood you up, Grandpops. There was business at the sorority. Everybody, this is my grandpops. Be nice to him. He's the new kid here, a freshman."

"Hi," said one of the girls in the line near Caroline. "I'm Beth."

"I'm Sandra." That introduction came from a beefy brunette whose smile, Pappy thought, could melt an ice sculpture at a wedding reception.

"I'm Ellie," said a blond cheerleader-type. She gave Pappy's hand a playful pat. "Ellie Esther Emma Easterling."

He patted her hand in return. "I'll bet your pop had fun coming up with that name. Friend of mine, when I was your age, was Karen Kathleen Kelley Katz. We called her Kitty."

"Oh, that's clever."

"It's true."

"Well, Ellie is my mom's name. Esther comes from a great aunt. Emma was my grandmother on my mother's side, and Easterling I inherited from Daddy."

"Ellie, that is a proud name." Pappy hauled Dempsey in. "I'd like you all to meet James Junior Dempsey, a tall drink of water from Bucksnort, Tennessee."

Puzzlement nudged an eyebrow up on Easterling's forehead. "I don't think I've heard of that."

Dempsey gave a one-shouldered shrug. "It's between Nashville and Memphis."

"Me, I'm from Goodno, Florida, way out in the swamps of the Everglades."

Pappy grinned. "I've done a little fishing in the Gulf off Naples."

"Naples, yes, Goodno's inland from there, about fifty miles."

"So, Ellie, why are you way up here rather than down at, say, Florida State?"

"My daddy. He's a UT graduate, Nineteen Sixty-One. Met my momma here."

"Ahh."

"They said this is the only place they'd ever let me go to college." Easterling patted Pappy's hand again. "Your Carrie kinda looks after me. We're in a lot of the same classes and the Theta Delts."

Sandra squeezed into the conversation. "Mister Brown, did you know we elected Caroline our president last night?"

Pappy turned to his granddaughter. He made a flourish with his hand and knelt before her. "Madam President."

Easterling giggled to the others. "Isn't he the cutest?"

"Grandpops, come on, you're embarrassing me."

Pappy pushed himself up. He took Caroline's hands in his. "I'm proud of you, Carrie girl."

Another girl nudged Caroline. "Move up. The line's moving."

Pappy let go of her hand. "You better go along. Junior and me, we're on the way to the bookstore. We gotta buy us a pile of books so we can do us some larnin' at this hyar university."

Another giggle rippled out of Easterling. "Oh, you're really cute, Mister Brown."

"Call me Pappy." He pointed to the name stitched above his shirt pocket as he backed away.

"Get used books," Caroline called over the crowd. "You'll save money."

"After what I left at the pay window, I need to do that."

"You'll come over for supper?"

"To your sorority house? You'll let a man in?"

"I'm the president now. I can do that."

"How about Junior?"

"Sorry. But he's invited to our first kegger."

Pappy slapped his forehead. "I'm shocked, Caroline, shocked. You drink in that place?"

"Grandpops."

"What time?"

"Six. Sharp."

He waved, then he and Dempsey plowed away through the mass of students waiting to pay their tuition and fees. "Your grandfather's cute as a button," they heard Sandra say. "Can I take him home to Goose Horn?"

Dempsey shook his head. "Pappy, you sure cut a swath with the girls."

"That's me, a devil on wheels."

"You got a wife, don't you? What's she say about this?"

"Very little."

"Why's that?"

"She's a resident at the Our Savior Baptist Cemetery."

"I'm sorry."

"Don't be. It's been nineteen years." Pappy, with Dempsey soldiering beside him, clipped up the steps toward the second-level exit. "We each only get so much time on this old earth, so we've got us a duty to enjoy it."

"My dad would like knowing you."

"Junior, if he's a wide-eyed wonder like you, I look forward to meeting him. Tell your folks to come up for Homecoming."

Chapter 2

Company at the Theta Delta Theta House

PAPPY JABBED the doorbell button of the Theta Delta Theta house, a white, three-story mansion that bore a curious resemblance to Tara of 'Gone With the Wind' movie fame.

While he waited, he listened to the chimes from the university's carillon play 'The Tennessee Waltz.' Pappy checked his watch—6 p.m. He patted his foot for a moment, then jabbed the doorbell button again.

This time the door opened. Sandra Kroizer, in a tight-fitting evening gown that showed well her generous proportions, stood there, her hair in a French twist.

Pappy sucked in a breath. "I didn't know this was formal. I could have gone home and put on a suit."

Kroizer took his arm. She drew him into the foyer. "You look just fine."

"In my baggy britches and my UT muscle shirt? I want you to know Junior made me buy this shirt. Mine's in the truck. I can get it."

"Mister Brown, you're fine. This dinner is only formal for the girls. It's our first time back on campus. Come on, let me show you around."

They strolled into what would have been the front parlor when the house was a private residence.

Kroizer flipped a hand toward the center of the room. "A couple years ago, when I was a freshman, we took out the wall between the front and back parlors to make this really big living room."

Pappy marveled at the size of it.

"A committee of alumni raised money for us. They bought the French provincial furniture we have here. Personally, I wanted beanbag couches."

"Do your dates ever sit on this furniture?"

"Very lightly, Mister Brown. If couples want to get passionate, we, uhmm, we find someplace else."

"Like the backseat of a car."

"How would you know about that?"

"Sandra, I've logged a lot of backseat time, but that was long before you were a glimmer in your parents' eyes."

Photographs covered one wall of the living room. Pappy went over for a better look.

Kroizer followed him. "Each year, we take a formal picture of the membership. If you count them, there are only twenty pictures up there. We retire the oldest picture when we put the newest one up. Here's last year's."

Pappy peered at the Theta Delta Thetas of Nineteen Eighty-Seven. He tapped the face of one of the members. "That's you, but why in the back row?"

"Haven't you noticed? I'm the giant economy size. Photographers always hide us big girls in the back."

"But you're so pretty. That's not fair."

"Carrie said you were a kind person."

"Speaking of my granddaughter, where is she in the picture?"

Kroizer leaned in until her shoulder touched Pappy's. She put her index finger on a person in the third row, near the end. "That's Carrie. She was historian last year, so she really should be in front with our officers. But she was late, dashed in, you know, and that's where she ended up."

"So this year she'll be in the front, huh?"

"Yes."

"How about you?"

"Me, too. They elected me corresponding secretary. It's a paperwork job, but it gets me to the national convention. Pretty good for a girl from Goose Horn."

Pappy glanced at Kroizer. "Where's that, anyway?"

"Macon County, not too far from the Kentucky border. Just a little south of Red Boiling Springs."

"We've got the damnedest names for towns in our state, don't we?"

"Well, I could have grown up in Difficult. That's where my momma's from."

"One last question." Pappy again peered at the Theta Delt picture. "Who's this old gal, sittin' here with the officers?"

A new voice answered. "That old gal is me."

Pappy and Kroizer swung around, Kroizer blushing. "I didn't hear you come in, Doctor Berry."

"Caroline sent me to get you two. They're serving."

Gray showed at the woman's temples. Glasses hung from a slender gold chain around her neck. She wore a red jacket and skirt that Pappy guessed were not off the rack at J.C. Penney's.

The woman held out her hand. "Ori-Anna Berry, Theta Delta Theta advisor."

Pappy shook her hand. "You wouldn't be related to Wilson Berry, would you, from down by Pistol Creek?"

"His daughter-in-law. I married Wilson Junior."

"Wilsy? I haven't seen him in years."

"Neither have I."

"I'm sorry."

"Don't be." Berry pulled at her sleeve, adjusting the cuff. "Come in, dinner's waiting. You wouldn't want your Veal Parmesan to get cold."

"Oh, you butchered the fatted calf for supper."

"Carrie warned me you'd say something like that. At least the chef didn't make blood soup or head cheese."

"Now that would have been good eats."

Berry slipped her arm through one of Pappy's arms and Kroizer the other. Together, they escorted the world's oldest freshman into a long, formal dining room where crystal chandeliers cast a soft light over the tables of Theta Delts. They rose and applauded their guest.

Berry leaned close to Pappy. "You see, you were expected."

"Oh Lord."

"Well, the muscle shirt is a bit informal."

"When Carrie asked me over, I thought it would be just she and me, and burgers and beans in the kitchen."

"Theta Deltas don't do burgers and beans."

Pappy gave a queen of England wave in recognition of the applause. Halfway down the room he stopped and squeezed the hand of Ellie Esther Emma Easterling.

Caroline Brown, at the head table, pulled out an empty chair.

"Kid," Pappy said when he got there and sat down, "you really know how to embarrass the old man."

She ran a hand over his buzz cut. "Grandpops, this is no big deal."

"But you're all so dressed up."

She sat next to him. "I'm sorry I didn't tell you. But I figured you'd beg off if I did and go to Taco Pete's."

"I'm not that desperate."

Berry slipped into the chair on the other side of Pappy. "Is there something wrong with Taco Pete's?"

"Not if you like heartburn."

Caroline interrupted. "Doctor Berry, the hotter the sauce the better for Grandpops."

"Then he'll love Chimmichunga's. You'll have to take him. Mister Brown, smoke will come out of your ears."

"Pappy. Call me Pappy." He reached for his napkin as a hand set a plate laden with veal, cheese potatoes, and glazed vegetables in front of him. Pappy looked up. "Junior."

"Mister Brown, isn't this great? My new roomie waiters here. He got sick this afternoon and asked me to take his place."

"Mister Dempsey, you're gettin' paid?"

"Absolutely."

"Your white jacket there seems a bit short in the sleeves."

"My roomie's not got as long of arms as I have, and they didn't have any other jackets here. But if I hunch in my shoulders and pull up my arms." He demonstrated to Pappy's applause. "What'll you have to drink tonight?"

"They wouldn't happen to have coffee back in the kitchen?"

"Yessir."

"Real coffee?"

"Real coffee."

"Not that instant stuff."

"No sir."

"Not decaf."

"Absolutely not. Genuine JFG coffee, I know because they made me the brewmaster."

"Well, bring it on, son."

"Doctor Berry?" Dempsey touched table in front of the advisor.

"I'll have white wine."

"My daddy says red wine with meat."

"White wine with veal."

Dempsey turned his attention to Sandra. "Miss Kroizer?"

"I'll have white wine, too."

He hurried off to a table at the side of the dining room, a table that served the waiters as a coffee station and wine bar. He returned with a demitasse cup and two wine glasses on a silver tray, all filled.

Pappy eyed the cup Dempsey set before him. "Damn small."

"Sorry about that. They only have girls' stuff here."

Pappy tossed the coffee back, swallowed, and held the empty cup up.

"Oh wow." Dempsey took the cup and departed.

Caroline put a hand on her grandfather's arm. "Grandpops, you're hopeless."

"When I want coffee, I want it in a really big cup." He held his hands out, indicating a container the size of a dishpan.

Berry touched the back of Pappy's hand. "Next time you come to dinner, we'll have a really big cup for you."

"That'd be right hospitable." Pappy sliced off a chunk of veal. He stuffed it in his mouth. "Mmm, this is good."

"We have a student chef. He's a major in the university's hospitality program."

"You should keep him."

"We will until May. He's a senior. He graduates then."

Pappy accepted the refilled demitasse. This time he sipped at it. "So, tell me, how did you become advisor to this bountiful bunch of beauties?"

Berry frowned.

"All right, these splendidly spectacular feminine students."

She set her fork aside. With grace, Berry touched her napkin to her lips. "I was a Theta Delta when I was a UT student. When I came back here to teach, the girls at the house asked me if I'd like to be their chapter advisor. The national office likes to have an alumnae do that job, so I accepted. That was twenty-one years ago."

"The year Carrie was born."

"A good year then."

"My boy's first child, my first grandchild, yes, a very good year. So what do you teach?"

"Narrative writing." Berry sipped from her wine glass.

"I don't have that class. Am I lucky?"

"Probably. It's an upper-level class, for students serious about writing."

Pappy cut another chunk from the veal on his plate. "Gawd, that's not me. The dun letter has been the extent of my writing. 'Pay your damn bill by Friday or I'll send my son over to rip out your plumbing.'"

"Did you ever have to do that?"

"No." Pappy pushed the veal into his mouth.

Caroline looked across Pappy. "Doctor Berry, he's never written a letter like that in his life."

"Is that true?"

"Fortunately." Pappy sampled the glazed vegetables.

Berry smiled as she set her wine glass down. "So you lie, Mister Brown."

"Not lie so much as tell stories."

"Are you ready for dessert, Grandpops?"

"Whaddaya got?"

"Sherbet."

"Not real ice cream? Carrie, I had my heart set on butter pee-can."

Caroline waved to the waiters.

They departed en masse for the kitchen, each to return with a tray of sherbet cups carried high above his shoulder. Dempsey came to the head table.

He yelped as he did, leaping, sherbet cups taking wing from his tray, like frightened wrens. Several cups spilled their scoops of lime green ice down the fronts of gowns. One cup hit the table and upset in Berry's lap. Another splatted on top of Pappy's head. The sherbet stuck, but the cup rolled off and shattered on the floor.

Dempsey clutched at his empty tray, his face ashen. "I'm fired, aren't I?"

Berry, with the consummate composure of a professional, lifted the sherbet from her lap onto her plate. She wiped the remaining liquid away with her napkin. "What happened?"

He pointed to a young woman at the end of the table, doubled over in laughter. "She pinched me on the butt."

"Someone's always pinching the new waiters, Mister Dempsey." Berry, stone-faced, stood. "It's a kind of an initiation. No, you're not fired, but will you please clean up this mess while some of us change?"

Chapter 3

The Blue Onion

PAPPY TOUCHED his can of Country Time to Dempsey's stein of Miller's. "Here's to sleep. I remember it vaguely."

"Yeah, sleep," Dempsey said, his words half-drowned by the raucous conversations of other Friday night celebrants. "I think I did that last summer."

Pappy sipped from his lemonade can. "When I'm not reading, I'm writing. When I'm not writing, I'm reading. These profs really pour it on."

"Yeah, and you're in those easy courses." Dempsey sucked up a mouthful of beer. He gargled.

Pappy squinted through the air hazy with cigarette smoke. "What are you doing?"

"Gargling. Bet I can blow beer up to the ceiling."

"You're not legal to be drinking that stuff, let alone spitting it around a bar. Kid, you're only eighteen."

"My driver's license says twenty-one."

"It's a fake."

"I know that, but he doesn't." Dempsey aimed his trigger finger at the bouncer carding students at the door.

Pappy chased an itch over the bridge of his nose. "You don't suppose my granddaughter had a card like that when she was eighteen?"

"Probably. All my buds back at Bucksnort High, we made up our own. Broke into the State Police drivers licensing office one night." Dempsey pantomimed taking flash pictures.

"My innocent Junior Dempsey."

"Oh, that's me, innocent and pure." The lanky youth drained the last of his beer. He tipped his stein back until a small blue onion rolled to his lips. He slurped the onion in. "Sweet."

"Junior, go for the Onion's yard-of-beer. Chug that down in one breath, my friend, and they give you the next one free." Pappy upped his Country Time. After he set the empty can down on the table, he maneuvered it with his pinky fingers to the center where the can joined company with a second empty and four wadded hamburger wrappers.

Dempsey belched. "Can't do a yard of beer. One regular for me or I'm up all night, peeing."

Pappy stretched. He shot his arms out to the sides and twisted his fists back. The long muscles of his arms shook as he ripped off with a mammoth yawn. "Speaking of night, what time is it?"

Dempsey craned around toward the clock behind the bar. "Five...four...three...two...one," he said, making the countdown. "Nine o'clock."

The sweep hand touched twelve. That triggered the musical clock to play a chorus of 'Rocky Top.' Everyone in the bar leaped or staggered to their feet, bellowing out UT's unofficial fight song.

The Vol Special, an HO-gauge model train, snorted off on its route around the Blue Onion, on tracks suspended from the ceiling, the engine's whistle shrieking and its headlight flashing.

"UT forever!" shouted someone in the crowd, holding his glass high, a student in an Austin Peay T-shirt.

"UT forever!" everyone chorused.

Over the heads of the partying crowd, the Vol Special chugged back into the rail yard above the bar where it wheezed to a stop.

People sat back down, except for the overflow. They milled around, some moving to new tables where friends or would-be friends waved them over.

"Jeez, I gotta get home." Pappy wiped a napkin over the tabletop in front of him, then threw it in the center with the other trash. "My son wants me to help him on a job tomorrow."

"You gonna skip the game?"

"Oh yeah, Vandy's here. Yeah, I guess I'll have to."

Dempsey leaned across his beer stein. "Got your ticket? I can sell it for you, make a couple bucks."

"You in the scalping business now?" Pappy pulled his wallet from his back pocket. He dug through the detritus it contained to unearth a game ticket hiding between his student ID and a Pizza Hut coupon he had torn from the Maryville Chief. He slapped the ticket on the table.

A shaggy-haired fellow pushed his way through the door of the Blue Onion. He held a card up to the bouncer and pushed his way past, swiveling around, apparently searching for a familiar face. He stopped on Dempsey.

"Demps!" he called out.

Dempsey peered up at the new arrival. He beckoned to him.

The student held out an envelope as he came over. "Demps, I found this letter in our mailbox. Thought it might be important."

Dempsey took it. He studied the front side. "Pappy, this is Frank Cauthern, my roomie in Massey Hall. Frankie, this is Willie Joe Brown."

Cauthern leaned across the table to shake hands. "The oldest freshman in the world. Demps talks about you all the time."

Dempsey tore open the envelope. He pulled out the letter it contained and scanned down the page. After some moments, he refolded the letter and tapped it on the corner of the table.

Pappy studied Dempsey's face. "Short news?"

When he didn't answer, Pappy shifted his chair closer. "Bad news then?"

Cauthern gestured at the envelope. "It's from Alpha Alpha Chi, you know, the ag engineering fraternity. They rushed Demps."

"The Alfalfas? Junior told me."

Dempsey sucked in a long breath. He held it, then let it escape, sounding like a tire with a slow leak, as he slipped the letter back inside its protective skin. "They don't want me."

Cauthern shrugged. "Demps, I'm sorry."

"Yeah, me too." Pappy waggled a finger for the bartender and pointed at Dempsey's stein. "Dumb asses. Dumb asses, Junior, not to know what a good man you are."

The bartender filled steins from his rim-full pitcher at tables on his way over. When he leaned in to pour for Dempsey, Dempsey waved him away. "One's it."

"Tonight, you have two. So what if you gotta pee more'n usual?" Pappy held a ten-dollar bill up to the bartender. "A stein for Mister Cauthern, too, and another Country Time for me."

The bartender took the bill and filled Dempsey's stein. "You're one hard drinker, Mister Brown."

"I used to be. Now I leave it to the kids."

Dempsey gazed at the foam running down the side of his stein, his face wilted. "I don't know what I'm going to tell my dad. I really wanted this."

Pappy gazed across at Cauthern. "I know what I'd tell him."

Dempsey raked a finger up the side of his stein. He stuck his finger in his mouth and sucked the foam off.

"I'd tell him I turned the dumb asses down."

"They're not dumb asses. They're some of the best engineers we've got in the ag school."

"They're still dumb asses."

"You hear from the T-Ups? They were more interested in you than the Alfs were in me."

"Ha, their president's more interested in my granddaughter than me. No, I haven't heard from the Tau Upsilons."

A new person appeared in the doorway of the Blue Onion, Caroline Brown, with Sandra Kroizer at her elbow. Both showed their cards to the bouncer, then pushed on into the sea of students priming their spirits and lung power for the next day's football game.

"Grandpops!" she called out when she saw Pappy opening a can of Country Time.

He looked up, held out an arm, and Caroline slipped into it. He hugged her, and she kissed him on the top of his head.

"Junior told me you two had made the Onion your annex."

Pappy massaged at the kiss on his scalp. "We like it. The owners discourage women from coming in here so we men can swear and scratch ourselves in rude places."

"They do not."

Pappy, still with his arm around Caroline's waist, squeezed her again. "So what brings you by, good lookin', you and that bodaciously beautiful friend of yours?"

Caroline opened her Day Planner. From it, she took an envelope. "Don gave me this for you."

Pappy released his granddaughter. He leaned over to Dempsey and bumped the youth's elbow. "Don is Mister T-Ups, El Presidente."

"Grandpops, don't you go ragging on him."

Pappy nudged Dempsey again. "He's a public relations major. I can't think of anything more useless."

Caroline wrapped an arm around Pappy's head and knuckle-rubbed his scalp.

"Heyheyhey!"

"Then read the letter."

"Why? He's only gonna kick me in the pants."

"Grandpops."

"All right." Pappy made a show of tearing off the end of the envelope. He peered up at Caroline as he blew inside, the sides of the envelope billowing out. He pushed two fingers in to capture the letter.

Pappy snapped the letter open.

Four pairs of eyes focused on him as he read. Without comment, Pappy folded the letter and slipped it back in its envelope.

Dempsey tilted his head toward Pappy. "Well?"

"I been kicked in the pants."

Caroline began to interrupt, but Pappy raised a finger.

Dempsey stared down at his beer. "I'm sorry, Pap."

The old student hunched forward. "What say we stick it in the faces of those dumb asses? We'll be independents." Pappy raised his lemonade can.

A smile niggled at the corner of Dempsey's mouth. He raised his stein, touched it to Pappy's Country Time. "Independents."

"Independents! Let's stand up and tell 'em all." Pappy kicked his chair back.

Dempsey did the same.

Pappy, his eyes gleaming, climbed up on his chair.
Dempsey joined him, only on his chair.
Pappy planted one foot on the table.
Dempsey did, too.
They slammed their drinks together in a toast, lemonade and beer splashing up and over their hands and down their arms.
"Independents!"

PAPPY AND CAROLINE did not talk while they strolled eastward out of The Strip, the four blocks of bars, fast-food joints, foreign restaurants, bookstores, and washeterias—Harvey Washbanger's Laundry & Pub the most prominent—that catered to the hunger, thirst, and other needs of the twenty-one thousand students who came to the university for an education, or so most told their parents was their purpose for being here. It was not until the two were on the skywalk, crossing over the traffic rumbling below on Cumberland Avenue, that Caroline took her grandfather's hand.

"Grandpops, that letter didn't say the Tau Upsilons didn't want you. Why'd you tell Junior they rejected you?"

Pappy stopped. He leaned on the handrail, the lights of the eastbound cars smacking him in the face for quick moments as each in the double lanes popped over the hill that divided The Strip from The Campus and started its descent toward the campus's north entrance and downtown Knoxville beyond.

Caroline stopped, too. She slipped her arm through Pappy's. Together, they watched the cars pass beneath them, most packed with students cruising, looking for parties or just riding on this spectacular fall night, talking about abs, buns, love, friendship, sex, and the universe.

"Carrie, the Alfs had just tossed Jimmy in the dumper. I'm going to hurt him more by telling him another frat wants me to join? Kid, not on your life."

"So you're going to turn the Tau Ups down?"

"No. Here's what I'm thinking. I'm gonna jack them up. Donny-boy wouldn't happen to be at the house, would he?"

"I asked him to come with me to find you, but he said he and some of the brothers and a couple alums were meeting tonight, to work out the details for a golf tournament."

"Oh, that will save the world."

"Grandpops, it's a fundraiser. We Greeks do a lot of that."

"Uh-huh, and it takes bodies to do the work, doesn't it? The more bodies doing the work, the more money comes in the front door." Pappy glanced at Caroline. "You want to see your old man's old man do a job on these junior geniuses?"

She shook her head, but grinned as she nudged Pappy on.

Four blocks and they came to Greek Row where thirteen frat and sorority houses faced a green and an intramural field. Two houses dominated, Theta Delta Theta's antebellum mansion and Tau Upsilon's equally impressive three-story red bricker. The two houses stood shoulder to shoulder, the power and pride of the district.

The Tau Ups had acquired their house after World War Two, a wreck of a place. They had the unlimited energy of youth, young men willing to put in long hours and gallons of sweat cleaning, painting, replacing rotted window and door frames, rewiring to code, changing walls on the second and third floors to create suites of rooms.

The Tau Ups had as their advisor at the time William Jennings Johnston, Ph.D., a prof in UT's architecture department. He made the house rehabbing a laboratory project for his drafting and design students, a five-year, do-the-work-as-you-raise-the-money endeavor.

On Halloween Eve, Nineteen Fifty-three, the Tau Upsilons celebrated the completion with a masked ball attended by, among others, the president of the university, four deans, the mayor of the city, the state's lieutenant governor, representatives of Tau Upsilon chapters at six other universities, the national Tau Upsilon president, and a half-dozen hookers. The stories handed down claimed the ladies of the city's red-light district had the best costumes, or was it the scantiest?

Pappy and Caroline strolled up the front walk and the steps to the porch that spanned the front of the house, a porch long enough that the brothers used it for a bowling alley during Rush Week, prospective pledges dodging flying pins as they took their turns as pin boys.

Two young men came out the front door, each with an open can in one hand and a six-pack in the other, appearing intent on getting to a party somewhere else.

"Wanna beer?" one asked. He held his six-pack out to Pappy.

"Naw, you enjoy it. President Donny-boy inside?"

"Yeah, in the card room." The youth saluted Pappy with his can of suds and passed on by, as did his partner.

The Tau Upsilon card room was famed on campus for having hosted the world's longest poker game back during the frat's wilder years. Tuitions had been won and lost there.

Pappy came on Don Wright huddled with six others at a long table, the table covered with mailing lists, form letters, and maps of the Farragut Country Club golf course.

Pappy leaned on Wright's shoulder. "Donny, I know you're busy, but we need to talk."

Wright straightened up. As he did, he took notice of Caroline a pace behind her grandfather. He touched his eyebrow in a salute to her, then focused his attention on Pappy. "I'd like you to meet these people. Everybody, this is Willie Joe Brown. We've invited him to become a Tau Ups. Pappy, you know Ed, Charlie, Ted, and Huey over there."

Each gave a nod.

Before Wright could introduce the remaining two, hands came out to Pappy.

"Asher Hanstead," said the first as he shook hands. "Class of 'Sixty-eight. I was house treasurer that year."

"Willie Joe, Andy Pipkin, Class of 'Sixty-three, past chapter president. Don's told us some excellent things about you. Glad you're going to be one of us. You play golf?"

"'Fraid I've never been much for chasing little white balls around cow pastures. I fish."

"We're planning a golf tournament for the alums for Homecoming weekend." Pipkin aimed his pointer finger at Pappy. "You're an old fart like most of those who will come, maybe you'd play a round with us."

"Depends on what I work out with Donny-boy."

Wright shucked himself of one of his lists. "Do you want to talk here? If not, we could go back in the kitchen."

"The kitchen."

Wright glanced around at his committee. "Go ahead and finish up without me." With that, he swung away to a side door that led to the dining hall and the kitchen beyond. Wright flipped on light switches as he went. In the kitchen, he opened the refrigerator and removed a two-liter bottle of Orange Crush. He held it out to his guests. "Want some?"

Pappy waved it off, but not Caroline.

Wright went to rummaging in a cupboard for Tau Upsilon mugs. When he found them, he handed one to Caroline and kept one for himself, then concentrated on filling the mugs. "So what's going on?"

Pappy leaned back on a preparation table. "Donny, I don't think I can join. Your Mister Pipkin was right out there. I'm an old fart. I don't think I'd fit in."

"The rush committee disagrees. They really like you. They think you'd be a heckuva Tau Ups."

"Yeah, sure."

"Look, you've got age, experience, wisdom." Wright waved his Tau Upsilon mug toward Pappy. "We'd all benefit from that. It's something else, isn't it?"

"All right, the rush committee wants me in because I'm a good guy. But let's be honest, Donny, you want me in because I can help you with Carrie."

"Heyyy, we're already dating. I don't need your help in that department."

"You're dating now, but what about next week?" Pappy let loose with a wicked laugh.

"You wouldn't."

Pappy folded his arms across his chest. He again leaned against the preparation table, waiting.

"Sonuvabitch, you would." Wright swirled the soda in his mug. He watched the bubbles spin. "All right, what do you want?"

"A deal."

"Uh-huh. What kind of deal?"

"Bargain day at the good old Tau Upsilon house, a two-for-one sale."

"And what would that be?"

Pappy picked up the Orange Crush bottle. He twisted the cap off. "Let me refill your cup for you."

"I've got enough."

Pappy raised the bottle to his lips. He tipped the bottle up and drained it. After he finished, he rubbed the back of his hand across his mouth. "You know, this stuff's not half bad."

"It's the house drink."

"I thought beer was."

"The nonalcoholic drink."

Wright took the empty bottle from Pappy. He tossed it at a recycle barrel across the kitchen. The bottle bounced off the lip.

Pappy eyed Wright. "You want me to join?"

"The rush committee does."

"Do you want me to join?"

"You're pushing it, Pappy."

"Here's the deal. If you want me in, you invite James Dempsey to join."

Wright scuffed the toe of his shoe at a spot on the floor tiles. "That freshman over in ag engineering?"

"That's the one."

"We looked at him, but we passed on him."

"Donny-boy, you're not hearing me. Let's go at this another way. When we first talked, at the kegger, what'd you tell me your goal was for this house?"

Wright peered up. "To have the highest GPA of all the Greek organizations on campus."

"I'm not going to help you there. Donny, I'm going to hurt you." Pappy strolled over to the recycle barrel. He recovered the errant Orange Crush bottle from where it had skittered away. "I'll be damn lucky if I get C's and D's. Now Junior, he's a straight-A student. So maybe he slips in one of his classes, he's still gonna come in with a three-point-eight or a three-point-nine." Pappy did a one-handed basketball shot over his head, dropping the bottle in the barrel. He stared at Wright. "No applause necessary for that shot, but, Donny, you need Junior to pull my average up, to pull the house average up as well."

"He's that good, huh?"

Pappy rapped on the table. "He may look like he's got hay behind his ears, but he's a Mensa."

Wright took his mug to the sink where he slurried it out under the faucet. "Well, I'll take it up with the rush committee."

"Donny, you're not listening. You, my boy, are the chief executive of this hyar outfit. El Presidente. Senior Supremo. You can make a decision. You tell the rush committee Junior's in, and Junior's in. And me, too."

Wright turned his mug bottom up in a drainer rack. He peered at Caroline. "Your grandfather always this tough a negotiator?"

"When there's something he wants. Don, he's right. You need every straight-A student you can get if you want this to be an academic house rather than a party house."

Wright rubbed his eyes with the heels of his hands. He drew his hands down his face, then gave Pappy a sideward glance.

"Deal."

Chapter 4

Mister Fudge Bar

SEPTEMBER MELTED under autumn's sun.
 Evaporated.
 Washed away. Gone.
 Disappeared, and four weeks of classes with it, seemingly in the flick of a mosquito's eyelash.
 In August, the country's major sportswriters had picked the Volunteers' football team to place high—second, most said—in the Southeast Conference. Three wins in four games suggested they could be right, that the university had at last one of the best football teams money could buy since the team of Nineteen Thirty-five. That team, playing for Robert Neyland, an honest-to-God U.S. Army general, had defeated Notre Dame in a game that drew national attention.
 One thing was certain. The university now had, by weight, the biggest football team in the nation. The front line averaged two hundred eighty three point six pounds per man—the Beef Trust.
 While the Tau Upsilons fielded a fair touch-football team and a crew team that won most of its meets, academics was the real competition at the house. Don Wright appointed a squad of monitors who collected and posted every quiz, test, and paper grade received by the

house's brothers. Additionally, the monitors devised a statistical model that weighted and averaged the grades on a one-hundred-point scale.

PAPPY SLOUCHED in a canvas chair on the flat roof above the front porch of the Tau Upsilon house, his feet propped on a plastic bucket turned bottom-side up. He scratched at his ear, then scribbled a calculation on a note pad. Displeased, he crossed it out.

A hassock flew out the window. It banged down near Pappy. Junior Dempsey, a bag of corn chips in hand, climbed out after the hassock. "Fritos, Pap?"

Pappy fished a handful out of the bag without looking up from the algebra problem. He popped a chip in his mouth.

Dempsey dragged the hassock over and sat down. "You wearing glasses?"

"Yup."

"Since when?"

Pappy took off his half-moons. He held them out. "Since I wanted to see. They're reading glasses. Bought 'em off the rack at Revco this morning."

Dempsey leaned forward. He studied the students passing in front of the house. "There's an Allison."

Pappy put his glasses back on. He peered over them. "She's a Barbara. Thirty-two B."

"Thirty-four."

"Junior, how close have you ever been to a woman?"

"Well, my mom."

"That don't count."

Dempsey pointed a Frito at another female student, this one in hip-hugger shorts and a tank top, a backpack slung over her shoulder. "How about that one? She's an Allison."

Pappy glanced over his glasses. "Agreed."

"Now I'd carry her backpack any day." Dempsey put his feet up on the railing. He nudged Pappy. "Like my new tennies?"

Pappy stared at them. "Gawd, I can see your knobby toes through 'em."

Dempsey grinned. He wiggled his toes. "Air conditioning. Ed was throwing them out. I rescued them from the trash."

"You're a real scrounge."

"Waste not, want not." Dempsey opened his mouth. He tossed a Frito in the air, but the Frito, when it came down, bounced off his cheek.

Pappy turned back to the problem on his notepad. "I got a dog that can do better than that."

"You have not." Dempsey tossed another Frito in the air. He missed that one, too.

"I put a cheese curl on Rufe's nose. He balances it there, watching me. When I throw him the okay sign, he flips the curl in the air and snaps it out. Never misses."

"You're putting me on." Dempsey tried again to catch a Frito.

"That dog loooves his cheese curls. Gawddammit." Pappy tore the sheet from his notepad. He crumpled it and pitched it over the railing. "Thirty-five years I ran my own business. I did all the math every day, most of it in my head. Gawddammit, I never needed this stuff."

"What's the matter, Pap?"

"It's this gawddamned algebra."

Dempsey leaned over. "Well, working yourself into a hissy fit doesn't solve anything. Gimme your book."

Pappy dug his textbook out of his lap. He handed the book over and gave Dempsey his pad and pencil, as well.

"Which problem?"

"Six-point-two, problem four."

"Oh, that's easy."

"The hell it is."

"Pappy, all algebra is is a way of thinking. It's equations, and every one is asking for the same thing—what is the value of 'x'? Look here, you plug in the givens." Dempsey jotted down a series of numbers and letters. "You do the operations. You get the answer."

He handed the pad back.

Pappy studied the pad. He traced the flow of numbers with his index finger through the four-step operation, silently sounding them with his lips.

Dempsey rapped the side of Pappy's hand. "Didn't your prof ever explain this?"

"We got a TA. I don't think he knows his fanny from the proverbial hole in the ground. Besides, he's Chinese."

"What's that got to do with anything?"

"He talks funny. We can't understand him."

Dempsey went back to his bag of Fritos. "Look, Pappy, you work the next problem. You've got to whip this. Your grades are stinking up the house."

"I know. Sixty-seven point three. I saw the latest posting."

"You've got to goose it up."

Pappy scratched down a series of numbers. "Junior, did you know you use up your brain as you age?"

"No."

"It's true. I'm more than three times as old as you. About all the brain I got left is enough to power a squirrel." He held the pad up.

Dempsey's gaze moved through the equation and the operations. "You've got it right."

"Well, gawddamn, it's about time." Pappy put his hand on Dempsey's arm, his voice changing to the hushed tones of a conspirator. "Hey, I looked you up on the posting. Ninety-eight point six. You even beat old Donny."

"I could do better."

Pappy rolled his eyes.

A student backed through the window, carrying one end of a small table on which rode a four-tiered chess set. The other end of the table followed, carried by a second student.

"Room out here for company?" the first asked–Fred 'Wicks' Wickingson.

Pappy motioned an okay. "Set up next to Junior."

The second–Ambrose Frye–went back inside. He handed out two camp chairs, then a cooler.

Wickingson opened the cooler. "Country Time, Pap?"

"You read my mind."

Wickingson pulled out a can and tossed it over. "Junior?"

"Miller's?"

"'Fraid not. All I've got in the beer line is Leinenkugel's."

"I guess I'm desperate enough."

He handed a cold can to Dempsey.

Wickingson had the build of a guy who could play varsity halfback. Pappy thought he would have if it weren't for the thick glasses he wore. Those glasses, though, didn't stop him from playing for the house team– fullback. Whoever played quarterback would slam the ball into Wickingson's gut. Down would go his head, and he'd run over anyone who got in his way.

Wickingson had trekked to Tennessee from Wisconsin, on scholarship in chemical engineering. Every time he returned from the North Country, he brought a trunk filled with Leinenkugel beer, bratwurst, and pepper jack cheese.

Frye, settling across the chess table from Wickingson, could have won his share of body-building contests if he'd cared to enter. He'd told Pappy he got his well-sculpted muscles wrestling tow chains for his father who owned Frye's Twenty-Four-Hour Towing Service in Strawberry Plains. Frye ran a Kenworth tow truck on weekends, pulling semis out of ditches in and around Knoxville.

Like Wickingson and Dempsey, too, Frye was a scholarship student—astrophysics.

The chess players, both sophomores, occupied the suite just inside the window. Their roommates of last year had graduated in the spring, so, with two beds empty, Wickingson and Frye spun the house's wheel-of-fortune. Whoever's names the pointer stopped on were their new roommates. They had won Pappy and Dempsey.

The first time the fraternity's monitors posted the grades of all the brothers, someone, reading down the list, gave the foursome a name, Limpbrain and the Three Geniuses. Wickingson and Frye invited the brother to a midnight poker game with their roommates—strip poker. He lost everything—shoes, socks, even his Fruit of the Looms. Wickingson and Frye then pitched the brother naked out the front door and locked it.

The four slapped hands in high fives, with Wickingson dubbing the roommates the Four Caballeros for the Steve Martin/Chevy Chase movie he had watched six times.

Wickingson motioned with his beer at the sidewalk. "A Darla coming."

Frye peered over the railing. "Darla for dog, yup."

Pappy glanced at the young woman. "You guys are nasty. She's at least a Constance."

"How about that one in the short shorts and skimpy halter top, coming out of the Theta Delt house? A Barbara."

Pappy turned in the new direction. "Hey, that's my granddaughter." He waved his note pad. "Carrie, you go back inside and get some clothes on!"

She looked up. "Hey, Grandpops! Some of us are going over to play volleyball on the sand courts. Come with us!"

Frye hopped to his feet. "Jiggle time."

"Sit down. You're not going over there to leer at my granddaughter."

"Ambrose, I'll get the field glasses." Wickingson hustled for the window and disappeared inside.

"My gawd, you are a lecherous bunch. Didn't your mommas teach you respect?"

Frye slapped Pappy's shoulder. "It's hormones, old man, raging hormones. Anyway, we're just teasin'. Wicks, you got those glasses?"

Wickingson came back out the window, a hand cupped behind his ear. "Hey, listen. Is that a bell I hear?"

Frye took the binoculars. "A bell? Have you been sniffing things in the chem lab, again? Come on back to the game. It's your move."

"It's a bell, I tell you. I hear a bell."

Dempsey scrambled to his feet. "Me, too. You hear it, Pappy?"

"No, but then I'm old. I'm near deaf."

Dempsey leaned out over the railing, scanning Volunteer Boulevard from west to east. "You're right, Wickie. That's ice cream music. There he is."

"Hey, it's Mister Fudge Bar." Wickingson came over, waving. "Mister Fudge Bar, over here!"

Dempsey jammed two fingers in his mouth and let loose with an ear-splitting whistle.

Mister Fudge Bar, an accounting student, shot up a hand. He turned his three-wheeler toward the Tau Upsilon house, pedaling on, stopping just short of the porch. He opened his trike's cooler and called up, "What would you like?"

Wickingson called down, "Got any Haagen Dazs?"

"Who are you trying to impress?" Pappy muttered.

"Sure! What flavor?"

"I don't care. They're all good. Surprise me."

Up flew a half-pint, a plastic spoon rubber banded to the carton.

"I want a Fudgsicle," Dempsey called down.

"That's more like it," Pappy mumbled. He started in on another algebra problem.

Up flew a Fudgsicle in its paper wrapping.

Wickingson kicked at Frye's shoe. "Ambrose?"

"Toffee bar."

"A toffee bar!"

Dempsey tapped Pappy. "You want something?"

"Drumstick."

"And a Drumstick!"

Up flew a toffee bar and a Drumstick.

"How much?" Wickingson called down.

"Five seventy-five!"

The three huddled around Pappy. They pooled their bills and coins until they hit the right amount. Wickingson dropped the loot over the railing into Mister Fudge Bar's cap. The future MBA counted the money and waved his appreciation to his porch-roof customers. He then turned to the ice cream needs of the dozen frat men and sorority women who also had heard the jingling bells.

The Caballeros settled back, each peeling the paper or plastic cover off his treat.

"You and Haagen Dazs," Pappy said, taking the first bite from his Drumstick.

"Hey, what can I say? I'm from Wisconsin. We know good ice cream. Besides, I'm a growing boy. I need my calories. Want some?" Wickingson held out a spoonful.

"I got my Drumstick. How's your Fudgesicle, Junior?"

Dempsey pulled the chocolate popsicle from his mouth. "As a kid, I could never get enough of these."

"Yeah?"

"In summer, we only got to town every other week, and Dad would ration me and my brother to one, you know, break it in half and you each get a stick."

"Only one?"

Dempsey licked at his Fudgsicle. "Once, Nathan and I took our money, and we sneaked off. We told Pap we were going fishing. But we went to Deke's, a crossroads store, and we each bought us a box of Fudgsicles. Oh, they were good."

"Uh-huh."

"And, oh, we got sick."

Pappy waved his Drumstick at Dempsey. "Too much of a good thing."

Dempsey bit off the end of his Fudgesicle. He chewed the ice. "Pappy, you know what I'd really like to get?"

"No, what would you really like to get?"

"An ice cream truck."

Wickingson put down his spoon, Frye his Toffee Bar. They stared at Dempsey.

Dempsey waved what was left of his Fudgesicle. "That guy does pretty good on his trike, but think what a guy could do if he had a real ice cream truck on this campus."

Pappy, too, stared. "Where the hell did this come from?"

"A buddy and I went to a movie over at the UC the other night, this Cheech and Chong movie. Funny, funny, funny. You know them?"

"I know Abbott and Costello."

"Who?"

"Never mind."

"Anyway, Cheech and Chong are in this ice cream truck, see, and Chong is driving, and it's wild. They're trying to outrun the police. We laughed ourselves silly." Dempsey studied his Fudgesicle. "That's what I want. It'd be cool."

Pappy took another bite from his Drumstick. "How prepared are you to be cool?"

"I've got five hundred put away for a car."

"That might buy you the tires."

"Well, it doesn't have to be new."

Pappy turned to Frye. "Would you go back in the room there and get the newspaper off my bed?"

Frye, when he came back out the window, held out the latest edition of the Maryville Chief.

"No, you look it up."

"Look what up?"

"The classifieds. Used vehicles. See if you can find something for this boy."

Frye leaned against the wall of the house as he paged into the paper. "Found it. Now what am I looking for?"

"You'll know it when you see it."

He scanned down the first column, then the second. Halfway down, he sucked in his breath. "Well, I'll be damned."

Wickingson looked over. "What is it?"

"Listen to this. 'Used ice cream truck. Nineteen Sixty-One Chev, bell, revolving light. Best offer. Two-eleven Chestnut' and a telephone number. Pappy, you knew about this."

"Maryville's a small place."

"Have you seen this, the truck?"

"Sure. Sam Kramer bought it new, ran it summers for fourteen years until he died. Martha just left it where Sam had parked it beside the garage." Pappy waggled his

Drumstick at Frye. "Now the town council's got itself on a cleanup jag, and they want it out of there. My bet is the rusty old wreck doesn't run."

Dempsey tapped his Fudgesicle against Pappy's Drumstick. "Can we look at it?"

"The number's there. Give it a call."

Chapter 5

The new Good Humor man

DEMPSEY PEELED the canvas back, revealing the doorless cab of the truck. "Where are the doors?"

Martha Kramer, a silver-haired wisp of a woman, stood nearby worrying a corner of her shawl. "I don't know. Sam was always having to get out and in every time he stopped. He thought the doors a nuisance, so he had them took off."

Frye lifted the hood and studied the mess before him. "Battery's busted. Probably froze in the winter way back when. And we've got a bird's nest in the wires."

"Nobody's run it since Sam died." Missus Kramer continued to worry the corner of her shawl.

Pappy took her hand. "He was a good man."

"The best. I miss him ever'day. I kept the old truck because it was his, you know, but the council says, if I don't get rid of it, they're going to have it hauled off and charge me the price. Don't know why anybody'd want it."

"Any offers?"

"Junk man. Two hundred dollars."

"You could always use two hundred."

"I suppose." A wistful look came over Martha Kramer's face. She turned away.

Wickingson opened the twin freezers, then the refrigerator. "These appear sound. The gaskets aren't the best."

Pappy stepped over to peer in. "Freon probably evaporated years ago, boys."

"Canvas roof over the box, pretty well shot."

"Wicks, go to my truck. You'll find a steel tape on the dash. Measure that top for us, would ya?"

Wickingson stepped down from the box of the ice cream truck and trotted off to the street where Pappy had parked.

Frye closed the hood. He came to Pappy. "Did you look at the tires? They're all flat."

"Now tell me you're surprised by that."

"I'm not. See, dry rot's pretty well spoiled the sidewalls. They're not just flat, they're shot."

Dempsey, in the cab, pounded dust out of the driver's seat. Two mice, apparently frightened by the thunder, abandoned their home inside. They jumped past Dempsey, hit the floor, and leaped for the weeds.

"The kid really likes this thing." Frye glanced at Dempsey. "Replacing the tires is nothing, and I could probably get the engine running. But I don't know about the freezers."

Pappy scratched behind his ear. "I know a guy who'd be willing to work on them, from back in my plumbing days."

"Davis?" Missus Kramer asked.

"That's him."

"He always took care of them for Sam."

Wickingson came over, wiping dust from his hands. "This is gonna be a lot of work, but I'm with Junior. I think it'd be cool."

"Junior," Pappy hollered.

"Yeah?"

"Get your butt down here."

Dempsey eased off of the seat. He ran his hand over the steering wheel one last time and tinkled the ice cream bell, a forlorn sound, as if the bell and the truck missed having laughing children clustered around, holding up nickels and dimes for ice cream cones. Dempsey stuffed his hands in his back pockets and shuffled away.

"You gonna buy it?" Pappy noodled at a weed with the toe of his work boot.

"I don't know if I should."

"It's up to you."

"I don't know what it's worth."

"Well, Martha's got one bid. Two hundred dollars from the junk man."

Dempsey peered at Pappy, questions in his eyes. "What do you think, two fifty?"

Pappy shook his head.

"Two seventy-five?"

Pappy again shook his head.

"Three hundred dollars?"

That got a nod.

Missus Kramer gave a weak smile, as if it were an effort to do so. "I got the paperwork in the kitchen. I think Sam would like knowing some young people were getting his truck. But I'm gonna miss it." She blew her nose into her handkerchief.

"Martha, Junior's check's good. He's my roommate, you know, up there at UT."

"Your word's fine by me. Always has been. Pappy, your boy Stevey tells me you like being a student."

"It sure beats fishing all day and drinking beer. Yeah, I like it, particularly being with these yahoos. My gawd, Martha, they're smart kids. Makes me feel good, thinking I can understand maybe half the stuff they talk about."

The group rambled on inside, Pappy and Missus Kramer talking about years past.

In the kitchen, she picked up a pitcher of lemonade. "Have some? I'm afraid I made it from a can, but it's good."

Wickingson, Frye, and Pappy scooped up glasses that Missus Kramer filled to the rim.

Dempsey, off by himself, took a chair at the table. He wrote out his check.

Missus Kramer, when free of her hostess duties, signed over the title.

Dempsey passed his check on. "Would it be all right if we didn't come back until Saturday to get the truck?"

THE FOUR, AT CURBSIDE, squeezed back into the cab of Pappy's pickup, a hellaciously tight fit.

He got his truck rolling out of town, toward the turnpike and north to Knoxville. "Junior, you call your pap tonight and tell him what you done. You ask him to set the insurance up for you."

"Insurance, right."

Frye stretched his arm across the back of the seat behind Dempsey. "I'll get the battery for you and some tires. There are always some laying around my dad's yard."

Pappy watched his side mirror, his attention fixed on the aluminum hauler booming up behind him. "Wicks, you got the measurements for the awning?"

"Yeah."

"There's an awning shop out on Kingston. Tomorrow afternoon, go out there and order what we need for Junior's ice cream truck, would you?"

"Can do."

"It may take them a week to make it up, to work it in with their other jobs."

The aluminum hauler yanked down on his air horn. He pulled over into the passing lane and roared past Pappy, the wind buffeting his pickup.

Chapter 6

A little tune-up

FOR DEMPSEY, the remaining days dragged by. He badgered Pappy to take him down to Maryville, so he could work on his ice cream truck, but Pappy put him off. He had a paper due for Freshman Comp and library research for Ornithology.

Wickingson and Frye put him off as well, both elbow deep in lab projects that required the bulk of their evening hours working with their engineering teams at Perkins and Dougherty Halls, two of the university's principal engineering buildings.

Saturday did come.

Pappy rose first.

He showered and shaved Army style—fast. When he came back to the room and found Dempsey snoring, his mouth open and an arm hanging out of bed, Pappy tiptoed back to the bathroom. He returned, carrying a shaving cream can.

Pappy filled Dempsey's hand with warm foam, then picked up a feather he had intended to take to Ornithology. He touched the feather's tip to Dempsey's nose. With the gentlest motion, he whisked the feather like one would a duster over delicate crystal.

Dempsey's nose twitched.

Another whisk.

Dempsey's nose twitched again.

On the third whisk, up came Dempsey's hand, splatting shaving soap into his mouth and across his face. He woke, spitting.

Pappy struggled to hide his laughter. "Morning, June. You weren't thinking of spending your life in bed, were you?"

Dempsey raked the suds away his lips. He spit to the side. "That's a cheap high school trick."

"So I recall. It works every time, doesn't it? Well, I'm going down to the kitchen, to make me some breakfast. Jump up and get your shorts on."

Dempsey picked up his table clock. He squinted at it. "Hell, man, it's five o'clock."

"And gettin' later."

Pappy left the room. He glided on his toes to the stairs and down, not wanting to disturb sleeping Tau Upsilons in the other suites. At the bottom, Pappy scouted the living room littered with spent beer cans and pizza boxes from the previous night's party.

He stopped to light a Camel. Pappy picked up an empty can and dropped his match in it, and dumped the can and an armload of others he gathered in a recycle barrel on the way to the kitchen.

In the kitchen, he pawed his way through the refrigerator, searching for what might be fit for a first meal of the day. Pappy grinned like a raccoon in a sweetcorn patch when he unearthed three eggs, a quarter-pound of Velveeta, some bacon, and one lonely onion. A cupboard yielded a can of mushrooms.

Pappy flicked on a burner on the stove. There he laid out the bacon in a skillet to fry. While the bacon crackled, Pappy beat the eggs in a bowl, the action shaking ashes from his cigarette into the golden liquid. He picked at the flecks but most eluded him.

"Aww, it'll just spice up the flavor," Pappy mumbled as he wiped his fingers on his trousers.

He went at chopping the onion into the egg mix. He also threw in a handful of mushrooms.

Coffee. Pappy remembered a battered coffeepot no one else used and found it neglected in the back of a cupboard. He half-filled the pot with water, dumped in some ground coffee, and set the pot on a back burner to boil.

Out came the bacon, almost charred, from the skillet. Pappy poured out the excess fat, then poured in his egg mixture, and set the skillet back on the hot burner.

He shook in some salt and pepper as he hummed a nameless tune, the pepper a bit more than the salt.

The egg mixture curled at the edges. Pappy tossed in a fistful of chopped cheese, then folded the egg over onto itself and sealed the edges. Perfection, he thought, as he slid the omelet onto a plate.

Dempsey stumbled in. "For me?"

"Hell no. It's Count Chocula for you unless you want to cook your own breakfast. I did boil up extra coffee if you want some." Pappy scrounged two cups. He filled them and set them on the preparation table.

Dempsey studied the selections in the cereal cabinet. He stopped on Frosted Flakes. He brought the box to the prep table where he sat, not on a chair or a stool, but on the table itself, eating the cereal straight from the box, by the handful.

Pappy gave Dempsey a look that appeared to question his sanity.

Dempsey shrugged. "It's candy. How's your omelet?"

"Don't you wish you had one?"

"Nope." He stuffed more dry cereal in his mouth. As he chewed, he sipped from his coffee cup. "Oh my God."

"What?"

"This is awful."

"Plumber's coffee."

Dempsey jumped down. He ran to the sink and threw half the mud down the drain. He then splashed hot water into the coffee that remained in his cup, stirred the new mixture with his finger and sampled it. "Well, I've got it half-way decent now. Pappy, how can you drink that stuff?"

"Have some bacon?"

"No thanks." Dempsey went back to his cereal box.

"June, when you pull an all-nighter, you're gonna be begging me to make you some of my famous plumber's coffee."

"I'll die first." Dempsey took another handful of cereal. "Ambrose and Wicks said they'd meet us in Maryville. They're going to Mickey D's for an Egg McMuffin, then on to Ambrose's father's garage for the tires and stuff."

Pappy set his plate, fork, and cup in the sink. He turned on the water. "We better get on the road. Who's cheffing this morning?"

"Andy Baker."

"He'll wash up the dishes for us." Pappy squirted in some soap before he turned the water off. He put the skillet, his mixing bowl, and other preparation tools in the sink. When Dempsey added his cup, Pappy wiped his hands dry on Dempsey's Tau Upsilon sweatshirt.

"Hey!"

"It's clean water. Don't have a cow."

A PINKING GLOW warmed the eastern sky as the two headed out of the Tau Upsilon house. In the pickup, Pappy turned on the radio and dialed in KNOX in time to catch Johnny Cash growling his way through 'Folsom Prison Blues.' Pappy whistled along as he drove out of the parking lot.

Dempsey stared out the window. "God, do I have to listen to this? That's my dad's music."

"Your old man's got good taste."

"Would you let me turn on One-Eleven-Seven, get some heavy metal goin' in here?"

"You can get heavy metal in your truck. In my truck, you get Johnny Cash and Merle Haggard."

Junior rolled his window down. He stuck his head out and screamed, drawing startled looks from two students jogging along Lake Louden Boulevard.

Pappy popped the turn signal down. "You still get Johnny and Merle."

PAPPY AND DEMPSEY found Davis Terheyden sitting in his refrigeration repair truck curbside in front of Martha Kramer's house, waiting for them, tapping his finger on the steering wheel in time to a Patsy Cline oldie playing on KNOX.

"Hear that?" Pappy nudged Dempsey as they walked up to the truck. "That man's got good taste, like your pap and me."

"Gawwwd."

Pappy rapped on the side window.

Terheyden rolled the glass down, a chubby, white-haired leprechaun of a man with a fringe of beard outlining his jaw.

"Davis, you work on those freezers all night?"

Terheyden flicked his radio's volume down. "Did it yesterday. Knew you were coming down early, so I came by to tell you about it on my way to my first call."

"You work Saturdays?"

"Like the doctor, every day of the week. This the new owner of Sam's truck?"

"That he is."

Terheyden opened his door. He slid down to the ground, a fair drop for a man four-foot-eight. He reached up to shake hands with Dempsey.

"Davis Terheyden," he said. The patch on the breast pocket of his blue twill work jacket read 'Cool Man Refrigeration.'

"James Dempsey," Dempsey said. "I go by Junior."

"How's the weather up there?" Terheyden cackled. "I suppose you get that one a lot."

"No. Never."

"Oh, well, come with me and I'll show you what I've done." Terheyden led the way up the driveway, hustling, outpacing the taller men.

"He's always in a hurry," Pappy murmured to Dempsey as they hiked after The Cool Man.

"Pappy, I got short legs, so I got to hurry." Terheyden hopped across a pothole. "If I didn't, Maryville's refrigerators and freezers wouldn't get fixed and the town would grind to a standstill."

"Or they'd call somebody else."

"No, they wouldn't. I'm the best, like you when you were plumbing."

"Can't argue with you there."

"Surprising, Sam's freezers and the refrigerator were in pretty good shape for not having been run for ten years." Terheyden climbed the steps into the back of the ice cream truck. He swung around, impatient. "Come on, come on, come on."

Dempsey shrugged to Pappy. He went on up the steps.

Terheyden motioned at the freezer on the driver's side of the truck. "Open that door, Mister Dempsey."

Dempsey lifted the door up and back.

"The gaskets were shot, so they weren't going to hold in any cold for you. Gaskets like those are hard to find today."

Dempsey studied the interior of the freezer. "I didn't know."

"Usually takes two weeks to track 'em down through some forgotten supplier in Nebraska or Washington State. But, for you, sonny boy, we were in luck."

"Why's that?"

"Because I made it a point to keep a spare set for Sam in my shop. Knew someday he'd need 'em. There they were, hanging up on a nail in the corner, still fresh inside their packages after all these years."

Dempsey held his hand inside the freezer. "It's cold in there."

"It is now. Pappy was right. All the Freon had leaked out." Terheyden pulled a stool from a cabinet beside the other freezer. He climbed the rungs and settled himself on the high seat. "You got a condenser and motor in each freezer and the refrigerator. I checked the condensers over. They're okay. I lubricated the motors and put on new belts, then filled the condensers with Freon."

Pappy leaned on the freezer next to Terheyden. "The motors get juice from the truck's engine?"

"No. Pull up that metal plate there, Mister Dempsey." Terheyden aimed his pointer finger at a plate in the floor, a plate with a ring handle folded flush.

Dempsey flipped the ring up. He pulled the plate away, revealing a small motor and generator below the floor.

"Sam talked to me when he was thinking of getting this truck." Terheyden took out a pad. He went on as he wrote a note to himself. "I told him the juice load to run the freezers and refrigerator was going to be hell on the truck's electricals, that he ought to get him an Onan generator to run everything back here, and he did. You get to it through this trapdoor or through the side underneath. Mister Dempsey, see that filler pipe?"

"Yeah."

"Screw the cap off."

Dempsey twiddled the cap off and got a noseful of gasoline vapor wafting up from the pipe. He sneezed.

"Well, excuse you." The Cool Man stuffed his note and his pad in his pocket. "The Onan's got its own gas tank, and you fill it up right there. You can close it up now and put the plate back in place."

"Why didn't they hinge this thing, Mister Terheyden?"

"If they did, you'd be tripping on the hinge. No hinge, you got yourself a flat floor."

Terheyden hopped off the stool. He took a key from his pocket and stuck it in a switch on the galley wall.

"Watch this." Terheyden twisted the key. As he held the key in, the Onan burred to life. "I changed the oil and the coolant in the motor for you, put in a new six-volt battery, lubricated the generator and put new belts on the unit for you. That little Onan is gonna run forever as long as you fill the gas tank every now and then. Now, tall man, lean down here."

Dempsey hunkered down on one knee, next to the refrigeration repairman.

"See this?" Terheyden swept his hand across a set of temperature gauges and controls next to the starter switch. "These are the controls for your freezers and your refrigerator. I'd set the freezers at thirty. Colder and your ice cream's gonna be awful hard. Refrigerator? Maybe forty-five."

Terheyden switched the Onan off. He gave the key to Dempsey as he wriggled past Dempsey and Pappy to the steps. He climbed down, Pappy following.

"What do we owe you for this?"

"Nothing. I did this for Sam, may he be enjoying his stay in Heaven." Terheyden turned back. He wagged a finger at Dempsey and cackled. "But next time—"

Terheyden backed away a couple paces, still snorting with laughter, before he hurried down the driveway.

Dempsey leaned on the freezer top, watching the retreating figure of the little man. "He's some fella, isn't he? Cool Man, huh?"

"About the best you're ever going to meet in this life."

"But, gawd, he's short. How's he ever drive that truck of his?"

"You ought to look inside sometime. He's got blocks on the brake and gas pedals, and he sits up on a parts catalog so he can see over the steering wheel."

Dempsey came down to Pappy. "Well, now what do we do to get the front end running?"

"Open the hood, I expect. See what kind of nasty business you got yourself into."

The two, as they strolled forward, spooked a rabbit that had been hiding in the weeds. It skittered away, zigzagging toward Missus Kramer's garden.

Pappy tramped down a path to the front of the truck. He stopped there, waiting on Dempsey. "You going to open the hood?"

Dempsey leaned down. He squinted through the crack between the hood and the grill. "I don't see a release. Is it in the cab?"

Pappy slipped his fingers between the first and second bars of the grill. When they touched a paddle-shaped piece of metal, he pushed up. The latch sproinged, and Pappy raised the hood. He gazed around.

Dempsey looked over his shoulder. "Something the matter?"

"There ought to be a rod just inside the fender, to brace the hood open. It's missing. Oh, looky there, that length of broom handle. That's what Sam used." Pappy jammed the broom handle between the top of the grill and the hood.

Dempsey lifted an empty bird's nest away from atop the air cleaner. He tossed the nest in the weeds, then checked the condition of the fan and generator belts while Pappy went over the spark plug wires and pulled the cap from the distributor. Pappy examined the rotor and points. "Looks like we're going to have to replace about everything."

"Yeah. The belts are all cracked."

"Make a list and we'll run over and see old Hubcap at Western Auto."

"Hubcap?"

"Hubby Dorr." Pappy slapped the cap back on the distributor. "He owns the shop. You got something to write on?"

"My arm."

"That'll do. Six spark plugs, the harness, points, generator and fan belt, air filter, oil filter, gas filter, three gallons of coolant, five quarts of oil or does this engine take six? A battery—"

Dempsey printed 'battery' on his arm. He stopped, wetted his thumb on his tongue, and erased the word. "Ambrose said he's bringing a battery."

"Oh. We better get new battery cables and clamps, though."

An air horn sounded, from a Kenworth tow truck rolling to a stop just beyond the driveway. In the time it took Pappy to wave, the driver had shifted into reverse and was spinning the steering wheel, guiding the big rig into the driveway and back to the ice cream truck.

Wickingson, in bib overalls and work boots, bailed out of the passenger door. He shoved his Badger cap onto the back of his head as he walked along.

Frye dropped down from the driver's side, he in blue twill trousers and shirt, and a Kenworth baseball cap that completed his work uniform.

"You boys ready to do this thang?" he called out as he opened the door to a side panel where the tow-truck operators kept their tools. Frye brought out two pairs of long-cuffed leather gloves. He tossed one pair to Wickingson and kept the other for himself.

Wickingson pulled down wheel rims on which someone had mounted half-way decent tires. He toted them over. "We didn't want to wrestle with changing tires, so we went by the bone yard and found a wrecked truck with the right size wheels. We bought the wheels and tires off it."

Frye unreeled two air hoses. He hauled them to the front of the ice cream truck. "Morning, Junior, Pap."

Pappy peered at Frye's shirt. "What's that say over the pocket?"

Frye laughed as he touched the stitching. "'Small Frye.' Dad always called me that, so when I came to work for him, he had it stitched on all my shirts."

He dropped the hoses and trotted back to the tow truck. Frye whistled to Wickingson.

Wickingson swung around in time to catch an air wrench Frye threw to him.

Frye opened a bin behind the cab of his truck and brought out an oversized rubber pillow. "Wicks, let's show these boys how we do it."

Wickingson attached the air wrench to one of the hoses. He hit the trigger twice, testing the wrench as he knelt by the ice cream truck's left front wheel. He rammed the socket over the first lug nut, hit the air, and broke the nut loose. Wickingson spun it off.

Frye threw the pillow under the front of the truck. He worked the pillow around until he had it under the first crossbeam of the frame. "Hand me the end of that hose, Pap."

Pappy passed the end to Frye, and Frye connected it to the pillow. He pressed a valve on the hose, and the pillow inflated.

Pappy watched the action, fascinated. "I been told about those pillows. Never saw one used."

"Pap, they're so much safer than jacks. And faster."

Wickingson hauled his air hose to the other side of the truck. He spun the lug nuts off the right front wheel while the front of the truck rose.

"Junior, pull the left wheel off," Frye said. To Pappy, he added, "It's amazing how much weight you can lift with one of these air bags." He rocked back on his heels. "Over on my rig, in the bin, you'll find an oil collection pan and a bucket. Would you get 'em for me? We'll drain the oil and the coolant while we've got the front of the truck up."

Pappy poked around until he found the requested items. He held them up for Frye to see, to make sure he had the right ones before he brought them back.

Dempsey slipped a new wheel and tire on the left front. He started the lug nuts on the stud bolts while Wickingson did the same on the right side.

Frye gave Pappy the eye as he returned. "You want to crawl under and take the drain plug out of the oil pan?"

Pappy stared at him. "I'm too old to be doin' that, Small Frye."

"Junior?" Frye called. "I've got a job for ya."

"I'm busy."

"Wicks?"

"I'll do it." Wickingson finished with the right front wheel and tire before he came around.

Frye flipped a quarter in the air. He caught it and slapped it on the back of his hand.

"Call it," he said to Wickingson.

"Heads."

Frye pulled his hand away. He held the coin out for his partner to see. "You lose. You get to crawl under the motor and drain the oil."

"Lucky me. Got a wrench?"

Frye pulled a closed-end wrench from his back pocket.

Wickingson grabbed the wrench. He got down on all fours, rolled over on his back, and wriggled his way in under the running board until he could reach the drain plug.

Frye pushed the oil collection pan toward him.

Wickingson got his fingers on the pan and worked it into position. After he got the wrench on the plug, he pulled down, straining, groaning. "Thing won't budge."

"Awful tight when they've been in that long." Pappy snatched up a blade of grass and chewed on it.

"How about the air wrench?"

"You can try it." Frye went around to the other side where Wickingson had left the air wrench. He put a smaller socket on it as he brought it around to the left side. Frye leaned over the fender and lowered the wrench and air hose down through the engine compartment.

Wickingson caught the gear. He positioned the socket on the plug.

Frye tapped on the cowling over the front wheel. "Easy now. Easy."

Wickingson jerked the trigger. The air hit the wrench with its full force, spinning the drain plug out, oil splurting into Wickingson's face. He jammed a thumb over the hole. "My God, what a mess."

"What happened?"

"Oil everywhere. Plug came out faster than I thought it would. Got it stopped, though."

"Get the pan under it?"

"Got it. You got a towel so I can clean up?"

Frye took two shop rags from his back pocket. He dropped them down through the engine compartment. "I'm going to drain the radiator. When the oil stops running, you put the plug back in, all right?"

"Gotcha."

Frye stuck Pappy's bucket under the radiator. He opened the petcock drain and watched the motor's coolant run out. Frye caught some in his hand. He put a penlight on the liquid. "Pappy, looks like rust flecks in this, don't you think?"

Pappy squinted at the coolant puddled in Frye's hand. "I'd say so."

"Then we better flush the radiator before we fill it."

"Martha's got a garden hose and a spigot by her back porch. I'll connect the hose up and bring it over."

Frye sent Dempsey to the far side of the engine compartment, to pull the wires from the spark plugs and the distributor cap. He rapped on the wheel cowling to get Wickingson's attention. "How you coming down there?"

"Oil's pretty well stopped running."

"Plug it and let's go on. I'll get you a filter wrench and you can take the oil filter off from down there."

"Right."

Frye trotted to the tow truck. He returned with a box. "Everything we need ought to in here," he said to Pappy.

"Junior and me were going to the parts store."

"Already been." Frye took a new filter from its box. He handed the filter and the filter wrench down through the engine compartment to Wickingson.

While Wickingson worked on that job, Frye hauled the air wrench up. He replaced the wrench with a jet and blasted dirt and debris away from the spark plugs. He then replaced the jet with the wrench and put a sparkplug socket on it. He zipped the plugs out.

Frye studied each plug. He held a couple out to Pappy.

"So?" Pappy asked.

"Well, look at the crud on them. From cylinders two and four. Junior could be looking at an overhaul job."

Pappy pulled Dempsey in. Pappy ran the tip of his finger around the open end of one of the plugs. "See this?"

"I heard. You think maybe we can get the motor to limp along for a month?"

"It's worth a try."

"If we can, I bet I can get some of my aggie buddies to help me rebuild the motor, you know, as a winter project." Dempsey turned away to an immediate job. He gapped the new spark plugs and screwed them in.

Frye came along behind, attaching a new harness to the plugs and the distributor cap. He pulled the cap off and examined the points. "We ought to replace these, June. You know how to do that?"

"Did it in auto shop."

"Excellent. There's a set of new points in the box. Go to it. Pappy, you want to change out the belts while I put on a new air filter?"

"Why don't I do the filter and you scrape your knuckles on the belt pulleys?"

"Chicken."

Wickingson wriggled out from beneath the engine. Pappy stared at him, a splatter of oil on Wickingson's glasses and face and a great blot in the middle of his bibs. Pappy erupted in laughter.

Frye arched an eyebrow at Wickingson. "I told you to take it easy."

"But that air wrench was so fast."

PAPPY GANDERED at his watch. "By golly, Miss Molly, we're done with the heavy stuff and in a shade under two hours."

Frye let the air out of the pillow. After the front of the truck sat square on its new tires, Wickingson air-wrenched the lug nuts tight. He then went to the rear wheels and spun those lug nuts off their bolts.

Frye tossed the pillow under the rear of the truck. He positioned it under a crossbeam and aired the pillow up.

The four, working like a NASCAR pit crew, changed out the rear wheels and tires.

Again, Frye let the air out of the pillow. While he packed it away and reeled in his hose, Wickingson air-wrenched the rear lug nuts tight.

Frye called back, "Anyone think to look at the muffler while we had the rear of the truck up?"

Pappy and Dempsey stared at one another, then at Wickingson and Frye. They shrugged.

Frye parked his knuckles on his hips. "Junior, you better crawl under there and see what you got."

Dempsey searched underneath until he located the muffler behind the cab and well forward of the rear axle. "Looks all right. Uh-oh."

"What?"

"I just rapped on it. The guts are rusted out."

Pappy looked over at Frye. "Ambrose, you got a muffler in your box of stuff?"

"That takes a cutting torch and a welder. I don't do mufflers."

"Well, we've got a Midas shop in town."

Dempsey crawled out from under the truck. He brushed himself off.

Frye came up with a ten-gallon gas can—empty—and a length of rubber hose. "The gas in this old truck is gonna be dead. Wicks, here you go. Siphon it out. I'll get the fresh gas."

Wickingson took the caps off the can and the truck's filler pipe. He peeked in the pipe. "Should I light a match to see how much we got in there?"

"Hey, don't you do that."

Wickingson pantomimed 'Ka-boom!'

Pappy pointed Dempsey toward the cab. "Turn on the ignition. See what the gauge reads."

Dempsey leaned in. He turned the switch and watched the gas gauge. When it didn't respond, he tapped the glass. "It's coming up now. Looks to be about a quarter."

Wickingson readied the hose. "What do you think, Pap, about five gallons?"

"About that."

He dropped one end of the hose in the tank. The other end he put in his mouth and sucked on it, pulling the gas up. Wickingson pinched the tube. He exhaled and sucked on it again. On the third pull, Wickingson spit, and at the same time he jammed the end of the hose in the can.

"Gawd, that tastes awful. Pappy, no smoking around me, please."

The gas flowed through the hose, up and out of the tank. When it stopped running, Wickingson pulled the hose out, and Frye poured the better part of five gallons of new gasoline in.

Pappy went around to the passenger's side and hoisted himself up on the seat. "June, you ready to start this thing?"

Dempsey slipped up on the driver's seat. "How about I try my bubble light first?"

"Have at it."

He fumbled around the instrument panel. Nothing. Dempsey scratched at the edges of his sideburn. "I don't see anything for that."

"June, where wouldn't a guy think to look?"

"Under the seat." Dempsey got out. He scrunched down, his ear on the floor as he peered up under. "There it is."

He pushed the switch, and an electric motor on the cab's roof set about grinding, a light revolving, flashing.

Pappy spun his hand in time with the rotating light. "Beautiful. Turn it off and get back up here."

Dempsey punched the bubble-light switch a second time, then again pulled himself up on the driver's seat.

Pappy patted the horn button.

"So?" June asked.

"Punch it. You're in for a surprise."

Dempsey pressed the horn button and grinned. "Would you listen to that, the Wilhelm Tell Overture, the first four bars?" He pressed the horn button again.

"Yeah, Sam was nuts for the Lone Ranger."

Wickingson came up. "Is that what I think it is?"

"Hi-ho Silver."

Frye leaned in. "Come on, you musical connoisseurs, get this thing going."

Dempsey looked at Pappy. He wiggled his eyebrows in Groucho Marx-fashion, put his fingers on the ignition key and twisted.

The starter whirred.

Pappy shook his head. "It didn't catch. Try it again."

Dempsey twisted the key a second time.

The engine cranked but didn't fire. Dempsey cranked the engine again, and still it didn't fire. He pumped on the gas pedal and kept the engine cranking.

The engine popped.

It crackled as the carburetor shot gasoline into the cylinders. Three cylinders fired, then a fourth, the engine shaking, a beast angered at being wakened.

Dempsey, laughing like a maniac, stepped down on the accelerator. The fifth and sixth cylinders fired, and the engine, smoothing out, screamed at a high rpm. He punched Pappy's shoulder.

Pappy yelled to make himself heard. "June, I think you got yourself a truck!"

Wickingson and Frye slapped hands in a high-five.

Missus Kramer came dashing out with tray of glasses and a pitcher of lemonade. "Oh, you got it going. Wonderful, boys. How about something to drink, to celebrate?"

Dempsey let off on the gas. He listened to the six-cylinder purr for some moments before he shut the engine off.

Missus Kramer poured the lemonade, hands grabbing up the glasses as rapidly as she filled them. The four Caballeros clicked their glasses together and gabbled on about what they had done.

Missus Kramer, though, helped herself to a pint of rum from her apron pocket. She patted Pappy's shoulder. When he turned to her, she held up her bottle and winked. "I take my comfort straight. In the right company."

Chapter 7

Meet Mister Sam

JUNIOR DEMPSEY'S ice cream truck became a Tau Upsilon project.

Steve Palusky and his girlfriend, Annie Beale, both art majors, created a splashy paint design for the truck that used swirls of orange and blue with star bursts, all overlaying a white base. They also convinced Dempsey and Pappy to change the color for the canopy top from candy stripe to UT orange.

Brian Hemphill, a mechanical/automotive engineering major, talked his Fountain City cousin into giving the fraternity one bay of his auto body shop for a week. The first day, Hemphill and his roommate, B.J. Castle, sanded out the rusted areas of the cab and box and laid down a primer coat. The next day, they sprayed the truck white. That done, they let the paint bake in the body shop's heat room overnight.

The morning of the third day, a Sunday, when most people were in church, Palusky and Beale taped the stencils of their paint scheme to the truck. Hemphill sprayed on the blue and let it bake that night. The next evening, he came back with the orange. He feathered it in, and let that bake.

The following evening Palusky and Beale painted the star bursts. They also hand-lettered 'Mister Sam' on the side of the box, the name Dempsey had given his truck.

Hemphill followed the next day with a clear coat.

On the last afternoon, Hemphill, Pappy, Dempsey, Frye, Wickingson, Castle, Palusky, and Beale returned to add the final touches to make the truck a show piece—fourteen-inch polished aluminum wheels and squat, low-profile Michelins, chromed twin exhaust stacks that ran up behind the cab to port the engine exhaust out over the canopy, the new orange canopy itself, and a placard they mounted above the canopy's centerline, reading 'Tau Upsilon's Frosty Treats.'

The group stood back, admiring the finished product.

Frye sniffed at the air. "Sure smells of lacquer in here, doesn't it?"

Pappy gave a tilt of his head. "Yeah, to get a buzz on all we have to do is breathe."

Wickingson brandished a thirty-five millimeter camera. "We gotta get pictures."

Up went the door to the body shop bay. In flushed fresh air as Pappy and Frye turned to the job of directing Dempsey backing Mister Sam out into the late afternoon sun.

Wickingson waved everyone around. "Palusky and Beale, I want you down here, each on one knee, your arms out like old vaudevillians, showing off your paint scheme."

He hustled Hemphill to the rear quarter of Mister Sam. "Put one foot up on the bumper. That's it, and your elbow on your knee."

He beckoned to Castle. "Get a paint gun for Hemphill, then stand behind him and wave at the camera."

Wickingson next grabbed Frye. He propped him against the front fender. "Pappy, I want you to stand on the running board. Junior, you're up in the box, leaning out across the freezer."

He caught Hemphill's cousin, Av Dellinger. "Mister Dellinger, I need you to take the picture so I can be in it. Is that all right?"

"Take it from here?" Dellinger asked.

Wickingson gave him the camera. Dellinger squinted through the viewfinder as Wickingson ran forward. He leaned on Frye's shoulder.

"Three, two, one," Dellinger called out and pressed the shutter button. The automatic winder advanced the film for the next shot. "I think somebody smiled in that one. This is serious. I'm going to take another picture."

Wickingson stepped around in front of the group. "All right, how about we make this like an old tintype family picture. Everyone, sober, a somber pose."

He stared at Dempsey and shook his head. "Junior, down here in front. Do your Napoleon."

Dempsey bounded out of the box. He twisted his cap to the side and stuck one hand inside his shirt.

"That's got it." Wickingson strolled back to his place next to Frye.

Dellinger again squinted through the viewfinder. "I like this. I like this. All right, three, two, one."

He pressed the button.

"One more. This time, everybody nuts."

Palusky dipped Beale in an embrace and planted the kiss of a lifetime on her. Hemphill and Castle, the painters, danced cheek-to-cheek. Frye throttled Wickingson, and Dempsey picked up Pappy as a groom would his bride.

"Three, two, one."

Snap.

Dempsey dropped Pappy and clapped his hands over his head. "All right, everybody, ice cream!" He ran back up into the box of Mister Sam and threw open a freezer. "I've got ice cream bars, Drumsticks, Haagen Dazs cups for the snooty, six flavors of Popsicles, and hand-dipped ice cream."

Frye lit up. "What flavors?"

"I've got chocolate, butter pecan, New York," which Dempsey pronounced New Yawk, "peach, the ever-popular vanilla, and Rocky Road."

"Rocky Road."

"One dip or two?"

"Two."

Pappy hopped up the steps to help fill the orders. "When did you stock up?" he asked as he handed Wickingson a Haagen Dazs and a spoon.

"Last night." Dempsey raked his scoop across the New York and packed the ball of ice cream into a sugar cone. "I called the Mayfield office. They put together a selection of stuff—this Mayfield ice cream is good, just as good as Haagen Dazs, Wicks."

Wickingson dug a spoonful of ice cream from his cup. "You'll never convince me."

Dempsey dipped again into the New York. "Anyway, they brought it out last night and helped me organize the freezers, even helped me work out my pricing. Pappy, I tasted every one of the ice creams, and it's really good stuff."

Pappy dug a scoop into the butter pecan. He made a cone for himself. "How you going to keep all this secure if you park your truck in the frat's lot at night?"

"They said I can leave Mister Sam at their Kingston Pike distribution plant. They'll rotate my inventory so nothing gets old." Dempsey handed a cone to Beale and reached back down in the freezer, to make up a double-dip for Palusky. "If I'm not going to use Mister Sam for more than three days, they'll empty the freezers and restock as long as I give them a day's warning."

"So you got this all worked out."

"Yeah." Dempsey handed Palusky his cone. He tossed his scoop in the truck's sink. "Think I'm gonna have me a Fudgesicle. You know Gibby?"

Pappy licked at a dollop of butter pecan hanging over the side of his cone. "Gibby Deets?"

"Yeah." Dempsey tore the paper from a Fudgesicle. "He's a business major, a freshman like us. For a cut, he's going to keep the books."

"How about your licenses?"

"Gibby got 'em, even the health department certificate. And since this is food, there's no sales tax to worry about, thank you Nashville for little favors."

Pappy put an arm around Dempsey's shoulders. "You're all right, kid. What say we head for the house? Let's break in Mister Sam and sell some ice cream to the brothers."

They made a parade of the return to campus, Dempsey, Hemphill and Castle in Mister Sam, Palusky and Beale with Pappy in his pickup, and, bringing up the rear, Frye and Wickingson in Frye's Kenworth wrecker, his rolling repair shop. Frye had borrowed it for the afternoon so he could put the new wheels and exhaust stacks on Mister Sam.

They ambled down Broadway, from Fountain City to the heart of downtown Knoxville. There they turned onto Cumberland and rolled past the site of the Nineteen Eighty-two World's Fair and the fair's signature attraction, the Sunsphere.

At the north entrance to the campus, Dempsey herded Mister Sam onto Volunteer Boulevard. He flipped on the bubble light and started the tinkle bell ringing.

Like the Pied Piper, he and Mister Sam led the mini-parade past the new library, past Glockner Hall, the old business building, past Claxton, past McClung Tower and the Art and Architecture Building where Palusky and Beale spent most of their time when they weren't in Palusky's room engaged in passionate sex.

Dempsey swung Mister Sam onto Greek Row. He hit his horn when he came within sight of the Tau Upsilon house, sounding 'The Wilhelm Tell Overture.' Pappy added to the cacophony by tapped on his horn, and Frye let out with a blast from his tow truck's air horn.

Greeks—male and female—rushed to doors and windows. Those on the front porches jumped down to the lawns. Students came running from all directions, converging on Mister Sam, shouting out orders even before the parade rolled to a stop in front of the Tau Upsilon house.

Dempsey, Pappy, Wickingson, and Frye bailed out of their trucks and into the back of Mister Sam where they scooped up ice cream and tossed out bars as fast as they could work, Palusky and Beale running the cash box.

Don Wright and his officers watched from the porch. After the last customer had been served, when Dempsey was at Mister Sam's sink, washing his ice cream scoops, they came down.

Wright put his hand up on the counter. "Junior, we've been talking it over, and we think your truck would make a heck of a float for the fraternity in the homecoming parade. What do you say?"

Dempsey glanced at Pappy as he gave him three wet scoops to dry.

"June, it's your decision."

"I think it'd be fun."

Chapter 8

The parade

NOBODY REMEMBERED how the tradition began. Maybe it was in one of those bleak football years when the Vols stood zero and four and the team faced sure slaughter by the Georgia Bulldogs that some of the band members took pity on the dispirited players who dragged themselves from their dorms to the stadium in rag-tag fashion and civilian clothes.

"Let's get out there ahead of them and play the fight song," a piccolo player may have said, and on that Saturday a dozen musicians and six cheerleaders ran out to lead the football players to the stadium.

Or perhaps General Neyland, UT's first great football coach back in the Nineteen Thirties, ordered a parade to the playing field.

One thing everyone agreed on, nothing had changed over the years except numbers. The band grew to two hundred members and became known as The Pride of the Southland Marching Band. Soon it was two hundred twenty-five, then two hundred fifty. The year The Pride fielded three hundred members made it the largest university marching band in the nation. Volume equated with size, and these musicians thundered out the music.

Parents and alumni drove in early on game days, from as far away as Nashville and Memphis, so they could pack the sidewalks along Volunteer Boulevard and the nameless block-long side street that connected the boulevard to Stadium Drive, just to hear The Pride boom out 'Rocky Top' on the three-block march from Gibbs Hall, the athletic dorm, to the entrance to the stadium, to cheer for the football players walking along behind The Pride, waving to the crowds swept up in Volunteer Fever. As always, the players were in civilian clothes. Neither the players nor the bandsmen wore uniforms in these pre-game parades.

Student-built floats preceded The Pride and the team on homecoming days. Still talked about was the Nineteen Forty-seven float of the aeronautical engineering students. In the dark of the night, they had hauled a wingless Piper Cub onto campus. They parked the flatbed truck on the intramural field and there attached the wings to the fuselage. The student engineers, and their girlfriends and wives, decorated the truck with hundreds of yards of orange and white crepe paper, and strung their 'Fly to Victory' banner above it all.

The float stunned the students and adults alike who lined the parade route that day, but what came next exceeded belief. The aeronautical engineers drove their float into the open north end of the stadium. There eighteen husky young men, most of whom were former GIs, lifted the Cub to the ground. They packed the football coach in the front seat and a pilot, another former warrior, in the back, then ran to the sidelines to watch the show.

The pilot started the engine, startling the coach.

The pilot stood on the brakes. He ran the engine up to the max, until it bellowed. The coach, wild-eyed, clawed at his shoulder harness—to escape—but before he could, the pilot released the brakes. He made a short run down the field, toward the south end of the stadium, and hauled back on the stick.

The Cub staggered into the air.

It scratched for altitude, climbing like a sick duck, finally clearing the goal posts by less than a dozen feet, the coach's eyes the size of saucers.

The pilot guided the Cub in a languid circle over the stadium, then side slipped it back in for a landing.

The coach, white as new snow, reportedly screamed at the pilot, "You're nuts! Certifiably nuts!" as he ran from the plane.

A reporter for the Daily Beacon learned later that the aeronautical engineers had not told the coach of the impending flight. They had instead told him the pilot was only going to taxi the airplane around the gridiron. "It'll make great pictures," they had said to him.

HOMECOMING MORNING dawned cold but clear, ideal football weather. Pappy and Dempsey turned out a herd of Tau Upsilons early to wax and polish Mister Sam one last time and hang the streamers. They put extension poles above the canopy and fastened a banner between them that read 'ice CREAM THE GATORS.'

At ten minutes before parade time, the temperature fifty-eight and climbing, Dempsey spread a blanket over the roof of Mister Sam's cab. When done, he motioned to a female student in UT shorts and varsity jacket, a beauty queen hopeful. "Liz, come up the ladder. I want you to sit up here."

"Why?"

"Cuz you're a stunner. We've got a Beacon photog here. He'll take your picture for the paper. Front page."

Liz Martin, Tau Upsilon's Sweetheart of Nineteen Eighty-eight, flashed a dazzler of a smile. She took Pappy's hand and stepped up on the ladder. "Do you really think the picture will make the front page?"

"With your legs, honey, guaranteed."

Two steps up, she grabbed hold of Dempsey's hand. He motioned at the hood. "Don't step on that. It's not that strong."

She worked herself up and settled herself on the blanket, beside Dempsey, where she went about displaying her bare legs at their curvaceous best.

Wickingson, on the ground, whistled.

"Ignore him," Dempsey said.

"Ignore him? That's what I want, whistles and applause and passionate sex. I'm a party girl. Par-ty, par-ty!" She blew kisses at Wickingson.

Wickingson picked up the Par-ty cheer as did other Tau Upsilons.

A parade captain beckoned to Dempsey. "Come on, get your truck in line."

Dempsey nodded to him, then turned back to Martin. "You hang on now."

"I'll hang onto you."

"Can't. I'm driving." He swung down and into the cab.

Pappy climbed into the passenger seat. "Mind if I ride along?"

"Wouldn't be right without you."

"Mighty pretty legs in the windshield."

"Ooo yeah. The rest of her doesn't appear to be bad either." Dempsey started the engine.

Wright and others cleared a path down the Tau Upsilon sidewalk to the curb while Dempsey idled Mister Sam along behind them. The truck rocked hard when it came off the curb, the fraternity's sweetheart scrambling for a handhold to keep from sliding off the roof.

At the end of Greek Row, Dempsey followed hand signals from a parade captain into the lineup, behind the Rodeo Club's horse unit and ahead of The Pride marching band. There the truck died.

Dempsey ground away on the starter, to no effect.

Frye, riding in the back with the fraternity's officers and a half-dozen other brothers, leaped over a freezer and ran for the front of the truck.

Pappy jumped down from the passenger seat.

Frye popped the hood latch and threw the hood up.

Pappy jammed the broomstick in place.

"Wiring." Frye leaned across the radiator. He set to wiggling sparkplug wire after sparkplug wire, searching for a loose connection.

"Damn, that doesn't seem to be it. Have we got juice?" Frye laid a screwdriver across the battery's terminals, and electricity arced, spraying up a shower of sparks. Frye leaped back, shaking his fingers. "Jesus H. Christ."

"You all right?"

"Gol-ley, that battery's hot. Yeah, I'm all right."

Pappy threw a spin-up sign to Dempsey. "Hit it again!"

Dempsey twisted the ignition key.

This time, not even the starter whirred.

A parade captain ran up, waving his hand radio. "You've got two minutes to get this truck running or we push it up on the curb and leave you!"

"Gotcha." Pappy grabbed Wickingson. "Run back to the house and get our tug-of-war rope. It's on the porch. And bring back every brother you can find."

Wickingson shoved through Tau Upsilon men and sprinted away, his legs pumping.

"Donnyyyy!" Pappy called out.

Don Wright, the frat president, leaned out over a freezer. "Yeah?"

"Get everybody up front. We're gonna pull this thing."

"You're kidding me."

"I said get up here! Bring everybody with you."

Liz Martin came forward on her perch. "How about me, Mister Brown?"

"Sweetheart, you just stay up there and smile and wave and look pretty. What're you wearing under that jacket?"

"A bikini top."

"Chuck your jacket."

Pappy slammed the truck's hood down as Wright and seven other Tau Upsilons pushed their way up.

"What's wrong?" Wright asked.

"The truck won't start. You want it in the parade, right?"

"Sure, we do."

"You remember that commercial for Twenty-Mule Team Borax?"

"Twenty-Mule Team what?"

Pappy threw up his hands. "Gawd, you kids are sooo young. Donny, get the brothers out in front of the truck. As soon as Wicks gets back here with the rope, we're the mules. We're gonna pull Mister Sam in the parade."

"You heard Pappy," Wright called to the Tau Upsilons, motioning for them to follow him.

Pappy pushed Frye under the front bumper. "You see tow hooks down there?"

"Yeah."

"You loop the rope around the hooks and I'll tie it off out here, then we pull."

"How much weight?"

"A couple ton."

"Good God, Pappy."

Wickingson trotted in, his legs wobbling, a massive coil of rope over his shoulder and a dozen other Tau Upsilons with him. He collapsed against the fender of Mister Sam.

"Hardest work you've ever done, huh?" Pappy took the rope from Wickingson. He gave a length to Frye who fitted it around the frame hooks. Frye held an end out, and Pappy tied the rope off.

He tested his knot, then hustled forward, unreeling the rope as he went. Every two feet a Tau Upsilon brother picked up the rope and wrapped it around his pulling hand.

Whistles sounded at the front of the parade.

The Pride's drum major raised his baton. On his downbeat, the drummers—twenty-six of them—struck up a cadence.

Floats began to move, then the Rodeo Club's riders.

A parade captain and six enforcers, all bigger than he and in Sigma Sigma Sigma jackets, charged up to Pappy. "Out of the way! We're pushing your goddamn truck off the street."

The Tau Upsilons on the rope circled back in as Pappy flipped the captain a middle-finger salute, Pappy's eyes closing to slits. "We don't much like you Sigs, so I'll tell you once—put a hand, even a fingertip, on our truck and you're in for a helluva fight. Are you up to it?"

"If that's what it takes." The captain elbowed in.

Wicks grabbed the man's wrist. He whirled him around in a wrestler's takedown and came down on the man's back with his knee.

Pappy glared at the remaining six. "Who's next?"

Two stepped forward.

Pappy waved to the Tau Ups. "Siggies, look around. We gotcha outnumbered four to one. Are you sure you wanna do this?"

The enforcers peered at one another. A beat slipped by, and they shuffled back.

Pappy wheeled to the brothers. "Back on the rope line. Come on, pull!"

Twenty Tau Upsilons dashed to their positions. Again they wrapped their hands into the sisal cord, and, on a second shout from Pappy, leaned their collective mass into it. Mister Sam edged along.

The drum major blew three sharp blasts on his whistle. The Pride responded with the opening notes of 'Rocky Top', people cheering.

The cheering rolled like a wave along the length of the parade route, Big Orange fever igniting all who had come to see a tradition, a tradition that carried many back in memory to homecoming-day parades and games when they were students at UT, to dances in the streets and kegger parties.

Young fathers hoisted their children to their shoulders, children in Vol sweatshirts, some wearing orange football helmets. Students, on passing floats, threw candy to them. Tau Upsilon men, not on the rope line, waded into the crowds, handing out discount tickets for Tau Ups Frosty Treats. "See us in front of the stadium. We'll be right across from the entrance," they told all within earshot.

A WBIR cameraman, videotaping the parade for the evening news, ran out into the street when he saw a line of students pulling an ice cream truck. He videotaped along the line and up to the Tau Upsilon Sweetheart for a tight closing shot. Liz Martin obliged. She leaned down and waved into the lens of the camera, producing a picture that wowed the news audience with her ample cleavage.

The cameraman ran back to Pappy. "Whose rig is this?"

"His." Pappy fired his trigger finger at Dempsey behind the steering wheel.

The cameraman said something into his headset, and, moments later, a reporter emerged from the sidewalk crowd. The cameraman gestured at Dempsey, and the reporter hopped on Mister Sam's running board. He stuck a microphone in Dempsey's face.

A horse lifted its tail, jetting out yellowish water. The splash, as it hit the pavement, showered Pappy, Wright, and the others at the front of the rope line.

They'd hardly dried themselves when a second horse dumped a load of manure.

Pappy saw it and twisted back. "Horse pucky, boys, and it stinks! Walk around it, over it or through it, but don't break the pace!"

ALTHOUGH NOT HOT—the temperature at game time reached only seventy-one—the sun that day in Tennessee's cloudless sky was a baker. Tau Upsilon men shuttled steadily between Mayfield's freezer trailer parked in the truck lot at the north end of the stadium and Mister Sam on Stadium Drive. They toted cartons, cases, and tubs of ice cream and frozen bars that sold as fast as each man made a round trip. Pappy and Dempsey stopped the runners ten minutes before game time, when the crowd on the street began to thin.

When, inside the stadium, The Pride played 'The National Anthem,' Pappy and Dempsey peeled off their Tau Upsilon caps. They stood at attention.

After the last notes drifted away, Dempsey slapped his cap onto the back of his head. He draped an arm around Pappy's shoulders. "Lordy, they ran us ragged, didn't they?"

"What say we go sit on the bumper?"

"Wicks, you clean up back here?"

"Yeah, I've got a crew."

Dempsey reached into the freezer for a Fudgesicle. "Want one, Pap?"

"Got a Drumstick?"

Dempsey dug down to the bottom. "One left."

"That's all I need."

Dempsey handed up the Drumstick, then led the way to the steps and down to the street. Dempsey and Pappy ambled past Don Wright and two others stripping the crepe paper decorations off the truck.

They settled themselves on the front bumper, like grackles on a telephone wire. Dempsey pressed the wrapped Fudgesicle against his forehead. "Ooo, that feels good."

Pappy bit into the cone part of his Drumstick. "You ever guess what you were getting yourself into when you said you wanted an ice cream truck?"

"A dead truck. Should I be calling Triple-A?"

"Naw, Ambrose has gone for his Kenworth. He'll tow Mister Sam to a garage for you."

"You arrange that?"

"Well, you were kinda busy there at the freezer with your big scoop."

"Thanks." Dempsey peeled the paper off his Fudgesicle. "Yup, all in all, I'd say it's been a right good day. Wonder how much ice cream we went through?"

"Don't know."

"Would you believe eighty-nine gallons?" A new voice entered the conversation, Gibby Deets coming from the back of the truck, an adding machine tape in his hand. Deets, thin and prematurely bald, looked every bit the accountant. "We also went through fifty-one cartons of bars and cups and other specialty items."

"What else?"

Deets reviewed his tape. "You know those coupons, those twenty-five-centers? We took in four thousand, one hundred sixteen of those little suckers. So we gave away one thousand twenty-nine dollars of our profit."

Pappy held up the stump of his Drumstick. "Cheap advertising. What's the bottom line?"

"After we pay Mayfield, three thousand six dollars and twenty-one cents. I don't know where that extra penny came from. Maybe somebody gave us a tip."

Pappy slapped Dempsey's hand. "Hot damn, son, you did well."

"I don't feel right keeping it. This was the fraternity's homecoming float."

"So split it with the frat. I'm sure Donny could find a good use for the money."

Deets stuffed the adding machine tape in his shirt pocket. "June, I'm going to take the money over to the student organization office in the Union. They've got a safe there we can keep it in until the bank opens Monday. I'll take Wicks the Hulk with me, kind of like a guard, you know, to scare off anyone who might be curious about what I'm carrying."

Crowd cheers interrupted. They welled up from within the stadium and spilled out over the near campus, and a cannon exploded.

Pappy, still chewing on his Drumstick, glanced at Dempsey. "We just got the first touchdown."

Chapter 9

Afterglow

THE VOLS of Tennessee and the Gators of Florida played to a twenty-one, twenty-one tie that day. The lack of a win took the edge off the post-game celebrations, and one person didn't celebrate at all.

Pappy.

Well after dark, he sat in his canvas chair on the porch roof of the Tau Upsilon house, his feet up on the railing. He lit a fresh Camel with the stub of one about to expire.

Don Wright and Caroline Brown, coming back from a party at the Greek Unity House, strolled together, he with his arm around her waist, she with her head against his shoulder. They turned up the walk toward the Tau Upsilon house. It was she who first saw the glowing end of a cigarette above them.

"That you, Grandpops?"

Pappy blew a lungful of smoke into the night air. "Sure enough, Sweetpea."

"You all alone up there?"

"Yup."

"You want company?"

"Sweetpea, you're always welcome on the porch roof of my house."

Caroline gazed at Wright. "Can we go up?"

"If you'd like."

"It's a nice night. He shouldn't be alone."

Pappy dragged on his cigarette. He took it from his lips, turned it and studied the accumulating ash on the fire end. Some of the ash fell off, down the front of his jacket. Pappy brushed the ash away.

Caroline stepped out through the window.

He gazed at her in the light that streamed from his room. "You're looking right pretty. Don come up with you?"

"Yes."

"Don," Pappy said in the direction of the window, "hand a good chair out here for Carrie and toss that old beanbag chair out for yourself."

Out came the chairs, and Wright.

Pappy flicked ash from his cigarette. "Come on, you two, sit and put your feet up. Want to spit and whittle some?"

"Grandpops." Caroline's tone sounded mildly of scolding as she put her chair down next to his.

Pappy opened Wickingson's cooler. "How about something to drink? I got Country Time, an RC–"

"An RC," Caroline said.

He fished up a wet can for her.

Wright looked over at the cooler. "You got a Bud in there?"

"Leinenkugel. All except for one lonely Miller's that Junior sneaked in."

"I'll have a Leinen-whatever."

"Here you go." Pappy tossed a Leinenkugel can across to Wright who had, by this time, been swallowed by the beanbag chair, all except for his legs and one arm.

Pappy pulled the pop-top ring on his lemonade. He made a studied effort at dropping the ring into the can.

Caroline opened her RC. "Where's Junior? You two are usually joined at the hip."

Pappy balanced his lemonade on his forehead. "You know what that rascal's done?"

"You're going to spill that, Grandpops."

"I haven't yet."

"What's Junior gone and done?"

"Remember our Tau Ups Sweetheart, Liz Martin, she rode on top of the cab of Mister Sam?"

"Yes."

"Ooo, Carrie, that kid's a knockout, drop-dead beautiful, even to an old man like me. Anyway, Junior talks her into dumping her date, and they're downstairs somewhere, probably in the kitchen, licking ice cream off each other."

"Grandpops, you're kidding."

Pappy lifted the can from his forehead. He sipped at the contents. "A little maybe. They are downstairs. The last I saw them, that hayseed had Miss Centerfold draped all over him."

"Grandpops—"

"So, all right, they're playing canasta."

"Playing what?"

"Canasta. Jesus, Carrie, it's a card game your grandma and I played by candlelight because Ben Franklin hadn't invented electricity yet."

"Oh." Caroline nudged Wright. She pointed her thumb at the window.

Wright rolled out of the beanbag chair onto his knees. He pushed himself up. "Pappy, I'm going downstairs and circulate with the alums. As president, it's kind of expected I do that."

Pappy gave an absent wave.

"See you in a bit?" Wright asked Caroline.

"Sure."

She reached for his hand. Their fingers touched, then Wright left.

Caroline sipped at her RC. She gazed out into the branches of the ancient magnolia that, five months of the year, shaded the Tau Upsilons' front lawn, the branches now almost naked.

Pappy tilted his chin up. "Smells of burning leaves, doesn't it? You suppose someone's havin' a bonfire somewhere?"

"Could be." Caroline continued to gaze up into the tree. "You want to talk about it?"

Pappy pulled on his cigarette. "About what?"

"Why you're sitting up here alone."

He stubbed the cigarette out. Pappy shredded the butt and sprinkled the bits of tobacco and paper on the roof. "Carrie, I'm an old man living in a young man's house. I don't fit in."

"That's not true."

"I mention canasta or Twenty-Mule Team Borax or I say I like Johnny Cash music, and I get stares that tell me you kids think I'm some old spook from the far distant past. And I don't understand half the stuff you talk about. Gawd, I sure don't understand your music and why you're not all deaf the way you crank it up so loud."

Caroline started to interrupt, but stopped, as if she had thought better about intruding.

Pappy let out a deep sign. "I miss your grandma. We had this big old house. It was a wreck, but we bought it cheap after the war. It had a porch on it like this, and she and I would sit out on the roof on hot summer nights and we'd just talk. Or the Paxtons next door had Bing Crosby on the radio, and their window'd be open, and we'd just listen...I miss that old gal. Gawddammit, why'd she have to go and drink herself to death?"

Pappy pulled a handkerchief from his pocket. He wiped at his eyes.

Caroline stared into her RC can. "I hardly remember her, other than the pictures at your house and the ones Dad's got."

"You were a tad when she died. She thought you were the best."

Caroline put a hand on Pappy's arm. Her hand slipped down and came to rest on his, her fingers curling into his palm.

Chapter 10

The plan

PAPPY, DEMPSEY, Frye, and Wickingson waded through the shoppers strolling from store to store at the Kensington Pike Center.

Dempsey hopped up, to see over the heads of others. "There it is, Ted's Trick Shop!"

He charged for the door and made it inside first, bug-eyed at what he saw. Dempsey lifted a Frankenstein head down from a shelf. He pulled the rubber structure over his head, turned to the Caballeros, and threw his arms out wide. "Ta-dah!"

Pappy snickered. "Gotta admit, June, it's an improvement."

Dempsey ripped the mask off. "Aw, come on, now." He pooched out his lower lip in an imitation of hurt.

Wickingson pointed to a Snow White head. "Hey, June, you wear that and a dress and we can go as Snow White and the Three Dwarfs."

"I don't think so."

Pappy moved further into the store. His gaze went up to a rubber head on high shelf. "Ooo, that's scary."

Dempsey looked his way.

Pappy thumbed at the head. "That one, right there."

"Who's that?"

"Richard Nixon."

"Richard who?"

"Gawd, you don't know nothing about history. President of the United States. Nineteen Seventy-three. Watergate. We ran the bastard out of office."

"Pappy, I was only seven years old."

Wickingson tried on a set of vampire teeth. "I remember him. We studied him in American History class when I was a junior at Westby High. Like my teeth?"

Pappy bowed to the young man from Wisconsin. "Our token Yankee, a man of wisdom and great intelligence. And, no, I don't like your teeth."

Wickingson spit them out. He gestured at the set of masks next to the Nixon mask. "Look, they've got Ronald Reagan, Jimmy Carter, and Gerald Ford."

Pappy clapped his hands. "We could go as The Four Presidents."

Dempsey touched Pappy's shoulder. "Cool."

Wickingson studied the Carter mask. "If we do it, I get to be Mister Peanut. I like his teeth."

"What's this thing you've got about teeth?"

Frye squared his shoulders. He jutted his chin out. "I wouldn't mind being President Reagan. I kinda look like him, don't you think?"

A man in a Dracula cape and dog fangs swept out of a back office. "May I help you, gentlemen?"

Pappy motioned at the masks. "We'd like to try on the four presidents."

"Excellent choices." Dracula picked up a yard stick. He poked the end up toward the top shelf where The Four Presidents resided next to mask heads of Al Capone and Scooby-Doo. He tipped the head of Reagan and caught it in the crook of his arm, like a football, when it fell. He handed the mask to Frye.

He next caught the Jimmy Carter head with its great toothy grin and tossed it to Wickingson.

Dracula held out the head of Gerald Ford, and Dempsey snatched it away.

That left sloop-nosed Richard Nixon.

Pappy wrinkled his nose, like he had stepped in a pile of dog poo. "Gawd, and me a Democrat." He pulled the head over his and spun around. Pappy thrust his hands high in the air. He waved two fingers on each in victory signs. "I am not a crook. I am not a crook," he said in his best Nixon voice.

Wickingson nodded in his Carter mask. "Hey, that's good. We saw that videotape in history class."

"Then your education wasn't a waste, kid." Pappy pulled off the Nixon head. "How much, Dracula?"

"Buy or rent?"

"Rent. Next year we might want to go as Goldilocks and the Berenstain Bears."

Dempsey put his thumbs up.

Pappy slapped at them. "I read those stories to my grandkids."

Dracula counted the sets of vampire teeth in a display bowl dripping with plastic blood by the cash register. "I'm missing a set."

Wickingson held them out.

"You put those in your mouth?"

"Uh-huh."

"I can't take 'em back. That's a buck and a half. For the head rent, Mister Carter, that's ten dollars each and twenty-five dollars security deposit for the lot of them. You'll get that back when you return the heads."

The Caballeros dug out their wallets. Each counted out enough bills to satisfy the rent and their share of the deposit, Wickingson an extra dollar and a half for the teeth.

Dracula scribbled out a receipt. He presented it to Pappy. "All you need for costumes are dark business suits and black shoes."

"I think we can come up with that."

Dempsey raised a hand. "Not me. I'm gonna have to go next door to the tuxedo shop and rent a suit and shoes."

Wickingson stood there, his face alight with a Jimmy Carter smile. "This is going to blow their minds, just blow their minds, when we come into the masked ball as The Four Presidents."

Pappy tucked the receipt in his wallet, next to his picture of Caroline. "Yes, particularly our distinguished university president. Lamar's got White House ambitions."

Frye checked his reflection in the window glass. "Well, he was our governor."

"And not half bad, even if he did make a hundred thou profit on a ten-thousand investment in the Knoxville News."

Wickingson turned on Pappy. "Are you implying that our university president is a crook?"

"Me? Never. A politician, yeah, particularly one who knows a good deal when somebody throws it at him."

"You're a cynic."

Pappy put his Nixon head on. He thrust his hands up, waving his fingers in vees. "I am not a crook! I am not a crook!"

THE CABALLEROS stopped at the Blue Onion on their way back to campus, for hamburgers and beer and a Country Time for Pappy. Wickingson, when he was well into his second Blue Buster Burger, mumbled to himself.

Pappy stared at him. "Something bothering you?"

"The Four Presidents is fine, but we've got to come up with something for Halloween that will have the campus jumping."

Frye lifted the top of his bun. He shot in a new squirt of catsup. "I'm game. Got an idea?"

"Nothing. Nada. Zip. Zero."

Dempsey leaned up on his elbows while he munched on his burger. "Gibby's got this buddy who's got this work-study job in the university historian's office, you know, doing research on stuff."

"So?"

"Well, he came across this article in a Nineteen-Oh-Six Beacon, about this bunch of engineering students who, for a prank, you know, took apart this big old farm wagon."

Wickingson sipped his beer. "What's this got to do with anything?"

"Hold on, I'm getting to it." Dempsey paused for another bite from his hamburger. He chewed and swallowed while the other Caballeros watched him. "Anyway, they hauled the pieces up on the roof of Perkins Hall–did it in the dark of night–and reassembled it up there. At least they think it was a bunch of engineering students. Nobody was ever caught. Think about it, a wagon on the roof of a building."

Pappy smiled, then snickered.

"What is it, Pap?"

The snicker rolled into a full belly laugh. Pappy slapped the table, upsetting Wickingson's beer.

"Come on, Pap."

"No, I gotta show you."

"Show us what?"

"When we go back to the house, I'll show you. I promise."

Dempsey tossed back his beer. "Come on, I'm ready."

"Well, count out your money for the bartender first."

Out came the wallets. The four, scanning down the bill, thumped folding money on the table until Frye announced, "Enough." He gathered in the cash and gave it and the bill to the bartender as the others hurried for Pappy's truck.

"Come on, Pap, you can tell us now," Dempsey said as he forced himself to become thin so Wickingson could yank the door closed on his side of the cab.

Pappy started the motor.

"Well?"

He shook his head as he pulled away from his curbside parking spot. The automatic transmission shifted from first to second, then into drive before he snapped on the radio to Johnny Paycheck belting out his one-and-only hit, 'Take This Job and Shove It.' Pappy hummed along.

Frye shrugged. "Give it up, Junior. He's not talking."

"I don't know what 'it' is."

Pappy turned onto Stadium Drive. He cruised past the University Center, tapping his horn button to get the attention of several students going into the building. When they looked his way, he waved.

Wickingson rubbed at his nose. "So he's really gonna make us wait."

"It appears so."

Pappy continued on past big C Thirty-nine, the parking lot where most of the commuter students and half the faculty left their cars for the day, on past the stadium and around the curve below the Communications Building's parking lots. He motioned through the glass of the windshield. "What do you see there?"

Dempsey peered ahead. "Andy Holt Tower."

"Remember that."

Pappy stopped at Lake Louden Boulevard. He checked for traffic before he turned right and started up the hill. Humming along now to 'Coal Miner's Daughter,' Pappy cut through a series of side streets that brought him into the back entrance of the Tau Upsilon parking lot. He put his pickup in next to Frye's ancient Beetle. Pappy pocketed the ignition key as he got out, his passengers boiling out the other door.

Dempsey squared around to Pappy. "You gonna tell us now?"

Pappy waggled his fingers for the trio to follow him. He led them through the maze of cars and out across Theta Delta's back lawn to the parking lot of the Sigma Sigma Sigma fraternity, the competition as most Tau Upsilons viewed the Sigs. Pappy made his way down the first line of cars to a vintage Isetta, a car smaller than a Volkswagen, a two-seater with a tiny motorcycle engine in the back, the car's most distinctive feature a huge door on the front that swung out to let a driver and one passenger inside.

Pappy held his hands out. "There she is, boys."

"The Sigs' Blue Streak?" Dempsey kicked a front tire. "You know, I always thought that was an odd name for a car. The best it can do is forty-five, and that's downhill with a wind behind it."

"Boys, I want you to put the Streak together with Andy Holt."

Wickingson elbowed Pappy. "You want us to put that car—that car—on the roof of Andy Holt?"

Pappy made his hand into a pistol. He fired it at Wickingson.

"Man, that's eight stories up."

"Right again."

"Pappy, you're nuts."

"Wicks, you three gentlemen are engineers. God gave you brains. Figure it out."

Wickingson stared at Frye, and Frye peered at Dempsey, then each pivoted to the car.

Dempsey got down on one knee. He perused the underside of the Isetta.

Frye went to a side window. He held his hands over his forehead, like a sunshade, so he could see through the glass. He gazed at the controls.

Wickingson walked around the car, studying it. At the rear, he stuck his hands under the bumper and lifted. The rear wheels came off the ground. "God, it's light."

Pappy pushed his hands in his pockets. "Whole thing weights less than seven hundred pounds."

"How do you know?"

"A prof at Maryville College bought one back when they were new. Students were always picking it up and carrying it off while he was teaching classes. He never knew where he was going to find that car at the end of the day."

"Ah-ha."

Pappy strolled away. He headed across lots back toward the Tau Upsilon house, while Wickingson, Frye, and Dempsey stayed behind in a huddle.

Wickingson patted the roof of the Isetta. "First thing we've got to do is steal this thing."

Frye rubbed at the back of his neck. "The Sigs aren't going to like that."

"*F* the Sigs. They're the enemy."

"And if we get caught?"

"We've got to figure out how not to get caught."

"Pappy's got us being criminals." Dempsey gazed around. He spotted Pappy moving across the Theta Delt's yard. "Pappy, wait up!"

The three galloped off. They caught up with him as he sauntered onto the Tau Ups' front lawn, moving toward the porch.

Wickingson's chest heaved as he worked at catching his breath. "Pap, you're gonna make us steal that car."

"They'll get it back."

"You know how to do this."

Pappy swiveled to his roommates. "Boys, I'm just a dumb jack hand at this student biz. You're the geniuses."

"You know how to do this, and you're not going to tell us."

Pappy grinned, the Cheshire cat of the Alice stories. "You'll excuse me. I've gotta go up and read some poetry, an assignment for a class tomorrow."

He backed away, turned, and trotted up the steps to the porch.

Wickingson worked his heel at the concrete of the sidewalk. "Can we get inside the tower?"

Frye checked his watch. "Yup, they don't lock the doors 'til nine."

"Shall we reconnoiter then, as my ROTC buddies would say?"

Dempsey gave a conspiratorial rub of his hands. "I'm game."

The three jogged off down the sidewalk toward the Communications Building and the administration building behind it, the eight-story Andy Holt Tower, the tower connected to the Comm building by a skyway.

At Lake Louden Boulevard, they trotted in place until a break came in the early evening traffic, then dashed across the four-laner and up the sloping lawn to the front of Communications. There they stopped.

Frye motioned Dempsey and Wickingson on. "Go inside and I'll look around out here."

Wickingson slapped Frye's shoulder. "It's a plan. See you in, what, fifteen minutes?"

Frye checked his watch. He waved and started back toward the sloping lawn.

Wickingson and Dempsey opened one of the two sets of double doors that formed the main entrance to the Communications Building.

"Oh, look at that," Wickingson said, "no center post. We can drive the Isetta right through the doors, right on inside."

They went in and down the wide hallway that led to the skyway and the tower, a straight shot, uncluttered, nothing to impede four men and a small car.

The skyway opened into a lobby, ahead a door to the offices on that floor, behind, in the lobby's back wall, four elevator doors.

Dempsey pressed the elevator call button. "None of these doors are wide enough to get the car through. Damn, we're going to have to take the car apart and take it up a piece at a time."

An electronic buzz sounded.

A door slid open and Wickingson leaned in. "Not a lot of room in here."

"Freight elevator?" Dempsey asked.

"Freight elevator, passenger elevator, the doors to the four are the same width. Looks like they didn't plan for taking up anything bigger than an office desk and that they'd have to stand on end. What say we ride up to the top floor and see if there's something up there Pappy knows about that we don't?"

"All right."

Dempsey and Wickingson stepped inside.

Wickingson pecked the eight button.

Almost as quickly as the elevator started, it stopped, and again the door slid open.

Wickingson and Dempsey stepped out into a lobby that led to a reception desk and the university president's and the chancellor's suite of offices. Someone stood there, locking a door. When the man turned, Wickingson reached out with his hand. "President Alexander."

Lamar Alexander, television handsome, in dress slacks, a blue blazer with a UT insignia on the breast pocket, and a knit shirt open at the throat, smiled with the ease of a campaigner. He shook hands with Wickingson. "Have we met?"

"No sir, I'm Fredrick Wickingson and this is James Dempsey. We're Tau Upsilon members. Our president sent us by to check with you, to be sure you're going to be at our masked ball this weekend."

"Oh, that's right. Yes, Honey, my wife, she did put it on our calendar. I'll be in San Francisco Friday night, raising money for our senate candidate out there."

"But you'll be back in time?"

"Absolutely. Vice President Bush will be there, and I'm to ride back with him on Air Force Two. I made him promise to get me back to Knoxville by mid-afternoon."

"If you like, we could have some of the brothers meet you at the airport with a car."

Alexander, smiling still, shook his head. "It's nice of you to offer, but I'll have my university car there. Have either of you been up here before?"

"First time for both of us," Wickingson said.

"Well, come on inside. Let me show you around." Alexander brought his key out and had it in the lock before either Wickingson or Dempsey could decline. He pushed the door open and flipped up a panel of light switches.

Desks for two secretaries guarded a glass inner door that opened to Alexander's office. He went on in with Wickingson and Dempsey following.

Alexander waved a hand toward the back of the office. "We've got a conference table back there, a conversation area in the front with couches and chairs, but mostly I work here." He ran a hand over the burled walnut top of his desk. "I had this desk when I was governor. I had it trucked over from Nashville."

Wickingson picked up a picture frame that had rested on the desk. He showed the picture to Dempsey. "See that inscription? 'Best regards. Ronnie.'"

Alexander puffed up a bit. "I'm proud of that. Did you know I gave his seconding speech at the 'Eighty national convention?"

Dempsey gazed out the glass walls on the south and west sides of the office.

Alexander stepped up beside him. "Some view from up here, isn't it? If we were to step out on the roof patio, you could see all of downtown Knoxville to the east. There to the south are the lights of the traffic coming up from Maryville—that's my hometown—and the airport, and down there, see that black ribbon?"

Alexander brought his company closer to the south wall. "That's Lake Louden. And look there, at those lights coming upriver, that's the Star of Knoxville, our paddlewheeler coming in from its evening cruise."

Dempsey let out a soft whistle. "My pap would sure like to see this."

Alexander scribbled some numbers on the back of a business card. He handed the card to Dempsey. "When he comes to visit you, you call my secretary at that number, and the two of you come up here, and you show him the sights. In the daytime," Alexander pointed off toward the southeast, "you can see into the Smoky Mountains. Of course, the office will be a bit different by then."

Wickingson glanced at Alexander. "How so?"

"You know I play the piano."

"I've heard you're good, sir."

"Well, I won a couple competitions back in high school. We're going to put some of this furniture in storage and put a piano in here."

"A spinet?"

"No, a grand."

"Sir, we came up on the elevator. It's small. I don't think you could get a grand in there. How're they going to get it up here?"

"A crane."

Wickingson peered at Dempsey. One eyebrow went up.

FRYE STOOD at the chain link fence that separated the Communications Building's parking lots from the construction area around the base of the Tower. He gazed up, studying the spindly structure that rose before him.

"You figured it out."

Frye jumped. He whipped around and found himself facing Pappy in his Brown's Plumbing jacket, the collar turned up to keep the cold breeze off his neck.

Frye aimed his thump at the crane. "You knew it all the time."

"Sure."

"The construction crane."

"Yup. A tall sucker, isn't it?"

"It's a tower crane. The cab's up there at the top."

"So?"

"You don't mean—" Frye waved his hand.

"I do mean. One of us is going to climb that tower, to get up there to run the crane. Nice thing about these tower cranes, they're electric, quiet as a kitten walkin' on cotton."

"You really think we can do it?"

"Where's your courage, Mister Frye?"

Wickingson and Dempsey came pounding down the sloping lawn to the parking lot, Wickingson shouting, "Ambrose, we know how to do it. We use the crane!"

Chapter 11

Not perfection

DON WRIGHT, dressed as Robin Hood, waved for silence.

"All right, everybody, all right. Time for the awards," he called out. "This is our thirty-third masked ball, thirty-three years since we completed the restoration of the Tau Upsilon house. Our university president was our guest of honor at our first ball and whoever's been in that office has been our guest of honor at every ball since, including tonight, President Lamar Alexander!"

Wright beckoned for Alexander, in buckskins borrowed from the university's mascot, to come to the platform.

The applause swelled as UT's top man came out of the crowd in the Tau Upsilons' dining room, the room festooned with black crepe and illuminated by candles burning in jack-o-lanterns carved to look like ghouls.

Alexander waved in appreciation for the applause. "Thank you. This is my first Halloween with you. Now I know what I'm supposed to do, so, Mister President, if you would, give me the names of the winners, please."

The drummer in the rock band at the side of the platform let off with a riff.

Gibby Deets, in the black tights and hood of the Lord High Executioner, stepped forward. He pulled a slip of paper from a blood-red bucket.

Alexander took the paper. He put on his glasses, read the slip, then announced, "Top prize for the best costumes, Caesar and Cleopatra—Lane Kunzelman and Elizabeth Martin!"

A drum roll and cymbal crash as the two came forward, Martin in an outfit that could be measured in square inches, with a boa constrictor wrapped over her shoulder and around her arm.

Dempsey elbowed Pappy as the two applauded. "She sure shows well, don't she?"

"How come she's not with you?"

"It was fun for a while, but, Pap, I found out she's old."

"What, a senior?"

"Yeah, twenty-two."

Alexander picked up a gold pumpkin, the first-place trophy. When he attempted to give the trophy to Martin, the snake moved. Alexander, shocked, wheeled on past and pushed the trophy into Kunzelman's hands.

Deets dipped into his blood bucket for a second paper. He handed it to the university president cum Mister Volunteer.

"Second place honors for costumes," Alexander read out, "go to the Headless Horseman and the Bride of Frankenstein—Howard Foster and Beebe Early!"

Another drum roll and cymbal crash.

Alexander held up the silver pumpkin award. Foster reached for it. As he did, he dropped the head tucked under his arm. The head bounced across the platform with Foster and his bride of Frankenstein scrambling after it.

Deets handed a third slip to Alexander.

"Third prize, the Three Stooges—Brian Hemphill, B.J. Castle, and Hunter Fox."

Hemphill, Castle, and Fox galloped to the platform, Hemphill and Castle doing their 'nyuck, nyuck, nyuck' and eye-poking routine. Fox produced a cream pie. He danced across the platform, holding the pie aloft for all to see, the audience chanting, "Throw the pie! Throw the pie!"

Fox whipped it at Castle.

Castle ducked.

Hemphill, too.

But not Wright, the Tau Ups president.

Fox gasped. He raced off the platform with Castle and Hemphill hard on his heels, leaving Alexander holding their green pumpkin trophy.

Someone tossed Wright a towel. While he wiped the shaving cream from his face, Deets handed Alexander yet another slip.

"What's this?"

Deets pointed to the top.

Alexander adjusted his reading glasses. "Well, it appears we have an honorable mention. The Four Presidents—Pappy Brown, Junior Dempsey, Fred Wickingson, and Ambrose Frye!"

Pappy, Dempsey, Wickingson, and Frye whooped. They slapped hands in high fives and dashed for the platform, Pappy 'Nixon' doing his victory wave and bellowing "I am not a crook! I am not a crook!"

On the platform, Wicks 'Carter' and Junior 'Ford' danced together while Ambrose 'Reagan' ran to Alexander. He swept the university president up and toted him around the platform, yelling, "Ronnie loves you, baby!"

PAPPY STOOD on the front porch, smoking a Camel, the other three presidents with him, without their masks. They sipped at bottles of beer.

Caroline Brown, still in her long, flowing Maid Marian gown, came out on the arm of one well-scrubbed Robin Hood. She stopped beside Pappy. "Grandpops, you were some kind of grandpops tonight, you, the forever Democrat, as Richard Nixon. And you, too, Junior, and Wicks, and Ambrose—the Four Presidents. You were a hit."

Pappy stubbed out his cigarette, "Leaving, Carrie?"

"It's late. Church tomorrow. You wouldn't want me to miss it."

"Well, you don't have far to go to get home, just next door."

She kissed Pappy on the check.

"Thank you, Sweetpea," he said.

Caroline and Wright went down the steps, Pappy calling after them, "Carrie, you watch out for spooks out there."

"Robin Hood will protect me."

"If he does a good job, you got my permission to smooch him."

"I was planning to."

"Figured you were."

Caroline and Wright turned at the end of the walk toward the Theta Delta house.

Pappy checked his watch. "It's time, boys."

Each of the four picked up a black gym bag. Wickingson and Frye took off toward the Tau Upsilon parking lot, Pappy and Dempsey to the sidewalk that would take them to Andy Holt Tower, a leisurely walk, although there was nothing leisurely about their pace.

Pappy and Dempsey stopped when they got to the gate of the construction lot. There they put on gloves.

"Bolt cutter," Pappy whispered.

Dempsey produced a long-handled device from his gym bag. Pappy held the padlock chain while Dempsey slipped the cutter over one of the links. He crunched the handles together, and the metal of the link gave way.

Pappy eased the chain down, then opened the gate just wide enough for the two to slip inside. They worked their way toward the shadows. There they took black coveralls from their gym bags and pulled them over their suits. They traded their dress shoes for black sneakers and put on black knit caps. Pappy pulled a flashlight from his bag. "Ready?"

Dempsey slipped a hand-held radio into his pocket. "What if the campus patrol comes by?"

"Fearless Fosdick?"

"Yeah."

"You ever see Fearless get out of his car to check anything?"

"Never."

"Forget him then."

Pappy stepped over to the base of the tower crane. He put his foot on the first rung of the ladder that would carry him on a nine-story plus climb to the top and the cab that housed the crane's controls. He put his hands on the side rails and pulled up. "Here goes nothing."

"What do you mean, 'Here goes nothing?'" Dempsey whispered.

"Nothing. You gonna keep up?"

"Sure."

Pappy and Dempsey climbed in silence, the night world opening out to them the higher they went.

"Pappy?" Dempsey asked in a strained whisper.

"Yeah?"

"That a helicopter out there?"

"Where?"

"Off there to the right, maybe a mile or so."

Pappy searched the sky until he saw the lights that had caught Dempsey's attention. "Slow movin'. Could be."

"You think he sees us?"

"Hell no."

They inched past the fifth-floor level, then the sixth.

"Pappy?"

"What?"

"Did you know I'm scared of heights?"

"Now you tell me."

"I don't like this."

"Junior, look out, look up, but don't look down."

"I'll try."

"Don't try. Do it."

Pappy pulled up two more rungs, then Dempsey slapped his heels. "Lights on on the seventh floor."

Pappy froze. He peered across the chasm between the mast of the tower crane and the building. "Who the hell's working at this time of night?"

"Lights just went out."

"Good. Come on, we still got twenty feet." Pappy put his foot on the next rung. As he pulled himself up, he slumped and instead pulled himself into the ladder. He clung to it, his arms shaking.

"What's the matter, Pap?"

"Nothing. Oh God—"

"What is it?"

"Pain—" Pappy squeezed his eyes shut. His jaw muscles tightened. The cords in his neck popped out. "Uhhth—"

"You're not having a heart attack, are you?"

"Uhhh—"

"I'm coming up. Hang on."

Dempsey pulled himself up rung after rung until he stood next to Pappy. He jerked Pappy's light from his pocket and shined it in the man's face. "You don't look good."

The cords in Pappy's neck relaxed some. "I'll be all right...Got to catch my breath...That light, turn it out... someone might see."

"You screw up, old man, you go and die on me—" Dempsey got an arm under Pappy's shoulders. He pressed him tight to the ladder.

Pappy panted, still with his eyes squeezed shut. "I'm not gonna die. Pain's easing."

"We're going down."

"No. Up...twenty feet...rest up there."

"Goddamn, you're stubborn."

"Yeah."

"You ready to climb, then?"

"Yeah."

"One rung at a time. I gotcha. You won't fall."

Pappy, with Dempsey pushing, hauled himself up a rung. "You're a good man, June, no matter what others say."

"Always the jokes."

The two hauled themselves up another rung, then another.

Pappy wheezed. "Gotta stop. Can you reach the door of the cab, open it?"

Dempsey peered up. "I gotta let go of you to do it."

"You can let go. I'm all right."

Dempsey took his arm away from Pappy. He clambered up two more rungs. When he reached over his head, he caught the door handle, a lever. He pulled down on it, and the door, the entire glass front of the cab, swung open. "Thank God, they didn't lock it."

"Why would they? Who's gonna steal anything up here?"

Dempsey reached down. He grabbed a fistful of Pappy's coveralls and pulled up, Pappy climbing with the assist. He got a hand through the doorway and grabbed the bar inside the cab. Pappy pulled, straining to hoist himself up and into the cab. Dempsey chucked a hand under Pappy's rump and pushed.

"I'm in! I'm in." Pappy flopped down on the floor. He laid there, panting.

Dempsey got hold of the bar and horsed himself up. When he got in, he, too, flopped on the floor, wheezing. "What do we do now?"

"Work this thing."

"What?" Dempsey asked after catching his breath.

Pappy rolled over onto his knees. He gripped the operator's seat and pulled himself up, still panting. "Whoo, not bad for an old man."

"I guess."

"My light?"

Dempsey fumbled Pappy's flashlight from his pocket. He held it up.

Pappy took it. He flicked the light on and played its beam across the control panel as he studied the pull-up switches, the handles, and gauges.

He slid into the operator's seat. "Make the call. Let's get this done."

Dempsey brought out his radio. He pressed the transmit button. "Eagle Two? Eagle One," he said into the radio.

Static crackled.

"Eagle Two."

The voice was Wickingson's.

Dempsey pressed the transmit button again. "Eagle One is in the nest. Roll."

"Eagle Two, rolling."

Pappy turned a key on the panel. That brought on lights imbedded in the instrument clusters. He touched the joy stick at the end of the right arm rest and the lever to his left. "June, these do everything we need."

"Do what?"

"The joy stick controls the jib—the arm out there—and the carriage under it. This lever, the cable drum."

"Brilliant."

"Not brilliant, simple, Mister Engineer." Pappy pulled up on a switch, and an electric motor behind the cab whirred to life.

Pappy pushed the joy stick to the left. The jib, in response, pivoted atop the tower.

Dempsey hauled himself up behind Pappy to lean on the back of the operator's seat. "How do you know when to stop?"

"We guess. In the daytime, there'd be a guy on the ground with a radio. He'd tell us when we had the hook over the pickup area." Pappy hunched forward, watching the elements of the night scene change in the glass below the control panel as the jib swung away from Andy Holt toward Lake Louden. He concentrated on the headlights of the occasional vehicle moving along the boulevard. When he felt he had the jib ninety degrees to the street, he allowed the joy stick to center itself, and the jib stopped.

He reached for the drum control lever. Pappy nursed it forward and listened as the drum reeled out cable, yard after yard.

"When do you stop it?" Dempsey asked.

"Guess...Unnth—" Pappy slumped in the seat.

"What is it?"

"Just a twinge. Ooo—" He massaged the ribs beneath his left arm. "I'll be all right."

Headlights, moving south on Lake Louden, swung onto an up-sloping drive that led to the Communications Building parking lot and the construction yard. The lights winked out.

Dempsey's radio crackled.

"Eagle Two. We're here. Gate just ahead."

"Ask him if he can see the hook," Pappy said, still rubbing his ribs.

Dempsey squeezed the transmitter button on his radio. "Eagle Two, can you see the hook?"

"Yeah. Looks to be about at the third floor."

Pappy leaned back. "Tell him to position the package under it, then we'll lower the hook."

"Eagle Two, whistle when the package is in place."

"Roger. Opening the gate now."

WICKINGSON SWUNG the gate wide. He waved for Frye to bring his tow truck through and the package riding on the wheel lift behind it, Sigma Sigma Sigma's Blue Streak. Wickingson trotted ahead of the tow truck, staring up at the crane's cargo hook. He stopped and wigwagged his arms.

Frye stopped his truck. He pulled on the parking brake, then jumped from the cab.

The two, dressed as were Pappy and Dempsey in black coveralls and knit caps, loped to the back of the truck. There Frye lowered the front of the Streak to the ground and snatched the safety straps from the Streak's wheels.

Wickingson hefted a length of steel beam from the truck. He slid in under the Isetta, behind the front wheels, then went back for a second beam. This he shoved under the Isetta, forward of the rear wheels.

Wickingson and Frye, working in silence, dropped spreader bars between the beams on either side of the car.

"Call 'em," Frye whispered.

Wickingson, his radio in hand, pressed the transmit button as he moved to the side, peering up. "Eagle One, lower the hook."

While he watched the hook descend, Frye snapped one-ton-test cargo straps to eye bolts welded to the ends of the beams on the driver's side of the car.

"Slow, now," Wickingson said into his radio. "Three feet...two feet...one foot...stop."

The hook bounced on the roof of the Isetta.

"Oh, jeez."

"What?" came Dempsey's voice over the radio.

"You didn't stop the hook fast enough. There's going to be a helluva dent in the roof of that car."

"You gonna tell anybody?"

"Not me."

Frye threw a strap over the hook. Wickingson caught the strap and attached it to the end of one of the beams on his side of the car. That done, Frye threw the second strap over. Wickingson attached that to the end of the second beam.

He keyed his radio's transmitter. "Up slow," Wickingson said into the radio. "That's it...that's it...stop. If I had a plunger, I'll bet I could suck the dent out of the car's roof."

"Pappy says he's got one in his truck back at the house."

"Lotta good that does us here."

Wickingson checked the straps and their hook ends one last time on his side of the car while Frye did the same on the other side.

Again Wickingson spoke into his radio, in as hushed tones as he could manage. "Up now, slow...that's it."

The cable and hook, spooling upward, lifting the Streak from the ground. Wickingson and Frye leaned further and further back as they watched the car ascend. When the Streak was half-way on its ride to the roof of Andy Holt, Wickingson's radio crackled.

"Trouble." Dempsey's voice, panic seeping through.

"What is it?" Wickingson said into his radio.

"Pappy's sick. We gotta get him down."

"Get him down, how?"

"I'll lower the package. You get in and I'll bring you up."

"What's that do for Pappy?"

"I don't know. Look, when you get up here, you take Pappy onboard. I'll send you both back down."

"Then what?"

"Pack Pappy in the scat wagon and tell Ambrose to drive like hell to the hospital."

"Is Pappy talking?"

"No."

"Do you know what you're doing?"

"No...I guess...The package's coming down?"

"Yeah, pretty fast. Too fast. Slow it. Slow it down. Slow it down! Slow it down! ...That's better...Slow it some more." Wickingson raked the sweat from his forehead. "Ten feet now, slower...five...four...three... two... one...stop."

The Isetta's wheels touched the pavement in the construction yard. Wickingson yanked the door open and jumped in.

"I'm in," he said into his radio.

"Going up."

Wickingson, peering out the Streak's windows, watched the construction yard and parking lot fall away. Ahead, the city lights appeared in the windows as the package rose above the Communications Building,

Wickingson's near horizon. "Hell of a view," he said into his radio.

"Yeah."

"I can see the lights on the Sunsphere."

"Wicks, count the floors on Andy Holt. Tell me when you're at eight. I can't see you real well."

"We're coming up on seven."

"I'm going to slow you."

"I can feel it...Coming up on eight."

"I'm going to creep you up now. Tell me when the hook hits the carriage."

Wickingson leaned forward. He twisted and stared up through the top of the windshield. "I see the carriage...There, we hit."

"I'm going to reel you in now."

Wickingson felt the carriage rolling, carrying the Streak toward the crane's mast. His radio crackled.

"Damn, it's dark out there. Tell me when you're close to the tower."

Wickingson raised the radio to his mouth. "Twenty feet I'd guess...ten. Stop. I gotta open the door."

He swung the great wide door out. The car swayed, swinging on the cargo straps. Wickingson edged up in the seat, to see over the front bumper and down. He pressed the transmit button. "Jiggers, man, it's sure one awful long fall to the ground."

"Tell me about it. I'll going to reel you in closer."

Wickingson felt the carriage move above him. "About five feet," he said into his radio. "Three feet... we're stopped. Junior, there's a gap of a couple feet between the Streak's bumper and the tower. Can you get me in closer?"

"No. We'll have to work with it. I'm bringing Pappy down the ladder."

"How is he?"

"Damn weak."

Wickingson sat back, minutes passing before he saw shapes coming down the ladder on the side of the mast. He shined his flashlight across the gap, picking up Pappy.

Wickingson leaned forward. "How ya doin', Pap?"

"Not good."

"Stop there. Can you get a foot on the bumper?"

Pappy edged to the side of the ladder, Dempsey holding onto him. Pappy reached out with his foot. He stretched it toward the car's bumper, touched it. But when he put his weight on the bumper, the car swayed away.

Wickingson waved Pappy back. "Goddamn, this thing's swings like a pendulum. Pappy, we gotta time this. Gimme your hand. You get your foot on the bumper at the top of the arc and push off for all you're worth. I'll yank you in. You want to go for it?"

"Not really."

"Tell you what, gimme your hand. I'm going to pull against you to stop the Streak's swinging. When it stops, you gotta jump."

"All right."

Pappy's arm came out into the gap.

Wickingson clapped his hand around Pappy's wrist. He braced a heel against the top edge of the front bumper and pulled.

The car's swinging stopped.

"Pappy, get your foot out there."

A foot came out. Wickingson watched it find its way to the bumper. "Pretty firm, Pap?"

"Yeah."

"On three, you jump....One, two, three!"

Pappy pushed away from the mast.

At the same instant, Wickingson yanked against Pappy's wrist for all he was worth, a fisherman hauling in a trophy muskie.

Pappy twisted. He ducked as he flew through the gap and slammed down in the seat beside Wickingson.

"Junior," Wickingson called out, "he's in. Get us the hell away from here!"

DEMPSEY SCRAMBLED back up the ladder, into the crane's cab. He slammed the door.

Once in the operator's seat, he pressed the joystick forward, and the carriage carried the Streak away from the tower. At the same time, he pressed forward on the drum control, letting the cable reel out at a hellacious rate.

"Slow us down!" came Wick's panicked voice from the speaker in Dempsey's radio. "Fourth floor!"

Dempsey eased the lever back. He let the joystick snap to neutral, stopping the carriage a third of the way out beneath the jib.

"Third floor."

Dempsey eased back more on the drum control.

"Second floor ...About ten feet now. Creep us down...Five feet...about three...two...touchdown. Man, a hard landing. Bet that hook dented the car's roof again."

Dempsey pulled the drum control to neutral. He waited and, with nothing to do, fidgeted.

"Scat wagon's away," came Wickingson's voice over his radio.

Dempsey peered down through the side window of the cab at running lights winking on a vehicle below, a vehicle moving out of the construction yard. The headlights came on and, when the vehicle turned onto

Lake Louden Boulevard, an amber bubble light, its rotating beacon warning others who shared the street to get out of the way.

Chapter 12

Headlines

PAPPY HEARD VOICES, someone somewhere saying something about how nice someone would look properly laid out.

He tried to open an eye, but the lid would not lift. It was as if it were glued. And there was that voice again..."He was a cheap old bastard. Just tell me when I can have the body."

"Well, I've got some paperwork to do," a second voice said. "Maybe fifteen minutes."

Who's cheap? What body? Where the hell am I?

Pappy forced his mind to locate his hand. He willed his hand to rise from where it rested, to come up to his face, to rub at the reluctant eyelid.

The lid, in response, lifted, but now he couldn't make his eye focus. Pappy sensed he was in a room, a white room—a brilliantly white room—and he sensed he was in a bed, on his back. He could feel that. Was that a sheet covering him?

He forced his other eye open. Those shapes, were they beyond the foot of the bed? Were they people? One? Perhaps two?

Pappy pushed himself up on his elbow. Whoever they were, they appeared to take no interest in him.

He squeezed his eyes closed, then forced them open again. Closed once more, and open.

Yes, there were two people there—men.

He was sure of it, one in white, the other in black. Pappy squinted at the man in black. "Digger?"

"When do you think they'll have the funeral?" the man in white asked.

"Couple days, I s'pose," the man in black said. "We gotta get a hole dug first, out behind his place, you know, to throw old Willie's carcass in."

That did it. "Digger!"

But the man in black did not answer.

"This ain't funny, Digger. I ain't dead!"

The man in black cupped a hand behind his ear. "Doc, you hear something?"

"No, just you and me," the man in white said. "It's quiet as a grave in here."

"Digger!"

The man in black burst out laughing. He fell into the arms of the man in white, then staggered around the bed to Pappy. He slapped Pappy's shoulder. "Gotcha."

"Gawddammit, O'Dell."

"Hey, Pap, would you deny your friendly undertaker a little joke?" The man in black snorted and cackled.

"Where the hell am I?"

Thomas 'Digger' O'Dell, Maryville's undertaker for a quarter of a century, pressed a finger to his lips. "Shhh, you're in a hospital."

"Maryville?"

"Fort Sanders."

"Since when?"

"Since two nights ago."

"Why?"

O'Dell motioned Pappy's family doctor, Rubble Muse, over. "Tell him, Doc, or he's just going to get crabby on us."

Muse twisted one stem of his drooping mustache. "Pap, one of your frat buddies brought you in. The ER docs told me you were three shades beyond white. After they got you stabilized downstairs, they called me because my name was on the health card in your wallet. You're damn lucky."

"I feel all right."

"That's because they knocked you out for forty-eight hours. Amazing what sleep does to heal a body. Your buddy says the two of you were out climbing rock walls or something." Muse leveled his gaze into Pappy's eyes. "You've got to quit that, Pappy. You're sixty-five."

"Hell, Rubble, you're seventy."

"You quit trying to be a twenty-year-old and maybe you'll make it to my age."

Pappy laid back on his pillow. "When are you gonna let me out?"

"What do you say to tomorrow?"

A hint of a smile curled at the corners of Pappy's lips.

Muse sat on the bed. "Pap, you're one tough old bird. You always were, and I hope you always will be."

"Is that a caution I hear?"

"Nope. You're going to do what you're going to do. Pap, here's the good news. I've looked at all the EKG tapes and the other tests they ran on you, and there's only a tad of damage to that heart of yours. I think the warranty may be good for another twenty years."

"That's it?"

"Not everything." Muse held out a pill bottle. "These are nitros. I want you to carry them with you every day, every night, wherever you go. You feel that twinge, that pain around your ticker, you pop one of these little suckers under your tongue and let it do its magic."

Pappy stared at the bottle. "Hope that's not one of those childproof caps. If it is, I'll be dead before I get it off."

"Then Digger gets you." Muse pushed a thumb up under the side of the cap. It popped off the pill bottle. He slapped the cap back on and once more held the bottle out.

Pappy took it and Muse's hand. He squeezed it as an old friend does when he doesn't want to say goodbye.

"Pap, I've got to go. I've got patients up here who really are sick. They're waiting on me to come by."

Pappy released Muse's hand, and Muse backed out of the room. He nodded to Pappy before he disappeared down the hall.

O'Dell settled near the foot of the bed. He swung his feet back and forth. "Doc's a good old boy. Cheats me out of a hell of a lot of business, though."

"And all the time I figured you two were in cahoots."

"You hungry?"

"Sure am."

O'Dell reached in his coat pocket. He pulled out something wrapped in butcher paper. "Sneaked a seven-layer burrito in for you from Taco Pete's. This hospital food will kill ya."

Pappy took it. He unwrapped the burrito and bit into it. "Mmm, warm."

"I've got friends in the right places. One of the nurses zapped it in her microwave before I come in."

"You know what would be good with this?"

"Beer, I know. But your boy tells me you've sworn off." O'Dell took a bottle and an opener from his coat's other side pocket. "How about a Doctor Pepper?"

"That'll do." Pappy sipped from the bottle, then went back at the burrito. As he ate, he gazed around the room, seeing for the first time bouquets of flowers and plants in baskets—dahlias and mums and a delicate African violet, not like him at all. "Gawd, you'd think somebody died."

"People were hoping."

Pappy put the cold eye on O'Dell.

"What can I say? Business has been slow."

Pappy set his drink aside. "Digger, how many people know about this?"

"About what, you being in the hospital?"

"No. About why?"

"Just about everybody. Doc can't keep a secret, you know. He blabbed it all over."

"The hell he did."

O'Dell shrugged. "Okay, so I blabbed it all over. Sue me."

Pappy peered at the tree next to his bed, poking up above the forest of flowers. A bag and a tube hung from the tree, a tube that looped down to a needle in Pappy's arm. He saw a second tube, too, one that snaked out from beneath the bed's sheet to a bag hanging at the side. "What's all this plumbing for?"

"Well, they didn't want you drying out, so that one on the tree there, that's a saline drip. And they didn't want you peeing the bed, so that other tube there, they tapped your bladder."

Pappy felt around his groin. "Oh, no. Digger, get me out of this stuff. I don't want no nurse diddling with my privates."

"They already diddled."

"I wasn't awake then."

"Mister Modesty."

"Gawddammit, O'Dell, you were a medic in Korea. You know all about tubes and needles."

"I don't do that stuff anymore."

"O'Dell!"

"Yeesh." O'Dell pushed himself off the bed. He came around to the plumbing side and slipped his hands beneath the sheet. He put one hand on Pappy's groin. With the other, he grasped the tube near where it entered Pappy's penis. "I can ease this thing out slow or I can yank it out and be done with it. You gonna complain?"

"Probably."

"My customers don't."

"That's because they're dead."

O'Dell pressed with one hand and, with the other, clipped the tab to let the water out of the balloon. Then he pulled on the catheter.

A nurse came in, studying a chart and carrying a blood-pressure cuff and a stethoscope. She glanced up at Pappy and at the man who had his hands under the sheet. "What are you doing?"

O'Dell grimaced. "Diddling with this man's privates. We're lovers."

"Get away from him."

O'Dell yanked the end of the tube from beneath the sheet. He held the tube up. "Don't get apoplectic. I've just unplugged him. Pappy wants to pee on his own."

"You can't do that."

"I already did it. You want to undo his arm?"

"No."

"All right." O'Dell went at the second tube. He disconnected it from the needle, then pulled the needle out and tossed it into a metal pan on the table.

O'Dell reached in his pants pocket for a Band-Aid. He tore the paper covering off and slapped the adhesive patch over the puncture. "These little doo-dads do come in handy when a health care professional won't do her job."

The nurse, heavy set and angry, bolted from the room. "Doctor!"

"We've done it now, Pap."

Pappy flipped the sheet aside. "Gimme a hand up. I want to see if my legs work."

"Of course they work."

"I want to see if they work good enough that we can gallop out of this place." Pappy swung his legs over the side of the bed. He grabbed O'Dell's shoulder and pulled himself up, but his knees buckled.

O'Dell caught him. "You better sit back down, old friend."

"Hell, no." Pappy hauled himself up. He pushed a foot forward and put his weight on it, then the other foot, all the time clinging to O'Dell. "I can do this."

"Oh yeah."

"Get the door open. We're outta here."

"You're serious."

"Yes."

O'Dell shoved the door open and held it with one hand while he and Pappy shuffled through. They made the turn into the hallway.

Someone, behind them, let off with a wolf whistle.

Pappy snatched the back of his hospital gown closed.

"Where are you going, Mister Brown?" a voice demanded.

"Damn, caught by the Gestapo."

PAPPY SAT propped up by pillows, his half-moon glasses riding the bridge of his nose as he paged through the Sentinel newspaper.

Fred Wickingson leaned in the doorway. He glanced to one side and the other before he waved for others to follow him in.

Wickingson tiptoed up to the bed. He peeked over the top of the newspaper, grinning. "Ready for company?"

"Wicks." Pappy chucked his newspaper aside. He gazed beyond Wickingson to Junior Dempsey in a wheelchair, making the turn into his room, Ambrose Frye pushing him. "What happened, June?"

"Nothing. We found out nobody bothers you in a hospital if you're in a wheelchair." Dempsey rolled up next to Pappy's bed. He whipped aside the blanket that covered his lap and legs. "Ta-dah."

"Oh, June, I sure hope that's pizza in that pizza box."

Dempsey opened the box on his lap. He held the box up to Pappy. "It sure ain't spinach salad. We smuggled it in."

Pappy took a slice as did Wickingson and Frye. He bit in, smiling like a child savoring his first chocolate-covered cherry.

He waved the pizza slice in the air. "I cannot tell you how good this is. For supper, I had a chicken patty and rubber jello. I swear the patty was made from ground-up pasteboard."

"Got your Country Time." Dempsey handed over a can that had ridden shotgun with the pizza. He brought out a can of Miller's Lite for himself and two Lone Star long necks, for Wickingson and Frye.

Wickingson swallowed a mouthful of pizza. "You get our flowers?"

"Which ones?" Pappy swept his hand around the floral wonderland that was his room.

"Spider mums. Junior stole 'em from the aggies' greenhouse."

"That them over there?" Pappy motioned at a bouquet on a side table as he reached for a second slice of pizza.

Dempsey rolled his wheelchair to the side table. He found the card in the bouquet and opened it. Rolling back, he held the card out to Pappy.

"They're yours, huh?"

"Yeah. Read the card."

Pappy adjusted the position of his glasses to bring the note's content into focus. He read the card aloud. "'From the Triple Sigs' parking lot to the roof of Andy Holt, we came, we saw, we conquered.'" Pappy looked back at Dempsey. "You didn't."

Dempsey flapped a copy of the Daily Beacon on the bed, open to the front page. The photo that drew all eyes to it was unmistakable—the Sigma Sigma Sigma's Isetta, the headline over it reading ROOFTOP PATIO MYSTERY STUMPS CAMPUS COPS.

Pappy held out his hand, palm up. Dempsey drew his palm across it, winking at Pappy as he did.

Pappy grinned in response. "You wascally wong-eared wabbit, you. Tell me how you did it."

Dempsey hunched forward. "After we got you out of there, I told Wicks to get back in the Streak."

Wickingson reached for another slice of pizza. "I thought I was done, but I wasn't."

"I hauled him up and reeled him out over the rooftop porch in front of the president's office, you know, and lowered the Streak down there."

"Yeah?"

"Old Wicks, he jumps out and disconnects the spreader bars and the beams, pulls 'em out, and lashes them to the hook."

"Excellent."

"Well, I tell him to climb on the hook and ride the hook down."

"I did." Wickingson slapped his puffed-up chest. "You'd think I was some crazed steel worker."

Dempsey wheeled back to the pizza box. "So there he is one foot on the hook, hanging onto the cable. I haul him and all that steel up, reel them away from Andy Holt."

Wickingson leaned in. "I tell Junior, on the radio, that we're clear of the tower, and he drops me and all that stuff eight floors. My God, what a ride. Beat anything at Six Flags."

Dempsey tossed back a slug from his Miller's before going for a wedge of pizza. "So he tells me on the radio he's on the ground. He gets everything off the hook, and I reel it back up. I check everything in the cab, to make sure it's all the way it was, and I climb down."

"I'm watching him. It took him forever."

Dempsey gave a jerk of his head. "A half an hour, man. I was scared, filled my pants at one time."

"He was shaking so bad that when we got him back to the house, we had to anesthetize him. How many beers did it take, June?"

"Oh, gawd, a six-pack at least. I passed out."

Pappy sat there, leaning back on his pillows, his hand over his mouth, holding back a smirk. "And nobody's figured it out?"

"They figured out the how, but not the who." Frye waved his Lone Star at Pappy. "So it won't happen again, they've got a guard on the gate all night now."

Pappy made a pistol of his hand and fired it at Frye, Wickingson, and Dempsey in turn. "This is one bodacious tale to tell your grandkids, boys."

Caroline Brown and Don Wright meandered in, she with a bouquet of red carnations, he with a Whitman Sampler under his arm. "Want more company, Grandpops?" Caroline asked.

Pappy stuffed the Beacon under the sheet. "You can join the party, have some pizza."

Wickingson and Frye got up. They moved to the side of the room.

Caroline passed them as she came to the bed. She hugged Pappy. "You gave us a scare, Grandpops."

"Scared myself."

"These flowers are for you."

He looked around the room. "I guess you'll have to throw some of these other flowers out if you want a vase."

Caroline went to the side table, to the spider mums. "These are nice. I can put the carnations in with them. Yellow and red, they'll look good together."

Wright took Caroline's place at the side of the bed. "How are you doing, Pappy?"

"Fine now, I guess. I tried to sneak out this afternoon, but they caught me."

Wright held out the Sampler. "For you."

"Hey, you shouldn't have."

"My mother tells me you old people like these."

"Oh, that's what I needed to hear. Why don't you give the box to Junior? I may have a piece later, after I put my teeth in."

Wright passed the box to Dempsey who ripped off the cellophane. He lifted the cover and inhaled the chocolate fragrance. "My favorite."

Dempsey shared the wealth with Wickingson and Frye.

Caroline nudged Wright to the side so she could sit on the bed next to Pappy. She put her arm around his neck. "Are you going to tell me how this happened?"

"It's my fault," Frye mumbled around a maple-raspberry nougat. "I dared Pappy to go wall climbing with me—yum, June, can I have another?—I guess it was too much for him."

"But at night?"

Frye picked an almond square from the box. "We didn't want the campus cops to see us. Some of them get real testy about students climbing walls."

"Where'd you do this?"

"Art and Architecture."

Caroline leaned away from Pappy. "Grandpops, you shouldn't be doing these things. You're not a kid anymore."

"Don't I know it." Pappy grabbed his chest. His face twisted.

Carolina snatched up the call button, but Pappy put a hand on hers, grinning as he did. "Just kidding. Doc Muse says I'm good for another twenty years."

"You better be. I want you and Poppie both to walk me down the aisle when I get married."

"You're not going to do this tomorrow, are you?"

"No, but someday." Caroline reached for Wright's hand. "Don's asked me."

Pappy's eyes popped. "El Supremo? Mister Tau Ups?"

"Grandpops."

"What did you tell him?"

"That I'd give him my answer the day I graduate."

Pappy pulled his granddaughter in. He hugged her and kissed her on the forehead. "You're one smart kid. You tell your mom and dad?"

"Yes."

"Good. I'm sure I was surprise enough for them."

Wright took a chocolate from the box. "When are you coming back to the house?"

"Tomorrow. Doc Muse says he's going to kick me out around sunup."

"We've had brothers attending your classes for you, taking notes so you won't be behind."

Pappy reached out. He shook Wright's hand. "Donny-boy, you're not half bad."

Caroline stroked Pappy's cheek. "We should be going. We don't want to wear you out. You'll come to dinner tomorrow night?" She and Wright moved toward the door.

"Only if Junior's invited."

"Hey, Pap, I'm going to be there," Dempsey said as he put the cover on the candy box. "I'm serving."

"Really?"

"They hired me for five nights a week."

"You wascal. Hey, just you keep your hands off your employers."

"Pappy–"

"You take care now." Caroline waved, as did Wright. They did a little two-step to get past a nurse coming into the room. She, a stern, square-jawed woman, gave the remaining visitors a hard look.

She sniffed the air. "Do I smell beer in here?"

Dempsey slid down in his wheelchair, but held up his can. Wickingson and Frye brought their long necks out of their jackets where they had hidden them. They held their bottles up.

She wheeled on Pappy. "Mister Brown?"

He held up his can of Country Time.

"Well, one saint among the sinners. But is that a pizza box I see?"

"Yes." Pappy set his drink can on the bed stand.

The nurse bustled over, Louise Krenshaw by the name on her badge. With a pen, she lifted the top of the box. "I'm going to have to confiscate this, Mister Brown. This is not hospital food."

"But there are two pieces left."

"Yes, from the Blue Onion, I see, with the works? Too bad for you." Krenshaw fixed Pappy with a stare so cold it would have frozen the soul of a fallen-away Baptist. "Put your arm out."

He raised his right arm.

She whipped a blood-pressure cuff around his biceps, then put the tips of her fingers on his wrist. She did not take her gaze off Pappy's eyes. "Good news. You've got a pulse. You're still alive."

She squeezed a rubber bulb, pumping air into the cuff. Krenshaw pumped the cuff up until the pressure had Pappy winching.

"Come on, Mister Brown, you're not a baby." She put the hearing end of her stethoscope over an artery bulging up just inside the elbow.

Krenshaw listened. She turned a knurled knob above the bulb, releasing air from the cuff, and listened again, counting, watching the needle in the cuff's pressure gauge as the air hissed away.

"Any more normal and we'll have to discharge you," she said, with no hint of a smile.

"How about tonight?"

"Hah."

Krenshaw removed the cuff. She stuck it in her pocket, swept up the pizza box, and made for the door.

"You're going to eat that, aren't you, Krenshaw?"

"Yes. Unlike you, I'm not on a hospital diet."

Dempsey gave a nod in the direction of the retreating nurse. "She's tough."

"I know her family. Raised her on sour apples. Now you know why I want to get the hell out of here." Pappy flipped the sheet back and swung his feet out of the bed. "Wicks, throw me my jumpsuit from the closet."

Wickingson slipped his empty long neck in his jacket pocket as he went to the closet door. He opened it and found, hanging on a hook inside the door, Pappy's black coveralls. He tossed them across the room.

Pappy grabbed them out of the air. He stepped into one leg, then the other, and pulled the coveralls up. He stuffed his hospital gown inside.

"Get the rest of my stuff, Wicks." Pappy zipped up the front. Done, he slapped Dempsey's shoulder. "Out of the wheelchair."

Dempsey pushed himself up, and Pappy slid in. He put his bare feet on the metal foot rests.

Wickingson dumped Pappy's suit, the rest of his clothes, and his shoes into Pappy's lap.

Dempsey handed over the blanket that had hidden the pizza and the drinks from prying eyes.

Pappy draped the blanket over his possessions and tucked it around his legs. "Look pretty good?"

"Good enough."

"All right, get me outta here."

Dempsey swung around behind the wheelchair. He wheeled Pappy toward the door and out, Wickingson and Frye at his heels.

"Mister Brown! Get your butt back in that room and back in that bed!"

Chapter 13

Santa and the six-foot elf

PAPPY RECLINED in a beanbag chair, his face buried in an ornithology textbook, his stockinged feet—a hole in one toe—up on his bed.

Dempsey came in, shucking his stocking cap. "Hey, Pap, we got snow out there. You should've been with us."

"I've seen snow." Pappy kept on reading.

Dempsey twisted around, as if searching for something or someone. He went back to the doorway. "Charlie!"

A person a bit more than half Dempsey's size came tearing in, bundled in a hand-me-down mackinaw and a dirty cap, his face swaddled in a muffler that, too, had seen better days. Dempsey grabbed the ends of the kid's mittens and yanked. After they came off, Dempsey helped the boy unbundle. "Pappy, this is Charlie. Charlie, this is the mean old man who's my roommate. You can call him Mister Brown."

The boy rubbed at his sniffly nose. "'Lo, Mister Brown. Junior and me, we been out makin' snow angels."

Pappy peered over his half-moon glasses at the short spectacle before him. "Who're you, kid?"

"Charlie Jackson." The boy puffed himself up to his three-foot-five and one-quarter-inch height.

Dempsey pulled off his own snow-spattered parka. He tossed it aside before whumping his butt down on his bed. "Come on, Charlie, let's get you out of those wet tennies and socks."

The boy ran to Dempsey, and Dempsey caught him under the arms. He swung the boy up onto his lap where the two half worked and half wrestled at unlacing the boy's soaked shoes. After they got them off, Dempsey stripped away Charlie's socks. He wrinkled his nose. "When was the last time you washed your feet, kid?"

"Last week."

"You gotta do better than that." Dempsey took the boy's hand, and the two marched off to the bathroom.

Pappy turned a page. He continued reading, pausing at moments to scribble words on a legal pad. He looked up when a squeal of laughter interrupted his thoughts.

In clomped Dempsey, Charlie under his arm, the boy laughing. Dempsey toted him like he would a sack of calf feed.

"Hey, Pap, this kid's ticklish." Dempsey wiggled his fingers in the boy's ribs, and the boy let out with another peal of laughter.

Dempsey carried Charlie over to his bureau. With his free hand, Dempsey pulled a drawer open and pawed through until he came up with a pair of gym socks. "Charlie boy, you can wear these."

He dumped Charlie on his bed. Dempsey gave him the socks and pointed a finger in mock warning when the boy hung the socks on his ears.

Dempsey sidled over to Pappy. He peered over his shoulder. "What're you studying?"

"Migration patterns. Chapter test Monday. Want to beat the rush." Pappy glanced over his glasses to the boy struggling to get his small foot into one of the oversized socks. "Who's he?"

"My Little Brother." Dempsey leaned down. "You know the house project, Big Brothers? I signed up. They matched me with Charlie. This is our first day together."

"Oh."

"He doesn't know who his daddy is. He's stuck in a little shotgun house with his momma and three sisters. Not much fun."

"How old is he?"

Dempsey straightened up. "How old are you, Charlie?"

"Six and a half."

"God, kid, you're ancient."

"No, I'm not."

"How you doing with those socks?"

"All right."

"Come on over here."

Charlie rolled onto his stomach. He slid off the bed and shuffled around, holding onto the tops of the triple-X gym socks.

Dempsey gave a wave at them. "Big, huh?"

"Yup."

Dempsey hummed his way over to his bureau where he once again pawed through a drawer. In a back corner, he found four clothes pins, the kind with springs in them that make them snap. He hummed back to the boy, bent down, and clothes-pinned the socks to Charlie's pant legs. "How's that?"

"Kinda dumb."

"Yeah, but at least your socks won't fall down. Show 'em to Mister Brown."

Charlie held a foot up for Pappy's inspection.

"Ah-ha, that's pretty good, kid."

"You think so?"

"'Course, I'm not an engineer like your Big Brother there, but, yeah, I think so."

Charlie put his foot down. He shuffled around, duck-footed, admiring his new socks. When he got to the far side of the room, he stared at a poster. "What's this?"

Pappy squinted at the boy. "What's what?"

"This." Charlie pointed to the poster taped to the wall.

"Oh. That's the Coors National Championship Beer-Case Stacking Team—Junior's heroes."

"The heck they are," Dempsey said. "Wicks put that up."

Pappy shrugged.

"You going down to supper, Pap?"

"Is it time?"

Dempsey held his Mickey Mouse watch out to Pappy. "Pizza night. Charlie, you ready for supper?"

The boy had his hand inside a Vols' *We're #1* foam hand. He waved it over his head. "Can I stay?"

"Your mother said you can as long as I get you home by seven."

"Oh." Charlie's laughing face drooped, and the foam hand fell to his side. "It's bath night."

Dempsey walked toward the door, his hand out for the boy. "Kid, you show her your clean feet. At least you won't have to wash them. Coming, Pap?"

"I'll catch up."

Pappy laid his book aside. He tugged on the end of his holey sock, doubled the fabric under his toes, and pushed them into a shoe. He tied the laces, then shod his other foot. Finished, he went to the mirror over his bureau.

"Mirror, mirror, on the wall—" Pappy picked up a hair brush. He brushed at his buzz cut.

"Junior," he said to his reflection, "you are growing up."

PAPPY HAD BURROWED himself deep in his ornithology textbook by the time his roommate returned.

Dempsey pitched his parka and stocking cap into his study chair, and flopped on his bed. "Got Charlie home. Where's Ambrose and Wicks?"

"Ambrose is still out, running a tow truck for his pap. Streets slick?"

"Pretty much."

"He'll have a lot of business then. I expect he could be out all night."

"And Wicks?"

"Over at Dougherty. Lab project." Pappy peered over his glasses at Dempsey sprawled on his Vols bedspread, his fingers locked behind his head. "You know Charlie's black."

"So?"

"It's all right by me, but some might give you a hard time."

"Then they got rocks for brains."

"Probably."

Don Wright and two of his fellow officers appeared at the doorway. Wright knocked on the jamb.

Pappy glanced up from his book.

"Pap, we want your help."

"Come to the old master, huh? What is it?"

Wright took a step in. "We need a Santa Claus."

"Me?"

"That's right."

"Wicks has got the better build, with that big jelly belly of his."

"We'll pad you. We've got the suit. We're planning a joint Christmas party with the Theta Delts, for their

Little Sisters and their families and our Little Brothers and families."

"Ahh. When're you thinking of doing this?"

"The night before we kick out for Christmas break."

WHAT WAS TO HAVE BEEN a small gathering for the Big Brothers and Big Sisters and their small-fry charges—roughly eighty people—changed and grew like Jack's beanstalk. First, someone suggested the parents of the children be included.

That upped the group by forty.

Then someone said they shouldn't leave out the other kids in the families."

Up eighty-six.

"And we want our members there who aren't Big Brothers or Big Sisters," said another.

Up fifty-four more.

Neither house could accommodate two hundred sixty kids, college students, and adults, so Wright and Caroline Brown booked a ballroom at the University Center.

That done, the Tau Upsilon officers and their Theta Delta counterparts handed out the assignments—you're doing the invitations, you're doing the decorations, you're doing the refreshments, you're doing the purchasing, etcetera, etcetera.

Purchasing. That was the big one, all agreed.

The planners decided each child should get a toy, an article of clothing and, at Pappy's insistence, a book. The Big Brothers and Big Sisters worked with the parents, developing wish lists.

The houses' number crunchers ran the totals for all the costs of the planned party—six thousand eighty dollars, well beyond the thirty-nine hundred the two houses had initially budgeted.

Wright and his officers went to work. They leaned on the manager of the local Toys R Us to fill the toy order at half price. Dempsey's district manager at Mayfield Dairy offered to supply ice cream at no cost. When that word got out, the route men who stocked the houses' Coke and Pepsi machines decided they weren't going to be outdone. They told Wright they'd supply the drinks.

Pappy took it on himself to stop in on James Proffitts, CEO of the Proffitts Department Store chain based in Maryville, Proffitts the grandson of the founder.

PAPPY SETTLED HIMSELF in the padded chair beside Proffitts's desk. "You shoot up your year's budget for good deeds, Jimmy?"

Proffitts, pouring coffee for his guest, didn't look up from his task. "If I say yes, you're still going to put the bite on me, aren't you?"

"Have I ever?"

He handed Pappy a bone china cup of premium Arabica. "Often. And when I go to turn you down, you remind me how you drove in the winning run for my daddy's baseball team, to win the Intercity championship in Nineteen Fifty-five."

"That was a good year and a good game."

"Uh-huh, and you did it again in Nineteen Fifty-six, yes, I know." Proffitts poured a splash of bourbon in his coffee before he took up residence in a leather armchair facing Pappy.

Baseball trophies filled a glass case at the side of Proffitts's office, the office that had been his father's until the old tiger retired. But it was the crossed bats that most people saw when they came in, and the autographs in the center of a display of plaques and team photos. Burned into each bat were the signatures of all the men who had played on the 'Fifty-five and 'Fifty-six championship teams. But as important as the crossed bats, at least to Proffitts, was the catcher's glove hanging from the handle of one—his catcher's glove.

Proffitts, a plump man with a salty cookie-duster mustache, smiled at Pappy. "What do you want?"

"Let me lay it out for you. I'm in college—"

"I heard."

"Good. My frat and my granddaughter's sorority are in Knoxville's Big Brother, Big Sister program."

"Uh-huh."

"We're throwing a Christmas party for the little brothers and little sisters and their families."

"Ah, yes." Proffitts sipped at his high-octane brew. "You've come up short on the money end, haven't you?"

"Jimmy, you are one perceptive fella."

"Skip the butter, Pap."

"Right. Here it is. We want to give some clothes to each kid, say about twenty dollars' worth, and the same to each of their real brothers and sisters." Pappy set his cup aside because his hands appeared to insist on punching up his words. "That's a hundred twenty-six kids, Jimmy. And most of them, they're from poor families."

Proffitts stroked his mustache. "So if I help, what do I get?"

Pappy touched his chest, just over his heart. "A warm feeling when you go to church that you done good."

Proffitts nodded.

Pappy pulled three folded sheets of paper from his pocket. He opened them and held them out. "I got lists, with sizes."

Proffitts took the pages. He slapped his pockets for his reading glasses. Failing to find them, he went to his desk. There he pushed aside a half-dozen reports before he unearthed them. He put his glasses on and scanned down Pappy's lists. "Leather shoes?"

"A lot of these kids have only tennis shoes, Jimmy, and most are hand-me-downs and not in good shape. They need something better for winter."

"Well, there's nothing here we can't handle." Proffitts went to a side door and opened it. "Axel, would you come in here, please?"

A young man, Pappy guessed him to be in his mid-twenties, entered. He wore a tailored suit of gray herring bone.

"Pappy, this is Axel Dumphrey. The company's getting so big the board made me take on an assistant and Axel's it. A damn good one."

Pappy rose to shake hands.

"You can see Axel in that picture right there." Proffitts gestured to one of the team photos. "He played second base for our company team, this year. Axel, Pappy Brown was shortstop for one of my father's teams way back when he and I were a helluva lot younger."

"It's good to meet you, sir," Dumphrey said as he shook Pappy's hand.

Proffitts leaned on the back of his chair. "Axel, you were in a fraternity up at UT, weren't you?"

"Sigma Sigma Sigma, yes."

"That your fraternity, Pap?"

"No."

"No matter. Axel, we're going to help this man with clothes for kids his fraternity and his granddaughter's sorority are throwing a Christmas party for. Here are the lists. Pull some employees and go shopping. Have every item you get boxed, wrapped, and ready by when, Pap?"

"Next week?"

"When next week?"

"Tuesday?"

Dumphrey flashed a smile at his boss, a smile a dentist would be proud of. "This won't be a problem. We'll tag each package with the child's name, and we'll bag everything to go." He turned to Pappy. "Mister Brown, colors and styles, what do you want to do about those?"

"I expect your good judgment would be just fine."

Proffitts moved back to his desk. "Axel, when you write up the bill, write it up for half our cost, not half of retail. Charge the rest to advertising."

"Yessir." Dumphrey swung to Pappy, his hand out. "Mister Brown, it was good to meet you."

Pappy clasped the executive's hand and gave it a firm shake, then Dumphrey left.

Proffitts rescued his coffee cup from where he had left it on a side table. "How's that, Pap?"

"Jimmy, you're as good a man as your father ever was."

"That's Grade-A butter and a high compliment, my friend."

CAROLINE STUFFED a feather pillow down in the waistband of her grandfather's Santa trousers. She stepped back and studied her work, shaking her head. "Grandpops, you just aren't fat enough."

She yanked the pillow out and tossed it aside for a foam pillow. Caroline pushed that into Pappy's pants.

She tilted her head to the side for a more critical look, then pulled his red jacket closed over the pillow. She fastened the Velcro strips beneath the white fur. "It would just be a lot easier if you were fat."

"I've got a paunch."

"Where?" Caroline grabbed for a love handle, Pappy twisting away. "Ticklish?"

"Darn right I am." He threaded his wide, black belt through its brass buckle and cinched the belt down.

Caroline reached in the Christmas suit bag and brought out a generous, curly beard. "Just right for you, wouldn't you say?" she said as she handed it on.

"Trying to make me feel old?"

"Never."

Pappy hooked the loops over his ears. He went to the mirror and adjusted the beard until he had it four-square. He ran his fingers beneath the mustache, raking fake whiskers away from his mouth. "Last thing I want to do is inhale this stuff when I got some kid on my lap."

He studied his image, tucking a bit more at one side of his mustache as he did.

Caroline dove back into the bag. She brought out a wig. "Your roof rug, Sir Grandpops."

He arched an eyebrow at her.

"Do you want me to help you with it?"

Pappy snatched the wig away and, while peering at his image in the mirror, positioned the wig over his own hair.

Caroline pulled gloves and a Santa hat from the bag and put the hat on her head. "How do I look?"

Pappy glanced at her in the mirror. "If all Santa's girl elves looked like you, he'd have no trouble hiring boy elves. But that skirt, isn't it kinda short, and that top, a little on the tight side?"

"Prude." She handed him the gloves and hat. "Now laugh for me."

"Ho-ho-ho."

"Deeper."

"HO-HO-HO."

"Deeper."

"HO. That's as deep as I can go. I'm not a bass."

"It'll have to do then."

"And it will do and do well. Who do you think Santa Claus was all those years you were a little kid?"

"You?"

"Fooled you, too, didn't I?"

She kissed Pappy on the tip of his nose. "Thank you, Grandpops."

"For you, kid, anytime."

Dempsey bounded into the room with Charlie riding on his shoulders, both in elf costumes and both wearing green slippers with curled-up toes.

"Ah, my giant elf," Pappy called out.

"Charlie and I been making the rounds of the house, spreading good cheer."

"And gettin' Christmas candy." The boy held out a fistful of candy canes.

Pappy gave a nod toward the door. "Let's go. Our sleigh awaits with Dasher Ambrose at the wheel."

Pappy, with Caroline on his arm, led the way out to the stairs. They trooped down, Pappy waving greetings to a half-dozen brothers who, like Santa, were bundled against the cold and about to depart for the University Center and the party. They held the house door open for him and his three assistants. Pappy, as he passed them, laid a finger beside his nose. "See you there, boys."

A Kenworth tow truck idled at the curb, Frye leaning against a fender. Three massive sacks of gifts swung from the hook at the back of the truck.

"Ready, Santa?" he called out.

Pappy reached for the handle of the passenger door.

Frye stopped him and pointed up to the roof of the cab.

"You want me up there?"

"That's right."

"You're kidding."

"I've got my orders." Frye snapped open a step ladder. "There's a rug up there for you to sit on."

He steadied the ladder while Pappy, hesitant, pawed his way up. Pappy settled himself, then reached down for Caroline.

She waved him off. "That's not for me, Grandpops. That's for Missus Claus."

Pappy fixed his granddaughter with a hard look over the tops of his glasses. "I don't have a Missus Claus."

"You do tonight." Caroline beckoned to a woman in red hurrying up the walk from the Theta Delta Theta house.

"Am I late?"

"Right on time," Caroline said.

Frye helped Missus Claus up the stepladder, and Pappy caught her hand when she reached the top. He guided her across in front of the windshield to a seat on the rug.

The woman slipped her arm through Pappy's and snuggled in close. "Thank you, my husband."

He stared at this stranger. "Doctor Berry?"

"You may call me Ori-Anna Claus."

"HO-HO-HO."

"Caroline drafted me."

"I'm a draftee, too."

Caroline, Dempsey, and Charlie climbed into the cab from the passenger's side while Frye trotted around to the driver's side. He, too, got in. After he closed the door, he rolled down the window and leaned out. "Ready to go, Pap?"

Pappy put a hand up beside his mouth. "On Dasher, on Dancer, on Prancer and Vixen—"

Frye fired up the diesel. He turned on the light bar and gave three quick tugs on the air horn's cord. "Now dash away, dash away, dash away all," he shouted to his passengers as he wheeled the big truck out into the street.

FRYE HIT THE AIR HORN every time he came on a cluster of students. They looked up and waved, and Santa and Missus Claus, riding on top of the cab, waved in return.

Frye took most of the turns easily, but on one, in front of Claxton Hall, he bounced the big truck over the curb. Missus Claus and Santa grabbed for the top of the passenger door frame, to keep from sliding off. When Frye straightened out on Middle Way, on the descent to Stadium Drive, the Clauses came up in each other's arms, laughing at the Mack Sennett comedy in which they had found themselves unwitting stars.

From Stadium Drive, Frye wheeled out onto Cumberland. Almost immediately, he swung left into the loop in front of the University Center and pulled up, lights flashing and horn blaring, to the building's massive front doors. He hopped down, grabbed the stepladder, and ran around to the passenger side. There he helped Missus Claus down and, in turn, Santa. Frye then pulled back on the power control, lowering the hook so Santa, Dempsey, and he could lift the bags of gifts off and heft them over their shoulders.

In they trooped and up the double-wide staircase to the second floor. They hustled ahead, down the long hall that led to the Orange Ballroom.

The closer they got, the more laughter they heard.

"Games," Caroline said.

Don Wright lounged at the door, waiting for them, a Cat-in-the-Hat hat on his head and an extra-long muffler, as striped as his hat, wrapped around his neck. "Ready, Pap?"

"Let's do it, Donny."

Wright leaned through the doorway. He threw a hand signal to Wickingson on the stage.

Wickingson, the games master, waved his hands over his head. "Hey, kids, who do you think is here?"

"Santa!" came the response from all corners of the chandeliered room.

Wright swung the door wide. "You're on," he said to Pappy and Missus Claus.

The two led the way in, waving and smiling, their faces glowing from the cold outside and the excitement inside, Pappy laughing his best and deepest ho-ho-ho.

They made their way through a wonderland of Christmas trees decorated by the university's varsity sports teams, past a tableau of toy soldiers and sugar plum fairies to the far end of the ballroom, to the stage on which sat two great red-cushioned thrones beneath an arch of pine boughs and mistletoe. Behind the thrones stood bands of Tau Upsilons and Theta Delts.

Pappy made a great to-do of seating Missus Claus, bowing to her before he went to the front of the stage and waved for quiet. "There's so many of you here!"

"Yea!" came the response.

"Tell ya how we're gonna do this—"

More cheers.

"I've got four groups of assistants here—"

The Tau Upsilons and Theta Delts, greeted by cheers, bowed and waved.

"They're gonna call out your names—"

Even more cheers.

"—when you hear your name, come runnin' up here 'cause they got something special for you."

More cheers still.

"And if you want to talk to me and Missus Claus and our little girl, Cornelia..." Pappy reached out for Caroline's hand and pulled her in. "...or our little boy, Jamie Jay..." Pappy caught Dempsey's arm and pulled him in as well. "...you come on up here, too. And somebody around here is gonna take a picture you can take home."

Cheers and applause went up everywhere.

Pappy scuttled to Santa's throne. As he settled in, a Theta Delt called out, "Justeen Davis."

At the side of the room, a child of five looked up, startled. Her father pushed her forward. Another Theta Delt carried a bag to the girl, a bag containing the three planned gifts plus a package of Reece's Pieces and a pass to 'A Christmas Carol' at the Tennessee Theater.

A boy–Frankie Long by the name tag slicked on his shirt front–found himself first in line to get to Santa. He swung and twisted from his mother's hand, too shy to climb up on Santa's lap, so Pappy swept him up and plopped him down. "You wanna talk to me?"

"Yeth." The boy took the sucker from his mouth. In waving the sucker around, he stuck it in Pappy's beard. Frye snapped pictures of Dempsey cutting the sucker away.

The next child became so excited, being with Saint Nicholas, that Pappy felt his pant leg beneath where she sat become suddenly warm and wet. He handed the leaker back to her mother.

Caroline laid a blanket across Pappy's lap. "Sorry, Grandpops."

"Accidents happen."

The line of children waiting to talk to Santa and his family lengthened. Most had something they wanted to ask, but some appeared only to want to hug the jolly old elf and be hugged by him. None hurried away.

Pappy lost track of time as the evening wore on. Only when he glanced up to find one final child–Charlie–standing before him did he realize his job was about done—Charlie, Dempsey, and a woman Pappy did not recognize.

Dempsey bent down. "Santa, this is Charlie's mom."

The woman, overweight and frayed from having kept control of her other children, smiled, her cheeks wet with tears. She held out her hands to Pappy, and he clasped them.

"Thank you," she said, "thank you. Thank you for all you done for my kids, particularly for little Charlie here. He really loves havin' a big brothah."

Pappy stood. He put an arm around the woman's shoulders and hugged her. "Your son's a good kid, you know that. And doesn't he look fine in his elf suit tonight?"

"He wants to ax you somethin'. He won't tell me what it is."

"All right." Pappy sat back on his throne. He beckoned Charlie over.

The boy eased up to Santa Claus, all the time holding onto Dempsey's hand.

Pappy lifted Charlie to his lap. He put his arm around the boy and leaned in close. "You want to ask me something?"

"Yes."

"What is it?"

Charlie picked at the fur on the cuff of Pappy's sleeve. "I don't know who my daddy is," he said so soft Pappy wasn't sure he'd heard right.

Charlie continued picking at the fur. "You think you might see him?"

"Your daddy?"

"Uh-huh."

"It's possible. I'm supposed to know everybody in the world."

"Would you tell him something for me?"

"What's that?"

"That I love him."

A tear slipped from the rim of Pappy's eye. He hugged the boy. "Charlie, I surely will. You got my word on that."

Charlie put his arms around Pappy's neck and hugged him in return.

It was only when Pappy felt the boy's hug relax that he motioned for Dempsey to come over. "Would you take Charlie to be with his sisters? I've got to talk to his mother."

"Sure, Pap." Dempsey lifted Charlie into his arms. Charlie clung to him as Dempsey moved away.

Pappy went over to the mother. "Missus Jackson, can we talk some?"

She gave a weak smile.

He guided her to a chair at the side, away from the crowd that was thinning as families said their thank yous to the college students and started for home. They sat together, Pappy and Charlie's mother, her skin of ebony where Charlie's was a light chocolate. Pappy took her hands in his. "Missus Jackson, who's Charlie's dad?"

"Oh Lordy." Nettie Jackson's lower lip quivered.

Pappy looked long into her eyes. "It's important."

She brought a hand to her mouth, whispering through her fingers. "Samuel. Samuel Phillips."

"Is he alive or dead?"

"Alive, though I've not seen him for six years."

"How do you know he's alive?"

"He calls me sometimes. Maybe once, twice a year."

"Is he in Knoxville?"

"I think so."

"Do you know where?"

"No."

"What broke you two up?"

"Oh Lordy, Lordy, Lordy—" Nettie Jackson wept. She squeezed Pappy's hand hard, her fingernails sinking into his flesh. "Samuel, he was in Nam before I knew him, a soldier. War screwed him up somethin' bad."

The tears rained down. "I'd hold him at night, and he'd cry and shake for hours. Other times he'd run off and scream at the moon. When I got pregnant with Charlie, he was convinced the gooks was comin' for him. That's what he said. Gooks. He said he had to protect us by leavin'."

"Where'd he go?"

"Under the Gay Street Bridge. Lived there with some other Nam crazies until the cops run them off. He come by a couple times after Charlie was born, to count little Charlie's fingers and toes, he said. Samuel was in terrible shape."

"When was the last time you heard from him?"

"Maybe a year ago."

"So he could be dead."

"I don't think so."

"Why's that?"

Nettie Jackson took a handkerchief from inside the top of her dress. She wiped at her tears. "His friends woulda got word to me."

"Samuel Phillips. He have a nickname or anything others might know?"

"Pooch. He said they called him Pooch because he could smell the Cong before anyone could hear 'em or see 'em."

"Ahh, a point man."

"That's what he said."

"Missus Jackson, I'm an old soldier, way too old to have been in Vietnam. I was in another war, and like Charlie's dad, I saw more killing than anyone should in a lifetime." Pappy glanced down at his boots, then back into the woman's eyes. "Look, I know where some of these boys hang out. I'm gonna try to find him."

"I wisht you wouldn't."

"What?"

"I said I wisht you wouldn't."

"Listen, I made Charlie a promise." Pappy helped Nettie Jackson to her feet. "He asked me to tell his daddy he loves him, but I intend to do that and better."

Pappy, an arm around Nettie Jackson's shoulders, guided her across the room to Charlie and his three sisters, who were laughing at Dempsey's ineptness with A Barrel of Monkeys, a game the youngest girl said was hers.

Pappy beckoned at the boy, to get his attention. "Charlie, you take care of your momma. And you keep watch at the window. You and me, we may see each other one more time before Christmas."

The boy he held up three monkeys he had hooked together, hand over tail. "You gonna come by?"

"Could be. I gotta go now. I got other things I need to do."

Charlie dropped the monkeys back in the barrel. He reached for Pappy's hand. "Bye, Pappy Claus."

Pappy touched a finger to the tip of the boy's nose and squeezed Charlie's hand. Then he left him to search for Missus Claus. Pappy found her on the stage, visiting with several of her Theta Delts. He went to the edge, gesturing for her to come over.

She broke away from her girls. "What is it, Santa?"

"You up to a little adventure?"

"Always."

"You know Charlie, Junior's Little Brother?"

"Yes."

"I'm going to find his dad."

Chapter 14

The search for Pooch

PAPPY AND DOCTOR BERRY hurried out to his pickup left by Wickingson in the University Center's parking ramp. He helped her in, then dashed around to the driver's side.

Berry watched him slide in behind the steering wheel. "Why're you doing this?"

"Every boy deserves to know his dad." Pappy started the engine. He backed the truck out of its parking slot, shifted into drive, and aimed the truck down the ramp. "I lost my dad when I was ten, but at least I knew him and I can remember him. Charlie doesn't have that."

"Aren't we going to change?"

"No time."

At the bottom of the exit ramp, Pappy turned onto Stadium Drive, then Cumberland and headed west.

"Where're we going?"

"Fourth Creek. There's a jungle camp out there where the bums and the hobos stay. Most are Vietnam vets who can't stand the indoors."

"Strange."

"Not really. You're inside and something goes haywire, you got only two ways to get out, the door or the window. To a foot soldier, that's not a good situation.

If you're outside, in the open, and your feelers are working, you got three hundred sixty degrees to escape."

"And you know this how?"

"I was in the big Number Two—the infantry, where war gets personal—and I got a nephew, one of the Nam boys who lives in the woods. He shows up on my doorstep every now and then."

"Oh."

"What do you mean, 'oh'?"

"Just oh."

Lights flashed up in Pappy's windshield and passed by.

"Look, Doctor Berry, Pooch Phillips may not even be at the jungle camp. If he isn't, chances are fair somebody will know where he is."

Pappy hit his turn signal, waited for a break in traffic, then swung across the on-coming lanes and into a Big John's Liquor Barn drive-up.

"Strange stop for Santa Claus, isn't it?"

Pappy winked at Berry. "Doin' a little Christmas shopping."

He idled up to the window, rolling down his own as he did.

The attendant leaned forward on his elbow. "After some Christmas cheer?"

"Jack Daniels, two pints."

The attendant put a knowing finger beside his nose. "Yea, Santa."

Pappy paid with a twenty. While the attendant counted out change, he said, "You know what I'd like for Christmas?"

Pappy shook his head, the bell on the end of his cap jingling.

"To get the hell away from all the drunks who drive in here. Sorry, I don't mean you."

Pappy chuckled. "May you get your wish, my friend."

He pocketed his change and drove on, out of the liquor store lot by way of a back entrance that brought him onto a side street. From there, Pappy cut left and right through a series of lesser streets, working his way south and west, south and west. After what seemed an eternity, he came out on a gravel trail that ended at a patch of winter-dried weeds decorated with piles of dog dew.

Pappy killed his truck's motor and lights. He and Berry sat in silence, Pappy listening to the distant whoop of an ambulance's siren, fading as it traveled north toward Fort Sanders Hospital.

Berry gazed at Pappy. "Are we here?"

"We're close."

He stuffed the Jack Daniels bottles inside his Santa jacket before he reached under the seat for a black, long-barreled Magnum flashlight. Pappy held the flashlight up for Berry to see. "Double duty. A good light and a helluva weapon."

He slipped out his door, holding the button in as he closed it so the latch would not click.

Berry opened her door. She, too, slipped out.

The two met in front of the truck. From there, they pushed out into a tangle of brush that did its best to mask a little-used path, a path that after some time twisted down the side of a ravine, twigs and branches snatching at the clothes of the intruders, the whole area with the musty smell of abandonment.

At the bottom, a creek—Fourth Creek—rippled over pebbles and stones as it made its way toward the Tennessee River, the smell here different, the air close in refreshed by the movement of water from a spring upstream. Here Pappy turned south, the direction in which the creek flowed, Berry two steps behind him.

It was eerily silent.

December.

No children playing late in backyards.

No night birds. All had migrated to warmer climates, to Florida, Mexico, Central America, except the snowy owls that had come down from the north.

Not even the city's sounds penetrated here, only the occasional burble of water where the creek swelled up and fell over a rock.

Pappy moved as silently as the night.

Thirty yards on, he put out his hand, and he and Berry stopped. Pappy flicked his flashlight on. He aimed its beam down, several inches ahead of his leg. The beam picked up a pale line not much thicker than a spider's silk. Pappy knelt to touch it, whispering, "Trip wire."

"What?"

"Trip wire. Fish line across the path, probably attached to some cans off in the brush. Cops come along, hit the line, the cans clatter and the bums scatter. Nobody gets caught."

Pappy's gaze swept from one side of the path to the other as he eased back up. He stepped over the line and took Berry's hand to help her across. He switched off the light after they were clear of the wire.

Twenty paces on, the flames of a campfire created dancing shadows in the near distance. The muted voices of men drifted toward Pappy and Berry.

He put a finger to his lips.

She nodded.

He went on, she behind him. They eased to the edge of a camp that was nothing more than a collection of cardboard shacks and a tarp stretched over a rope. Four men sat on milk crates around a fire.

Pappy stepped into the circle of light. "Hello, boys."

Three glanced up from their cigarettes and their bean cans of coffee, the air laced with the smell of smoke from cheap tobacco.

"Good gawd, Sherm," said one, "is that a commie there in that red suit or is that old bugger Sandy Claus?"

One of the men got to his feet. He stepped in front of Pappy, towering a head over him. "Who the hell are you?"

"As your buddy says, Santa Claus."

"And I suppose that gawddamn slut's Missus Claus?" The man jerked his head toward Berry.

"No slut, but you're right. She's Missus Claus."

"Smart ass."

Pappy stretched up. He pushed his face into the face of the taller man. "You lookin' to have me scratch your name off the good-little-boys' list?"

"I don't give a damn what you do."

Pappy settled back on his heels. His eyes scanned the man's faded and patched camouflage jacket. "You Army?"

"Hell no. Marine."

"Vietnam?"

"The DMZ."

"When?"

"What's it to you?"

"It's important."

"Sixty-eight."

Pappy pulled his beard off. He stuffed it in his pocket. "Army, 'Forty-two to 'Forty five, all the hell over Europe."

The ex-Marine sneered down at Pappy. "So we measured each other's dick. What the hell you want?"

"Samuel Phillips. Maybe you know him as Pooch."

"Never heard of him."

Pappy eased around the big man. He moved closer to the fire. "How about you boys? Any of you know Pooch?"

Pappy pulled a pint of Jack Daniels from inside his jacket and held it up. "A reward for the man who helps me find him."

Two peered at one another and shrugged. The fourth man, the one who had not looked up nor had he glanced at the others, raised a hand. "I know Pa-Pooch."

Pappy hunkered down. He cradled the bottle in his hands. "Son, where is he?"

"I da-don't know. I ain't sa-seen him for th-th-three months."

"Guess you don't get this fine whiskey then." Pappy straightened up.

The vet, in patched jeans and a Goodwill mackinaw, rose up with him. "Ba-but Stick pra-probably knows."

"Who's Stick?"

"He's one of our ba-boys, but he's ca-crazy, all those ch-chemicals in Nam and the wa-wack weed he smokes."

"Where can I find him?"

The vet shifted his weight to his other foot. He pointed downstream. "He st-stays pa-pretty much to himself, ca-closer to the river. Got a ha-hooch he made outta ca-corrugated metal. Fa-for that bottle, I'll ta-take you to him."

"Think I can get along without you."

"He na-knifes strangers."

An eyebrow went up on Pappy's forehead. "Tell you what, you can split the bottle with Stick if you take me to him and he knows where Pooch is. Deal?"

The vet rubbed his hands on the sides of his coat, his gaze fixed on the bottle. "Da-deal."

"What's your name, son?"

"Ca-Cooter. Wa-William Henthorn."

"Call me Pappy."

"All right, Pa-Pappy."

"Lead on, Cooter."

Henthorn started down a path that led south out of the jungle camp, but turned back. "Yer not ga-gonna renege now, are you?"

"No sir. You got point. I'll watch your six."

"All right, I ga-got point." Henthorn turned and again moved down the path.

Pappy reached back for Berry's hand, and the two followed.

Minutes passed. The waning moon, now overhead, slipped behind low, scuddy clouds filled with snow.

Henthorn stopped. He cupped his hands around his mouth and let out a bobwhite whistle.

Silence.

Henthorn gave out with another bird call.

A bobwhite whistle echoed back.

"Stick?" Henthorn called out. "It's me, Ca-Cooter."

A scratchy throated "You alone?" came back.

"Na-not exactly."

"What do you mean, 'Na-not exactly'?"

"I got Sa-Sa-Sa-Santa Claus wa-with me."

Pappy glanced around, searching for the voice.

"You jiggin' me, Coot? I'm a crazy sonuvabitch. Don't you jig me."

"I wa-wouldn't jig you, Stick. I ra-really do have a ga-guy here in a red suit."

"I'll kill him if he isn't Santa Claus."

Berry put her hand on Pappy's arm.

"He ra-really is, Stick," Cooter said to the night. "He ra-really is. Ca-can we come in?"

Silence, except for the rhythmic scraping of steel on stone, someone whetting a knife.

"Yeah," the voice came back.

Henthorn turned to Pappy. "If you ga-got a beard, mister, you ba-better put it on."

Pappy took the beard from his pocket. Berry helped him hook the loops over his ears, then straightened the beard.

Henthorn moved on, Pappy and Berry again following.

Seconds ticked off into a half-minute, then a minute.

"That's far enough." The scratchy voice came now from behind the trio. Pappy turned. As he did, a light flashed in his face.

"Sonuvabitch," the voice croaked. "You makin' house calls in the bush these days, old man?"

"Appears so." Pappy flicked his Magnum on. Its beam shot down the other's and burst into a face that was more hair than skin. A hand came up to shield its eyes.

"Goddamn, that's bright."

"Yours ain't no sick candle either," Pappy said.

Stick lowered his flashlight, and Pappy did the same.

"What you want?" Stick said.

"I'm looking for a friend of yours, Pooch Phillips."

"Why?"

"He's got a little boy he's not seen since the boy was a baby."

"What's his name?"

"This a test?"

"Yeah."

"Charlie—Charlie Jackson."

"That's right."

"Damn right it's right."

"What do you want with Pooch?"

"The boy, for Christmas, he'd like to see his dad."

Stick waved his light for Pappy and the others to follow him. He led them off the trail to a shack of metal back under a rock overhang, a shack masked from the outside world by a thick tangle of brush and a honey locust tree standing sentinel.

The vet struck a match. He put the flame to a candle in a snuff can. "Pooch ain't here as you can see."

"Where is he?"

Stick, in railroad overalls, denim jacket and fatigue cap, flopped in a canvas camp chair. The muzzle of Kalashnikov poked from beneath a blanket on the ground, the weapon within reach of the vet's hand. "VA hospital. I carried him in sometime back."

"What's wrong?"

Stick slipped a hand in his jacket pocket. Pappy watched the man's fingers fumble beneath the fabric until they fell on something, a sliver of wood, it turned out. Stick poked the sliver into the crevices between his teeth. "He's dying."

Pappy hunkered down. He brought a Jack Daniels bottle out and set it next to the candle. "What of?"

"Nam." Stick stretched the corner of his mouth back into his cheek as he worked the wood sliver around a molar. He spit to the side. "Nam's killed all my friends."

Cooter stepped forward. "It ain't ka-killed me."

"It will, Coot. It's gonna kill you and me both. We just don't know when."

Pappy stared at a line of books on the rock wall behind Stick.

Stick eyed Pappy. "Like 'em?"

"Yeah. What's that big one, 'Plato's Republic'?"

"Uh-huh." He reached back for the book and tossed it to Pappy.

He caught it and ran his hand over the cover before he opened it. "Leather, nice. You read this?"

"Sure."

"It's in Greek."

"Uh-huh. And I got books in I-talian, French, German, and Russian. I read 'em all. I may be bugs, man, but I ain't stupid."

"How you with poetry?"

"Shakespeare's sonnets, Shelley, Robert Burns if I want to practice my brogue."

Pappy laughed. "Fella, you're way beyond me. I'm about at the Robert Frost level. 'Two roads diverged in a yellow wood, / And sorry I could not travel both / And be one traveler, long I stood / And looked down one as far as I could / To where it bent in the undergrowth, / Then took the other–'"

Stick leaned forward. He braced his elbows on his knees. "Pretty puny stuff, man. You have to go deeper. If you want to stick with an American, you go with Whitman or Sandburg–'Pile the bodies high at Austerlitz and Waterloo. / Shovel them under and let me work – / I am the grass; I cover all. / And pile them high at Gettysburg, / And pile them high at Ypres and Verdun. / Shovel them under and let me work. / I am the grass.'"

Pappy picked up a twig. He doodled in the dirt. "Sandburg?"

"He's plain, man. Plain. Powerful. Speaks to the soul, like old Uncle Walt."

"You Army?"

"Yeah."

"I got one for you–'In Flanders fields the poppies blow / Between the crosses, row on row, / That mark our place, and in the sky / The larks, still bravely singing, fly / Scarce heard amid the guns below. / We are the Dead. Short days ago / We lived, felt dawn, saw sunset glow, / Loved and were loved, and now we lie / In Flanders fields.'"

Stick nodded, his chin on his fists. "Two May Nineteen-fifteen. Canadian surgeon, a major, name of John McCrae. He had just buried a former student of his, a lieutenant, killed in a shell burst. Took McCrae twenty minutes to write that poem while he sat by the grave."

Pappy tilted his head toward Stick. "He threw the poem away. Didja know that?"

"I didn't."

"If another officer hadn't pulled it from the trash and sent it off to the newspapers, we wouldn't have it."

Stick gazed out over the bushes that shielded him from the world beyond, his eyes fixing on the first flakes of snow drifting down from the scud clouds.

"Might be a white Christmas," he said. He closed his eyes. "'Watch your step, little child. / Pungee sticks, straw dolls booby trapped, / Shells—shining brass—unexploded. / Claymores, Bouncing Bettys, / Death is everywhere, little Christmas child. / So watch your step, / So watch your step.'"

Pappy rubbed at his sleeve. "I've not read that one," he said, his voice low, hushed.

Cooter leaned down. He motioned at Stick. "It's ha-his."

Pappy waited for the scholar and poet of the jungle camp to leave the world inside his being, to open his eyes. When he did, Pappy put the Plato book in Stick's hands. "Pooch. When did you see him last?"

The Vietnam vet held the book as one would a baby, before he slipped the book back in its place among its compatriots, between Aleksandr Solzhenitsyn's 'Gulag Archipelago' and Niccolo Machiavelli's 'The Prince.' "Couple days ago."

"How's he doing?"

"Weak, coughing up his guts. Pooch was in the back country, like a lot of us, when they were spraying that Agent Orange stuff. Soaked him and his platoon time and again."

"I've been told it's bad."

"Blisters, headaches that go on forever, pain, deformed children. Gawddamn right, it's bad. Pooch is the last of his platoon that he knows of. All the others—" Stick's hand flicked out flat.

Pappy tapped the vet's knee. "I'm going to see Pooch. You want to come along?"

"You got room in your sleigh for a mean old fart like me?"

"Always." Pappy stood up.

Stick gazed from the white-bearded man in the red suit to the bottle in its black label. "That for me?"

"For you and Cooter."

"Think I'll stay here. Coot an' me, we'll kill that old sucker." Stick picked up the bottle. He held it aloft in a salute to Pappy. "Merry Christmas."

Chapter 15

Reunion

ORI-ANNA BERRY stared at Pappy as the windshield wipers swished in a metronome beat, whisking away snowflakes that wanted to cling to the glass. "Where'd you come up with the poetry?"

Pappy leaned forward, his forearms on the steering wheel. He glanced past Berry, looking for approaching traffic as he came on an intersection. He saw none and rolled through. "You think we plumbers work all the time when we're on the job?"

"If I've hired you to fix my kitchen drain, you'd better."

Pappy half smiled. "Sure."

"That's not the answer you wanted, is it?" Berry said from the dark comfort of her side of Pappy's pickup.

"It's sure not the one I expected." He popped the cigarette lighter. Pappy pulled a Camel from the open pack on his dashboard and put the tip between his lips. When the lighter snapped out, he touched it to the end of his cigarette. "Mind if I smoke?"

"Yes."

Pappy's hand stopped in mid-air. "I shoulda asked before I fired up, shouldn't I?"

He slid the lighter back in its socket, then traded hands on the wheel so he could roll his window down. He flicked the cigarette out into the night air, the glowing end spinning away.

Berry picked up the conversation after Pappy had rolled the window back up. "All right, I'll concede. Plumbers don't work all the time."

The half-smile returned to Pappy's face. "Yeah. Well, as I was going to say, I remember complaining to my wife once about idle time on a job we were doing."

"What was it?"

"The job?"

"Yes."

"A new office building. We were way the hell ahead of the carpenters. Next day, I opened my lunch box and down under the pickle-and-pimento-loaf sandwiches and the slice of rhubarb pie was this little book you could slip in your shirt pocket."

Lights flashed in the windshield. A city truck passed by in the opposite lane, a plow on the front, the blade up.

"'Poetry for Working Stiffs,'" Pappy went on, "and a note from Lorene saying I should bend a few pages when I had nothing better to do."

"Did you?"

"Uh-huh. Some neat stuff in that little book, including 'The Road Not Taken.' I memorized it that day."

"Oh."

"I worked through that book and the poetry books we had in our town library, which wasn't much. Then I bummed a card off Maryville College for their library. That place was pure gold."

Berry interrupted Pappy's reverie. "VA Hospital coming up."

He slowed and spun the steering wheel to the side. Pappy guided his truck into a traffic circle that swung past the central building on the VA campus, the only new building in the complex. The three that laid beyond were nothing more than World War Two barracks—wood painted white, fronted by massive, century-old oak and hickory trees that shaded the barracks and their residents in the summer.

Pappy wheeled his truck into a parking space that had a 'Reserved for Doctor' sign attached to a post in front of it. "The old soldiers and the mobile patients live in those buildings."

"Mister Brown, you can't park here."

"You're a doc."

"Not that kind."

"Who's going to know?" Pappy shut off the lights and cut the motor. He opened his door. "Come on, Missus Claus, let's go hunting."

Berry sighed.

She opened her door and stepped out and down into a skiff of snow sufficient that one could track a cat, a bear or an elephant through it. But there were no cat, bear or elephant tracks, not even shoe prints of humans.

"Is the door going to be open?" she asked when the two met on the sidewalk.

"There's always the night buzzer."

The central building, military-plain brick and glass, thrust itself up three stories. First floor, administration offices and cafeteria. Second, medical and operating rooms. Third, rooms for the critically ill. Pappy knew the place well, not from being a patient, but from being a visitor to the survivors of his war.

He knew well, too, the cemetery at the rear of the campus, the destination for the old men who lived out their last years, months, and days here, those who had no families to carry them home when they died. Pappy served in the rifle squad that fired the last volley at their funeral services.

The reception desk was vacant when the two came in out of the weather. Pappy glanced first down the hallway that led to the cafeteria, then down the side hallway that led to the elevator, both dimly lit and as vacant of people as the lobby. A hint of Pine Sol hung in the air.

He leaned on the desk, drumming his fingers.

"Oh, the hell with it." Pappy marched around to the nurses' side. There he opened the master book and ran a finger down the pages of patients.

Berry reached across to him. "You can't do that."

"You've never helped yourself when the help was off somewhere else, swilling coffee?"

"How do you know they're drinking coffee?"

"I don't." Pappy's finger stopped. "He's here. Barracks A, Room Six. He's got a bunk mate, Cyril Roberts. My gawd, I know old Cyril, one of the old bachelor boys from down at Greenback. Hmm, lists him as eighty-eight. World War One."

Pappy came around the desk. He took Berry's hand and the two set off at a dog trot for the front door and Barracks A. When they got there, they found its door, too, had not yet been locked.

The hall light, as in the central building, was on night dim. Televisions glowed from several of the rooms, the sound turned low. Most rooms, though, were dark and quiet, except for the soft sounds of breathing and someone, in a distant room, snoring. The air smelled of Pine Sol mixed with the gaseous odors of the living.

Pappy and Berry moved with stealth. They stopped in front of Room Six. There Pappy tapped on the door frame.

A bedside light snapped on.

"Yeah?" a voice asked.

Pappy leaned in. "Cyril?"

A big-framed old man pushed himself up on his elbow, the man rail thin, a craggy nose prominent on his face, slightly offset, a nose that looked more like a beak, and beneath it a handlebar mustache as white as Pappy's beard. "Good golly, is that you, Sandy Claus?"

Pappy pulled his beard down as he came in. "Pappy Brown. You remember me?" He sat on the bed.

Roberts's visage brightened. He hugged Pappy, slapped him on the back with his boney hands, the fingers bent to the side by arthritis. "Willie Joe, how could I forget you? When the county condemned my shit house, you built me an indoor toilet and a septic tank, and you wouldn't take a dime."

"Hell, Cyril, you were on an Army pension. You didn't have any dimes to spare for nuthin'."

Roberts leaned back. He clamped Pappy's shoulders in his hands and looked deep into his eyes. "I ain't dead yet, Old Scout. I hope you ain't come up here to be in my funeral."

"I hope I'm not in your funeral until you reach a hundred."

"Twelve years, Willie boy. Twelve years and I'll be a century man." Roberts peered over Pappy's shoulder. "Who's that behind you? Missus Claus?"

"A friend. We've been Mister and Missus Claus for a bunch of kids tonight."

"Well, what brings you by?"

Pappy threw a look to the side, to an empty bed, the blanket folded back, the pillow undisturbed, precisely placed an equal distance from both sides of the bed. "You got a roommate?"

"Pooch?"

"We've come to see him. Where is he?"

"Out back, smokin'. You know, they won't let us old boys smoke indoors anymore. The hospital's gone and got all health conscious on us. Won't even let me chew snuff like I used to." Roberts beckoned for Pappy to lean in. He spoke at a low volume. "Between you an' me, Pooch shouldn't be smokin'. Got this gawd-awful cough."

As if it were a cue, coughing came from the hallway, a harsh, hacking cough repeating itself, moving toward Room Six. It stopped and a man, wheezing now, more emaciated than Roberts, entered, his gaze fixed on the floor before him, the man in faded jeans, a khaki shirt and slippers, his shoulders hunched, a hand holding a handkerchief to his mouth.

"Pooch, you got company."

Pooch Phillips jerked his head up. He backed out into the doorway.

"It's all right, Pooch. These is good people."

"Maybe so, Sarge. I'll talk from here. Who you, mister?"

Pappy stayed where he sat on the edge of Roberts's bed. "Pappy Brown. You got a little boy?"

"Yeah. Something happen to him?"

"He's all right. When did you see him last?"

"Six years ago."

Roberts squared his shoulders. The softness in his eyes disappeared, replaced by fierce anger. "You got a boy, an' you ain't seen him fer six years? What in the name of good gravy is wrong with you, Pooch?"

Phillips raised a hand. "Sarge, it's hard to explain."

"By gawd, it's time you did. If I had a boy, I'd be outta here faster'n you could throw Nurse Gilson across the room."

"Look at me, Sarge. I'm in a helluva shape. I don't want no son of mine seeing me like this."

"Stick says you're dying," Pappy said, still not moving from his seat on the bed. "That true, Pooch?"

"You know Stick?"

Pappy bobbed his chin.

Phillips leaned against the door jamb. "Ain't we all dyin'? Some of us just sooner than others."

"Charlie wants to see you."

Phillips's gaze went down to the floor, then to the dull steel sink in the corner of the room. "How would you know, mister?"

"I'm Santa Claus. I know everything."

"No, really, how would you know?"

"Look at me, son. I'm a student at UT, an oooold student. You may find that hard to believe, but believe it. I got a roommate and he's Charlie's Big Brother—you know, the Big Brother, Big Sister program?"

Pooch tilted his head to the side, his eyes near vacant.

Pappy leaned an elbow on his knee. "Charlie having a Big Brother is not the same as having a father, but it's a help. So, yes, I know Charlie, and I know he's got one wish for Christmas, for me to tell you he loves you, but you owe it to this little boy you created to go see him."

"I can't."

"You want Charlie's only memory of you to be of you laid out in a box?"

Phillips moved the toe of his slipper over the pine flooring. "I didn't know my father."

"So you want that for your son?"

"No."

"Pooch, come here." Roberts paddled his hand for Phillips to come to his bed. "Look, you get your bee-hind in gear and you go see that boy. I don't know if yer a believin' man, but I am, and I can tell you you're not long from having ta explain ta God a whole lotta things, and you want to explain this one right."

"I can't do it, Sarge."

"You want to live out the rest of your days with me, son?"

"'Course I do."

"Then git. Willie Joe, where's this boy live?"

"Couple miles from here."

Roberts, his hand quaking, motioned to a locker at the far side of the room. "Pooch, ya put yer coat on. This man an' this woman, they'll take you by right now."

"Maybe tomorrow."

"Pooch, son, none of us knows we got tomorrow. You go now."

Phillips gazed into Roberts's watery eyes, softening, about to spill over with tears. He started to open his mouth, but Roberts raised a bent finger in warning. "You cain't run. You cain't hide no longer, Pooch."

Phillips's shoulders slumped. He went to the locker, rattled the door open, and took a winter-weight camouflage jacket off a hook. He pushed an arm into a sleeve, then struggled to find the other sleeve behind him, his hand thrusting back for the arm hole.

Berry glided to Phillips. She lifted the shoulder of his coat.

Phillips's hand found the arm hole and slipped down in, but the zipper fought against him when he tried to hook an end into the slider. He ground his teeth, pulled a fatigue cap from his coat pocket and slapped it on his head, then hugged the coat around him.

"Shoes, son?" Pappy asked.

"Slippers is all right."

"It's snowing."

"It's all right."

Pappy handed his ignition keys to Berry as the two guided the vet toward the door. "Missus Claus will take you out to my truck. I gotta make a call."

Phillips glanced to the side, to Pappy. "You ain't got a sleigh?"

"A Dodge Ram. I'm a modern Santa."

BERRY HAD THE PICKUP running and the heater blasting out hot air by the time Pappy caught up. She sat behind the steering wheel while Phillips, still outside, paced in the snow. Berry rolled the window down. "He won't get in."

"Nuts." Pappy went over to Phillips. He tried to put an arm around the man's shoulders, to ask what the difficulty was, but Phillips pulled away. Pappy, angered, squared around in front of him. "What the hell is your problem?"

Phillips shook like a dry leaf in the wind. "I can't ride in that cab. It's too close in there."

"Well, you sure can't ride in the box. You'll freeze yer britches off."

"I can't sit in the center of that seat."

"Oh, that's it." Pappy ran his tongue along his teeth, the lower first, and then the upper. He sucked at them. "Tell you what, what if I was to sit in the center and you take shotgun? That puts you next to the window. You get to feeling too closed in, you roll the window down. How's that?"

"We can try it."

Pappy shot a hand in the air. He spun around, opened the passenger door, and hopped in. He slid in next to Berry. "You're driving."

Phillips followed Pappy, hesitating, his gaze roaming the interior of the cab as he let himself down on the seat.

"Gawd, Pooch, close the damn door before all the heat gets out."

Phillips eased the door into its frame. The latch clicked, and Phillips jerked around.

"Pooch, it's all right." Pappy put his hand on Phillips's knee, to assure him, but Phillips pushed Pappy's hand away.

Berry moved the shift lever from park to reverse. "How do I get there?"

"Go downtown, then hook north on Gay."

Berry backed out of the parking slot. The truck slid when she stepped on the brake pedal. "Lordy, it's slick."

"The city streets will be better."

Berry with care pulled the shift lever into drive. She pressed down a tiny amount on the gas, and the truck crept away.

Phillips's wandering gaze came to rest on the cigarette pack on the dash. "Could I have a stick?"

"Sorry, the doc here—Missus Claus—she don't allow any smoking in here. Now if you and me were alone—"

Berry shot a look at Pappy meant to pierce armor as she herded the truck out onto the street. She picked up the speed in the snow milled to slush by the tires of other traffic.

Phillips stared out the side window. "Nettie still live in that little house of hers?"

"On New Street?" Pappy asked.

"Yeah."

"She does."

"First couple years, most nights I watched that house from across the street."

"Nobody complain about you hanging around?"

"Nobody saw me."

"That I can't believe."

"I was invisible, man. In Nam, if they could see you, you were dead. I got real good at being invisible. Once, on a bet from the lieutenant, I hid for three days."

"How'd you do that?"

"Dug a hole in the hillside and pulled the grass in after me. Had to give it up when the ants moved in. They can chew your hide off."

A rotating yellow light came up in the windshield. It passed by, attached to a city truck, its blade down now, slush curling off to the side, splattering the sides of parked cars.

"Why'd you watch the place, Pooch?"

Phillips shrugged. "I s'pose I thought I was protecting what was mine."

"But why not just go in?"

"I couldn't bring myself to do it." A tremor ran through Phillips's shoulders. He cracked the window, then rolled it down halfway. The cold night air washed over his face. "Closed places. Can't stand closed places."

"But you stay at the hospital."

"Huh?"

"I said you stay at the hospital."

"That's different."

"How different?"

"They let me come and go. If they said, 'Pooch, you gotta stay in that damn room,' I'd be jumpin' out the window. I'd be gone, man. Nettie, she still pretty as I remember?"

"Gay ahead," Berry said.

"Go left. At Summit Hill, it's a right."

Berry signaled and slowed to turn.

Pappy glanced at Phillips. "Pretty? Let me put it this way. She's had a hard life, trying to raise those four little children by herself. That takes a toll on a body, Pooch. But I think if you were to ask your boy, Charlie would tell you his mamma's the prettiest woman in the whole world. There's a lotta love between those two."

Phillips grew silent. He gazed out the passenger window.

Berry stopped at the red light at Summit Hill Drive. She pushed the turn signal handle up. When the light changed, she turned right.

Summit Hill curved down through an old warehouse district that had not seen prosperity for a third of a century. Then it climbed away east, up over the James White Parkway to Summit Hill proper.

"Left on Old Vine," Pappy said.

Berry slowed. She pulled the turn signal handle down.

"Old Vine's gonna curve a couple times. Beyond the second curve, it's left on New Street. New Street, that's a joke. There's nothing new about it."

South of Summit Hill Drive, high on the hill, stood a series of apartment complexes, the residents largely white and largely young.

North of the Drive, on the land that fell away toward First Creek, were the projects, the residents largely black, all ages and lots of children.

New, for its short length, paralleled First Creek. A kid in his backyard, armed with slingshot, could loft a stone into the water.

"There's New," Berry said when the headlights flashed on a street sign.

"Left. Third house on the left, next to the alley."

Berry again signaled. She made the turn and guided the truck toward the curb.

"No. NO!" Phillips threw open the passenger door. He bolted from the truck.

Pappy lunged for him but missed. He, too, leaped from the truck and hot-footed it after the vet racing away, up the sidewalk.

Phillips slid in the snow. He made the turn into the alley and pounded off.

Pappy came after him, less than a dozen paces behind but fading, his arms milling at the air as he ran. *What the hell am I doing this for?*

He saw a silver trash can ahead. Pappy grabbed the lid as he passed and whirled, flinging the lid as hard as he could at Phillips's fleeing figure.

The massive frisbee sailed out flat. It clipped Phillips behind the knees, knocking him off stride. He stumbled, then fell, sprawling, sliding face first in the snow, a coughing fit racking his body.

Pappy trotted up, his chest heaving. Before the vet could rise, Pappy stepped on the man's shoulder. "You sonuvabitch. I'm too gawddamn old for this. You tryin' to give me a heart attack? I've already had one and it wasn't fun."

He grabbed Phillips by the collar and hauled him up, the vet still coughing. Pappy shagged him back up the alley.

"Lost my slippers," Phillips said, his voice hoarse from hacking.

Pappy looked down at the snow squishing up between Phillips's toes. "Serves you right, knothead."

"I ain't no knothead."

"Coward then. You prefer coward?"

Phillips raised his arm to his face. He coughed hard against his sleeve, doubling forward as he did.

Pappy stopped.

Phillips gasped for air. "I prefer not bein' here."

"The hell with what you prefer. You're here so your boy can see his dad, to know he's got one. You want to argue about that, I'll beat hell out of you."

"I can't go in there without shoes."

"Charlie's not going to notice. Come on." Pappy hauled him along.

"I don't know what to say."

"It'll come."

"You going to wait on me?"

"Knothead. The way you ran on me? And that damn Stick said you was weak."

"You going to wait on me?"

Pappy and Phillips moved through the beams cast by the headlights of Pappy's truck, Pappy not loosening his grip on the man's collar. "Yeah, I'm going to wait on you."

He pushed Phillips up the steps to the porch of a bungalow, its paint peeling, a bare yellow bug-light bulb on above the door.

Pappy banged on the side of the house.

Seconds passed, then the door creaked open. Nettie Jackson, in a terry-cloth robe and flip-flops, stood before the late-night callers.

Pappy's chest still heaved as he worked at catching his breath. "Missus Jackson, I brought Charlie an early Christmas present. His pap."

He dope-slapped Phillips. "Take your cap off."

Phillips pulled his cap from his head. He held it before him. "Nettie?"

She stepped back. "You better come in, Samuel, a-for you catch your death of cold. Charlie's in the bed, but I'll get him up."

Barefooted, Pooch Phillips shuffled in. He turned and stared at Pappy hanging onto the door jamb.

Nettie Jackson, too, stared at him. "Comin' in, Mister Brown?"

"No, I'd be in the way. My truck's across the street. I'll wait there, to take Pooch back to the VA."

"You look like you been runnin' some."

"Yeah."

"You know you're welcome."

"I know. That's all right."

Pappy stepped back and Nettie Jackson closed the door, but not before Pappy saw the aluminum Christmas tree in the corner and the presents in their opened wrappings under it, the presents from the Tau Upsilon, Theta Delta Theta party.

He grimaced as he turned to leave. Pappy grabbed for the calf of his right leg and crumpled against a porch post.

Berry came running from the truck. "What is it?"

"Charlie horse. Gawddamn it hurts." Pappy massaged the muscle.

Berry got an arm under his shoulder. Together, they limped down the steps and across the street, but he stopped her when she reached for the truck door. Pappy again grabbed for his paining calf muscle. "Just let me down on the running board."

She helped him turn and sit, then she sat beside him, Pappy kneading his calf muscle.

"Hard work being Santa Claus, isn't it?"

"Yeah. No wonder he's old."

Book Two
CHAPTER 16

The Meistersingers

DEMPSEY AND CHARLIE, sprawled on their bellies on the floor, glanced up from their checker game when Pappy rattled into the room loaded down like a prospector's mule. He dropped his computer case in a chair.

Dempsey returned his attention to the game. He tugged at his earlobe. "Welcome back, Pap."

"Hi-dee, June, Charlie." Pappy dumped his backpack of books on his desk.

Dempsey looked across at the boy. "You going to give the old man a hug?"

Charlie bounced up. He ran for Pappy and threw his forty-eight pounds into Pappy's arms, knocking Pappy back on his bed, still hugging him. "I love you, Mister Brown."

"Gol-ly, kid, if I'm gonna get this kinda welcome, I'm gonna have to go away more often." He wiggled his fingers into Charlie's ribs, the boy squirming, howling as he tried to get away from the tickling digits.

Dempsey pushed himself up to his feet. "Hey-ho, you two. Charlie, show Mister Brown your Christmas present."

The boy rolled around and up on his butt. He pushed a foot into Pappy's face. "New shoes."

Pappy ran his hand over the leather. "These are good, Charlie. What else you get?"

"A picture book."

"You got it here?"

"It's at home."

"Well, you bring it by sometime and read it to me."

"Okay."

Dempsey slipped his hands under Charlie's arms and lifted him away. "Come on, kid, let's get back to the game. I'm beatin' the pants off you."

"No, you're not."

"Am, too."

"Am not."

The two settled back on the floor, Charlie moving the red checkers and Dempsey the black.

Pappy sat up. "Anybody going to ask me what I got for Christmas?"

"Ignore him. All he wants is attention. Give it to him and he'll never leave you alone."

"All right." The boy pushed a red checker forward.

"Thank you, kid." Dempsey jumped a black checker over Charlie's red and set the red off the board.

"Hey."

"Hey, what? You gave it to me."

"Did not."

"Did, too. Now pay attention." Dempsey tapped his checker, then a red checker kitty corner from it, an open space, and a second black checker.

"Oooo, yeah." Charlie jumped his checker over Dempsey's and jumped the second black as well.

Dempsey clutched at his heart. "You're killing me."

"Am not."

"Am, too."

"Am not."

"Does anybody want to know what I got for Christmas?" Pappy asked a second time.

"Not me." Dempsey slid a checker into an open square.

Charlie whipped around. "I do!"

Pappy stood. He threw out his arms and did a pirouette as a clothing model might.

Charlie screwed up his face. "What?"

Dempsey waggled a finger at Pappy. "He's got a new jacket."

Charlie clapped his hands. "You get a new coat?"

Pappy bowed. "Caroline gave it to me. She said she was sick of me wearing my plumbing jacket to classes, that I can't do that anymore. Get this, now that I've got this school-bus yellow blinder, she wants me to go skiing with her."

"You'll break your leg."

"That's what I said." Pappy went out in the hall. He returned carrying a banjo case and holding up a tin. "Cookies."

Charlie's eyes lit up. "Can I have some?"

Dempsey gave the boy a stare that said no.

"Can I, Mister Brown?"

"I think your Big Brother wants you to wait until after supper." Pappy shucked his ski jacket and his knit cap. "Know what's on the menu?"

"P-and-J sandwiches and tomater soup. Our cook's not back. Your move, isn't it, kid?"

Pappy set the banjo case on his bed. He opened the case and took out a five-stringer and a handful of metal picks. He slipped the picks on the fingers of his right hand, then proceeded to tune the instrument, picking a G and twisting a tuning nob, alternately loosening and tightening the string. He continued to pick and twist.

Dempsey pulled a king back one space. "Didn't know you played, Pap."

"Not for a lotta years. Started fiddling with it over Christmas." Pappy picked a C on a second string and twisted the tuning knob that controlled that string.

Dempsey glanced up at Charlie. "Should I show him?"

"Yeah."

Dempsey hefted himself up. He went to his closet and took out a guitar case that he laid on the bed next to Pappy's banjo case. When he opened the guitar case, the gleaming blond wood of a Martin D Forty-five showed itself to the world.

Pappy gazed at the instrument. "You play that?"

"Yup."

"You never told me."

"You never asked." Dempsey lifted the guitar out. He put it on his knee and strummed through A-minor, B, B-minor, and C chords. "I was in a garage band in high school. I've got an electric at home—a Gibson—but I like this one better. Not so dang loud."

"That guitar's older than you are. Where'd you get it?"

Dempsey picked a C, wincing at the off-key note. He picked again at the string, twisting a tuning knob as he did. "It's my grandpaw's. Says he ordered it from the Sears Roebuck catalog for ten bucks way back before electricity ever came to the farm. Taught himself to play, listening to the Grand Ole Opry on a battery radio. You tuned up, Pap?"

"That I am."

Dempsey turned to Charlie. "Whose birthday is it, kid?"

"Mine!"

Dempsey strummed a C chord, and Pappy picked in.

"Happy birthday to you, happy birthday to you," Dempsey and Pappy sang.

They sang and played all the way to the end, Pappy finishing with a riff that ran from a C chord up through a G, Charlie clapping and laughing.

Dempsey pulled the neck of his guitar up against his shoulder, all smiles. "You're pretty good for an old man."

"And you're not half bad for a young pup hardly paper trained."

AMBROSE FRYE STUMBLED over the door sill as 10:32 flicked up on Pappy's digital clock, Frye with a book bag over his shoulder, a gym bag in one hand, and a bass guitar case in the other.

Pappy gazed up from his ornithology text.

Frye, bleary-eyed, dumped his load. He spun around and flopped on his bed. "Gawd, I'm shot."

"Hard vacation?"

"Don't you know it."

"That ice storm east of Strawberry Plains?"

"I've been dragging semis out of the ditch for the last thirty-six hours. Helluva mess."

"No breaks?"

"Not even to pee."

The guitar case drew Pappy's curiosity. He left his studies and wandered over to where Frye had dropped it. He opened the case. *Lordy, a Fender Mustang. A beaut. But where's the amp?* "Ambrose?"

A fluttering snore answered.

Pappy gazed at Frye, asleep. He came over to the foot of the bed and unlaced Frye's work boots. He pulled them off, took them to the closet, and returned with a blanket. Pappy draped it over Frye's length. "Morning comes early, pard. Sleep while you can."

WICKINGSON CAME IN the next evening, fresh off the plane from Wisconsin, to the thumping beat of 'Folsom Prison Blues' and Frye doing his best Johnny Cash on the lyrics.

Wickingson dumped his gear on his bed and shoved a Christmas-wrapped case of Leinenkugel's underneath. He shucked himself out of his storm coat. "What the hell have I missed?"

Frye continued the driving beat with his bass guitar, his eyes closed. "Junior and I had garage bands. We didn't know Pappy picked a mean banjo. Says he played in a group when he was our age, at fire department picnics. Can you believe that?"

"Yeah. My dad plays in a polka band."

Frye stopped dead. "That does it. Nope, no polkas, no way. Not for me."

Dempsey set his guitar aside. "You play, Wicks?"

"Three years' piano lessons. I got real good at 'Twinkle Twinkle Little Star' before the teacher gave up on me. I sing, though."

"What part?"

"Tenor."

Dempsey shrugged. "Should we try something?"

Pappy pulled the picks off his fingers. "I'm game."

Dempsey took up his guitar. He picked out a C chord. Frye took the bottom, Wickingson the top, and Dempsey and Pappy fit themselves in between on lead and baritone. They held the chord, harmonizing until Dempsey said, "Happy birthday."

The Caballeros woodshedded their way through the birthday song, applauding themselves for their guts when they reached the end.

Frye grinned to the others. "That's not half bad."

Pappy pulled his compatriots into a huddle. "Let's try it again. Jazz it up, give it a syncopated beat. Ah-one, ah-two, ah-one two three—"

Frat brothers, passing by, leaned in the doorway. They, too, applauded the quartet when they reached the end of the jazz version.

Frye waved his hands. "We could do it as the Four Presleys." He swiveled his hips as Elvis would, beginning a slow rendition. "Ha-ha-ha-happy birthday to you-hoo-hoo-hoo-hoo—"

Don Wright pushed his way into the room as the quartet ground through this latest version, leading the applause when they hit the end. "You guys, you guys, the frat's doing a revue in February for a fundraiser. Give yourselves a name. You're in it."

SUNDAY NIGHT. Dempsey, at his desk, scribbled notes on the side of a blueprint for a tobacco harvester.

Wickingson, in the beanbag chair, turned a page in a chemical engineering textbook, reviewing reaction control systems.

Frye, on his bed, slept, the sports section of the Knoxville Sentinel open over his face.

"Easy now, Grandpops," came a young woman's voice from the stairway.

Dempsey peered up from his notes.

"I can do this, Carrie," came another voice.

Wickingson lowered his book.

Dempsey leaned toward the doorway. "Pappy?"

"I'm all right, Junior."

Dempsey stared at Wickingson, then shoved his chair back. He went out into the hallway. "The hell you're all right." He hurried to Pappy and got an arm under his shoulder. "What happened?"

"He got twisted on his skis and fell," Caroline said, the first voice from the stairway.

Dempsey helped Pappy hobble into the room, Pappy in his school-bus yellow ski jacket, cap, jeans, and a cast on his right leg. Caroline followed, carrying a pair of crutches, she, too, in skiing togs.

Wickingson rolled out of the beanbag chair. He got a hold of Pappy's other arm and, working with Dempsey, lowered him onto his bed, Pappy wincing and moaning.

"What the heck happened to you?"

"Not much."

Wickingson turned to Caroline. "How bad is it?"

"I never should have insisted he go with us. It's all my fault."

Dempsey punched up Pappy's pillow. "Accidents are no one's fault. Pap's tough. God, do I know that."

Wickingson grabbed Frye's newspaper. He whacked his sleeping roommate with it. "Wake up, bro. Pappy's hurt."

Frye's eyes snapped open.

Pappy half sat, half laid back, his bound leg out straight. He horsed himself around and worked his fingers into the Velcro fasteners that held the two halves of the instant cast together.

Dempsey slapped his hands over Pappy's. "What are you doing?"

"I've got an itch. I want to scratch it."

"Your leg's broken, man. You open that cast, you're gonna do real damage."

"June, you're not my doctor."

"Maybe I should be."

"Gotcha, old buddy."

"What do you mean, gotcha?"

"Just that, gotcha. Nothing happened to me. Carrie and me, we faked it."

Chapter 17

Singing for bucks

DEMPSEY RACED into the Caballeros' suite, still in his waiter's white jacket from his dinner stint at the Theta Delta Theta house. "Tomorrow's Liz Martin's birthday! Let's sing for her."

Pappy turned away from his laptop. "You still hung up on her?"

"No. She's just a good kid."

"I thought you thought she was old."

Frye, at his desk, set his fluid dynamics textbook aside. "Pap, ease up. Liz is fun, and she's real easy on the eyes."

Pappy scratched at the side of his face. "Well, I have to agree with you on that one."

"So you'll do it?" Dempsey asked.

"Why not?"

"Count me in." Frye went back to his textbook.

Dempsey shed his jacket for a UT sweatshirt. "Do you think Wicks will?"

"Junior, you can sell him on anything. Nail him when he gets back from the library." Pappy returned to his computer. After a glance at the screen, he clattered away at the keyboard.

"Pap, you're fast at that thing."

He held up his index fingers, wiggling them. "Sixty words a minute, no errors."

Frye looked over. "I don't do much better, and I use all my fingers."

Dempsey pulled his sweatshirt on. "We gotta do something special."

"What do you mean?"

"For Liz's birthday, we gotta do something special."

Frye stared at the wall in front of his desk, as if there might be an idea there.

Dempsey studied the floor.

Pappy turned to the window. He gazed at a streetlight while he massaged the back of his neck. "Johnnie Ray. We could do the birthday song like Johnnie Ray."

Dempsey came over and leaned on Pappy's shoulder. "Who's Johnnie Ray?

"Do I have to teach you everything that happened before you were born? Johnnie Ray. He was big in the 'Fifties. He would cry when he sang." Pappy pulled open a desk drawer. He took a videotape from it and held it up to Dempsey. "Stick that in the VCR. Caroline's in a pop culture class. I got the tape for her."

Dempsey glanced at the sleeve as he pushed the tape into the video player. "'Ed Sullivan Highlights.' I've heard of this guy."

He turned the television on and punched the play button.

On the screen came Ed Sullivan introducing Mister Wences.

"This is black-and-white."

"Junior, that's how television was back then."

"I supposed you watched it by candlelight."

"Advance it to the third cut."

Dempsey punched fast forward. He rocked with the VCR as it spooled up to triple speed, Mister Wences silently ripping through his ventriloquist act. Then Elvis Presley came on, gyrating, his shoulders going like a shimmy dancer's.

"Hold it. We gotta see the king." Dempsey punched the stop and rewind buttons in succession.

Feet of tape whipped past the reading head as the VCR spooled up in reverse.

Dempsey punched play.

There on the screen, Elvis belted out 'You Ain't Nothing but a Hound Dog,' his band behind him.

Dempsey cranked the volume up. "How come we only see him from the waist up? Where are those hips?"

"Too racy," Pappy said. "Sullivan wouldn't show that."

"You're kidding."

"No, it's true."

The three watched the man who blended the blues, country, and gospel into something new wail away on his early hit, and then it was over.

While Dempsey and Frye applauded, Ed Sullivan introduced Johnnie Ray. Ray came on screen, Sullivan's orchestra playing a four-bar intro. Ray threw a hand toward his knees, then hit the lyrics, "If your sweetheart sends a letter of goodbye—"

He sobbed and cried through two-and-a-half minutes of song.

During Ray's bows, the camera swept over the audience, stopping on teenage girls jumping in the aisles, screaming.

Dempsey hooked his thumbs in his belt loops. "I can do that."

DEMPSEY CARRIED a two-layer cake above his shoulder, the cake complete with pink-frosting roses and twenty-three candles, all burning, to the table where Liz Martin sat with her table mates. Frye, Wickingson, and Pappy followed, dressed, as was Dempsey, in waiter's jackets, white shirts, and bow ties. They hefted trays of ice cream in crystal cups.

Dempsey set the cake down in front of Martin. "Happy birthday, Liz. You can't blow the candles out just yet."

"Why not?"

"We've got something special for you."

Other waiters trotted up. They took the trays of ice cream, and one handed Frye a guitar. Frye slipped the strap over his head onto his shoulder, then strummed a C chord, the quartet taking their notes. On a downbeat from Pappy, they went into a weeping, sobbing rendition of the birthday song, Johnnie Ray style. Dempsey, at the end, whipped off his jacket. He flailed it from side to side and threw it to the ceiling when the applause went up, the jacket snagging on a chandelier.

"One more? One more?" Dempsey waggled the fingers of both hands at audience, applause greeting his request.

He leaned into Pappy, Frye, and Wickingson. They took their notes for the opening chord of their encore and held it until Pappy touched a thumb and forefinger together, the cutoff. He nodded the downbeat—"When I get older, losing my hair / Many years from now / Waa-waa-waa-waa-waa—"

The Meistersingers went into the Beatles' funky 'When I'm Sixty-Four,' performing it complete with hand motions and choreographed steps through three verses. Applause erupted that Pappy thought would not stop.

Caroline rushed down from the head table. She hugged him. "Grandpops, you're great."

"Didn't embarrass you, did I?"

"Could you ever?"

"Oh yeah—"

DEMPSEY OPENED an envelope he had picked up from mail central at the Tau Upsilon house. He pulled out a note on pink stationary and read down the page. "Holy smokes."

Dempsey ran for the stairs, taking the steps two at a time. "Pap, you're not gonna believe this. Somebody wants us to sing for them, and they'll pay!"

Pappy came out of the bathroom, toweling off. "What's that?"

"Somebody will pay us to sing for them." Dempsey waved the note in Pappy's face.

"I can't read it. I haven't got my glasses." He raised a foot and ran the towel between his toes.

"Omicron Rho wants us to sing for them, a birthday bash for one of their members. You gonna walk around here naked all night?"

"June, I just got out of the shower." Pappy flipped the towel behind his neck. He toweled down his back, ending his dry-off with a vigorous rump rub. "Carrie tells me that's a pretty wild bunch, a lot of women athletes in that sorority."

"But they'll pay."

Pappy went in search of his shorts and socks. "How much?"

"Fifty bucks."

"We could give the money to the frat's Big Brother fund, I suppose."

"Then you'll do it?"

Pappy, now on his knees, rooted under his bed for shoes. "You an' me, we're only half. Check with Ambrose and Wicks when they come back from Perkins. My gawd, look at all the dust bunnies under here. Dust bunnies, they're more the size of turkeys. And what's this?"

He brought out a Tonka dump truck.

Dempsey snatched it away. "That's Charlie's. We wondered where it got to."

FRYE AND WICKINGSON agreed to the gig.

For the show, the foursome added two numbers to their repertoire of two, so they could do a ten-minute set. Pappy taught his fellow meistersingers Meredith Wilson's 'Lida Rose,' a barbershop standard, and Hank Williams's 'Hey Good Lookin',' an upbeat country tune. They changed the name Lida Rose to Linda Rose, for Linda Rose Musselmann, the Omicron Rho's birthday person and reserve center for the Lady Vols basketball team.

The men closeted their waiter's jackets, white shirts, and dark trousers for UT-orange silk shirts, white ties, and white slacks.

Their first rehearsal drew hoots from other frat members on the floor. Pappy, his frustration boiling, leaned out into the hallway. "Gawddammit, will you shut up? The frat gets the money from this gig, forcrissake."

THE CABALLEROS, chatting among themselves, strolled up to the Omicron Rho house at the requested hour. They went inside and laid their coats, jackets, and caps over the back of a couch in the living room. From there, they drifted over to the dining room door–closed.

Wickingson cracked it and peeked in.

Pappy leaned against the doorjamb. "Well?"

"Cake's coming out now." Wickingson waved to someone in the dining room.

Pappy punched him. "What's that all about?"

"The Omicron Rho president. She waved to me."

"You know the sorority president?"

"Hey, I get around."

A clinking of spoons on water glasses interrupted.

"Attention, girls, attention," a voice inside the dining room called out. "Tonight is our sorority's anniversary dinner, and it's also a birthday dinner for one of our sisters, Linda Musselmann. So we have booked something special."

A smattering of applause came.

"Here to entertain you, Linda and everyone, are four guys from the Tau Upsilon house, James Dempsey, Ambrose Frye, Fredrick Wickingson, and William Joseph Brown, the Four Caballeros."

Wickingson pushed the door open, and the four dashed into an open area in front of the head table, waving to the young women.

Dempsey swung his guitar up. He riffed an introduction, then the four hit it–"Say hey, good lookin'. What ya got cookin'? / How's about cookin' something up with me?–"

The Omicron Rho president pointed to the birthday person.

Dempsey went straight to Musselmann. He leaned across the table to her on the next line–"Hey, sweet baby. Don't you think maybe / We can find us a brand new recipe?"

Chorus, verse, chorus, verse. And applause.

Musselmann, a wine glass in hand, slipped away from the table. She stumbled. "Am I a li'l drunk?" she asked as she waved a five-dollar bill to the girls around her. Then, with a sweeping movement, she stuffed the bill in the waistband of Dempsey's pants.

Dempsey's eyes popped. He pivoted to Pappy.

"A tip," Pappy mouthed.

Staggering, Dempsey took the group into 'When I'm Sixty-Four.'

That brought whistles and a response equal to 'Hey Good Lookin'' and a five-dollar bill that another girl stuffed in Frye's waistband.

The quartet rolled on into 'Lida Rose,' Dempsey again singing to Musselmann.

She, however, hailed the attention of a waiter and thumbed at her empty wine glass. When she did turn around, Dempsey was there, warbling, his necktie swinging in front of her. She latched onto the tie and reeled Dempsey in, came out of her chair, swaying and dancing to the rhythm of the song. She cupped her hand behind Dempsey's neck.

He flushed and skittered away. Dempsey ducked back into the group, between Frye and Wickingson. Musselmann danced after him, but Frye and Wickingson blocked her.

Dempsey sang the rest of the song to Musselmann long distance. When the applause and hoots came up, he handed his guitar to Frye and raced from the room, hands waving dollar bills, reaching out for him.

Dempsey returned almost as quickly as he left, wearing a white jacket.

The Caballeros went into their finale, their weeping Johnnie Ray rendition of the birthday song. At the end, Dempsey whipped off his jacket and flailed it at the floor.

Musselmann came up out of her chair again. She grabbed Dempsey by the necktie and kissed him hard, loosening the knot in his tie while she caressed his tongue with hers. Then she snatched the tie away.

"Why don't you take it all off?" she said through a lascivious smile.

Dempsey leaped back, but other hands grabbed him, and Frye and Wickingson as well.

Frye went down in an attempt to wrench himself away, losing his slacks as he scrambled under a table.

In the rush at the Caballeros, someone pinched Pappy. He whirled and his shirt ripped away. Pappy grabbed for his belt when he felt a hand on his back pocket. He twisted and fabric tore.

In desperation, he seized on a tablecloth. He snatched it away, sending dishes, wine glasses, and cake flying. Pappy wrapped the tablecloth around himself and fled, Wickingson and Frye at his heels, they clutching at the remnants of their clothes and dragging Dempsey with them.

They bolted through the living room and on outside, the Omicron Rho girls in pursuit, laughing, waving, blowing two-handed kisses to the Caballeros.

"Y'all come back!" Linda Rose Musselmann called after them.

Dempsey, in little more than his socks and shorts, shivered in the January air whistling around him. "What the hell happened in there?"

"They wanted your body, June," Pappy said.

"Yeah, I can understand that. But yours?"

Pappy managed a laugh as he cinched the tablecloth more tightly around himself. "Amazing, isn't it?"

A PACKAGE and Dempsey's guitar lay on Dempsey's bed the next day when he and Pappy returned from classes.

Dempsey picked up the Martin. He examined it, found no damage, then strummed a few chords. "Thank God, they didn't hurt Grandpaw's guitar. It's getting to be worth something."

He packed the Martin away in its case before he undid the strings on the package.

Pappy peered around Dempsey's shoulder. "Hey, that's my ski jacket and my cap." He carried them to his closet.

Dempsey continued to paw through. "Looks like all our coats are here."

He took out Wickingson's trench coat and Frye's towing jacket and laid them on their owners' beds.

He then picked up his own winter coat. An orange shirt came with it, torn and minus one sleeve.

"Would you look at this?" Dempsey held the shirt up for Pappy to see, a message scrawled across the back in hot pink lipstick, *Love stud*

Chapter 18

The whiskey runner

THE BELL RANG, ending the class.

While the students around Pappy evaporated like mist before a July morning's baking sun, he took extra care to place his books and notepad into his backpack. His ballpoint? Pappy stared at the ink end. He watched it disappear when he snapped the retractor.

Pappy slipped the pen into his shirt pocket, then glanced up to the front of the lecture hall. He had a question, but wondered whether maybe he should skip it and head for the Blue Onion.

Doctor Berry, at the front, looked up from a paper another student had given her. She beckoned to Pappy.

That decided it. He slung his backpack over his shoulder. Pappy gathered his coat and wandered forward to a desk in the first row. There he took up residence.

He could wait.

He didn't have to hurry away.

This was the final class of his day, and the lecture hall would be vacant for the next several hours, until students began filtering in for the first of two night classes.

He studied his watch. When it appeared to him the professor and the student still had more to review, he pulled the course syllabus from his backpack and reread the description of the semester paper he was expected to write.

"You wanted to see me, Mister Brown?"

Pappy looked up. Doctor Berry, at the lectern, stood alone now, putting papers into a valise.

"You motioned for me to come up," he said. "I thought maybe you wanted to see me."

"No, I saw you back there. I thought you had something." She closed the top of the valise, but did not secure the latching strap. "I didn't want you to think you should leave because I was talking to another student."

"Oh. Yeah, well, ahh, the big paper—"

"Yes?"

"You know, I'm only taking this course because Caroline insisted."

"I know." Berry sat on the desk beside the lectern. She crossed her legs at the ankles and swung her feet while Pappy worked up to asking the question that had concerned him.

"Could I buy you a cup of coffee out at the machines?" he said.

"It's pretty awful stuff." Berry opened her valise. She brought out a small vacuum bottle. "This is a two-cupper and it's full, so it's hot. Why don't I share with you?"

"I don't have a cup."

Berry reached back into her valise.

"I always have a spare." She brought out a mug that had a Theta Delta Theta shield on it. Berry placed it on the desk.

Pappy watched her pour. "Caroline says you carry the world in that valise."

"Just about. Never know what I'll need and when I'll need it." Berry held the mug out to Pappy.

He took it and settled back on his desk.

She filled her Thermos cup. "It's decaf."

"Can't have everything." He sipped at the brew. "Not bad."

"That a left-handed compliment."

"Well, all right, it's okay."

"Am I embarrassing you?"

Pappy glanced away. "I'm probably embarrassing myself."

"Well, let's get to the business of whatever it is I can do to help you."

Pappy set his cup aside. "This semester paper, it's a big thing, isn't it?"

"Half your grade."

"Well, what do you want?"

"Just what I've asked for. You have it there in the syllabus, a personal narrative, a story from your life at least ten pages long, and you list any documentation and sources you draw on, other than yourself, in an appendix. The format's in the textbook."

"How many sources?"

"What's the syllabus say, three?"

"Five."

"Then five. What's the problem, Mister Brown?"

Pappy put his fingertips on his forehead. He massaged the one deep crease that was there, then drew his hands down his face. "There's nothing in my life worth writing about."

"Carrie wouldn't agree."

"She's my granddaughter. I lie to her a lot."

"Somehow I don't think you do." Berry shifted on her perch so one foot touched the floor. She leaned to the side, bracing a hand on the desk top. "How about your World War Two experiences?"

"Another soldier's story. Who'd want to read that?"

"I would. And Carrie. And probably your son."

"It's a thought."

"Or how about the story of someone in your family?" Berry again shifted on her perch, her hands now talking. "You'd have to write in the first person, from that person's point of view, get inside his or her head just as you're inside your own head."

"Hmm."

Berry's hands opened out. "Have an idea?"

"Maybe."

"What is it?"

"My pap."

She returned to her coffee. "He died when you were ten, didn't you tell me?"

"He was a whiskey runner in his last years. Nobody's ever told me about the circumstances of his death."

"Is there anyone still living who knows?"

"One man."

PAPPY SPUN the brass handle on the old-timey doorbell. While he waited, he picked up a rolled newspaper from the porch floor. He had hardly gotten the rubber band off the paper and the front page snapped open when footsteps approached inside, and the door swung open.

There before Pappy stood a hawk-nosed man, gaunt and ramrod straight. He smiled and extended his hand, his hand trembling. "Pappy, how are ya, boy?"

"Doin' fine." Pappy shook the old man's hand. "How about you, Sheriff?"

"Aw, you shouldn't call me that," Quill Rose said. "I haven't been in that office for—how long has it been?—twenty-eight years now? See ya found my paper. Anything interesting?"

Pappy glanced at it, embarrassed for having opened it. "Just looked at the headlines." He rolled the paper up and handed it to Rose.

Rose stepped back from the doorway. "Come on in out of that February chill. I'll see if Martha'll brew us up a cup of tea."

Pappy entered. The aromas of gardenia potpourri swirled around him as Rose closed the door.

"She won't let me drink coffee anymore. God knows, the coffee we used to make down at the courthouse would tar your innards, so I can't say I miss it much. Martha?" Rose called out.

"Yes?"

"Company."

A small woman, a bit better fed than her husband, bustled in, her arms out to the caller. "Oh, Willie Joe, how nice of you to come by."

She hugged Pappy as a maiden aunt might, with a gentle touch. "Take off your coat. Why Quill's got you standing out in the hall, I don't know. I think he's forgetting his manners. He's eighty-nine, you know."

Pappy shed his jacket.

Rose took it with the intention of hanging it on the hallway coat stand, but Pappy stopped him. He pulled off his knit cap and stuffed it in a pocket.

Rose admired the jacket as he hung it up. "Certainly is a bright thing."

"School-bus yellow. Carrie gave it to me for Christmas.

"Oh? How is she?"

"As good as ever."

Martha Rose latched onto Pappy's arm and ushered him into what had been the front parlor when the Roses bought the house, her eyes sparkling from behind Coke bottle glasses. She patted the back of a Queen Anne's chair.

Pappy took it as an indication that's where he was to sit.

Rose came through and took a seat in an old oak office chair. "Remember this?"

"Yours when you were the sheriff."

"The new sheriff felt he deserved a leather chair, so I snitched this when he wasn't looking."

Martha Rose cleared her throat. "Willie Joe, would you like some tea?"

"That'd be nice."

"Well, you just talk to Quill a bit and I'll make us some." With that, she bustled away, out of the front room.

Rose gazed after her. "I swear Martha seems to move faster as I move slower."

Pappy cocked his head to the side. He studied the old man. "Really, Quill, how are you?"

"All right, I guess. I've outlived three doctors." Rose chuckled, then leaned forward on an arm of his chair. "Now you didn't come by to get a health report on me. What is it you really want?"

"You know I quit my business."

"Sold out to your boy. I heard."

"I'm taking classes up at UT now. I've become a student."

"Know that, too. Better than drinkin', isn't it?"

"You heard."

"Uh-huh."

"Went on one awful tear last year, but that's past." Pappy shook his head. "Quill, you're as sharp as ever."

"I like to think so. Truth is I'm not."

"Well, let me get to it."

Martha hurried in with a wicker tray on which rode three steaming cups on saucers, a plate of sweets, and napkins at the side.

"Baklava," she said when Pappy peered at the sweets.

He took one and a cup and saucer. "When did you go gettin' so fancy?"

She laid a napkin on the arm of Pappy's chair. "Just in case you need it."

"Martha's always trying new recipes," Rose said.

"Keeps me young." She turned to her husband and held the tray out to him. After he took a saucer and cup and a sweet, she went to the love seat by the front window. She set the tray on a coffee table half covered with seed catalogues. As she sat down, her foot bumped a knitting basket beneath the table, the basket overflowing with an unfinished afghan. She pulled up a portion. "Making this for my great grandniece."

Rose dipped his finger in his tea. "Ahh, just the temperature. Martha, Pappy was just telling me he's taking classes up at the university."

She huffed. "Pappy. How you can call him that when he was Willie Joe to us all those years he was growing up."

"Willie Joe's just fine, Miss Martha," Pappy said.

"Well, I'm glad to hear it." She stuffed the afghan back into the basket. "You like being a student?"

"Yes, but it's a helluva lot of work—pardon—a heckuva lot of work. Miss Martha, that's why I've come by, to ask Quill for some help."

"How's that?" Rose asked.

Pappy picked up the baklava. He examined it before he put a tooth to it. He chewed. "Ooo, this is good. I taste honey in here."

Martha Rose worked herself into a more comfortable position on the love seat. "Have another?"

Pappy popped up to help himself. "You're going to spoil me for lunch," he said as he put a second square on his saucer. He motioned at the seed catalogs. "You planning your garden?"

"They're the best winter reading, Willie Joe. And the pictures of what you can grow, oh, they're just so beautiful."

"I always left the garden to Lorene. She said my only value was scaring the crows away." He went back to his chair. As he did, he directed a question to Quill Rose. "You remember my pap?"

"I do."

"What can you tell me about him I don't know?"

Rose sipped at his tea. "Well, let's see. We grew up neighbors in Townsend. Your pa was, what, two years younger than me. I liked him, though I was closer to Homer and Harold Wright. They were neighbors as boys on the other side. Your pa was a devil of a kid and a devil of a man."

Martha Rose shot a look of disapproval at her husband.

"Martha, I mean that in only the nicest way. You see, Pappy, there wasn't nothing your pa wouldn't do."

"I'd heard he was fearless."

"That's true. Once, Homer and Harold talked him into wing walking for them when they were doing that little air show up at Elkmont. Remember that, Martha? That was what, Nineteen and Twenty-five?"

"Nineteen and Twenty-six."

"That's right, he was working for them at the time in their sawmill." Rose shifted in his chair. "'Course, you know that from Homer and Harold raising you and your brother after your pa died. Your brother, now he was as wild as your pa."

"Yes."

"Shame he had to die in the war."

Pappy stared into his cup, his elbows on his knees.

"You were there, weren't you?" Rose said.

"We were in the same platoon. Shared a foxhole a lot of the time."

"You've never talked about it, have you?"

Pappy swirled his cup. He watched the tea spin. "No, that was a terrible time—for all of us there."

"But it's your pa you want to know about."

"Yeah."

"Why?"

Pappy set his cup and saucer on the floor, next to his chair. "I'm taking a narrative writing class, and I have to write this story. Thought I'd like to write it about how Pap died."

"Oh." Rose tilted back in his chair, a spring squeaking.

"You ought to oil that, Quill."

"I don't bend too good. I'm afraid oiling squeaky chairs and starting lawn mowers are things I've given up."

"I can take care of that for you."

"That's not necessary. I hardly notice it."

Martha Rose arched an eyebrow. "I do," she said as she piled the afghan onto her lap, her fingers working the needles and the yarn.

Rose rubbed a bony knuckle against the tip of his nose. "Pappy, what do you remember about your pa?"

"Not a lot. I know he was a whiskey runner in his last years."

"'Thirty-one and 'Thirty-two. Timbering was petering out in the mountains. You may not have known that at the time, being a kid and all. But your pa could see that Homer and Harold were going to have to shut down their mill, so he quit 'em, to save them his pay, he said."

"How'd he get from that to the whiskey trade?"

"Prohibition."

"Ahh."

"There were a lot of stills up in our mountains. For every two I'd dynamite, three more would pop up elsewhere in the county. I slowed 'em, but I couldn't stop 'em. None of us lawmen could. They were turning out shine by the barrel, much of it worse than skunk pee, but people back then, they'd drink anything."

"They still do."

Quill Rose, smiling, tugged at his ear. "I s'pose. Anyway, the shiners needed to get the stuff out of the mountains, to Nashville and Memphis. They hired men who had trucks, but trucks were slow. We could catch 'em. Your pa went to them and said he'd haul it out on halves, said he had a fast car."

Pappy whistled.

"Halves, that's right. Expensive for a shiner to give away half his load, so all turned your pa down but one. So your pa made that first run, and he sold that hooch at a premium. Well, that old shiner was so tickled when he got his half of the money that word got around, and everybody was throwing business at Willie."

Pappy's gaze drifted up toward where the floral wallpaper met the ceiling plaster, his eyes not focused, yet there was his father bent across the fender of an old car, his hands twisting a screwdriver on something. He heard his father's voice calling out, "Floor it, son."

Pappy half-smiled at the memory. "He was always tinkering on his car, wasn't he?"

"Oh yes, your pap was a top mechanic. He had a little Chevy coupe. First thing he did when he quit the sawmill was get him a straight-eight, you know, out of a wrecked Overland. He dropped that in the coupe and that little machine just flew."

Pappy turned back to Rose. "Couldn't haul much with a coupe, could he?"

"That was a problem. He took out the seat, and, even at that, he could only get eighteen cases of shine in there, not much when a decent truck would haul two hundred fifty gallons and a tanker with a false bottom, three thousand. A shiner who lost a truck of booze was hurt, and a group of shiners who went in on a tanker and lost that, they were out of business. The loss of eighteen cases, if someone caught your pa, well, some of those shiners drank that much of their goods in a year."

Pappy ran a finger along a nonexistent crease in his trouser leg as images of a succession of cars drove through the back reaches of his mind. "He didn't have that little coupe for long as I remember, did he?"

"Pap, this all going to stick," Rose asked, "or had you best take a note or two?"

"Oh jeez, I was supposed to record this. Where's my tape recorder?" Pappy touched a finger to his forehead. "It's in my coat pocket. Just a minute while I get it."

He hurried to the hallway. When he returned, he had a micro recorder in his hand, the recorder no larger than a pack of cigarettes. He fiddled with the buttons, checking the battery's power, speaking into the machine, "Testing one, two, three, four."

Pappy pressed a button and all heard the sound of a chipmunk chattering as the tape rewound.

He pressed the stop and the play buttons. "Testing one, two, three, four" came from the miniature speaker in the recorder.

"All right, it's ready." Pappy pressed the record button and placed the recorder in Rose's hand.

Rose stared at it. "No microphone?"

"It's built in." Pappy tapped the top of the recorder. "It's right here. You go ahead and talk. The machine will pick you up."

Rose turned the recorder over, then back. "Tiny thing, isn't it? I don't have to do anything, just talk, huh?"

"That's right." Pappy went back to his chair.

Rose brought the tape recorder up, as if he intended to sing into it. "Story is your pa made three runs to get the money he needed to buy a Packard, a big tan four-door job."

"I remember that car. Ma yelled at him for a week for spending the money. It must have been a fortune to her."

"That car had an eight in it, like the coupe, but for the load your pa wanted to haul, it wasn't enough, not and have any speed. He blew the engine on the first run out of the mountains and wrecked, almost killed himself."

"I didn't know that."

"Shiners found him and patched him up. They hid him until he could walk out and get him another Packard."

"Oh, the black one."

"Black as coal. Now your pa got himself a V-sixteen from a Cadillac. He dropped that under the hood, and he had a machine nobody could catch. I know. I tried, and I thought I had a fast car, a little light Ford with a five-speed transmission I got out of a truck. When I wound that car up in fifth gear, I thought I was flyin'."

Martha Rose's fingers twirled her needles, the needles clicking together as they knitted and purled the yarn, lengthening the afghan row upon row. The hall clock chimed, and she looked up. She turned to Pappy. "Willie Joe, it's coming on lunchtime. You'll have a bite with us, won't you?"

"Oh now, Miss Martha, I don't want you to go to any trouble. I'll get something at Taco Pete's."

"I won't hear of it. That's not real food and you know it. Now I got chili on the stove and cornbread about ready to come out of the oven."

Rose winked at Pappy. "Better say yes."

"Be a pleasure then."

Martha Rose worked herself up out of the love seat as she laid her afghan and needles to one side. On her way to the kitchen, she collected the tea cups and saucers.

"So you never caught Pa?" Pappy asked Rose.

Rose stared at the recorder. "Come close. Once we were sitting up on Seventy-Three, waiting for him to come down. We didn't know it, but the day before, your pa cut a road to a creek. That night he ran out on the creek bottom. Then twice he run out on the railroad tracks, but we stopped that."

"How so?"

"Got the railroad to leave lumber cars on the mainline at night, outside of Walland." Rose chuckled. "For a time, your pa had a cousin clerking in my office. We didn't know she was a cousin 'til we found out she was feedin' him information on where we were setting up. I fired her fanny for that one. 'Course, like your pa, I had nothing against getting an advantage when I could."

"How's that?"

"Sometimes I'd catch a shiner at his still. Caught like that, he knew he was going to jail and maybe the penitentiary, and he didn't want that."

"Uh-huh."

Rose leaned forward. He dropped his volume a notch. "So he and I'd have a little heart-to-heart, and, to keep out of jail, he'd end up telling me everything I wanted to know about his competitors and the runners hauling shine."

Martha Rose rapped a spoon on a pan.

"Enough of that, Quill," she called from the kitchen. "You shag yourself in here and bring Willie Joe with you. Lunch is ready."

Rose aimed his thumb in the direction of the hallway. "Better not keep the boss waitin'."

"Not if you want to eat regular," Pappy said as he got up.

Rose horsed himself up as well. He handed the recorder to Pappy, and the two ambled to the hallway and back toward the kitchen.

"I usually wash up at the sink," Rose said, "but if you want the bathroom, it's upstairs."

"I remember when a bathroom was a path with a little house at the end of it."

"Wasn't all that long ago, was it?"

"I can wash at the sink if Miss Martha doesn't object."

The two shambled into the kitchen to see Martha Rose with a ladle in her hand.

She shook the ladle at them. "Hurry and sit."

Rose held his hands up. He wiggled his fingers. "Thought maybe we'd wash first."

"Well, be quick about it. Everything's ready." Martha Rose dipped chili from her kettle at the stove into bowls, white bowls that had a blue Currier and Ives pattern baked into the glaze as did the plates and cups on the table. She glanced over at Pappy. "How do you like my table?"

A treadle table made from red maple. He recognized the wood and ran an approving hand over its surface gleaming with newly buffed wax. The waxy scent was there, too.

"Quill made that for me when he retired. Wouldn't know it's a quarter-century old, would you?"

Rose, his hands in a towel, motioned for Pappy to go to the sink.

Rose polished his fingernails. "I wanted to make the chairs, too, but I never was a hand at turning wood, so Harold Wright made them. He learned from Wilmer Johanson, the old cabinetmaker up in Townsend. You remember him?"

Pappy soaped his hands. "I do. I lost track of him during the war, though."

"By the time of the war, Townsend was little more than a shell. Wilmer still had a family to support, so he took a job at Alcoa. Hated the noise, so he hired on at the Secret City as a carpenter when the feds started to build the atomic factory at Oak Ridge. 'Course, that was all hush-hush at the time, so none of us knew what he was doing. Worked there until he died in 'Fifty-six."

Pappy took the towel from Rose. He dried his hands before he laid the towel by the sink.

Martha Rose pulled a chair out for him, and Pappy slid onto it. She then sat down. "Quill asks the blessing."

Pappy bowed as did his hosts.

"Great God in Heaven," Rose said, his voice hushed, "You've given us one more day in Your world, and we thank You for that. We also thank You for bringing our friend to us so we might reminisce about what it was like when we were younger and more spry and had fewer pains. We're not complaining, Lord, it's just that Martha and I have come to be the old folks our parents once were and our grandparents before them. Well, Sir, I especially want to thank You for Martha. You could not have given me a finer mate and better cook. Would You please bless this food she's prepared that it may keep us strong and healthy? It's in Your Son's most holy name that I ask it. Amen."

"Amen," Pappy mumbled. When he looked up, Martha Rose was holding a plate of cornbread out to him.

"And I got pickled corn from last summer's garden," she said, passing him that bowl as well.

Pappy attempted to steer the conversation back toward moonshiners and bootleggers, but Martha Rose parried it away, to other things—Pappy's grandchildren, the new minister at the Methodist church, the Lady Vols' winning streak. Pappy came to understand that Martha Rose was a feminist and a rabid basketball fan.

She gave him a sweet smile. "Are you seeing anyone?"

"Afraid not."

"Willie Joe, you've been alone so long you really ought to find you a new wife, someone to take care of you like I take care of Quill. I'm a firm believer that God meant for us to live two by two."

Pappy buttered another piece of cornbread. "Quill won't give you up, Miss Martha, so I guess I doomed to batch it until they carry me to the bone yard."

"Bone yard. That's not nice."

"Miss Martha, you know why they put fences around cemeteries?"

She looked up from her nearly empty chili bowl.

"Because people are dying to get in," Pappy said.

She patted his arm. "Willie Joe, you never could be serious. How about dessert? I got apple pie."

Before Pappy could answer, she was up and at the side counter, lifting slices of pie onto dessert plates. "I'm ashamed to say it's not mine. It's Missus Smith's, but it's pretty good. Heat it up for you?"

"That'd be fine."

She put a plate in the microwave and zapped it. A bell rang at the end of forty-five seconds.

Martha Rose removed that plate and put a second in. Again she punched in forty-five seconds and pushed the start button.

She brought the first dessert plate to the table and set it before Pappy. "This radar range is so nice. I thought it was a revolution when we hauled off my old Home Comfort wood cook stove and replaced it with a gas range from Southern States. But this thing cooks like—" She snapped her fingers.

And the microwave's bell rang.

Out came the plate with the wedge of pie for her husband and in went the plate with the wedge of pie for herself. Again she punched in forty-five seconds.

The dessert conversation continued on, as had the main-course conversation, on inconsequential subjects—the prospects for an early spring, the Sunshine Café changing hands, Martha Rose's thimble collection.

She beamed. "I have thimbles from every state, all given to me by friends in the D.A.R. They had swapped Tennessee thimbles for them at national conventions."

Pappy put his fork down for the last time. He jerked his thumb toward the sink. "Why don't I wash the dishes?"

Martha Rose waggled a finger. "I'll have none of that."

"But I want to do something to pay for my lunch."

"No, no, no. You're dying to get back to what took your pa from us. Go in the other room. I don't want to hear it."

Pappy pushed himself away from the table. He got up and slouched out of the kitchen, his hands stuffed in his pockets, Quill Rose beside him. Rose said, his voice low, "Martha was never hot for me sheriffing all those years. She spent a lot of scared nights alone, worrying she might be having to call the undertaker the next day to arrange my funeral. Me talking about it brings back the memories."

"What say we talk in my truck? I'd like to see where Pa died. Maybe you'd show me."

"It was on the west side of Knoxville."

"No matter."

Rose turned back to the kitchen. "Martha?"

"Yes?"

"Pappy wants to take me out riding. That be all right with you?"

"When will you be back?"

"Late afternoon, evening, maybe."

Martha Rose came to the hallway, drying her hands on her apron. "You want me to hold supper for you?"

"What do you think, Pappy?" Rose asked.

"Miss Martha, we're going to run up to Knoxville. Why don't we call you in late afternoon from a saloon and tell you how we're doing?"

"Quill doesn't drink, Willie Joe."

"I'm a lemonade man myself, so no bartenders are gonna get rich off us."

She went to the coat stand. There she took down her husband's mackinaw and helped him into the sleeves. "You wear your cap now and your gloves. I don't want you gettin' cold out there."

"Mother, you worry too much." Rose's stiff fingers fumbled with the zipper.

She turned him around, took hold of the zipper, and zipped up the coat for him. "Worrying about you is what's kept you coming home alive, old man."

"Guess it has." Rose leaned down. He kissed his wife.

She stroked his thin cheek, then hurried back to the kitchen while Pappy pulled on his own jacket and his knit cap.

Rose pushed his guest toward the front door. "Why don't you go ahead and start your truck? There's something I want to get from my desk for you."

Chapter 19

The last run

PAPPY TURNED OFF the main road to take Quill Rose past the Alcoa aluminum complex, the old sheriff rubbernecking. "Sure not seen that place for some time. Just read about it in the papers."

"Lot of our people worked there over the years, but we better get on." Pappy pulled the clicker down for the cutover to the Alcoa Pike, the four-laner that ran north to Knoxville.

As they came up on McGhee Tyson Airport, a high-wing aircraft loomed up in Pappy's windshield, the airplane on an approach to Runway Two-Five Left. Rose ducked, as if he feared a wheel might thump the roof of Pappy's truck.

"Exciting drive, isn't it?" Pappy said.

"You didn't think he was gonna get us?"

"None have so far."

The old man straightened up. He shook his shoulders. "I guess. I remember when there was nothing but open fields up here on the high ground. Then the war came and everybody said we needed an airport out here, so we could train pilots. The Army Air Force come in and built a training base."

"Yup, and now the Air Guard flies out of the military side. I'm told we've got Guard pilots who come down on weekends from as far away as Wisconsin to fly with our unit."

Rose scanned the skies ahead. "You know, I've never been up in one of those things."

"We can fix that. I'll turn around."

Rose grinned. "'Fraid I'm a little too old. Just happy to be out on a nice day, riding in your truck."

The highway dipped down into a curve that came out in bottom land next to the Tennessee River. Rose gazed to the west, to the flat, gray waters. "You fish much there?"

"Some last summer."

"I would, but there's no one to take me. Martha won't let me drive no more."

Pappy peeled off to east, onto the John Sevier Highway, named for the state's first governor who had settled on a farm outside of what would one day become Knoxville, Sevier a farmer, Indian fighter, politician, and one of the leaders of the Overmountain Men who defeated the British at the Battle of Kings Mountain.

Another mile on and Pappy turned north onto the two-lane Maryville Pike. That road fed into Chapman Highway, coming up from the southeast, from Sevierville.

Pappy took out his tape recorder. He pressed the record button and handed the small machine to Rose.

"You want me to talk into this again, huh?"

Pappy waved an okay.

Rose held the recorder up toward his mouth. "Well, once, some months before your pa's last night, my deputy and me had good information on him."

"What did you do?"

"We set a trap for him. We knew if we let him hit pavement anywhere there was little chance of catching him, so we trailed behind when your pa went off onto a woods road that led to a still." Rose paused. He massaged the stubble on his cheeks. "Now this still was a good three miles back, so I sent Tommy Jenks, my deputy, ahead in his pickup. I told him to go in two miles and pull off in the brush and hide."

Pappy pointed at the windshield, at the Gardener baking plant beyond.

Rose sniffed the air. "Mmm, fresh bread. Isn't that wonderful? Turn right up here at Blount."

"Why?"

"In your pa's day there was no Henley Street Bridge. They were just building it in 'Thirty-two. Anyone coming into Knoxville from the south turned right on Clifton—that's Blount Avenue now—to get over to the Gay Street Bridge."

"I didn't know that."

Pappy slowed for the turn. Once on Blount, he drove past Baptist Hospital, then turned again, left onto the Gay Street Bridge.

"This is the route your pa took that last night." Rose motioned with the tape recorder through the windshield. "Up ahead, he turned left onto Main Street which becomes Cumberland, as you know. The Knoxville police were looking for him. I'd called ahead and told them he'd outrun me. Actually, your pa fooled me. That's how he did it."

At the far end of the bridge, Pappy drove past the massive concrete, brick, and glass City-County Building the planners had built into the side of a bluff that overlooked the Tennessee River. A block on, he passed the sixteen-story Andrew Johnson Hotel, vacant, its business killed off by the automobile and the Interstate. Another block on and Pappy stopped at the Gay

Street/Main Street traffic light in the heart of the city's central business district.

He waited for the light to change. "You were telling me about setting a trap for Pa."

Rose peered at the recorder. "Well, I followed Tommy in my Ford. I was just going to go in a mile and stop, use my car to block the woods road. Tommy had a flare pistol with him."

The light changed, and Pappy turned left onto Main.

"Long after sundown," Rose said into the recorder, "I see this flare rise up over the woods, and I knew your pa was coming out. He'd just passed Tommy. I heard that big sixteen-cylinder growling my way. With that load, he musta been in low gear."

"Uh-huh."

"When your pa's headlights came 'round the bend, I pulled my headlights on and stepped out with my shotgun. Pappy, your pa sure enough saw me because he slammed that Packard into reverse, his transmission howling as he backed away, but there were the headlights of Tommy's truck in his rear window. We had him boxed it."

Pappy glanced to the side, to Courthouse Park, to a particular tree where vigilantes had once hanged a man, a tree where people, on certain eerie nights, reported seeing the spectral being of the dead man swinging from a limb. "How'd he get away?"

"That old devil jammed the car into first, floored it, and rocketed off into the brush."

"You give chase?"

"Yup, but on foot. Your pa knew there wasn't any road he could pick up, and we knew it, too, so we hotfooted it after him. We weren't about to wreck our vehicles on the stumps and rocks in that little canyon we'd forced him into."

"What happened?"

"When your pa got to the end, he jumped out, set his car on fire and skedaddled like a scared fox up and out of there on an old Indian trail."

Pappy laughed. "I guess people didn't call him 'Gone Again' Willie for nothing."

"Not at all. We got there just as the whole thing blew up. No car, no booze, no evidence. Two weeks later, he was back with two Packards and your brother driving for him."

"I remember that. Pa would never let me go along."

"You were only nine or ten at the time and a bit on the small side."

Pappy held up his hand, then motioned to the right. "World's Fair Park. You get there for any of the big show back in 'Eighty-two?"

"Nope. You?"

"No. Too many people. I watched some of the fair on television, though."

"Same for Martha and me. Building it there sure got rid of a lot of rundown housing that was an embarrassment to everybody, didn't it?"

"Uh-huh. The amphitheater gets a good workout in the summer. Now if we could just find some use for the big building here on the end of the park."

"The Sunsphere gets some use, doesn't it?"

Pappy glanced up toward the Sunsphere towering eight stories above the fairgrounds, its gold-tinted glass glowing in the afternoon sun. "A couple have tried to make a go of the restaurant up there, but it's just never drawn enough people. But I tell you, Quill, I've been up there and you get one spectacular view of the city. It's really something at night."

Cumberland dipped down to a bridge over First Creek—once known as Scuffletown Creek—then rose up

Barbara Hill into the university district where great stone buildings on either side of the boulevard housed warrens of classrooms and laboratories.

Pappy slowed for a traffic light going yellow at Stadium Drive. He stopped when it turned red. "So what did you do?"

Rose again brought the tape recorder up. "Yeah, back to your story—Pappy, we set up on Tater Ridge. We knew your pa was going to be coming out of Cades Cove with a load of shine. By then, we had a new road in from Townsend that everyone drove, but you remember Tater Ridge was a twisty old wagon trail, dirt and gravel what wasn't ruts, and we knew your pa would run it 'cause he would be expecting us to be miles away, over on the new road."

The light turned green, and Pappy stepped on the accelerator.

"I don't know how he knew we were there," Rose said into the tape recorder, "but just as he should have been cresting the ridge, we heard something crashing through the brush off to the side, and there went those two Packards around us. We turned around and gave chase and caught up with them, but we couldn't get ahead of them because the trail was only one-car wide."

"Uh-huh."

"We followed 'em for miles up hill and down, around switchbacks, sometimes fast, most of the time in second gear. We just couldn't pass 'em."

Pappy tapped his horn button. He waved at a young woman hurrying along the sidewalk, a book bag over her shoulder.

She waved back.

"That's Caroline," Pappy said.

"Your granddaughter?"

"Yup, but you were telling me about the chase."

"Right. Finally, down we come off the north side of Rich Mountain, rolling out of the last switchback into Dry Valley. The road straightens out there, and the two Packards floored it with me and Tommy on the bumper of the second car. We were going flat out. You know where Dry Valley Road forks into Seventy-Three?"

"Yes."

"Take the left fork and you're heading out of the mountains toward Maryville and Knoxville. Take the right, you're heading for Townsend and deeper into the mountains. The lead Packard went left. The second went right."

"You went left."

"I hollered to Tommy that the lead had to be your pa, and we took after him. We passed him finally and cut him off going into Kinsel Springs. But it wasn't your pa."

Pappy snickered. "Jimmy?"

"Right. Your brother, all of twelve years old, and not a jug or a bottle of shine in his car."

Pappy topped Cumberland at Seventeenth Street. "That's The Strip ahead," he said. "Four blocks. You would not believe how many students pack in here come supper time and early evening. Thick as ants at a picnic."

"S'pose you got a favorite place."

"Yeah, right there on the right, see it? The Blue Onion? Makes killer hamburgers and pizzas."

"Barbecue?"

"No barbecue."

"Too bad. Beer?"

"Any brand you want."

"Hmm."

"It's legal, Quill. Beer's been legal for most of my lifetime."

"Just as well. You know, prohibition was a dumb idea. Killed a lot of good people on both sides of the law."

"But you were out there, catching the violators."

"It was my job, Pappy, to enforce the dumb laws as well as the good ones. I cut some slack for the moonshiners, though. All of us did, but when they endangered people, making busthead whiskey, we went after them. We went after the runners, too. The way your pa drove, it was only a matter of time before he'd hit someone with his car, maybe kill 'em, maybe some young couple with little children. I determined that wasn't gonna happen, and I told your pa that one day up on the street in Townsend. He just laughed, said he'd found a good way to put food on the table in these hard times. Pappy, it was the Depression. The times were hard."

Cumberland dipped away from the strip, down toward Third Creek and back up to where the boulevard intersected with Neyland Drive going left to the agricultural college and Concord Avenue going right to the state garage.

Pappy gave a nod toward a slim building thirteen stories high. "Married student housing, Kingston Apartments. Most call it the Cereal Box. I call it the Fertility Hilton."

"You envious?" Rose asked.

"I raised Stevey. That's enough."

"You did a good job with your boy. Your pa would be proud."

Beyond the university district, Cumberland ambled away through long blocks lined with trees and wealthy homes. It also passed Saint George's, the Greek Orthodox Church. The boulevard then descended into Bearden where the street was no longer Cumberland, but Kingston Pike.

Bearden, once a small farming town, now was a business district in the sprawl of Knoxville to the west where one could buy everything from Danielle Steele novels in paperback—used—at McKay's on the south side of Kingston Pike to Mercedes Benz automobiles—new—at Knoxville Motor Car across the street.

Pappy put his hand on Rose's shoulder, to jog him back to the story. "Pa went out the long way, didn't he?"

"What?"

"Out of the Tuckaleechee."

"Yeah, he did. Townsend, the Wear Cove Road to Sevierville and the road that's now Chapman Highway into Knoxville."

"And?"

"And the next week, he and your brother did it to us again."

"How?"

"This time we were waiting for them in Miller Cove, and they run around us through Hint Parker's tobacco field. We heard them mowing down the tobacco and saw their taillights come back up on the road behind us."

"So you went after them."

"Darn right. I wheeled my Ford around and let out the string. We came through Walland and Chilhowee Gap at an awful speed, slowing for Melrose. Then the lead Packard takes off onto County One-Twenty-Seven, east for Sevierville. The second whips left onto Seventy-Three for Maryville and Knoxville. I yell to Tommy your pa's not going out through Sevierville twice, and we take after the second car. And we caught it just outside of Rockford, and damn, it's your brother again."

"Ooo, that had to hurt."

Pappy's pickup climbed away from Bearden, up Mansion Hill. At the top, Rose waved the recorder at a restaurant parking lot to the left. "Pull it in there."

Pappy snapped the turn signal on. He waited for a city bus approaching in the opposing lane. After it passed, he turned into the lot and wheeled his truck around until he and Rose could watch the Kingston Pike traffic going both east and west.

A fire department crash truck and an ambulance, running lights and sirens, raced up the hill. They passed in front of Pappy and Rose and continued on west.

"Must be an accident," Rose said.

"Likely. So this is when you called for help?"

"Yeah. Tommy and me, we drove on to Asa's General Store. I pounded on the door until Asa come downstairs to let me use his telephone. I called the Knoxville police. That done, Tommy and I went back to Maryville, home to bed and glad of it. It was something like three in the morning."

"And Pa?"

"We followed his track today, up Chapman Highway into Knoxville, Gay Street, Main, Cumberland, and Kingston Pike west. It all ended down there, at that curve."

Rose pointed the recorder to the west, down the backside of Mansion Hill to where the pike made a sharp turn as it started up into the West Hills district, home to the mammoth West Town Mall and a half dozen of the metro area's largest car dealers whose lots sprawled for a mile as Kingston moved on toward Cedar Bluff and Concord, bedroom communities for Knoxville.

"How'd it happen?"

"A patrolman, coming off a side street near the university, saw this black Packard shoot by at too fast a speed, so he gave chase. Speeds increased—fifty, fifty-five, sixty in places. Coming down into Bearden, your pa really stepped on the gas. The patrolman said he was holding seventy and falling behind. They streaked past another patrolman coming out of an all-night diner at Papermill and the pike."

"So now there's three in the chase."

"Yes. Your pa and the first patrolman crested the hill right here." Rose gestured toward the windshield. "The patrolman started to brake for that curve down there, but your pa didn't, not until the last second. The patrolman said he saw the brake lights come on, then saw the car whip into skid and roll. It took to the air and came down in that ravine at the bottom of the hill. All trees and brush down there then, none of those buildings you see now. The Packard smashed into an oak tree and exploded."

"My gawd—"

Rose sucked in a long breath. "Next morning about ten, a Knoxville captain called me. I called Homer Wright—he was one of our fiscal court judges at the time—and the two of us drove up together. There was nothing in that ravine but charred wreckage, some of it still hot."

"Pa in the car?"

Rose looked off to the side. "Just bones. Everything else had burned away. We went up the pike to a feed store and bought a silage basket and a rake. We came back to the crash, and Homer and I raked through it. We picked up every bone we could find, a lot of them broken, all burned badly. We put them in the basket and took them back home, up to the cemetery at Townsend and arranged to bury them."

"Do you know, Quill, if Pa was killed right off?"

Rose fell silent for a long moment.

"The patrolman said your pa was pinned in there, screaming, 'Shoot me! Please, God, shoot me,' when he ran up."

"Omigawd."

"The patrolman got in as close as he could, but the fire kept him back. He said your pa saw him, and he saw your pa's eyes pleading with him through the flames. He took out his gun and aimed, but his hands, they were shaking so bad he couldn't pull the trigger."

"So he burned to death."

"No. The second patrolman runs up, hearing your pa's screams, too. He brings out his revolver and puts a shot in there." Rose pulled a handkerchief from his pocket. He wiped at his eyes. "They both saw your pa's head snap back. The first patrolman said he got sick then, staggered off in the brush, and threw up his guts."

Rose put the handkerchief on the seat. Free now, his hand went inside his coat, to his shirt pocket. He brought out two sheets of paper yellowed from age, the sheets folded. "A copy of the patrolman's report. I kept it all these years, figuring someday you might want it."

Pappy took the papers, and Rose slipped his hand into his side pocket and brought out a pocket knife, most of its bone handle burned away. He held it out to Pappy.

Pappy took the knife. He examined it, rolled it over in his fingers. "Pa's?"

Chapter 20

Oh, for a little heavy metal

DOCTOR BERRY rapped on the door frame. "Will they let any woman come in here?" she asked when Pappy turned to her.

He rose as did his granddaughter, Caroline, she hiding a longneck Miller's behind her back.

Pappy held up his can of Country Time. "'Course, you're welcome, Doc. Have a lemonade or a beer? Carrie's having a beer."

Caroline's face flushed.

"Well now, Carrie, your advisor might as well know that sometimes you get sick of white wine and come over here to whittle and spit with us good old boys and toss back a low-wattage brew."

Berry took off her rain-soaked coat and hood. She shook them out in the hall. "You know, it's really coming down out there. I think I saw some kittens falling from the sky."

"Something to warm you if you don't want a cold one?" Pappy asked.

"I might consider that."

He took a Budweiser mug from his book shelf. Pappy dumped the pencils it contained onto his desk and wiped out the mug with his shirttail. "Wicks has a microwave here. We can brew you a coffee or a hot cocoa."

Berry stared at the mug and at Pappy still polishing the inside with his shirttail. "On second thought—"

"Well, come, sit. Take my chair." Pappy held it out for her. "And toss your coat on the bed over there. That's Junior's."

Toss it she did not, but laid it out, lining down, then sat.

Caroline settled on the edge of Pappy's bed. She cupped the Miller's in her hands.

Pappy stood by Caroline, a hand on her shoulder. "So, what brings you to the boars' nest?"

"Good news, and I didn't want to wait until class tomorrow to tell you."

"Ahh, I'm going to get my first C, huh?"

"Better."

Pappy gazed down at Caroline. "For a D student, what could be better?"

"Being published."

Pappy sat down.

"Remember the story you wrote about your father?"

"Yes, but that was just a first draft."

Caroline elbowed Pappy. "Can you believe it, Doctor Berry, he wouldn't let me read it, and it was about my grandfather."

"You'll read it now."

Pappy fidgeted with his glasses. "Meaning what?"

"I submitted it to the Appalachian Journal of Culture and History. The editor called me this afternoon. He wants to publish it."

Caroline slipped her hand over Pappy's hand. She squeezed it. "Grandpops, this is big."

"Really?"

Berry waggled a finger. "Of course, there are some sections he and I want you to rewrite, but this is a coup, Mister Brown. I've gotten a couple papers of my graduate students in that journal, but never an undergraduate, certainly never a freshman."

THAT EVENING, when Wickingson learned of his roommate's good fortune, he noodled at his computer. He read the words on his screen, then noodled some more, changing type faces and point sizes. At last, he punched the print command, and his printer spewed out a long sheet of paper, a banner Wickingson taped in the hall over the door to the Caballeros' suite: SHHH! NEXT CORMACK McCARTHY WRITES WITHIN.

WICKINGSON TWIDDLED the tuner on his stereo, flitting from AM station to AM station, then he turned through the FM band, glum. "Not one frickin' station plays Mayhem, Stormwitch, or Helloween. What kinda hick town are we in?"

Pappy closed his ornithology textbook. "What's fried your fanny?"

"I'd just like to get some heavy metal, man. K-Nox, your favorite, country. The FM stations, Golden Oldies and classic rock. WUOT, our university's own, Mozart and, when they're really daring, Bach. Gawd—"

Wickingson punched back to the AM band and twisted the tuner knob some more. He stopped when he came on a screeching electric guitar, a wild drumming behind it. Wickingson rocked in his chair as he pounded out the rhythm on his desk.

Pappy side-armed a sock across the room. It slapped Wickingson in the ear.

Wickingson's hand shot up as he jerked around. "What did you do that for?"

"The whole house doesn't want to listen to that."

"It's Pestilence."

Pappy whipped another sock at Wickingson.

He dodged it, then opened a desk drawer. He grubbed around until he found a headset. Wickingson fired Pappy a smug look as he put the muffs over his ears and plugged into the tuner. He rocked and drummed along on his desk top.

Pappy returned to his textbook. He turned a page and read on into the author's theory on clutch size, why four eggs seemed to be the ideal number for most species of birds in order to assure survival.

"Goddammit!"

Pappy glanced over at Wickingson in a fury, twisting the tuner knob again. "What's the matter?"

"Station faded out."

"What was the frequency?"

Wickingson leaned into his tuner. He squinted at the numbers. "Looks to be Six-Twenty, Six-Twenty four or five maybe."

"That's Nashville. You're getting a skip signal off the atmosphere."

"Hell."

"Hey, if your music means that much to you, start your own radio station. Pirate radio—Harrr, matey!—that's for you. You're over there in engineering. You know that stuff."

"I'm chemical, not electrical, but, hey, Pap, I know who is." A steely glint came into Wickingson's eyes. He chucked his headset aside and hustled from the room.

Pappy went back to his reading only to be interrupted by Dempsey coming in. "Hi-dee, buddy. Saw Wicks running up the stairs. Where's he going?"

"I dunno."

"Ooo, you're a bit gruff."

"I'm tryin' to read."

"Oh, sorry." Dempsey dropped his backpack on his bed and went about shucking his muffler, coat, and cap. He tossed them in the general direction of his closet as he made his way over to the suite's mini-refrigerator, whistling.

Pappy glared at him.

Dempsey looked over. He stopped, turned, and mouthed the word 'sorry.' At the refrigerator, he pushed cans of Leinenkugel's and Country Time aside and found a lone can of Miller's in a back corner.

He brought it out and pulled off the pop top.

Dempsey also took two bendy straws from a box on top of the refrigerator. He worked them together to make one. With a can of beer in one hand and a super-long straw in the other, Dempsey ambled over to his bed. He twirled and flopped down on his back. Dempsey stuck one end of the straw in the Miller's balanced on his chest and bent the other end of the straw down to his mouth. He sucked on the straw until he had a mouthful of brew.

Dempsey pinched off the straw. He swallowed and let off with a long ahhhhh and a belch that rattled the window.

Pappy glared over the tops of his glasses. "Junior, you don't go to all that trouble unless there's something you want to brag about."

"How'd you guess?" Dempsey sucked in some more beer.

"How long we been bunkin' together?"

"Six months."

"I know you, kid. Spill it so I can get back to the birds and their eggs."

"Doesn't sound very interesting."

"It isn't."

Dempsey, grinning like a bear with his paw in a honey tree, looked over to Pappy. "Know that tobacco harvester blueprint I've been working over?"

"Yeah."

"I came up with a modification that minimizes leaf damage. The prof likes it. He wants me to work with a group of senior engineering students to draft it and machine the parts—to build a prototype."

Pappy slapped his book closed. "By gawd, June, you're going to make me proud of you yet."

Wickingson burst back into the room. "Hey, June, Pappy. Pappy, Randall Cunningham upstairs—he's in electrical engineering—he says I could cobble together a tape deck, a couple mics, a mixer, and a low-watt transmitter for a couple thousand bucks." He threw out his hands, an open-mouthed 'ta-dah' smile on his face.

Dempsey raised an eyebrow. "What's he talking about?"

"Wicks is going into pirate radio, so he can play Stormwitch, whatever that is, for all the world to hear."

"Pirate radio, cool." Dempsey sucked up another mouthful of beer. "But why not just hijack a real radio station? Wicks, that would put you on the air on the cheap."

Wickingson sauntered over. "What would you know about radio?"

"Last summer, I was weekend DJ for our local five-watter. Nobody listened, so the station owner let me do anything I wanted so long as I didn't broadcast foul language, dead air or burn the station down. Tapping into somebody else's transmitter, that's easy, man."

Wickingson took Dempsey's beer. He chugged a couple swallows.

"Hey, man," Dempsey barked.

"You tell me how this works, I'll give you a supply of Leinies for a lifetime."

Dempsey rolled over on his elbow. "Well, you get yourself a CD player and wire it through the amplifier in your stereo. You run a line from the amplifier out to the line going from the studio to the station's transmitter, and you patch into that line. Put a little servo switch there and you can cut back and forth from the studio to your setup anytime you want. Of course, if you get caught—"

Wickingson went to the refrigerator. He took out a Leinenkugel, opened it, and handed the new beer to Dempsey. "What do I do not to get caught?"

"You put the patch and the switch where you can pull it out when you need to."

"And where would that be?"

"When they find out someone's on their air, they're going to shut down the transmitter and go searching for the trouble."

"Yes."

"Engineers are logical. You know, you're one." Dempsey patted the side of his bed, and Wickingson sat down. "Look, they're either going to start at the transmitter and work back to the studio or at the studio and work out to the transmitter. You put your patch in the middle. That way you've got maybe a couple hours before they get to it. By then, you've got it out."

Dempsey held up his hand and Wickingson slapped it.

Pappy covered his face.

WICKINGSON, pacing, shot out his beer hand clutching a Leinenkugel. "WUOT in the Comm Building, that's the one we hijack. It's only four blocks away."

Dempsey snatched a tennis ball out of the air, the ball he had bouncing off the edge of his desk. "Could work, Wicks, but how do we get our signal from here to there?"

Randall Cunningham, a new recruit to the pirate radio team, a tall, thin kid with mechanical pencils and ballpoint pens in a pocket protector and a calculator on his belt, pushed a mop of blond hair back out of his eyes. "Please, please, nobody say string a wire on the telephone poles."

"Why not?" The question came from Wickingson still pacing.

"Hey, man, isn't it obvious? We go running up and down telephone poles tacking up a wire, someone's going to see us, even if we do it at night."

Wickingson stopped. "Dammit. All right, then, we use a telephone line."

"You're gonna call your program into the station? I don't think so."

Dempsey squished the tennis ball between the heels of his hands. "How about this? We microwave the signal over. A little dish here, a little dish there."

Cunningham snorted. "Oh, now you're talkin' really big bucks."

"Got carried away, didn't I?"

Pappy leaned in from the hallway, a backpack over his shoulder. "What are you yahoos going on about?"

Wickingson came over. "Our radio show. We've agreed we're going to commandeer WUOT. I want to use a telephone line to get our signal to the station. Junior, there, he want to use microwaves and dish antennas."

"Boys, you open to a suggestion?"

"Sure."

Pappy eased into the room. He set his backpack on his desk and shed his ski jacket. "What's the job of an engineer?"

Wickingson looked over at Cunningham. Cunningham, in turn, looked over at Dempsey doodling at his desk, and Dempsey stopped doodling.

Pappy swung his chair around. He sat a-straddle the seat, his arms folded across the back. "Do I have you geniuses stumped? The engineer's job is to simplify. Boys, you're making this thing way too complicated."

"But we've got to get our signal over there, Pap." Wickingson aimed his beer can in the direction of the Communications Building.

"Sure you do. So why don't you walk it over?"

"What do you mean?"

Pappy pulled a pack of Camels from his shirt pocket. He shook a couple out and held the pack up to Cunningham who took a cigarette. Pappy took one as well. He lit his with a match from a book of matches on his desk, then tossed the matchbook to Cunningham.

After Pappy sucked on his cigarette, he blew out a lungful of smoke. "Junior, how does UOT get its signal from its studio to its transmitter?"

"A dedicated telephone line probably. Most stations do it that way when their transmitter is at a remote site."

"Now we're getting somewhere."

"What do you mean?"

"In most buildings, all the telephone lines come together at a central box in the utilities room." Pappy opened his hands out, waiting for the lights to turn on in the minds of his cohorts.

Cunningham tapped the ashes from his cigarette. "Oh."

"Oh what?" Wickingson asked from where he'd settled, on a window sill with his back to the glass.

Cunningham raked his fingers back through his hair. He toured around the room, giving himself a brisk scalp rub. "It's so simple. It's so elegantly and beautifully simple. Pappy, why couldn't we see it?"

"See what?" Wickingson asked.

Cunningham, with his cigarette crammed in the corner of his mouth, took a mechanical pencil from his pocket protector. He turned the lead up as he hustled to Dempsey's desk. There he nudged Dempsey aside and sketched on a blank sheet of paper. "All this stuff's small, Demps," he said as lines flashed out.

Wickingson left his perch. He chugged the last of his beer as he came over.

"CD player, mixer, microphone, amplifier..." Cunningham drew a rectangle around the assortment of symbols and lines. "...we can fit it all in a briefcase, a studio in a briefcase. We wire a power pack in. We go into the utilities room, open the briefcase, plug into any old wall outlet for ee-lectricity, alligator clip onto the phone line, and we're on the air."

Dempsey stared up at Cunningham. "God, this is going to be fun."

Wickingson tapped his beer can on the diagram. "How do we know which telephone line?"

"Clips and a handset. We test the lines one at a time. If we get a dial tone or a voice, that's a regular line, squalling, that's a data line, music, that's the one we want. That's the studio line."

"How do you know?"

"You get into this stuff in your junior year. It's all a part of circuits and testing."

"I'll be damned."

"And we got the clips and handsets in the lab at Perkins."

Pappy stripped off his shirt. He started for the door. "'Scuse me, boys, I'm going down the hall and brush my teeth." He stopped at Dempsey's desk. "Just a couple questions from a dumb old man."

Wickingson glanced up from the drawing. "Yeah, what is it?"

"When are you going to do this?"

Cunningham twirled his mechanical pencil across his fingertips, as if the pencil were a baton. "Well, it can't be in the daytime. Too many people around."

"So at night."

"The later the better, I'd say."

"After ten o'clock?"

"Yeah."

"The building's locked, and the utilities room is locked all the time."

"Damn."

Pappy marched out of the room.

Wickingson stuffed his hands in his back pockets. He studied the floor.

Dempsey leaned back. He gazed up at the ceiling.

Cunningham, with precision, while still puffing on his cigarette, folded his sheet of diagrams into an airplane. He sailed it away, the paper plane looping, then diving toward a wastebasket on the far side of the room.

Pappy strolled back in, scrubbing his teeth. "Don't you boys know how to lay your hands on a key?"

Wickingson and Dempsey turned to one another. Each, and at the same moment, fired an index-finger pistol at the other.

PAPPY IGNORED the Pie-rat radio team, as he called the trio of Wickingson, Cunningham, and Dempsey, while they soldered, fit, and tested the various parts of their studio-in-a-briefcase over the next several evenings.

Wickingson and Dempsey disappeared on one of those evenings. When they returned, sometime after eleven, Dempsey tossed a key on Pappy's notebook, startling Pappy engrossed in the sonnets of Elizabeth Barrett Browning. Pappy picked up the key. He held it up to his desk lamp. "Very good."

"You gonna ask me how I did it?"

"No."

Dempsey hung his coat in his closet, then went to his bureau for a mug and a packet of Instant Swiss Miss. "You want cocoa? I'm making."

"Fine."

"Wicks?"

"Yeah."

Dempsey took out two more Tau Upsilon mugs. He filled the three with milk from the refrigerator. "Where's Cunningham?"

Pappy set the key down and returned to his book. "He had the good sense to quit a couple hours ago. He's over in Perkins, said his team was meeting to work on their miniature remote-controlled car, for some kinda competition."

"Ambrose?" Dempsey asked as he put the mugs in the microwave. He punched up three minutes.

"Date. Said not to expect him home before tomorrow."

"Oooo."

"Pap, you're not going to believe how we did it," Wickingson said.

Pappy put a hand over his eyes.

"Junior and I went over to the Communications Building, and we found one of the janitors taking his coffee break in the sandwich room, you know, down on the first-floor level. You wouldn't believe it. There were his keys, laying on the table next to him. Well, I get him in a conversation, and June takes his keys."

Dempsey picked up the story. "I've got this block of wax. I find his master key and make an impression of it, both sides, while he and Wickingson are talking. I read about this in a spy novel. Anyway, Wicks and I go over to the fabrication shop at Ag Engineering, and I make a key."

He put both thumbs up.

Pappy peeked between his fingers. "Does it work?"

"By cracky, old timer, it sure does. Wicky and I go back to Communications, and we let ourselves in, into the building and into the utilities room as well."

A 'meep-meep' sounded in the hall.

Dempsey swung around as a four-wheeled platform came over the door sill, the platform no more than a hand long, on which rode a collection of servos, electric motors, and a small battery, nine-volt by its appearance. Cunningham followed, maneuvering a joystick controller. "How do you like our car?"

"Cool." Dempsey went down on his hands and knees and studied the little machine.

Cunningham put the unit in reverse. He backed it through a figure eight.

"Set your pen on the floor," Cunningham said to Dempsey. "Now hold it there."

The little car, responding to Cunningham's controller, edged up to the pen. A wheel eased up, without the platform rising, and dropped down on the other side. A sister wheel followed, rising. It, too, went over the pen and down. Still the platform remained level.

"Four-wheel independent suspension," Cunningham said. "One of our guys figured out how to rig it and scrounged the parts."

Dempsey, with his finger, traced the wiring from the radio receiver to the motors and servos. "What's left to do?"

"We have to mount an arm on the platform that will pick up a ping-pong ball or scoop up a ping-pong ball—we don't know which way we're going yet—and drop it in a cup at the end of an obstacle course. The course is precise, so we're going to blow everybody's minds."

"How?"

"We talked one of the computer engineering students into working with us, and he's going to write code and a computer's going to drive the car for us."

"Neato."

Pappy bent down. He placed a key on the rolling platform.

Cunningham stared at it, then at Dempsey. "You did it."

"Yeah."

The microwave dinged.

"Ahh, we've got hot milk for cocoa." Dempsey pushed himself up and went to the oven. "Cunning, you can have my mug. I'll heat up another for myself."

Dempsey distributed the mugs, cocoa packets, and spoons, then went after a fourth mug.

Pappy tore open his packet. He dumped its contents into his cup of steaming milk. "Love the smell of chocolate. Hey, boys, I hate to be the one always asking the tough questions, but—ahh—doesn't the guy at the station listen to what's going out over the air?"

Dempsey took his mug to the microwave. "Of course he does. He's got it on the monitor."

"So the moment Wicks cuts in, the guy's going to hear something other than what he's supposed to be hearing."

Dempsey swung around. "Omigod. If he can't fix it in twenty seconds by flipping switches and twisting knobs, he's gonna cut the transmitter."

Wickingson stopped stirring his cocoa. "I'm only going to get twenty seconds of air time?"

Dempsey waved his spoon. "Waitaminute, waitaminute, waitaminute. We loop the studio into the monitor. That way he's always hearing what's coming out of the studio, never what's going out over the air. We can do that."

Pappy raised his hand, as he might if he were in a class. "When, and not get caught?"

Dempsey tapped his spoon against his forehead.

Cunningham stirred his chocolate. "I know when."

Wickingson eyed him as did Dempsey. Pappy leaned back in his chair.

"I've got a friend who works at UOT. He told me the guy on the graveyard shift always loads in a symphony CD at one o'clock. While it's playing, he goes to the can, then outside for a smoke. He may not come back for half an hour. He locks the studio, but we've got a key."

Chapter 21

Black-bag job times two

PAPPY AND DEMPSEY hunched together, reviewing the duty assignments for that night's double break-in, as they walked back to the Tau Upsilon house from classes unaware that Caroline was hurrying up behind them. When she got close, she slowed her pace. "What're you talking about, Grandpops?"

Pappy jumped. He grabbed at his chest as he wheeled around. "Gawd, Carrie, you scare a body to death, sneaking up like that."

"I wasn't sneaking up. I saw you two, so I ran to catch up, so we could walk together."

"Oh, well–"

Caroline slipped between the two. She put her arms through theirs as they started off once more for Greek Row. "What were you talking about?"

"Nothing."

"I heard you mention UOT. You've never been interested in Public Radio. You're going to break into the station, aren't you?"

Pappy slapped his chest. "Good ol' Honest Willie Joe and his buddy, Junior 'Take-a-Bite-Outta-Crime' Dempsey?"

"Don't you kid with me, Grandpops. I heard some of what you two said."

The trio continued on, in silence now, Pappy not daring to make eye contact with his granddaughter.

She elbowed him. "Better tell me and tell me now, or I'll turn you in to keep you from getting into bigger trouble. Come on."

Dempsey glanced across to Pappy. "She's not going to quit, is she?"

"Not likely."

"She's like you, stubborn, bullheaded—"

"Loyal, honest, true, a heart of gold with a love for all peoplekind."

"Quit dancing, Grandpops. Fess up."

Pappy led the group off the sidewalk, to Hercules's Boulder. The boulder, called Greek Rock by others, was a massive stone at the edge of the green in front of Greek Row. The fraternities and sororities competed to see who could paint the gaudiest logo on Hercules.

"You caught us," Pappy said when they got to the rock. "We're going to break in and steal all their gawd-awful collection of classical music and replace it with Johnny Cash and Whalen Jennings."

"Come on, get serious."

"All right." Pappy peered around to see whether anyone was within eavesdropping range. "I'm gonna tell you, but if you so much as breathe a whisper, I'll cut you out of my will."

"Oh yeah. What were you going to leave me, that old truck of yours?"

Pappy squinted at Caroline. "Have you been talkin' to my lawyer?"

"You're not really going to leave me that old truck?"

"Hey, you have a boy someday, he's gonna love it."

"You're still dancing."

Pappy leaned on the boulder. He motioned for Caroline to come in closer. "Look, Wicks wants to do a little pirate radio, spin some heavy metal. We're gonna help him."

"And you're going to do it on UOT?"

Dempsey turned away.

Pappy tilted his head.

"When are you going to do this?"

"We do the setup tonight. Tomorrow night, it's Wicks to the world."

"Ohhh, this I've got to see."

"Oh nonononono."

Caroline raised a finger. "It's either me or the police."

THE PIRATES bailed out of Ambrose Frye's Beetle, like it was a clown car–Dempsey, Cunningham, Pappy, Caroline, and Wickingson, all in black and each with a small bag, except Wickingson. He carried a briefcase.

They hurried to the glass double doors beneath the skyway from the Communications Building to Andy Holt Tower, the doors to the ground floor of the Comm building, as Frye drove away.

Dempsey slipped his key into the lock. He turned it, and the locking mechanism pulled the deadbolt out of its secure home in the center door post.

Once inside, Pappy took the lead. He moved without a sound up a short hallway and to the right, into the center hallway that split the curved building, two football fields long, right down the middle. As he went, he checked the doors and windows, to make sure the lights were out in the business offices and the warren of cubbyholes that lined the hallway on either side. The cubbyholes were the worst, Pappy knew from conversations with Don Wright. These were graduate-student offices, for journalism and communications majors, each office barely big enough for a desk and a chair. Graduate students, particularly those who taught classes, frequently worked in those cubbyholes late into the night.

Light came from beneath a door. Pappy raised a finger, and all stopped.

He cupped a hand behind his ear. When he heard the sound of typing from the other side of the door, he signaled for all to continue on.

At the elevators, Pappy pressed the UP button. A door slid open, and Dempsey and Cunningham stepped in.

After the door closed, Pappy, Caroline, and Wickingson continued on down the hallway. At the midpoint in the building, they cut right, down a short hall that led to the loading dock, receiving area, and the all-important utilities room.

Pappy took his long Magnum flashlight and a duplicate of Dempsey's key from his bag. He unlocked the door and shined his light into the room.

In they went, Caroline last. She closed the door, then pulled a towel from her bag and laid it across the bottom, to prevent light from escaping into the hallway.

"All right," she whispered.

Pappy flipped the wall switch up for the room's lights. Next, he took his radio from his pocket and pressed the transmit button.

"Moles are in," he said into the radio.

"Roger that," came back Frye from where he had set up watch outside, in the shadows of Andy Holt.

"Eagles, where are you?" Pappy spoke into his radio.

"On fourth," came Dempsey's voice.

"Roger." Pappy went looking for the telephone junction box and found it on the other side of a three-foot square support pillar. He opened the box, revealing a rat's nest of wires.

"Eagles?" came Frye's voice on the radio.

"Yeah."

"Music Man just came out on the loading dock. He's lighting up."

"We're going in."

"Roger that."

Pappy fished in his bag for the handset and alligator clips Cunningham had borrowed from the electrical engineering lab. He found them and put the handset to his ear, scrunching his shoulder to hold it there, freeing his hands to touch the clips to connections.

Caroline came around. She took Pappy's flashlight and aimed it into the box. "This help?"

Wickingson, working behind them, laid his briefcase open on a beat-up metal desk, then went searching for a power outlet. He found one under the desk. Wickingson plugged the cord to his power pack into one of the receptacles.

As he backed out, he banged his head on the center desk drawer, setting off a great rattling of the drawer's contents. "Goddamn."

"You all right, Wicks?"

"Yeah, but I'm gonna have a headache in the morning."

"Just be glad the DJ's out on the dock. If he were smoking from the door, he would have heard you and been in here." Pappy touched a connection, listening. "Dial tone," he muttered.

He touched another.

"Dial tone."

"Dial tone."

"Data line."

"How many lines coming in?" Caroline whispered.

"Sixty, maybe more."

Pappy continued moving his clips from connection to connection.

"Dial tone...dial tone...dial tone...oops! What's this?"

He put the handset to Caroline's ear.

She listened and smiled. "Beethoven's Fifth."

"Bingo."

The two touched pinky fingers.

"Carrie, I need a small piece of red tape from my bag."

She went in for a roll of plastic tape, found it, and clipped off a piece no more than a quarter-inch long. She gave it to Pappy.

He wrapped the tape around the studio's broadcast line, high in the box where the tape wouldn't be noticed. Pappy, now finished with his job, closed the box and went over to Wickingson hunched over his briefcase studio, listening through a headset to a CD he had put in his player. Pappy tapped on the desk. "Everything working?"

Wickingson raised a thumb.

"I'm done here. Pack up."

Wickingson motioned an okay.

Pappy spoke into his radio. "Moles finished."

"Roger. Eagles?"

"Loop's in."

"Roger that. Eagles, Music Man's on the move. Get out."

"Out now."

"He'll take the stairs. Go for the elevator."

"Almost there."

Pappy pressed his transmitter button. "We're coming out the loading dock."

"Going for wheels," Frye came back.

Wickingson snapped his case shut. He came around the pillar to Pappy and Caroline waiting for him by the door.

"Didn't leave anything behind, did you?" Pappy asked.

Wickingson slapped his forehead. He ran back and returned waving the CD case for his Stormwitch album.

Pappy rubbed at his nose. "Okay, let's go then."

As if they had rehearsed it, he snapped out the lights, Caroline snatched up the towel, and Wickingson eased the door open while she stuffed the towel in her black gym bag.

"Clear," he whispered after he glanced left, then right.

He went on out into the hall, turning left. Pappy punched him and jerked a thumb in the other direction, toward the loading dock less than five yards away.

Caroline came out, leaving Pappy to lock the utilities room door. Done, he hurried on and unlocked the loading dock door. The three shot outside where they hunkered in the shadow cast by the loading dock's roof.

A minute passed before Pappy heard the sewing-machine whirr of an air-cooled engine—Frye's Beetle. The running lights came around as the rusty car traveled through the S-Thirty parking lot. It stopped under the skyway to Andy Holt.

Two figures in black dashed from the shadows and slipped into the Beetle.

That distinctive whirr came again, and the car rolled forward into the G-Five lot, coming toward the loading dock.

Pappy, Caroline, and Wickingson held in place. When the Beetle stopped, Pappy shoved Wickingson into the lead and the trio made a run for it.

The passenger door swung open, and Wickingson thrust himself into the backseat with Dempsey and Cunningham. Pappy took the front passenger seat.

Caroline, the last, wriggled her way in, onto Pappy's lap, and pulled the door closed.

As the Beetle whirred away into the night, she hugged Pappy. "God, this was fun."

Chapter 22

Pie-rat radio

HANDBILLS CIRCULATED in the bars on The Strip. Students read them, then slid them face down to others, each handbill with the same message...
Shhh!
Top Secret!!
Pie-rat Radio experiment in heavy metal
Tonight . . . One a.m.
Ninety-One-point-Nine FM
In the middle in red, an oversized luscious kiss print.

HEADLIGHTS OUT, Frye guided his Beetle through the Communication Building's parking lot, under the skyway to Andy Holt Tower, and on to the loading dock. There the Pie-rat crew, all in black and all wearing latex gloves as they had the night before, bailed out. They trotted up the steps to the door.

Frye drove off, intent on losing his car among others in the parking lot next to the university's steam plant, diagonally across Lake Louden Boulevard from the massive Comm building.

Dempsey, at the door, worked the lock.

They had come a half-hour before air time, to set up and clip into WUOT's broadcast line.

Cunningham studied the line Pappy had marked with red tape.

"If I clip in here and here and cut the line in between..." He jutted his side cutters where he intended to snip. "...I've got the signal coming in through my patch. When we're ready, I flip the switch. UOT goes off the air, and we go on."

Pappy looked hard at the wires. "You're sure of this?"

"I tested the patch in the lab. It worked."

"How fast can you splice the telephone line back together when we're done?"

"Fifteen seconds, no more than half a minute." Cunningham wiggled his fingers in front of Pappy's face. "These are the instruments of a magician."

He turned back to his job of attaching the clips to the line.

"Wicks, turn on your radio," Cunningham said after he had the second clip in place. He opened his side cutters over the telephone line, ready to cut. "Shall we see what happens?"

Wickingson found the station, on it a voice reading a public service announcement, inviting listeners to write to a New York address for literature on organizing an anti-smoking crusade.

"Patch is open," Cunningham whispered. At the end of the PSA, in the moments of dead air before the final musical selection of the hour came up, he sheared through the telephone line.

The music came up the way the DJ, in the studio three stories above, punched up a CD of the Berlin Radio Orchestra playing a Saint-Saens's composition.

Pappy nudged Cunningham. "You're good."

"Thanks."

Wickingson stared at his watch. He raised a handful of fingers, indicating five minutes to station break.

Dempsey and Caroline pulled chairs next to the desk, to wait with Wickingson. Cunningham and Pappy stayed at the junction box, babysitting the patch.

Dempsey jabbed Wickingson. "Isn't that boring music?"

"Bor-ring," he answered. "Bored, boring, boringer, boringest."

"Dull, pallid, ponderous," Dempsey said.

"Interminable, insipid, humdrum, vapid."

"Vapid? Ooo, that's a good one. Vapid—flat, dull, lacking interest—vapid, vapidity, vapidness."

Wickingson glanced up from his watch. "Have you been memorizing the dictionary, again?"

"Yeah. That's what I do, walking to class. I figure, if we ever have a Scrabble tournament at the house, I'll clean up. Vacuous, now there's a word—lacking expression, unintelligent, empty."

Caroline, mesmerized, gazed off into the gloom of the dank, cavernous utilities room. "Actually, I like this music."

Wickingson and Dempsey shot a glance at one another. They shook their heads.

A tone came over the radio, followed by "This is WUOT-FM, ninety-one-point-nine in Knoxville, your station for classical music. It's one o'clock. This hour, music of the opera, Wagner's Ring Cycle."

Wickingson, waving his hands, called to Dempsey, "Ooo, opera."

Dempsey laughed. "The story uf Br-r-r-ruhilda und Siegfried und r-r-r-ring, r-r-r-ring, who's got dah r-r-r-ring."

"Und a leettle R-r-r-reingold beer."

Caroline turned on them. "You clowns, have you ever gone to an opera?"

"In Bucksnort? Afraid not." Dempsey and Wickingson slapped hands.

A short crackle of static came in on Pappy's radio, followed by Frye's voice. "Moles?"

Pappy pressed the transmit button. "Yeah?"

"Our guy should be on the way to the can. You've got five minutes to rock, then he's out on the loading dock, sucking in cancer."

"Roger."

Pappy fired a 'go' sign at Wickingson.

Wickingson opened the pot on his microphone and threw a hand signal to Cunningham.

Cunningham, his lips pursed, flipped the switch on the patch.

"Good morniiiiiiin', Knoxville!" Wickingson screamed into his microphone. "This is WUOT piraaaat radio, rockin' with Stormwitch!"

With one hand, he punched up the CD player. With the other, he turned the pot off on his mic. Over his radio came a squalling guitar.

Wickingson and Dempsey slapped hands again.

Pappy plugged his ears. "Turn it down. We don't want him hearing it when he walks by the door."

"Excellent," came Frye over Pappy's radio.

Pappy pressed the transmit button. "Anybody outside?"

"No. Wait a minute. The loading dock door's opening. Oh jeez, he must need a smoke more than he needs to tap his bladder."

Pappy went to the desk. There he leaned down to Wickingson, Dempsey, and Caroline. "Our boy's outside," he whispered. "Keep it quiet."

Wickingson mouthed 'gotcha.'

Pappy's radio crackled again. "We've got company."

"More?" Pappy said into his radio.

"Fearless Fosdick just rolled up. Our guy's going around the car."

Pappy raised a finger to Wickingson. "Get ready to shut down. Cop's outside."

Wickingson sat up. He moved his hands to the controls in his briefcase studio.

"It's all right, moles. The two are just gassing, sharing a cigarette."

Pappy sighed.

Wickingson leaned back.

Cunningham relaxed.

Caroline reached in a pocket. She brought out a CD and held it out to Wickingson.

"What's this?"

"Hootie and the Blowfish."

"What?"

"Hootie and the Blowfish. Have you been living under a rock?"

"Of course not."

"Wicks, they've been playing the bars on The Strip for a year. They're good. This is their first album."

"And you want me to play a track from it?"

"Why not? Look, one day they're going to be doing stadium shows. You'll be able to tell everybody you were the first to put them on radio."

Dempsey waved his hands. "And it alllll started here in Knoxville."

"Huh, Hootie and the Blowfish." Wickingson turned the CD over, the copy there a list of the songs.

"Try 'Only Want to be With You'," Caroline said.

"Sounds mushy to me."

She slipped her arm around Wickingson's shoulders and gazed into his eyes. She gave him a sultry smile.

"Oh what the hell," he said.

"You're sweet."

"Yeah, sure. How long's this group been playing?"

"Two years. Started out at the University of South Carolina. They were students there."

"Okay, here we go."

Wickingson waited while the first Stormwitch track played out. The moment it did, he opened his pot, punched out the Stormwitch CD, and went into his spiel while he called up the track Caroline wanted on her CD.

"All right, you bar crawlers on The Strip," Wickingson said, loving his microphone, his voice deep and sexy, "this one's for you, Hootie and the Blowfish with 'Only Want to be With You'."

He punched 'Play.' At the same moment, he turned his microphone's pot out.

Static came over Pappy's radio. "Fearless is leaving. Our guy's going back up on the dock. Uh-oh."

"Uh-oh, what?" Pappy said into his radio.

"He tossed his ciggy. He's going inside."

"This is too soon."

"Maybe he's gotta take a whiz after all."

"Let's hope so. The telephones sure must be ringing upstairs by now." Pappy pocketed his radio. He tiptoed to the door and put his ear against it, listening.

He raised a hand to the others, and all ceased breathing. The room became silent.

Pappy inched his thumb and forefinger into an okay sign.

Caroline and Wickingson released their breaths. They hugged.

Dempsey closed his eyes. He dropped his head forward until his chin came to rest on his chest.

Cunningham let out a low whistle.

Pappy hurried to the desk. "Five minutes and we bug out. He's not going to stay in the can long."

Wickingson shook his head. "Maybe he'll take a newspaper with him."

"Maybe, but we can't risk it. Five minutes." Pappy waggled his hand at Cunningham and mouthed the words 'five minutes.'

Wickingson dug in his case for CDs. He came up with three and fanned them like playing cards. He held them out to Dempsey. "Pick one."

Dempsey glanced over the choices. He touched the Sex Pistols album.

"What, you couldn't pick Mayhem?"

Dempsey touched the Sex Pistols album again.

"Good Lord, so we go out with a little punk rock." Wickingson turned up his radio monitoring the broadcast coming off WUOT's transmitter. He held up his hand and started a countdown with his fingers.

Hootie played out on zero.

Wickingson punched out the CD. He turned up his mic's pot, slapped in the new CD and cued it up, all the while screaming into his microphone, "WUOT way-out-there piraaaat radio, countingdowntoscramtimewith the Sex Pistols!"

He punched 'Play' with the fingers of one hand while he turned the microphone's pot down and off with the fingers of his other. He then scooped his microphone and its table stand into his case. "Well, guys and girlie-gal, it's been fun."

Wickingson hopped up from his chair and did a victory dance. Midway through, his radio monitoring the transmitter went dead.

Pappy's head snapped around. "We been found out. Now, Cunning."

Cunningham ripped the clips and patch from the telephone line. He plunged into the junction box, stripping insulation from the ends of telephone wires and twisting the wires together. He pulled a roll of electrical tape out of his pocket.

Pappy threw the patch and its line to Dempsey who jammed them into the briefcase.

Wickingson yanked the power plug. He coiled that line. In one fluid motion, he dropped the line on his CD collection, closed the case, and snapped the latches shut.

"Done," said Cunningham as he slammed the junction box cover closed.

"Trouble," came Frye's voice over Pappy's radio.

Pappy whipped the radio from his pocket. He mashed the transmit button. "We know."

"Not this. Fearless is back. He's brought friends."

"Where are they?"

"Fearless is at the loading dock, came in from the east. A car, with his light bar on, just went up the hill toward Circle Park. I think he's going for the front door. Hey, here comes one in from the west. Get out."

"How? Where's Fearless?"

"Still at the loading dock. He's not gone in."

"Great. We can't go out in the hall with him there."

"Here comes another car from the east. He's stopping at the far door. All the exits are covered on your level."

"Shit."

"Lay low."

"Beetle, they'll eventually come here. Scram. No need you get caught."

"You sure?"

"Yes. Get out of here."

When Frye didn't answer, Pappy stuffed his radio in his coveralls pocket. He motioned for the others to gather at the desk. "Cops at all doors on this level, and at least one at Circle Park. Who knows this building best?"

Cunningham raised a hand.

"Any other ways out?"

"Three exits on this level, three on the next—onto Circle Park. That's all I know of. Wait a minute."

"What?"

"If we can get over into Andy Holt, we could go out through the basement, through the parking garage."

"That's a long way, a lot of chances to be seen, and we can't even go out in the hall with Fearless on the loading dock."

Wickingson fidgeted. "Look, I say we just stay here. They've gotta go back to the cop shop sometime."

Pappy paced. "They're going to search this building."

Wickingson gathered up his briefcase. "Pap, this was my idea. I've got everything right here. I'll go out and let them catch me. Then when they leave, the rest of you can leave."

"Bad idea. If anybody does that, it's me. You all need to graduate. Other ideas?"

Caroline wandered off.

Dempsey went to the door. He opened it a smidgeon. "Lights flashing," he whispered. He peeked down the hall. "Cop's still at the door."

"Grandpops?" Caroline called from a far corner of the room. "What's this?"

"What's what?"

"This plate in the floor."

"Voices out here," Dempsey whispered, still at the door.

"Then shut up." Pappy hurried to Caroline and followed her gaze down to a steel plate recessed in the concrete floor, a plate some three feet square, hinged on one side, two holes drilled through on the side opposite.

"Wellwellwellwellwell. Gimme that hook." Pappy shot his fingers toward a steel rod in the corner, a hook on the end of the rod.

Caroline handed it to him.

He inserted the hook in the holes and pulled up. Pappy next aimed his flashlight into the blackness of the opening. "Ah-ha, the plumber's friend."

"What's that?"

"The sewer. Carrie, we're outta here."

A key scratched in the lock of the hallway door. Dempsey, panicky, looked across the room to Pappy.

"Kill the lights, June. Everybody over here, now."

Dempsey reached for the wall switch. He pulled it down, plunging the room into darkness except for the light from Pappy's flashlight. Pappy kept that aimed down the shaft that led to the sewer. Dempsey started over, but reached back to snatch up the towel from the bottom of the door.

When he got to Pappy, Caroline and Wickingson were well down the shaft's ladder, and Cunningham was working his way down after them.

"Junior," Pappy whispered, "get in there."

"You first."

"No. Git."

Dempsey turned. He extended a foot into the shaft, feeling for the ladder. His foot came down on the first rung.

As soon as Dempsey disappeared, Pappy climbed down. Four rungs and he reached back up for the plate. He pulled on it, and it came over. Pappy hunched and let the plate fall on his back, preventing a clang of steel on steel.

He eased down the ladder, lowering the plate into its metal frame as the door to the utilities room opened.

Pappy snapped his flashlight off. In that instant, the room light came on. He froze and clung to the ladder like a chameleon to a wall, holding his breath, straining to hear the voices in the room above.

Two rays of light slanted through the holes in the cover. The moment Pappy became aware of them, they went out. And the door closed.

He exhaled. Then and only then did he again start down the ladder, a long ladder it seemed. Twenty-five feet? Thirty feet? Pappy couldn't be sure.

When his foot did come down on concrete, he snapped on his flashlight and there, where the shaft opened into the sewer proper, huddled Wickingson, Cunningham, Dempsey, and Caroline, Caroline wrinkling her nose. "It stinks in here."

"Sweetpea, no worse than the barnyard on Dempsey's farm. It's just wastewater and some of that clumpy stuff we all drop from our rear ends. Just watch where you step."

Dempsey nudged Pappy. "Which way?"

Pappy swept his light around the area where they stood. "Well, the ladder's got to be on the north wall of the shaft, based on the way the Communications Building's laid out."

He aimed his light to the left.

"That would be east, maybe northeast, a little upslope." Pappy swung his light around to his right. "West. Downslope. The sewer plant's about a mile that way as I remember. We go that way."

Wickingson squared his shoulders. "You've got to be kidding, to the sewer plant?"

"No, to the next shaft going up. Could be a manhole that would let us out on a street. Shall we?"

With that, Pappy led out, down the sewer. He kept to the side, out of the trickle of water and the occasional flush. He counted his paces while all behind him followed without speaking to one another.

"—one forty-six, one forty-seven, one forty-eight—Ahh, look above us." Pappy turned his light up, into a shaft. "Got to be a street up there. Stay here while I go up and see where we are."

Pappy handed his light to Caroline, then grabbed the sides of the ladder. He climbed, counting the rungs.

"—sixteen, seventeen, eighteen, nineteen—unnth." Pappy stopped.

Pain clutched at his heart, and he squeezed his eyes shut.

"What is it?" Caroline called up from below.

"Nuthin'." Pappy held to the ladder, an arm hooked through a rung. With his free hand, he fumbled a pill bottle out of his shirt pocket. He popped the top, and it fell away.

"Something hit me, Grandpops."

"You think?" He shook a pill into his mouth and worked it under his tongue. Pappy sucked in a breath, swallowed, and sucked in another, the pain easing.

"Grandpops, I found a pill bottle cap. Is this what I think it is?"

"Dunno."

A vehicle passed above, its tires banging on iron.

Pappy reached above his head. With his fingers working like an insect's antennae, he felt around. They touched something—hard, cold. His fingers explored the surface—flat, round.

"Grandpops, you get down here."

"I've found a manhole cover." Pappy pushed against it. He lifted it enough to snatch a quick look. "Oh Christ."

Headlights flashed in his eyes. He hunched down, and the cover fell back into place as another car's tires kabump-a-bumped across it and rolled on.

Pappy let himself down the ladder, slowly, tentatively, rung by rung.

"What happened up there, Grandpops?"

Pappy's foot touched concrete. "Nothing other than Lake Louden Boulevard. Enough cars to get us mashed if we try to climb out."

"This pill bottle cap." Caroline held the cap in the light.

"Stuff it."

"Grandpops."

"I said stuff it." He snatched his flashlight away and aimed it left, then right. "This is a main sewer." He stopped for a breath. "If I'm right and we're under Louden..." He stopped for another breath. "...We could go right, north, up into the campus. From there, maybe we try to find our way over to Greek Row, but if we get lost—"

"We could get lost down here?"

"Carrie, I don't have a map. Yeah, we could get lost."

Dempsey slid down on his haunches, his back against the sewer wall.

"If we go left..." Pappy aimed his light in that direction. "...that's south. That should take us to the city sewer under Neyland. But there should be a branch sewer before then. I say we go that way, any objections?"

When no one spoke, Pappy moved out, Caroline behind him, Wickingson and Cunningham next.

Dempsey, alone, pushed himself up and trotted after the others.

Not fifty yards on, by Pappy's count of his paces, he swung his flashlight to the left, into what he had been looking for, a second sewer, one that ran east. "Bingo."

"What is it, Grandpops?"

"Salvation for us, unless there's an alligator that way."

"In a sewer?"

"Amazing what you find down here. Alligators, snakes, rats—big ones." He held his hands out, far apart, indicating size, a tremor in one hand. "Carcasses of dogs, dead bodies killers are trying to get rid of."

Caroline pressed against Pappy. "You are kidding, aren't you?"

He shook his head.

Again he aimed his light into the side sewer. "That should be under Stadium Drive. Let's go."

Pappy hopped across the water flow and into the side sewer. He reached back for Caroline's hand. She came in a quick jump, but not Wickingson. He stepped out into a surge of wastewater flushing down from the north. It filled his shoes. "Aw jeez—"

"What's the matter back there?"

"I stepped in the stuff big time."

"At least you didn't get swept away."

"Fun-ney." Wickingson sloshed out of the main sewer into the side sewer.

Cunningham and Dempsey jumped across after him.

Thirty paces on, Pappy stopped. "I don't like this."

Caroline peered around his shoulder. "Did I see up there what I think I saw?"

"Some kinda critter, the snout, yeah. Backed off in that side sewer."

"What is it?" Wickingson asked.

"I don't know, but I don't want to mess with it. You wanna go back?"

"I wanna get outta here."

"The short way is ahead. If we do it, we run like the devil's behind us. You wanna go for it?"

"Maybe."

"No maybes."

"All right."

"We go on three. One, two, three."

Pappy took off, his legs pumping, the sound of tennis shoe-clad feet pounding after him. He lost track of the time, maybe it was just a minute, when he shot his flashlight up. "New shaft," he called out, stopping. The others piled in on him.

Again Pappy passed his light to Caroline. With his hands once more free, he clambered up the rungs, twelve before he banged his head against a manhole cover.

Pappy eased the cover up. He slid it back enough to poke his head up through the opening. He swiveled around, searching for landmarks, then patted his pockets for his radio. When he found it, he brought it up. "Beetle One," Pappy said into the radio.

No response.

"Beetle One," he said again.

A static burst.

"Mole One? Pappy, that you?"

"You bet your Aunt Fanny."

"Where the hell are you?"

"Not where you think."

"Where?"

"Manhole on Stadium. I can see Andy Holt Tower due north."

"Gotcha. Be there in two minutes."

Pappy stuffed the radio back in his pocket, then hollered down the shaft, "Everybody, topside! Now!"

He pushed the cover the rest of the way back and scrambled up and out of the manhole. On the pavement, he pivoted, prepared to kick the cover back over the sewer opening if a car came around the curve from the east or turned onto the drive from the west.

Caroline's head appeared above street level.

Pappy grabbed her hand and pulled her clear.

Wickingson came next. Pappy and Caroline each grabbed a hand and hauled him up.

Cunningham pushed himself out after Wickingson. Then came Dempsey.

A sewing-machine whirr sounded from the west, and a Beetle shape turned onto Stadium Drive, its lights out.

Pappy shoved the manhole cover back toward its receiving ring. He kicked the cover hard, and it dropped in, iron clanging on iron.

The car's brakes squealed as the Volkswagen pulled up next to the collection of pirates.

"Howdy, strangers," Frye called out as he shoved the passenger door open.

Wickingson, Cunningham, and Dempsey bailed into the backseat. Pappy lowered himself into the front, and Caroline wriggled her way in and onto his lap.

"I envy you," Frye said as he started the VW up the street. "You guys get all the little pleasures."

Pappy laughed.

Frye sniffed at the air. He glanced up at his mirror. "What stinks back there?"

Chapter 23

Surprise

PAPPY AND DEMPSEY returned from afternoon classes to find the doorway to their room blocked by black balloons, each proclaiming 'Over-the-hill.'

Dempsey swatted at one. "Your birthday, Pap? It's sure not mine."

"Did you have a hand in this?"

"A hand? A hand?" Dempsey threw up his hands, his face swathed with an expression of surprise.

"What's in there?"

"You gotta go through the balloons to find out, I guess."

Pappy unshouldered his backpack. He took his time in setting it beside the door before he parted the balloons. He made his way into a dark room, dark until someone threw back the window curtains and someone else snapped on the lights.

"Surprise!!!"

There before Pappy, all wearing party hats and blowing horns or singing 'Happy Birthday' full out were Wickingson, Frye, Caroline, Ellie Easterling, Sandra Kroizer; Steve Palusky, Annie Beale, Brian Hemphill, and B.J. Castle—the ice cream truck painting crew; Pappy's son Steve and his wife Mavis and their sons—Pappy's grandsons—Will and Joey; and Walter Stackpole and Digger O'Dell. Outside, Don Wright and a dozen Tau Upsilon brothers crowded in from the hallway.

The songsters roared into a chorus of "How old are you? / How old are you?"

When they finished, Pappy hollered out, "Older than anybody in this room, and that includes you, Walter and O'Dell!"

He grabbed his Maryville buddies, standing by Dempsey's study desk. He hugged them as they toasted him with cans of Country Time.

Randall Cunningham backed in from the hallway. "Outta the way. Cake coming through."

The crowd parted as if Cunningham were Moses holding a staff aloft. Instead he toted a sheet cake with Gibby Deets carrying the other end, the cake covered with a forest of candles, their flames dancing.

Stackpole clapped Pappy on the shoulder. "Make a wish and blow 'em out before they set off the fire alarm."

Pappy closed his eyes.

He pulled Stackpole and O'Dell in even closer as he concentrated on his wish. Then he sucked in a monstrous quantity of air and, with his cheeks puffed out like a crazed chipmunk, blew at the candles.

The closest went out, then more, and finally all to the applause of everyone in the room until one lone candle, on a far corner of the cake, sputtered back to life. That brought 'aws' from several in the crowd.

Pappy sucked in a new lungful of air.

He blew once more, and that candle went out.

He turned and waved in victory, exalting in the cheers coming from the crowd.

O'Dell poked the birthday boy's shoulder. "Pap, the candle."

Pappy swung around to be greeted by the lone candle again sparking.

He blew it out a third time.

It came back to life once more.

Pappy collapsed in laughter in Stackpole's arms, gesturing at the eternal flame. "It's one of those you can't blow out, isn't it, you devils?"

Caroline held up her thumb and forefinger. She wet their tips on her tongue and pinched the candle out. Just as quickly, she, Easterling, and Kroizer plucked up the candles to reveal a wish the cake baker had piped on in blaze-orange frosting over chocolate, *Happy birthday, world's oldest freshman!*

Easterling and Kroizer cut into the cake. They lifted pieces onto napkins that Caroline and her brothers handed around to the crowd.

"Surprised, Grandpops?" she asked when she put a square of cake in Pappy's hand.

"Down to my socks. You engineered this, didn't you?"

"I had help. You're not upset, are you?"

He hugged her. "How could I be upset with you? You're the best gift I've got."

"Speaking of gifts—" Caroline led Pappy over to his bed. There piled high were packages, each wrapped in newspaper. "You can see we spared no expense."

"Cheap, cheap, cheap, cheap, cheap," Pappy chirped to all who were once more applauding.

"You have to open them."

"Now?"

"Yes."

Dempsey came over. He took Pappy by the arm and made a production of helping him sit down. As Pappy settled, a farting sound erupted beneath him.

He leaped up.

Dempsey, just as quickly, reached under the bed cover. He brought out a whoopee cushion and danced around the room, laughing like a maniac as he showed the cushion off.

"What else did you put in my bed?"

"Nuthin'. Nuthin'."

With that for an assurance, Pappy again sat down—eased down—ready to spring back up if anything untoward should happen. Relief showed on his face when nothing more did. He picked a package from the pile. Giving off a crooked smile to those nearest him, Pappy tore into the newspaper wrapping. From it emerged a book.

He held it up, Jerry Peterson's 'Early's Fall.' When Pappy opened it, a bookmark fell out, twisting and spiraling toward the floor. Pappy chased after it.

He recovered it, turned the bookmark over, and found a signature—Ellie Esther Emma Easterling.

"This from you?" he called across the room.

"Yes." Easterling came over and kissed Pappy on the top of his head.

"How did you know I like this guy?"

"Carrie told me. I found it at McKay's. I think we were all out there."

The next package yielded J.R.R. Tolkien's 'The Lord of the Rings' trilogy and a bookmark with James Dempsey's name on.

"My favorite books when I was a kid," Dempsey said to Pappy between swallows from his Miller's beer can.

Michael Shaara's Civil War novel, 'The Killer Angels,' came out next.

"Always wanted to read this." Pappy waved the book at Don Wright.

The Tau Upsilon president saluted him.

There were more books, a writing journal, a silver Parker pen, the University of Tennessee edition of

Monopoly, a windup set of chattering teeth—a gift from Wickingson—the brain teasing Tri-Bond, a first edition of John Steinbeck's 'Travels with Charley' signed by the author.

"Where'd you get this?" Pappy asked Walter Stackpole. He opened the book to the flyleaf so others could see the signature.

Stackpole grinned. "Year after Steinbeck wrote 'Travels,' we had him at Maryville College to give a talk. He signed the book for me then. Huh, that was twenty-seven years ago."

"You sure waited long enough to give it to me."

"Well, I had to read it first."

From the next package came a framed photo of Caroline, Will, and Joey, Pappy's grandchildren.

Joey sidled up. "You like it, Gramps?"

"Couldn't be anything better. You know where I'm going to put this?"

"No."

"Right over there." Pappy pointed across the room. "I'm going to put it up on the wall there, over my desk. Every time I get lonely for you, I'll look up there and see your puss smiling back at me."

"I made the frame in wood shop."

Pappy ran his hand over the finely sanded and oiled wood. "Cherry, isn't it?"

"Yeah."

"You did a really nice job. You're not too old for a hug, are you?"

"Guess not."

Pappy stood up and wrapped his arms around his younger grandson. He hugged him, then pulled Will in. "You're both good kids. Will, you comin' up here next fall?"

"I've been accepted, and I've applied for the scholarship at Mister Stackpole's bank."

"Good."

Stackpole leaned in. He whispered to Pappy, "He's won it, but don't tell him yet."

Pappy nodded. To Will, he said, "We'll have to get you in the T-Ups."

"That'd be neat, Gramps."

The last package contained a slim volume with the odd title 'We're the Last to Let You Down.' Pappy opened it to the first page, and there he read the book's subtitle, 'Grave Jokes from the Funeral Parlor.'

"Digger, I should have known." Chuckling, Pappy held the book up for all to see.

With the last of the packages opened, people began drifting away.

Steve and Mavis Brown, and Will and Joey pulled on their coats. Pappy hurried over to them. "You're gonna stay and have supper with us at the frat, aren't you? It's rib night."

His son winced. "Pop, we'd like to, but we can't."

"Why not?"

"We've got plans. We're taking the boys to Squirrely Shirley's Shrimp Shack. We don't have anything like Squirrely Shirley's in Maryville."

"Maybe I could tag along."

"Naw, I think there's still something planned for you."

Pappy leaned into his son. "What do you know that I don't know?"

"Sorry, sworn to secrecy."

"Stevey—"

Brown just threw up his hands and backed toward the door. "I've got to get these boys fed. I don't want them gnawing on the car seats."

"Well, I'm glad you came, son, all of you." Pappy waved to his departing family.

Stackpole and O'Dell, also in their coats, came over. O'Dell slapped Pappy on the shoulder. "Old man, you got to have another birthday."

"Guess I will if I want to keep myself off your slab. But, hey, won't you stay around? We'll go out for a soda pop."

Stackpole put his duffer's cap on. "That'd be nice, but you know our wives are going to raise hell with us as it is for keeping supper waiting."

"Yeah, well, I guess."

"You come by the bank. We'll roust Doc and Digger out, and I'll take you all to lunch."

O'Dell perked up. "Ooo, a banker spending money. That's news. Excuse me, I gotta call the editor."

"Digger, it's easy for me to spend money. It's not mine. I just take it out of your account."

Pappy walked Stackpole and O'Dell to the door. "Well, I'm glad you boys came, even if you do have to skedaddle."

"You couldn't have kept us away."

"I spread my business card around," O'Dell said, "but these kids, you know they're so young, I'll be dead before I see any business from them."

Pappy stood in the doorway. He watched the Maryville stalwarts amble on toward the stairs, then down. Loneliness began to settle over him, a chilled mist that makes a person's bones ache.

Dempsey, in his white waiter's jacket, brushed by. "'Scuse me, Pap. Gotta get over to the Theta Delts. See you after supper."

"All right now."

Dempsey hurried on to the stairs and down.

Pappy, feeling abandoned, turned back to the room. There sitting on the beds were Wickingson, Frye, and Caroline, Wickingson grinning. "Some party, huh, Pap? Did we really surprise you?"

Pappy shambled over to the beanbag chair and flopped down in it. "You surely did."

Caroline leaned forward. "What'd you wish for, Grandpops?"

He looked over at this attractive young woman so at ease in her jeans and Theta Delta sweatshirt, pleased that she was hanging with him. He half smiled. "You know I can't tell you."

"Why not?"

"Remember when you were a little kid, and we'd go out in the backyard in the evening, and I taught you to say, 'Star light, star bright, first star I see tonight—'"

"'—I wish I may, I wish I might have the wish I wish tonight.'" Caroline carried the childhood rhyme on.

"And I always told you—remember?—never tell your wish to anyone or it won't come true."

"That was then, Grandpops."

"You really want to know?"

She gazed into his eyes. "Yes."

"Well, all right, here it is."

Pappy kicked off a shoe. He hiked his stockinged foot up on his knee and scratched at the underside of the arch. "I wished for three more years. One, to see you graduate. The second, to see my two roomies here get out of here legally. And the third, so Dempsey and I can suck up the pleasure of seeing the astonished looks on our profs' faces when we collect our diplomas."

Frye giggled. "You're going to do it, Pap. And the three of us, we're going to be in the front row, hooting and hollering and yelling our heads off when you go across the stage. Well, I will at least."

Wickingson bumped shoulders with Frye. "I'll be there, too. You can count on it."

He stood and Frye, as well, Wickingson stretching. When they started toward the door, Pappy rolled out of the beanbag chair. "Say, why don't we blow this joint? I'll treat you to dinner at the Blue Onion."

"Tempting, Pap, but my stomach's set on barbecue." Wickingson rubbed his ample belly. "Coming Ambrose?"

The two strolled out together. Pappy listened to them chatting as they clattered on down the stairs.

Caroline came over. She slipped her arm through her grandfather's. "Grandpops, there's one more birthday gift."

"What's that?"

"I'm buying you dinner tonight."

"Really?" Pappy put his hand over hers and squeezed it. "Where we going?"

"Calhoun's On The River, only you're going. I'm not."

"Well, that's no fun."

"You won't be alone. I've set you up with a blind date and don't ask who. She's a very nice person." Caroline nudged Pappy toward the door. As she did, she tucked something in his shirt pocket. "My credit card."

"You got a credit card?"

"Grandpops, I've got a lot of things you don't know about. Now you put this on my credit card, and don't you go ordering the cheapest thing on the menu." She tweaked his nose and kissed him on the cheek. "Your table is thirteen."

"Couldn't you have done better?"

"It's the last they had for six o'clock."

"Well, then I'll just have to avoid black cats, walking under ladders, and slipping on banana peels."

Caroline punched her index finger into Pappy's chest. "Change, Grandpops. Dress up. I don't want you looking like some raggedy old college student out there."

"Yes, ma'am."

He watched her leave. She moved so easily, so gracefully. For a moment, Pappy envied her youth, but only for a moment. He'd been eighteen, nineteen, twenty. He had no real desire to do that again.

Now he was alone, and he knew it with a certainty.

He turned back into the room. As he did, he caught his reflection in the mirror. He stepped over and, leaning in, examined his fierce five o'clock shadow. A shave was in order, so he gathered up his kit and went down the hall to the bathroom.

Pappy nicked himself shaving in that hardest of all places to work with a blade, beneath his chin. He peered around the bathroom, spotted a roll of toilet paper. He tore off a small piece and dabbed it at the blood. Aside from the nick, he decided he looked all right.

He brushed his teeth and gargled, then dug around in his kit for his Old Spice. He splashed on some of the aftershave before he headed back to the room to see what might be in his closet that wasn't overly wrinkled and could pass the sniff test.

Pappy settled on gray trousers, a knit shirt he chose to wear open at the throat, and his Tau Upsilon blazer, the only dress-up jacket he owned.

"You'll do," he told his reflection as he checked himself in the mirror one last time.

Chapter 24

The blind date

"TABLE THIRTEEN," Pappy said as he shed his ski jacket.

The maitre-d'hotel, resplendent in a tuxedo, stared at the jacket, an eye-blinding school bus yellow. "Are you going to take that in with you? Perhaps you would allow me check it for you."

"Fine, Clyde." Pappy handed his jacket over.

"The name is Edison."

"Sorry."

The maitre-d' passed the jacket through a Dutch door to the coat check girl who gave him a numbered token. This he held out to Pappy.

"Your first time here, sir?" the maitre-d' asked as he led the way into the main dining room glowing in warm light from red-shaded wall sconces and candles on the tables, the air alive with swirls of aromas ranging from steak tartare to bourbon whiskey.

"Yes. I usually eat at Taco Pete's."

"How nice."

"My granddaughter's treating me to dinner, even set me up with a date. There wouldn't be someone at my table, is there?"

"Yes, a lady."

"Do you know who she is?"

"I do not. She did not give me her name, nor did I ask."

"Well, nothing like surprises. Can I get a beer?"

"A beer? Sorry. Wine, perhaps, or a mixed drink?"

"How about I just have sweet tea?"

"An excellent choice."

The maitre-d' stepped around a table for two, on the side of the room next to the river window, midway down. A woman was there in a silver evening gown, seated, her back to Pappy.

The maitre-d' laid a menu on the table and pulled out a chair. He held it, waiting, but Pappy had bent down to introduce himself to his guest. "Willie Joe Brown," he said.

"I know." Ori-Anna Berry turned to him. She gave her hand to Pappy. "Are you as surprised by this as I?"

"Damn right."

"Is this going to be awkward? We're adults. We don't have to do this."

"Hey, Doc, I'm game if you're game."

Pappy went to his chair. He gave a fishy look to the maitre-d', still standing there, holding the chair out. He decided it was poor form to argue, so he allowed the man to slide the chair under him as he sat down.

"Your wait person tonight is Raymond." The maitre d' bowed and swept away from Pappy and Berry, away to the front, to guide the next guests to their table.

"Thanks, Clyde," Pappy called after him.

The maitre-d' turned back. "The name is Edison."

"Forgive me. I'm an old guy. My memory's shot."

Berry leaned forward, an elbow on the table. "Are you teasing him?"

"Me tease? But he does walk like he's got a stick up his butt. You have a chance to look over the menu?"

"I did."

Pappy opened his. He put on his half-moon glasses and read down the choices. "What are you having?"

"The butterfly shrimp." Berry touched Pappy's hand.

"Yes?" he asked, glancing up.

"I don't know how to put this, but—ah—did you know you have a piece of toilet paper under your chin?"

"Oh gawd." Pappy felt for and found it. He pulled it off. "Cut myself shaving. Why didn't Edison tell me?"

"You know, my father used to do the same thing."

"Oh?"

"He and razors didn't get along. Most mornings, he'd come down to breakfast with three, four, sometimes five little bits of white on his face and neck. My sister said he looked like he had the white measles."

Pappy chuckled. "That's good. But back to dinner, the shrimp, is that expensive?"

"Not particularly."

"Why don't you step up to lobster? Caroline's buying." He cackled and held up her credit card for Berry to see, then went back to the menu. "Ooo, look at this, Alaskan king crab. I always wanted to try that. And look at the price. Caroline's going to have a heart attack."

"You wouldn't do that to her."

"I wanted a BLT tonight, but she told me not to order anything cheap, and, Doctor, I always do what I'm told."

A young man in a jacket tux appeared beside the table with two crystal glasses of ice water on a tray. One glass he placed in front of Berry, the other in front of Pappy. "I'm Raymond, but you can call me Ray."

"Ahh, Ray," Pappy said to Berry, pleased. "After meeting an Edison, it's nice to meet a Ray."

"You'll have to forgive our maitre-d'. He's a bit formal, but he runs a top dining room."

"Don't you get sick of him?"

"We did once, last summer. Three of us took him out and threw him in the river." Raymond gazed at Berry, a quizzical expression on his face. "Excuse me, but, you're Doctor Berry, aren't you?"

"That's right."

"You don't remember me, do you?"

Berry studied the waiter for a moment. "Oh yes. Third row, second seat from the window. You were in my short story class, two years ago."

"Ray Marquis."

"Of course. How are you?"

"Just fine. I'm a senior now, graduate in May." He tugged at his jacket.

"Are you still writing?"

"No. Money got tight for me, so I'm having to work two jobs. There just isn't time. Would you like something from the bar?"

"Sweet tea for me," Pappy said.

"The maitre-d' told me. I'll have it for you in a moment. Doctor Berry?"

"White wine, please."

"Any particular variety or brand?" He gave Berry a wine menu.

She opened it and read down, her finger following the choices. It stopped on one. She showed it to Raymond. "The Chardonnay."

"Ah, from Monteagle Wine Cellars. Did you know they opened their salesroom only two years ago, and they've already won a national medal for their Chardonnay? That wine is better than anything you can get from New York and better than most of the Chardonnays you can get from California."

"I'm impressed. You know your wines."

"Well, we have regular tastings for our staff, and to top that, Edison has brought in most of the Tennessee winemakers to teach us about their products. I've met the Marlows from Monteagle, good people. I'll get your wine, and your tea, sir, while you look at the menu."

"Oh, we're ready to order." Pappy peered over the tops of his glasses.

The waiter brought out his pad.

"The butterfly shrimp for the lady, or can I talk you into the lobster?" Pappy said to Berry.

"No, the shrimp will be fine."

"Salad?" Raymond asked Berry.

"The house salad."

"And you, sir?"

Pappy raised his hand. "There are no sirs in my family. Call me Pappy."

"All right, Pappy."

"The Alaskan king crab, and do you have that jello salad with the little marshmallows in it?"

The waiter raised an eyebrow.

"Right, I should have asked Edison. I would have gotten a real snort out of him."

"Yes, and he would have spilled ice water in your lap."

"All right, what do you recommend?"

"You look like you're a daring person. How about something with fire in it?"

"Ahh. Three alarm?"

"Well, I don't want you running out and sticking your head in the river. This is a salad, after all. How about two alarm?"

"What do you have?"

Raymond touched his pen on an item on the menu.

"Hmm, Southwestern Caesar salad."

"Yes, with chilies in the dressing."

"Go for it."

"Excellent. I'll be back in a moment." With that, the waiter departed.

Berry leaned forward again. "Do you know what you're getting yourself into?"

"Hey, it's as Ray said, I'm a daring fellow. He was a student of yours, huh?"

"Yes."

"He any good?"

"Very. We entered one of his pieces in a New Yorker short story contest. He won second place. Unfortunately, the magazine published only the first-place story, but Ray did get a check for a hundred dollars."

The waiter came dodging through the maze of tables, carrying a tray with glasses of wine and tea and two plates of salad. He set them out. "If you don't mind, I'm going to create an appetizer for you right here at the table that will have you bragging for days about dining at Calhoun's on the River."

Raymond sped away.

"Something special?" Pappy again peered over the tops of his glasses. "You must have given him an A."

Berry took a bite of her salad. "Yes, I did. He earned it."

"Do you remember all your students?"

"Most of them."

Raymond wheeled a chopping-block cart in. "Showtime," he announced.

He gestured at the burner on top of cart. "Doctor Berry, I need a few magic words."

"How about abracadabra?"

Raymond gazed at the burner. "I'm afraid that's not it. That didn't make any fire."

"Ala-kazam?"

"No."

"Any suggestions?"

"How about Calhoun's on the River?"

"All right, Calhoun's on the River."

"Knoxville, Tennessee."

"Knoxville, Tennessee."

"Now point to the burner with the fingers of both hands, like you're a magician."

Berry aimed her hands at the burner, her fingers splayed out.

"Not good enough. Do it again, only with more determination."

Berry gritted her teeth, then threw her hands at the burner one more time.

It burst into flames that shot above Raymond's head before the fire settled back.

Berry's mouth gaped. "How did you do that?"

"I didn't. You did." Raymond took a wok hanging at the side of the cart and placed it over the ring of fire.

"What are you going to make?"

"Watch." He splashed in some water. It whooshed into a cloud of steam.

Next he spilled in a mixture of thinned honey and caramel. Sweet aromas rose and spread out over the tableside chef, Pappy, and Berry.

"Now a few secret ingredients." Raymond threw in three pinches of something he took from a bowl beneath the burner top.

Pappy couldn't identify the new aromas.

"And chunked pineapple." Raymond poured in a small dish of the fruit with a splash of juice.

He picked up the wok, slurried the ingredients and flipped them all into the air. He caught them and flipped them again and flipped them a third time. Raymond then raked the hot pineapple into two small bowls. The excess liquid he poured into a cup.

He placed the bowls before Berry and Pappy. "Caramelized pineapple."

Pappy rubbed his hands at the prospect of tasting this treat.

"But that's not all." Raymond mopped out the wok and again splashed in water. And a new burst of steam arose.

He brought up a bowl and tipped its contents toward Berry. "Liquefied butter with a dash of black pepper and another ingredient that I won't tell you because it's also a secret."

He poured this around the edges of the wok and watched it wash down to the bottom. Next Raymond dumped in the liquid from the caramelized pineapple. He whisked this together with the liquefied butter, sweet steam rising, then threw in a handful of peeled shrimp, followed by a second handful.

Again Raymond picked up the wok. He slurried the contents, flipped it all in the air, caught it and flipped it again, then raked the shrimp and the liquid into another pair of bowls for Berry and Pappy.

"This is shrimp scampi like you've never had before," Raymond said after he killed the fire. "Applause is welcome, but tips are better."

Pappy clapped. "Yes, and there's gonna be a good tip, too. Count on it."

"What do you do, Pappy?" Raymond asked, making conversation while he cleaned his wok.

"I'm a student like you, only a freshman."

"You're pulling my leg."

"My hands are above the table." Pappy wiggled his fingers.

"Kind of old to be a student, aren't you?"

"Retired. I was a plumber and got the itch to study."

"Ahh. Have you pick a major yet?"

"No. What's yours?"

"English, with a teaching minor. You didn't know that, did you, Doctor Berry?"

"Not the teaching part, no," she said.

"Figured I always ought to be able to get a job with that." Raymond slipped the wok onto a shelf beneath the burner top.

Pappy nibbled on a hot shrimp. "This is good. My friend, you should consider Maryville when you get out. Gawd knows, we always need good teachers."

"Actually, there is an opening at the high school. I've applied."

"Really?" Pappy dug his wallet out of his back pocket. He opened it and thumbed through until he found a business card. He gave it over. "You call me. I live over at the Tau Ups house. Let's get together and talk. Maybe I can help you."

"Thanks." Raymond slipped the card in his jacket pocket. "You'll have to excuse me. I've got an order up for one of my other tables. I'll be back later with your main courses."

He wheeled his cart away, through the leather-covered swinging doors into the kitchen, and almost as quickly came back out carrying a tray with four steak dinners.

Berry gazed at Pappy. "You'd really help him?"

Pappy tried the caramelized pineapple. "Ooo, this is good."

She speared a chunk and placed it in her mouth. She chewed, smiling. "It is, isn't it?"

"Back to Raymond. You're his recommendation. If he could pull an A from you, he's gotta be beyond excellent because, if you don't mind me saying it, Doc..." Pappy held up a shrimp scampi. "...you're real stingy with A's."

"That's because I have high standards." She took a shrimp scampi of her own.

"How well I know. My grandson Joey's coming up to high school. He's gonna need a good English teacher, and this guy's a showman to boot."

"Ahh, you have a selfish motive."

"Darn right I have. You have children? Grandchildren?" Pappy switched to his Southwestern Caesar.

"Afraid not. Sam and I parted before that could happen."

"Sorry I asked."

"Don't be. As a teacher, I've got children by the hundreds. It's just that every one of them belongs to somebody else." Berry reached across to touch Pappy's hand. "Maybe I have them on loan."

He smiled at that idea.

Raymond breezed in with a tray balanced on one hand above his shoulder.

"Butterfly shrimp for you, Doctor Berry, and the mighty king crab for you," he said as he put their plates down. "More sweet tea, Pappy?"

"You're reading my mind."

"No, I'm looking at your glass."

Onto the tray went the empty tea glass and off to the kitchen went Raymond.

Pappy cracked the crab legs apart. "How's your shrimp?"

"Raymond's scampi was excellent. This is even better. Try one." Berry lifted a shrimp onto her fork and held it out.

Pappy, still wrestling with a crab leg, took the shrimp in his lips. He chewed. "Mmm, you're right."

After one more tussle, he got the leg open enough that he could pull out some of the snow-white meat. He dipped it in the butter sauce and ate it. "Ooo, you gotta try this. Just a hint of garlic in the sauce."

"I thought your taste buds would have been burned away by your salad."

"Not hardly."

Pappy cracked another leg open. He laid it on Berry's plate.

She took some of the meat in her fingers and dipped it in the butter sauce. "Ummm, Caroline will never know what she missed."

"Oh, yes, she will. I'll tell her every last gastronomic detail."

Raymond swept past, a flaming dessert on his tray. He set it before four guests at a nearby table. Pappy stopped him when he came back. "What was that you just took over there?"

"Cherries Jubilee."

"Oh, we want that."

"I'll bring one when you're ready." With that Raymond charged off to help a busboy clear one of his tables.

"You're enjoying this, aren't you?" Berry said.

"You can say that again."

"You're enjoying this, aren't you?"

Berry laughed when Pappy glanced up from his king crab, perplexed. He, too, then chuckled.

"You're good," he said, still chuckling. "If you don't mind me asking, what happened with you and Sam?"

She stopped eating. Berry instead toyed with the shrimp on her plate. "How can I put this? Sam was like a dog, always running off, looking for a female in heat. I couldn't keep him home. When I'd had enough, I changed the locks on the house and set everything he owned out in the driveway, down to his golf tees and his Reeboks."

"Oh."

"The next day, I had him served with divorce papers. He was a lawyer, did you know that?"

"Yes."

"I had him served right in the middle of a trial, right when he was up questioning a witness. I wanted everyone to see it."

"That was a bit nasty, wasn't it?"

Berry touched her napkin to the corners of her mouth. "He had it coming, and for spite, I kept his name. That I had to do."

"Why?"

"I was Doctor Berry in the profession, and I had published under that name. To start over under my family's name would have been a lot of bother." Berry picked up her fork. She stabbed a shrimp and put it in her mouth.

"And your family name was?"

"Cashdollar."

"Cashdollar. I don't know that one."

"There are just a few families of us, up around Puncheon Camp in Claiborne County."

"Flatlanders."

"More or less. I understand you trace back up into the Smokies."

"How did you know?"

"Caroline."

"Yup, the Tuckaleechee Cove. Townsend specifically. That all went to hell when logging ended in the 'Thirties and the national park came in. Actually, for me it ended with the Big Number Two."

"Oh?"

Pappy pulled out some more crab meat. "When I came back, I settled in Maryville. There was work there for someone willing to learn the plumbing trade."

"I see. And what happened to Missus Brown?"

"I'd rather not talk about that."

Berry placed her fork beside her plate. "Look, if you can ask me about Sam, I can ask you about Missus Brown."

Pappy pushed his plate aside. "Yeah, I guess I opened myself up for that."

"What was her name, her first name?"

"Lorene."

"A lovely name."

"Lorene Diehl." Pappy glanced away, then back. "Came back from the war. Walter Stackpole and I were running around together. We'd been in the same platoon for three and half years. We met Lorene and her sister at a dance at some roadhouse one night. Jody's—yeah—Jody's it was. The Diehl sisters, Big Diehl and Little Diehl. Within a year, I had married Lorene and Walter had married Clare."

"And?" Berry asked.

"You know, I could use a cigarette."

"I don't think they let you smoke here."

"They don't. I saw the sign."

"This really bothers you, doesn't it?"

Pappy pulled the bowl over that held the sugar packets. He picked out four, tore them open, and dumped their contents in his tea. He stirred it with a fury, the spoon clinking ice cubes against the sides of the glass.

"You don't have to go any further," Berry said.

"Yeah, I do." Pappy took in a mouthful of tea. He swallowed it. "Gawd, this stuff's like syrup."

He waved at Raymond coming out of the kitchen and held up his glass.

"You know why I drink tea and lemonade?" Pappy asked Berry.

"You're an alcoholic. Caroline told me."

"That's a gawd-awful polite term for it. After the war, Walter and I were roaring drunks. He got smart and sobered up. By the time I quit drinking, Lorene had become a drunk." He shook his head over the memory.

Raymond glided in. "Fresh tea," he said as he exchanged glasses, one full for the half-empty. "Doctor Berry, more wine?"

She put her hand over her glass.

"Very well." He went off again.

Pappy gazed at the new glass, at the Calhoun *C* etched into the crystal. He ran a finger over its form. "Lorene fell into the bottle I'd just climbed out of. She drowned there. Ten years, drank herself to death."

A flash of lightning lit the river and everything around it. The thunder clap that followed shook the restaurant.

The sconce lights snuffed out. Several people gasped. Not Pappy. He motioned Berry closer to the candle. "If this goes out, I've got my lighter."

Edison stepped up on a chair in the center of the room.

"Please do not be concerned," he announced, turning as he spoke. "Power will be restored momentarily I am sure. Until it is, please enjoy your dinners by candlelight. Perhaps Cupid planned this."

Nervous laughter rippled through the room.

"March thunderstorms," Pappy said. "They seem to come out of nowhere."

"And go as fast." Berry worked her fork around her plate. "At least it's over."

"Yeah, the rain's stopped, at least for the moment."

She touched Pappy's hand. "I'm sorry I asked about your wife."

"That's all right." He pulled his hand away.

A tray of flame came from the kitchen, through the swinging doors, carried by Raymond the waiter—Cherries Jubilee. He set it down on Pappy's and Berry's table as they pushed things out of the center, to make way for the dessert.

"How's this for when we have a power outage?" Raymond said.

Berry clasped her hands together. "It's beautiful."

"I'll just take your dinner plates, then I'll be back to serve it up."

The flames on the Jubilee, raging red and yellow just moments before, now became blue, flickering and dying, and then they flickered out.

Raymond returned with dessert plates. He scooped the flamed cherries and cherry brandy sauce over the Jubilee and put half on a plate for Berry and half on a plate for Pappy. "Surely, you'll want coffee with this."

"Please," Berry said.

"Pappy?"

"Oh yes, black."

The conversation drifted over no particular direction during dessert and coffee. When Pappy and Berry could eat no more, Raymond appeared. "Has everything been all right?"

Pappy gave him an okay sign.

"Then your check."

"Ahh." Pappy opened the black cover. At the bottom, he wrote in a hefty tip and gave the dinner check and Caroline's credit card to Raymond.

"I'll be back in a moment," he said.

Pappy gazed at Berry. "Normally, at this point I'd ask you if you'd like to go out to Swenson's for ice cream, but with the Jubilee—"

"I couldn't even if you asked. I need to get home. I have papers to read."

"Well, all right."

Raymond returned with the credit card receipt. Pappy forged Caroline's signature.

Raymond looked at it as he snapped out the yellow copy and the carbon. He handed the copy and the carbon to Pappy. "I didn't know your first name was Caroline."

"That's my granddaughter. It's her card. She's buying tonight. My birthday dinner."

"I wish I had known. We would have brought out a cake for you and sung 'Happy Birthday.'"

"Others already did that."

"You'll come back?"

"Yes. And you'll call?"

"Absolutely."

Raymond pulled the chair back for Pappy and then for Berry. They strolled out to the cloakroom where they recovered their coats.

The lights came on as Pappy and Berry stepped out into the night air washed clean by the sudden rain. The aromas of steaks grilling over hickory drifted their way from the kitchen. Somehow it smelled better now.

"Nice night," Berry said.

"Where you parked?" Pappy asked as they walked along.

She nodded ahead. "Right up there."

"Which one?"

"The LeBaron."

"The white one with the soft top?"

"Uh-huh."

Pappy whistled.

"It's the one luxury I've permitted myself."

"And a nice one it is."

At the car, Berry unlocked the door.

Pappy opened it and held it while she slipped in behind the steering wheel.

"Thank you," she said.

"Been fun," he said.

"Well?" She gestured at the door that he still held open.

"Oh."

Pappy closed the door and stood watching as Berry started the motor. When she turned the headlights on, he rapped on the window glass.

She pressed a button on the armrest, and the glass slid down. "Yes?"

"Would you like to do this again sometime? Maybe?"

"I'd consider it."

"Good."

When he said no more, she pressed the button that raised the window glass. After it closed, she drove away, a back tire splashing through a pothole filled with rain water. The wave it sent up drenched Pappy's slacks.

Chapter 25

Death of a soldier

PAPPY, AS HE TROTTED down the Tau Upsilon house's steps, saw him across the green, pacing at the edge of a pool of light cast by a street lamp, Cooter Henthorn, his shoulders hunched, his hands stuffed in the pockets of his Goodwill mackinaw, unshaven and unchanged from when he had seen him last in the hobo camp back in December.

Pappy made his way across the grass. "Cooter," he said when he came near.

Henthorn jumped.

"Didn't mean to scare you, Coot. You wanted to see me?"

Henthorn's lower lip quivered. "It's Pa-Pa-Pooch."

"What about him?"

"He's da-dead."

"When?"

"Af-af-afternoon. Stick wa-wa-was with him. He sa-sent me, says S-s-sergeant Roberts wa-wanted you to know."

"Old Cyril?"

"Uh-huh, his ra-roommate out at the VA."

"They set the funeral?"

"Tomorrow, yeah. Stick sa-says S-s-sergeant Roberts wa-wants you in the rifle squad."

PAPPY, IN HIS dress uniform from World War Two, corporal chevrons on his jacket sleeves and the crossed rifles insignia of the Infantry pinned above his breast pocket, leaned against the tailgate of his pickup. He took a drag on his cigarette. There had been a break in the day's showers.

From his vantage point, he could see Dempsey seated with Nettie Jackson, Charlie, and Charlie's three sisters under an awning by an open grave. Behind them stood Wickingson, Frye, Caroline, and Don Wright. Further back, a squad of VA residents–pallbearers–lounged by a flag-draped casket, Cyril Roberts among them in a wheelchair, he in his uniform from World War One, his trousers riding britches with puttees–bound leggings.

Pappy also saw the four Vietnam vets from the hobo camp and the giant they called Stick shamble out of the tree line at the edge of the VA cemetery. They remained there in the distance, a cluster far from everyone else.

The rifle detail leader came up. "It's time, Pappy. Ditch the smoke."

Pappy flicked his cigarette away. He reached in the back of his truck for his M-1 carbine that lay in its open gun case. Weapon in hand, he moved into line with the other riflemen, four in all.

"Forward, harch," the leader said in a voice soft, so no one other than the detail would hear him.

The riflemen stepped out through the wet grass in silent cadence, the air washed clean, their movements parade-ground crisp. When they arrived at their designated position, they halted. "Right face," the leader said. "Parade rest."

Pappy stood, as did the others, with his carbine at his side, the butt on the ground, the barrel held forward.

The VA chaplain came next, leading the pallbearers carrying the casket, Roberts rolling along beside them. When they came up to the grave, they set the casket on a bier, then formed a line in front of Nettie Jackson. The pallbearers saluted and moved to the side.

The chaplain took his place at the head of the casket, two steps away from the military's memorial to a fallen soldier, an M-16 with a bayonet fixed to it, the bayonet stabbed into the sod so that the rifle stood upright, its barrel pointed at the earth, a helmet placed on the rifle's butt. He waited until everyone was focused on him before he opened his notebook. He proceeded to read aloud, "Private Samuel John Phillips, born Eighteen January Nineteen Fifty, served with distinction in the Vietnam Conflict from Four February Nineteen Sixty-nine to Twelve February Nineteen Seventy as a member of Delta Company, Twenty-third Infantry Division—the Americal Division. Private Phillips passed from this earth on Sixteen March of this year. The last surviving member of his platoon, he has now joined his comrades in arms for that final long rest before being called before God on Resurrection Day. Would you please join me in prayer?"

He bowed. "Dear God," he said, "please receive into Your hands the soul of Samuel Phillips, a good soldier during his time here among us. Give him the peace he has so richly earned as an honored member of the United States Army. Amen."

The chaplain closed his notebook. He turned away from the casket and the assemblage before him, to the rifle squad, issuing the order, "Rifle detail, fire three volleys."

The detail leader snapped to attention. He called out, still in a soft tone, "Detail, ten-hut. Right face. Port arms. Aim. Fire on my command. Fire one."

Pappy squeezed his M-1's trigger and felt a light kick from his weapon.

"Fire two."

Pappy's weapon popped back into his shoulder a second time.

"Fire three."

The final shots, and, as the sound carried off across the cemetery, Taps drifted back, played by an unseen bugler. The 'Nam vets by the tree line came to attention, their right hands firm at their foreheads. They held their salutes until the final note of Taps faded.

"Port arms," the detail leader said to Pappy and his fellow riflemen. "Left face and parade rest."

A fine mist began to filter down from the scud clouds, adding a new chill to the air.

Two pallbearers, oblivious to the mist, lifted the flag away from the casket. They proceeded step by patient step through the ceremony of folding the flag and presenting it to Nettie Jackson, Nettie fighting hard against her tears.

The presenters, their job done, moved back in line with the other pallbearers and marched away. Cyril Roberts, though, rolled up to Nettie. He took her hands in his.

From his distance, Pappy could not hear what the old soldier was saying, surely something comforting.

"Detail, dismissed," the detail leader said, breaking Pappy away from his thoughts. The other riflemen ambled off to their cars, and Roberts rolled away in his wheelchair toward the VA's barracks. Pappy, though, stood alone for a quiet moment. He hated military funerals. He'd been to too many, yet he continued to come, as a rifleman out of respect for the dead. He put his weapon away in its case and went off to see the tight knot of people still with Nettie Jackson at the grave. Half way there, he sensed someone moving along with him. He glanced to the side.

There strode Stick in lock step, Stick in his railroad overalls, fatigue cap, and a battle jacket, hardly an arm's length away. A sneer curled at his lips. "Served with distinction, honored member of the Army—bull crap by the truckload."

"You think?" Pappy said, not breaking his pace.

"All Pooch did, like the rest of us, was to keep himself from gettin' shot or blown up so he could get the hell out of 'Nam at the end of his hitch."

"He made it."

"He did, but then that Agent Orange kills him anyway."

"Stick, it's good you're here."

"I guess. Pooch was one of us, we residents of the bush. That guy who spoke, that damn chaplain, he has no idea. Sure no ground-pounder. Probably never been outta Tennessee."

Pappy gave a tilt of his head, his sign to Stick that he likely was right.

When they came up to Nettie Jackson and her children, Pappy reached out for Charlie. He pulled him in close. "Charlie, how you doin'?"

"It's kinda hard, Mister Brown. I never said it, but thank you for lettin' me see my father on Christmas."

"That's a memory you should keep hold of. Charlie, this fella, this is a friend of your dad's. Goes by the name of Stick." Pappy turned to the vet. "I don't honestly know your real name."

"Sallison Timmerod," Stick said. He focused on Charlie's mother. "Miz Jackson, I've got something for you."

She gazed up into the eyes of the big man, her eyes questioning.

He brought out a fistful of fabric from inside his battle jacket. Stick let the fabric fall open. "Miz Jackson, this is Delta Company's campaign flag. Pooch wanted something to remember his time in 'Nam by–frankly, I don't understand why–so he stole it. I found it among his things."

He passed the flag to Nettie, and she wrapped it around her U.S. flag that had covered Samuel Phillips's coffin.

Stick slipped a hand into his pocket. "Pooch never got any medals for his time in the Army other than a good conduct medal, and they took that away from him when they found him high on weed. Miz Jackson, Pooch deserved something because the war hurt him bad, as you know, so I want you to have this, too."

He brought out a presentation case. Stick opened it, revealing a pillowed velvet lining on which rested a medal–a Purple Heart.

"Mistah Timmerod, I don't know what ta say."

"You don't have to say a thing, ma'am. It was my honor to have known Pooch, to have marched into hell with him and out again."

Stick stepped back.

Pappy expected him to salute Nettie Jackson. He didn't. Instead, he snuffled up a tear and bowed his head, nodded a couple times as if agreeing with some thought he could not put into words, then left.

Pappy hiked after him. "That medal–yours?"

"Not no more."

Chapter 26

The stranger

PAPPY SAT at a small work table, oblivious to others in the city library and everyone beyond its walls, two fingers flying over a keyboard, tapping notes into his laptop's memory. He had spent much of the afternoon here, pulling down books from the Lawson McGhee's regional collection, paging through, reading, gathering information on death customs in the Smoky Mountains.

The sun had slipped low in the west, beyond the Sunsphere three blocks away, beyond the university, beyond Knoxville itself. Street lights had come on, to push back the shadows that had commandeered the last remnants of the day. And still he typed, unaware that evening had come and unaware that his stomach craved food.

Papers spilled to the floor, not Pappy's. Yet their rustling broke his concentration.

He peered over his half-moon glasses, to the side, to a woman there on her knees, doing all she could to corral the errant pages. He bent down to help.

"Thank you," she said.

"Not a problem," he said as he gathered the several pages under his chair and handed them to her.

She bunched them with hers, tapping them on their ends and sides to settle them.

Pappy went back to his typing.

She pushed the pages into a bag and got to her feet. The woman, unremarkable in her smock and sweat pants, gathered up the books she had laid on the table beyond his and headed for the circular stairway that led down to the checkout desk.

Pappy stopped typing.

Something about that woman was familiar.

He leaned over the railing and looked down into the open area near the front door. There at a long desk, three librarians ran library cards and books past scanners before they gave them to waiting patrons.

The woman he had helped was there.

There was something about the way she stood, balanced on one foot, her other hooked behind her ankle, something about the way she tilted her head as she chatted with the librarian processing her books.

Was it pentimento, a memory long painted over, yet still wanting to bleed through?

Pappy swore.

He put a save on his file, then hustled toward the circular stairway, but by the time he got down to the first floor, she was gone.

He went up to the counter, to the librarian who had checked out the woman's books. "Who was that person?"

The librarian gave him a puzzled look.

"The woman, the one that was just here, checking out books."

"Uhm, I'm sorry, sir, but we're not permitted to give out the names of patrons."

"But I think I know her. Couldn't you just look on your screen? I'm sure her name is still up."

"I can't do that, really, sir. Maybe if you hurry, you can catch up with her on the street." The librarian motioned toward the door.

Pappy wheeled and ran.

He burst through the door and down the steps, out onto the sidewalk, glancing down the street and up, but she was gone.

A man shook a Denny's cup in Pappy's face. "Spare change, mister?"

Pappy smelled him before he even looked. The man had dirty clothes, a three-day growth of beard, and, by his ripe aroma, was long overdue for a shower. "You see a woman come out here a minute ago?"

"Yeah."

"Which way'd she go?"

"Ahh—"

"It's worth a fiver." Pappy pulled a bill from his pocket. He held it up.

The man wobbled to the side, motioning with his knobby fingers up the street. "That way, toward Krutch Park, ya know, only she turned at the corner. Yeah, that's what she did, went right."

Pappy stuffed the bill in the cup and ran.

He swung around the corner, but the sidewalks on both sides of the street were empty, as empty as the street itself.

He trotted on until he came to a parking lot. Perhaps she had driven to the library and had parked her car there. If so, she was gone, and there was no one Pappy could ask. After five o'clock, a sign said, the lot was unattended.

He stood there, hands jammed in his pants pockets, wondering, thinking, remembering.

My gawd!

"I WILL NOT be the Easter bunny. Gawddammit, Don, get somebody else."

"But the kids love you, Pappy."

"Oh yeah, I let you rook me into being Santa Claus and kids stuck candy in my beard and peed on my britches. Not again."

"But Pappy—"

"No!"

CAROLINE HELD a rabbit's head out to Pappy. "Grandpops, you look fine. Now put this on, please."

Dempsey pulled the fluffy tail on Pappy's backside, and Pappy swatted him.

"Boy, you are getting crabby in your old age."

"You'll be crabby, too, when you're sixty-six and some kid's diddling with your bee-hind. Get in your chicken suit."

That was the deal. Pappy had agreed to play the Easter bunny for the Tau Upsilon/Theta Delta Theta Big Brother/Big Sister Easter egg hunt only after Dempsey agreed to go as the Spring Chicken and Caroline as Raggedy Ann.

But Caroline went one better. She made Don Wright, the instigator of the egg hunt, agree to dress up as Raggedy Andy.

Wickingson, Frye, and Cunningham volunteered to be Polaroid photographers and shoot instant pictures of the Little Brothers and Little Sisters with this quartet of holiday characters.

It had rained the night before—hard. Wright and his officers stayed up, kicking around ideas on how and where they could do the event indoors if the day was a rain-out. But dawn brought the sun and a stiff breeze out of the west. At ten a.m., they walked the park in front of the fraternity, the sod squishing beneath their Air Jordans.

At eleven, they tried it again. They found the sod still spongy, but it no longer made sucking sounds as they walked along.

At twelve, they found the sod firm. Wright and his officers sent the word out through the houses, "We're on for two."

It was now one forty-five.

The park had been roped off with yellow tape Frye had lifted from a campus police car, and the eggs had been hidden, plastic eggs with candy and tickets for stuffed toys inside.

Pappy could see them from his window, dozens of kids, small and not so small with their moms or dads and their Big Brothers and Big Sisters, some kids running races, others playing catch, still others playing hide-and-seek, doing fun stuff, Dempsey said, until showtime.

And now it was showtime.

"Quit fussing, Grandpops," Caroline said.

He hunched down, and she settled the oversized rabbit's head over his head.

She adjusted the head. "Can you see me?"

"Gawd, looking through the mesh of these eyes is like looking through a window screen. You need more red on your nose."

"I do?"

Caroline peered in the mirror. She took out her lipstick—Poppy Red Gloss—and painted in the sides and bridge of her nose up to where the bridge met her eyebrows. "How's that?"

"Good. I like your braids."

"I'm thinking of keeping them."

"All right, gang, let's go." Pappy held his arm out to Dempsey. "Come on, chicken, gimme your wing."

"Bwuuk, bwuuk-bwuuk-bwuuk."

"You fixin' to lay an egg?"

"Bwuuuuk."

The trio trooped out into the hall and down the stairs. Outside, on the Tau Upsilon's front porch, they added to their numbers, Wright as Raggedy Andy, and two Pappy had not expected–twin Bo Peeps.

"Doc?" he asked as he stared at the nearest shepherdess.

"Are you surprised?" Ori-Anna Berry said.

"You got a sister there?"

"My niece."

Berry drew the second Bo Peep away from the Tau Upsilon men with whom she was flirting.

"This is Cindy," Berry said, making the introduction. "She's staying with me for the weekend. Cindy, this is Mister Brown, one of my students."

With his hand, Pappy flapped one of his ears. "A party girl, huh?"

"No more than my aunt."

Berry put a hand to the side of her face. "A lot more than her aunt. But we thought this would be fun, so we went out to the costume shop yesterday, and here we are."

"With our shepherd's crooks, ready to go catching little kiddies," Bo Peep Cindy said.

"Then let's do it."

Pappy and his colorful collection of cohorts headed across the street.

A cry went up from the waiting children, "The Easter Rabbit!"

They charged Pappy, running, screaming, laughing.

He braced himself, yet staggered back under the weight of the first wave. "Hey, heyheyheyhey, waitaminute, waitaminute, waitaminute! Idon'thaveanycandy, thecandy'soverthereintheeggs!"

Raggedy Andy blew his referee's whistle hard, stopping the children. "All right, listen up! This is what we're going to do. Toddlers and kids a year old, you're going with the Easter Bunny and the chicken. They have a hunt area for you. Two years old to five, you're going to go with the Bo Peep sisters, and age six through twelve, you're coming with me and Raggedy Ann. Got it?"

Children and mothers carrying babies milled around, getting with their leaders.

A small boy tugged at Berry' sleeve. "What's a Bo-pee-pee?"

The older children raced to the park, to the egg hunt, only to find themselves blocked by Big Brothers and Big Sisters and their teenage charges patrolling the tape lines.

Pappy motioned the chicken to the far end of the tape line in front of the toddlers' area. Only when Dempsey got there did Pappy look over to the other areas. When he saw the Bo Peeps and the Raggedies standing, waiting, he shot up his front paw and held it high.

"Ready!" Pappy glanced at the Bo Peeps and the Raggedies one more time, then swept his paw down like an official starting a race.

Raggedy Andy and Ann, the Bo Peeps, and Pappy and the chicken all broke their tape lines as the children dashed in, the toddlers not so much dashing as stumbling, mothers and dads helping the smallest of the small.

Tau Upsilons and Theta Delts, with stuffed animals under their arms, waded in among the masses of hunters, to give their prizes to children who found the eggs with the award tickets. Each scream of delight announced another lucky hunter.

Ten minutes and it was over. Children ran to their parents and their Big Brothers and Big Sisters, waving what they had found. From there, they ran to Pappy, the chicken, the Bo Peeps, and the Raggedies to get their pictures taken.

Charlie Jackson charged through. He wrapped his arms around the Easter Rabbit's neck. The chicken crowded in just as Wickingson was about to take the picture.

"Know who this is, kid?" the chicken asked. He lifted off his head.

Charlie squealed. He threw himself into Dempsey's wings. "I thought you wasn't here!"

Wickingson shot two pictures of Charlie in the middle, his arms around the necks of Dempsey and Pappy, both men still in their costumes, their fake heads now propped on their knees. Wickingson gave one to the boy's mother and kept the other for the wall of the Caballeros' suite.

Families drifted away after Wickingson or one of the other shooters took pictures of their children with the storybook characters. In the background, Tau Upsilon men policed the park, picking up candy wrappers and yellow tape.

Pappy lifted his rabbit's head off and mopped at the sweat beaded out on his forehead. "Some afternoon," he said to Bo Peep Number One.

"It was nice, wasn't it?" Berry said.

"'Spose we ought to walk around and see if there's any eggs the kids missed?"

"You think there are?"

"Only one way to find out. Best chance will be in the toddlers' area."

The two strolled away toward that end of the park, passing Gibby Deets coming in with a bag of debris he had harvested. "We got everything picked up, Pap."

"You're a good man, Gib."

Berry took Pappy's arm and turned him to the side. "See Junior and Charlie out there? Looks like Charlie's with Big Bird."

"If Big Bird were a Plymouth Rock."

"Junior's teaching Charlie the bunny hop."

"You'd think he'd teach him the chicken dance."

A glint of color from beneath a bush caught Pappy's eye. He hunkered down on his knees and groped beneath the branches with his paw. He brought out an egg. He held it up before he tossed it to Berry.

She caught the egg and twisted the halves apart. "We've got a Cadbury here. Want a bite?"

"You enjoy it. I see another egg in the tulips."

Charlie came charging up as Pappy started for the new egg. "Whatcha lookin' for, Mister Brown?"

"Eggs, Charlie-boy. Just found one and I see another."

"I see it!" The boy bolted for the egg. He cut in front of Pappy, tripping him. Both twisted in each other's legs and went over.

Charlie came up laughing. He scooted off after the egg, but not Pappy. He laid where he'd fallen.

Berry hurried to him. "Are you all right?"

"Don't think so." He reached for his knee, grimacing as he did, and fell back.

Dempsey ran up. "What happened, Pap?"

"Think I busted my leg. Hell, I know I busted my leg."

Chapter 27

Second sighting

BERRY OPENED her car's passenger door. She held it for Pappy. "Come on, cripple, get out." He stared up at her, frowning at the name. Pappy got a hand under his knee. He lifted, turning, setting his plaster-wrapped leg out of the car. He brought out his good leg, then, grabbing the door and pushing against the back of the seat, he forced himself up.

Berry brought his crutches out of the back seat. She chucked them under his arms and pointed him toward the park.

While Pappy hobbled on up to the sidewalk, she got a picnic basket and blanket from the trunk.

"You know, we don't have to do this," Pappy said.

"Look, you put up with me dragging you to the symphony last night—"

"—And it was a gawd-awful bore."

"Mozart can be dark, I'll admit that."

"Gimme good ol' Jerry Lee."

"Who?"

"Jerry Lee Lewis. He would have set his piano on fire."

"Well, anyway, after what I made you sit through, you deserve a good meal, and I made everything myself."

"Now that tickles my interest."

Pappy and Berry moved on into the park, Pappy with care.

This was Krutch Park, Knoxville's smallest at half a city block, walled in and gated at night to keep the winos out. The sots who had the temerity to wander in in the daytime usually found themselves rooted out by a policeman on foot patrol.

The park had come to be a refuge for those who worked downtown. At noontime, when the weather was fair, as it was this day, secretaries from the Tennessee Valley Authority, clerks from the courthouse, and tellers from the nearby banks flooded into the streets and down to the park to eat lunch.

The place was a mosaic of brick walks, green spaces, trees, and bermed gardens, the dogwoods fragrant now in full bloom, most of them pink, but a few old-fashioned whites, wild trees brought down from the mountains and planted here.

Berry stepped off a walkway and onto one of the park's small lawns. She flapped her blanket open and watched it settle to the grass.

"Come on," she said, taking Pappy's arm.

He dropped his crutches. With Berry hanging onto him, Pappy did his best to lower himself to the blanket, wobbling on his good foot as he reached back, feeling for something to grab hold of. Pappy lost his balance. He went down with Berry falling on top of him.

Pappy laughed at the silliness of it all. Berry, too.

And he kissed her.

Pappy pulled back, not an easy thing to do with Berry on his chest. "I'm sorry. I shouldn't have done that."

She touched his cheek. "Why don't you let me be the judge of that?"

"What if the mayor comes along?"

"It's Sunday. I don't think he's downtown today."

"The beat cop?"

She pushed up on her elbows, the better to peer into his face. "You're embarrassed, aren't you?"

"No—yeah—I suppose—I don't know."

Berry rolled over and sat up. She brushed her hair back from her eyes.

Pappy, too, struggled up. He gazed at his cast. "Hope you don't mind me wearing these damn walking shorts. They're the only pants I can get my cast through. Any of my long pants, I got to split the leg to get 'em on."

"Must be difficult."

"I tell you I'd be in one helluva fix if it weren't for the guys. They help me get in my shorts and pants in the morning, and did you know you're not allowed to take a shower with this damn thing on? It'll fills up with water."

Berry shook her head.

"I got to take a bath in a bathtub, and I can't get down in by myself. Then I'm in and my leg's hanging over the side and I'm all wet and I can't get out—"

Berry broke out laughing.

"Gawddammit, it's not funny."

"Oh, yes, it is." She tried to regain her composure but couldn't.

"You got no sympathy at all."

Berry broke out laughing all over again. She got to her feet and staggered off, one hand on her face, the other holding her ribs. "Poor little boy with his boo-boo—"

"Oh gawd."

"I'm sorry, I shouldn't laugh at you." She sat back down. "But you're an easy target."

"Target, hell. You haven't signed my cast."

Berry peered at it, studied it. "You've got quite a collection of signatures there."

"Everybody in the house, half the Theta Delt girls, Charlie—"

"Is that—?"

"Yeah. I ran into the university president the other day. I mean I really ran into him. I didn't see Lamar coming around the corner, and I whacked him with a crutch."

Berry giggled, a hand to her face again.

"He's from my town," Pappy went on, "so we know each other. So after he retrieves his briefcase that goes flying off across the hall, I ask him to sign my cast."

"And now you want me to sign it, too?"

"Sure." Pappy took a pen from his pocket. "I got a Sharpie here."

He lifted his leg and swung it over onto her lap.

Most who signed just wrote their names and maybe a couple words, but Pappy watched Berry write on and on. "You writing a book?"

"No."

"Well, what is it? I can't read it from here."

"'Breaking one leg is enough. Your student insurance doesn't cover a second.'"

"Funny. Oh, that's verrryyy funny. How are you signing it?"

"I'm thinking Doctor Berry is a bit formal."

"Your first name's all right with me."

"Ori-Anna? People reading that on your cast might get ideas."

"Ideas of what?"

"That I care for you something more than just as a student."

"Never thought of that."

"As long as we're on names," Berry said, "we've been showing up at the same events together, and then there was your birthday dinner at Calhoun's and the symphony last night, I can't go on calling you Mister Brown."

"Does make me sound ancient."

"And I can't call you Pappy. That's silly when we're not that far apart in age."

"Some call me Willie Joe. I grew up with that."

"I'm sorry, that's juvenile, Mister Brown."

"Well, my grandson goes by Will."

"Will," Berry said, tasting the name. "That's, ah, that's all right."

Pappy pulled a paper from his shirt pocket. "If we're getting down to names, there's one more thing you better sign."

She took the paper. "What's this?"

"I'm withdrawing from your class."

"Why?"

"If we're going to go on seeing each other—"

"Don't you think you ought to ask me about this first?"

"I'm in trouble, aren't I?"

"I don't know, are you?"

Pappy fixed Berry in his gaze. "Look, I kissed you and you didn't slap me. I don't think it's a student-and-teacher thing anymore. There could be something here."

"Don't you think you ought to ask me?"

"Ask you what?"

"If there could be something for you and me."

"Well, could there?"

"Yes, but I have to decide these things for myself, Will. You can't go around making decisions for me. And back to this withdrawal slip..." Berry shook the paper at Pappy. "...you have three weeks to go in the semester. If you quit now, you throw all that away."

"A 'W' isn't gonna hurt my grade point average. And I'm not throwing away what I learned in your class or from you. That I keep."

"You're sure you want to do this?"

Pappy took a deep breath. "Yeah, I'm sure."

Berry signed the paper with a flourish. She folded it and handed it back. "You'd better not mess up, Will Brown, or you'll be sitting in your room at the Tau Upsilon house with the boys an awful lot of nights."

"Yeah, well, ahh—what did you put in the basket?"

Berry glanced at Pappy as she opened the hamper. "Chicken a la Berry, Southern potato salad, baked beans, a lettuce salad from my garden—"

"You have a garden?"

"Doesn't everybody?"

"Lorene always said I had a thumb of an appropriate color for a man named Brown, and she'd plant some scrawny little shrub out in the yard, and I wouldn't be paying any attention and mow it off. Gawd, I caught hell."

"No doubt you deserved it."

Pappy stared at Berry. "Why, Miss Ori, you do have a mean streak in you."

"As you would say, damn right. If you mowed off one of my shrubs, you'd do more than catch h-e double-l. You'd sleep in your truck for a week."

Pappy's mouth fell open.

"Cat got your tongue?" Berry asked as she set a plate on Pappy's lap. She held out the salad so he could help himself.

Slowly, he forked a modest portion onto his plate. "Ah, dressing?"

"Sweet Vidalia onion. I made it myself." Berry brought out a bowl. She pulled off the cover.

Pappy dipped a spoon in and tasted it. "Gol, this is good."

"Of course, it is."

"And you're so modest."

"Of course, I am."

His glance at her caught her smiling.

Pappy spooned on the dressing and ate.

Out came a bowl of fried chicken and bowls of potato salad and beans. Out also came thermal cups and a jug of sweet tea. Biscuits, butter, and honey followed.

"Tell me about your niece who came to visit back on Easter." Pappy bit into the crispy skin of a chicken leg. "Ooo, this is good. How did you make it?"

"Like the Colonel, secret spices and batter, but I skillet fry mine, like my mother did."

"You could go into the restaurant business."

"If I wanted to work harder than I already do, but you were asking about Cindy." Berry took in a mouthful of potato salad. "She's a hard case. My brother and sister-in-law wanted a break from her and asked me if I'd take her for the weekend."

"Hard case?" Pappy reached for a biscuit. He broke it open and slathered on the butter.

"She smokes weed—marijuana. She's addicted to all kinds of pills, and she's alternately anorexic and bulimic."

"She seemed so nice."

"Oh, our Cindy's a very good actress. At home, she's a terror."

"How do you handle her?"

"Firmly. I don't let her get away with a thing. Of course, it's easy for me to be the Wicked Witch of the West. I get to send her home at the end of the weekend."

Pappy helped himself to a second chicken leg. "She must make you glad you don't have kids of your own."

"I don't know." Berry sipped her tea. "I think I would have made a good mother. I certainly get a lot of practice with my Theta Deltas. How did you and your son get along?"

Pappy didn't answer. He had his gaze fixed on a woman moving along just beyond the park's wall.

Berry glanced that way, then turned back to Pappy. "Who are you staring at?"

"I know her." He scrambled up. He rammed his crutches under his arms and hop-stepped away, stumbling when the tip of one of his crutches caught in a crack between two bricks.

Berry ran after him. She caught up to him at the park's gate, but by then the sidewalk was empty.

Pappy stood there, leaning on his crutches, shaking his head. "Dammit, dammit, dammit."

Berry put a hand on his arm. "What is it, Will?"

"That woman, did you see her?"

"Yes."

"Forty-four years ago, I asked her to marry me."

"What?"

"Forty-four years ago, I asked her to marry me."

Berry stared at Pappy. "How long were you going to keep this secret?"

"What secret?"

The sound of a tinkling bell came around the corner at Gay Street and Clinch—Mister Sam, Junior Dempsey in the pilot's seat and Charlie next to him. They waved.

The bell broke through Pappy's confusion and funk. He looked up, and, when Mister Sam registered with him, he brought his hand up in a tepid waggle.

Dempsey herded Mister Sam over to the curb. "Caroline told me you two were having a picnic here."

"So you're just out tooling around?"

"Charlie and me have been out selling ice cream and having a good day, haven't we, Charlie?"

"Yeah," the boy answered from his place on the passenger's seat.

Dempsey killed Mister Sam's engine, then hopped down and came around. He held out his arms, showing off his bleached jeans, orange shirt that had white sleeves and a white collar, and an orange duffer's cap emblazoned with the UT logo. "How do you like my new outfit?"

He motioned for Charlie to stand up. The boy, too, was dressed the same way.

For the first time in some minutes, Pappy smiled. "You two guys are really sharp."

"Well, are you ready for dessert?"

"Almost I guess. Doctor Berry?"

"I've never said no to ice cream."

"What'll you have?" Dempsey asked.

"What do you have that's special?" Berry asked.

"I make a mean banana split."

"All right, two. One for each of us."

Pappy jerked toward Berry. "You ever see how big he makes those? One feeds three people."

"All right. Mister Dempsey, one banana split and two spoons."

"Oooo," Dempsey said as he crossed in front of Pappy on his way to the truck box.

Pappy swatted him with one of his crutches.

Dempsey only laughed. "Come on, Charlie, give me a hand."

The boy scrambled up and into the box.

"Go back to your picnic," Dempsey said. "We'll bring the split when we've got it ready."

Berry slipped her arm through Pappy's and aimed him back to the park. "Doctor Berry indeed," she said.

"Well, I gotta get used to this."

PAPPY AND BERRY set their plates aside when Dempsey and Charlie came marching their way, Dempsey calling the cadence, "Heup, heup, heup-two-three," and Charlie carrying a banana-split boat heaped above the gunwales with ice cream, three kinds of toppings, whipped cream, and maraschino cherries.

"Companyyyy halt."

Dempsey and Charlie stopped next to the picnic blanket. They clicked their heels.

"Preseeent dessert."

Charlie held the boat out to Berry.

"Thank you," she said as she took it.

"At ease, soldier," Dempsey said to Charlie.

"Yessir."

Dempsey handed Berry and Pappy spoons and napkins.

Pappy opened the napkin on his lap. "What do you know about marching?"

"Saw it in a movie."

Berry dug into the ice cream. "We have some chicken left. Would you like it?"

"Charlie?" Dempsey asked.

The boy grinned so broadly the world could see the gap where he had lost a tooth.

Berry put the banana split aside and got out the bowl of chicken and extra plates. "Come, sit down."

The newest arrivals helped themselves to the bounty while Berry and Pappy went back to their banana split.

Charlie tore into a chicken breast.

Dempsey chewed on a leg. "What do you say, kid, pretty good grub?"

"The best."

"Well, don't tell me. Tell the lady."

"Thank you, Doctor Berry. This is real good grub."

"You're welcome. And the banana split you made is really good, too."

Dempsey dug into the potato salad. "You quit her class?" he asked Pappy.

Berry swiveled. "You discussed this with him?"

"I may have."

"Anyone else?"

"Wicks, possibly Ambrose."

"And?"

"Caroline."

"And?"

"That's about it."

"You're amazing. Why didn't you just take out an ad in the Beacon?"

Dempsey sampled the baked beans. "Well, did you?" he asked Pappy.

"Did I what?"

"Quit her class."

"Yes."

"Aww, puppy love." Dempsey ripped out with a wicked laugh. He elbowed Pappy.

And Pappy swatted him. "What would you know about love?"

"Hey, I could have had any one of those girls at the Omicron Rho house." Dempsey waved a chicken wing as he went on. "They were stuffing money in my pants. They ripped my clothes off. Pappy, they wanted me."

"Oh gawd."

Chapter 28

Obsession

PAPPY CAUGHT a city bus back to campus, a bus that traveled what was known as the circle route. He boarded the Number Fourteen on Cumberland—Knoxville's Main Street—in the central business district.

The bus idled now at Gay and Wall, the driver waiting for the light to change. Pappy, in the fourth row back, found himself contending with an itch inside his walking cast, an itch that would not quit no matter how he tried to rub the cast against the irritated skin. He couldn't reach his fingers inside even though he tried. Then he remembered the tool, a slender scratcher Dempsey had made for him in the ag engineering machine shop.

He dug in the side pouch of his backpack until he found it. Pappy inserted the tool down into the cast until its blunted spring-steel fingers reached the itch, then he worked the tool with the vigor of a dog scratching fleas.

The air brakes released. Pappy, still working his scratcher, leaned into the turn as the bus swung onto Wall and rolled on down the street.

Itch relieved, he returned Dempsey's tool to his pack and settled back to gaze at the cityscape beyond his window, here dominated by the twin granite TVA buildings that commanded the south face of Bingham Hill. A broad sweep of steps led from Wall Street up to the plaza and the front entrances to the buildings.

Pappy noticed someone on those steps, going up, a woman in a pale blue dress, clutching a purse under her arm. He watched her, casually at first, then with increasing interest.

It was her.

He grabbed the emergency cord and yanked on it, yanked on it until the driver stopped the bus.

Pappy hobbled forward to the exit steps. "Thanks, buddy," he said as he clambered down and out the door.

The woman continued on up, well ahead of Pappy now, she perhaps fewer than a dozen steps from the top. He heard the door close behind him, the *chssshh* of the air brakes releasing, the diesel engine ginning up as he started across the sidewalk toward the steps, the engine blasting out oily fumes that fogged Pappy, filled his nostrils.

He sneezed and rubbed at his watering eyes.

Could she work there, he wondered.

Pappy clomped up the first series of steps. The cast, it was so damned awkward that it slowed him. If she did work there, why had he never seen her here before? Thirty-five years, the county planning commission had sent him to meetings at the TVA. He knew a lot of the mid-level managers.

Half way up now, Pappy's breath came hard. His chest hurt. Two-thirds of the way, he could go no further. He eased himself down on a step, puffing, blowing, fumbling in a pocket for his pill bottle.

"You look pretty green, old fella," someone said.

Pappy gazed up.

A young man stood before him, twenty-something, he guessed, in a suit. Where had he come from?

"Phew, yeah," Pappy said as he struggled with opening the bottle. He shook out a pill and stuffed it under his tongue.

"Can I give you a hand, maybe carry your backpack?"

"Appreciate dat, but gimme a minute—catch my breath."

The young man sat down next to Pappy. He had a roll of paper under one arm.

"Whazzat?" Pappy asked.

"Oh, this?" The young man unrolled the paper to reveal something that looked like a blueprint. "We've been doing studies on river elevations, what happens along the banks when you release water from our dams."

"Huh. Looks inneresting."

The young man glanced up from the drawings. "You care about this stuff?"

"I fish some."

"Well, you know how you get hacked off when the water's really low or really high. You and the others out there in boats, you want a level pool. But, like our dam at Norris, we're managing that for power generation and flood control, not boating." The man's hand danced over the drawings. "We let a lot of water out in the winter, so we've got capacity for the spring rains and runoff—"

"Yeah, to keep it from flooding downstream, I know," Pappy said.

"You know that? Of course, you do. I know that, too, but most city people who've got vacation homes up there don't understand what we're doing. We're draining the pool, and one morning they wake up and their dock's twenty feet from the water. They get prickly as porcupines."

"I bet. Well, I'm feelin' some better."

"Changing needs, we may have to change the way we do things." The young man rolled up his drawing and helped Pappy to his feet. He took Pappy's book bag, and, together, they went on up the steps.

"You an engineer?" Pappy asked.

"Uh-huh, hydrologist."

"And they make you wear a suit for that?"

"The boss's rule. Someday maybe I'll be the boss, and I'll get to change that."

"Name's Willie Joe Brown," Pappy said.

"Matt Eldridge. Good to meet you, Mister Brown."

At the top of the steps, Eldridge opened the door of the East Tower for Pappy. "You here to see somebody?"

"Hope so."

"What department?"

"I don't know. I just got a name."

"Well, let's get you over to the information desk. If anyone can find your person, Alice can."

The double-doorway entrance to the TVA building opened into an overly large lobby, its marble floor polished to a high gloss. In the center, to the side of a hall that led away to banks of elevators, stood a curved desk and a middle-aged woman behind it talking to several other women. Pappy guessed they were secretaries.

"Alice," Eldridge called out.

The woman turned away from her conversations. "Yes, Matt."

"This is Mister Brown. He needs to find someone. Maybe you can help him."

"I'll certainly try."

Eldridge set Pappy's backpack on the information desk. "Well, Mister Brown, Alice is the best there is, so you're in good hands. I gotta get on upstairs."

"Thank you." Pappy turned to Alice. He noticed the nameplate on her desk. "One of the Jones girls, I see."

"I guess you could say I am."

"Missus?"

"Yes. I married John Jones. Can you believe that? And me a Smith. How may I help you?"

Pappy leaned on the desk. "Do you have a Grace Ferguson working here?"

"Well, let's get out the personnel roster and see." The woman took what appeared to be a small telephone book from her desk drawer. She opened it to the F's and ran a pencil down the names. "We've got a George and a Granger, but no Grace."

Pappy's face sagged. "Well, before she married, she was a Clarke, with an *e*. Maybe she's going by her maiden name."

"Some women do that. Let's look." The woman turned to the C pages. Again, she ran her pencil down the names. "Clarke with an *e*, yes. We have one and only one, a Deborah Clarke, works at our Tellico office."

Pappy rubbed at his face. "Maybe she's a visitor. She came into the building just a couple minutes before I did. Maybe you saw her."

"I didn't, I'm sorry. I just came back from break, and I was visiting with some of the girls I'd been on break with."

"I just wanted to say hello." He peered around the lobby. "Would it be all right if I sat over there, maybe wait a few minutes? She might come out."

"Certainly."

Pappy gathered in his backpack and limped across the lobby.

"Could I get you a cup of coffee while you wait?"

"Oh, that's not necessary."

IT STARTED as a trickle at four-thirty and, by a few minutes after five, it was a flood, TVA employees pouring out of elevator cars and stairwells, hurrying toward the exit doors and home. One—Matt Eldridge—saw Pappy sitting alone. He came over.

"You find your friend, Mister Brown?"

"Not yet." Pappy got up from his chair. He stretched. "Your information person and I thought she might be a visitor, so I'm waiting. Thought I might catch her as she leaves."

"Well, good luck. And it was nice to meet you."

"My pleasure."

Eldridge moved away to the doors that led down to the employees' parking lot.

Ten minutes and the TVA flood tide was no more. Alice Jones put her books and notepads in her desk drawer. She took out her purse and, seeing Pappy still waiting, came over to him. "She's still not come out yet?"

He shook his head.

"I'm afraid I don't know what to tell you. The night guard's going to be coming on in a few minutes. He's going to be locking the doors."

"DOES THIS MAKE up for the concert chorale?" Berry asked as she and Pappy slipped into the crowd flowing out of the Tennessee Theater.

"Johnny Cash? In spades. And we didn't have to dress up."

"It was rather loud, though, wasn't it?"

Pappy cupped a hand behind his ear.

"I said it was kind of loud," Berry said with a boost of volume.

"Maybe a little."

The crowd swept them into the long marble lobby that was the theater's entrance. There they slid out of the tide and onto the landing of the grand staircase that led up to the balconies. Berry handed Pappy her jacket, and he held it for her so she could slip her arms in.

"Thank you," she said.

"Anytime."

"Maybe we should wait here a minute while it thins out. Then it won't be so crowded for a wounded old man like you out on the sidewalk."

"Oh, thanks. That really builds my spirits." Pappy put his hand in his jacket pocket. He brought out a small box. "Jujubes?"

"Thank you."

Pappy shook a candy into Berry's hand before he took one for himself. "You know, I think I saw her yesterday."

"Oh, Will–"

"On the steps, going up to the TVA."

"Tell me you didn't follow her."

"I did, but with this damn cast on my leg, I couldn't catch up."

"So then you waited for her to come out, didn't you?"

"Two hours."

Berry tilted her head toward Pappy. "You're obsessed. You've got to stop this."

"Yeah. Well, the crowd seems to be petering out. Maybe we can get outside."

They plunged back into the flow. It carried them through the double sets of doors, past the now empty box office and onto the street–State Street. They broke away to the right, they and several other couples.

At the corner, Pappy and Berry went right again, onto a side street–Clinch–to a city parking ramp on the east side of Central, the next cross street. A policeman stood there, directing traffic coming out of the ramp. He raised a hand for the cars to stop, and, with his other, beckoned for Pappy and Berry and the others to cross the street.

"Thanks, Robbie," Pappy called out.

The policeman touched a finger to the bill of his cap in salute.

"You know him?" Berry asked as they went on into the ramp.

"He's one of our Maryville boys. We trained him up right, then the Knoxville PD thrust a fistful of cash at him and he came north."

At the white LeBaron, Berry unlocked the passenger door. She opened it for Pappy. After he got in and settled his cast-bound leg, she went to the driver's side and slipped behind the steering wheel.

Berry put the key in the ignition. "You're going to burst if you don't tell me the rest of the story, aren't you?"

"I don't have to."

"All right." Berry turned the key.

The little six came to life.

She waited for a break in the string of cars coming up from a lower level, then backed out and drove on. At the entrance, as she guided the LeBaron onto the street, Pappy again waggled his hand at the policeman.

Central to Cumberland to—"You want a burger?" Pappy asked as the LeBaron rolled toward campus.

"Big spender tonight, huh?"

He cast a baleful look at his driver.

"Yes, I'd like a burger, a veggie burger."

"The Blue Onion all right?"

"I've never been there."

"Ori, you're what, fifty-three? It's time you walked on the wild side."

Berry drove on, on past Stadium Drive and Volunteer Boulevard, on beneath the pedestrian skyway, up the hill and into The Strip, squinting at the lights of the cars coming her way. "Lots of traffic tonight."

"Students out getting lubricated for exams."

"They're a week away."

"Good drinkers start early."

Berry slowed at the Blue Onion. She turned onto a side street and ahead found a parking space being vacated by another car.

The hike back to the Onion was less than half a block. There Pappy, with Berry in his wake, pushed through the gaggle of students clogging the doorway. Inside, he spotted an empty table near the back. He grabbed Berry's hand and hop-footed it on before someone else could claim the table.

He stared at it—the empty steins and glasses, the overflowing ashtrays. "Gawd-awful mess," he said as he pushed it all aside.

A waitress rushed over, a dish tub under her arm. She raked the leavings of the last customers into the tub. "Sorry, Pappy. It's been a panic tonight."

He pulled a chair out for Berry. "Raylene, that's all right."

"Haven't seen you in here for a while."

Pappy swung his cast up on a chair. "Busted leg. It's kept me from coming down to dance with you."

The waitress brushed Pappy's cheek. "You're sweet for an old man."

"We do get better with age. Raylene, this is Doctor Berry."

The waitress wiped her hand on her bar apron before she held it out to Berry. They shook hands.

"The good doctor teaches over in the English department."

"I'm pleased to meet you," the waitress said.

"Raylene's an old cow milker from down in—where you from?"

"Beans Creek. How can you forget that?" She bumped Pappy with her hip, laughing as she did. "Doctor

Berry, Beans Creek is outside of Winchester, in Franklin County—dairy country."

"Raylene's a vet student."

Berry edged some crumbs aside on the portion of the table in front of her. "Large animal or small?"

"Large. I intend to go back and work with my neighbors." She brushed a sweat-soaked strand of hair from her eyes. "One more year and I'm outta here."

"Good for you."

"You two ready to order?"

"Sure," Pappy said.

"What'll it be?" The waitress set the tub on a chair and went to wiping down the table.

"A hamburger. Put real meat in it, wouldja? The works."

"And a Country Time, I know." Raylene tossed the damp cloth in the dish tub.

"Right. And for the doctor, a fake burger."

"A veggie burger," Berry said.

"I'm sorry, we don't have that, but O'Charley's makes a good one. I'm not supposed to, but I'll call down there, and they'll send one up. Something to drink?"

"Peach wine cooler—Bartles and Jaymes."

"I'll have that for you in a minute." The waitress gathered up her tub and headed for the kitchen.

After she had gone, Berry leaned forward. "Is there anybody you don't know?"

"Just seems that way because we're in my circle. When we're in your circle, I'm the stranger."

"But never for very long I've noticed."

The minute hand on the Blue Onion's clock touched twelve, triggering 'Rocky Top.' Everybody seated jumped to their feet, including Pappy, but not Berry. They sang at a volume that could be heard outside, on the street, while the Vol Special chugged around its route beneath the bar's ceiling.

"UT forever!" the waitress shouted, throwing a fist in the air as she came out of the kitchen.

"UT forever!" all in the bar chorused.

Berry put her hand to her face, her eyes wide. "What was that?"

Pappy settled on his chair. "An Onion custom, every hour on the hour."

"Amazing, absolutely amazing."

The waitress came by with the wine cooler and Country Time. "You've not been here before, huh?" she asked Berry as she handed the cooler to her.

"Any more surprises like that?"

"Bound to be. It's a Friday night." The waitress set the Country Time in front of Pappy. "If you'll excuse me, I've got to get on to another table."

She prodded a beefy six-footer in the ribs, the student lounging between her and where she needed to go. When he turned to see what gnat had annoyed him, she pushed on by.

Pappy hunched forward over his Country Time, toward Berry. "Did I tell you I remembered the woman's name?"

"The mystery woman? The will-o-the-wisp? The now-we-see-her, now-we-don't?"

"You're making fun of me."

"I'm sorry." She settled back in her chair.

"She was Grace Clarke when I knew her. Gawd, she was beautiful, and wild."

"And this is the woman you wanted to marry?"

"It was Nineteen Forty-three, Ori. The war was on. Yeah, I did." He pushed his finger around the top of his drink can. "They furloughed us all for two weeks before we were to ship out to Italy. I came home, spent most of the time with her. Is it warm in here?"

Pappy pulled at his collar.

"It is."

"Fred's chiller must be busted again." Pappy rubbed the cold lemonade can across his forehead, then held the can against the side of his face. "We went to dances at the USO—we had a USO club here at the time—went to shows at the Tennessee Theater, paddled the swan boats on the lake up at Fountain City. Then night would come and we'd go to the Andrew Johnson. Man on the desk didn't give a hoot you weren't mister and missus as long as one of you wore a uniform."

He shook his head as those nights came back. "We sure didn't get much sleep, I'll tell ya for true."

The six-footer, laughing at another's joke, backed into Pappy's chair. He swung around, spilling his beer. "Sorry, buddy."

He bent down to mop the foam and wet off the leg of Pappy's jeans.

"Hey, at least you didn't pour it down my cast."

"I didn't do that to you, too, did I?"

Pappy jigged a thumb at the glass. "How many of those didja have?"

"I dunno. Six, maybe eight."

"Maybe you ought to quit."

The student parked his elbow on Pappy's shoulder. "Not as long as I can stan' up."

"How about standing over there, then?" Pappy waved in the direction of the far wall.

"Yeah, okay." The student stumbled off.

Berry gazed at Pappy for a long time, an odd expression holding court on her face. "I don't understand you."

"What? That I'm not upset with him?"

"Yes."

"That was me at his age. As long as I could stand up, I'd keep pouring it down. Of course, I had more I wanted to forget than he does."

"Will, why don't you forget this woman?"

"I can't." Pappy sipped some from his Country Time, then he rolled the can between his hands like mountain kids do a stick when they're trying to start a fire and they don't have any matches. "I proposed to her, you know. Gawd, I loved her, I mean I'd fallen hard. She turned me down."

"Why?"

Pappy pushed the can aside. He opened his hands out. "Said she wouldn't marry a walking dead man, didn't want to be a war widow."

"I'm sorry, Will."

Pappy took the can back. He tilted it on its bottom rim, his finger above on the top rim, steadying the can at an angle. "We were having coffee at some little café—I forget the place—and she up and walks out. I tell you, I wasn't fit to be with friends nor strangers, so I found me a bench at the Southern depot and made camp there, waiting for my train. I didn't care much if I was killed in Italy or not."

Berry put her hands on Pappy's. "Look at me, Will. Are you going to keep chasing after this woman?"

"I don't know."

"I take that as a yes."

"No. Ori, I really don't know."

"Look, you've got to make a decision. You say you're interested in me, and I think you're a very special man, maybe the last good man I know, but I can't be around you, not as long as she's got a claim on you."

"She doesn't have a claim on me."

"She has, Will. That's why you're chasing after her."

"I'm not."

"You are. Just telling me this, you are. It's an obsession, and I won't have any part of it. For all you know, that woman might not be Grace at all. It could be someone who just looks like her."

"It isn't."

"Will, you're chasing shadows. You've never been able to catch up with her, no matter how hard you've tried. Think of it, sitting in TVA's lobby for two hours, my God." Berry stood up.

"Where you going?"

"Home. I don't want anything more to do with this."

"But—"

"You can get back to the Tau Ups on your own. Beg a ride, take a taxi, I don't care." Berry stormed away, brushing past students who stood between her and escape.

The waitress hurried in with a tray of hamburgers. "She coming back?" she asked when she didn't see Berry.

"No." Pappy, on his feet, patted his pockets. "I gotta go. Let me pay for this."

She ran a total in her mind. "Seven sixty-three."

Pappy pulled a fistful of bills and change from his pocket. He shoved it all in the waitress's hand. "Better count it. I don't feel none too good."

"You don't look well, Pappy."

He stumbled, one hand grabbing for the back of a chair, the other his chest. Pappy hauled himself up, his face twisting, his eyes glazing.

He lurched from the table, only one step before he collapsed against the waitress. She dropped Pappy's money as he rolled and fell to the floor among the night's detritus.

"Fred! Call an ambulance!"

Chapter 29

The pirates return

O'DELL SAT next to the bed while, out in the hall, Caroline and the Caballeros prodded Doctor Muse for information.

Muse, in his pajama tops, wrinkled trousers, and a suit coat that didn't match anything, stared at the floor. "What can I tell you, Carrie, it was a heart attack."

"Was it bad?"

"They haven't done the tests yet."

"Is my grandfather going to wake up?"

Muse pulled at his drooping mustache. "Carrie, you're asking me to predict the future. I think he will, but I can't guarantee that. Nobody can. Look, I'll put it to you straight. Pappy could come out of this fine, or his heart could seize up again and we lose him altogether."

"Should I call Pops and my mother to come up?"

"I already have."

THE MONITOR PEEPED each time a line spiked on the screen and fell back.

To O'Dell as he sat beside Pappy's bed, his elbows on his knees, the peep was steady, predictable, comforting.

A hand touched his arm, and he jumped. "Good God, Pap, you trying to give me heart failure?"

Pappy put a trembling finger to his lips.

"Shh, nothing. I've got the wagon out back. I thought sure this time I was gonna have to haul you off to the mortuary."

Pappy motioned O'Dell to lean in. When he did, Pappy whispered, "We have to quit meeting like this."

"That's for damn sure."

"Shh-shh-shh-shh."

"What?"

"Where am I?"

"The hospital, Fort Sanders," O'Dell whispered.

"What happened?"

"Someone said you got liquored up at a college bar and passed out, that an ambulance crew had to sponge you up in a bucket."

"You believe that?"

"No. Rubble says you had a heart attack. He called me when the hospital called him. We came up together."

"Digger, I'm awful tired."

"I don't know why. Hell, you been out for hours."

Pappy closed his eyes.

"Pappy? Pappy?" O'Dell shook Pappy's shoulder, to no effect. He put his hand on Pappy's chest, felt it rise and fall. O'Dell looked up at the monitor, at the spiking line sliding across the screen, and hustled out to the hall, to Muse, Caroline, and the Caballeros. "Doc, Pappy just woke up, but he's out again."

Muse bolted for the room. He glanced at the monitor as he rushed in, then whipped his stethoscope from his pocket. He stuffed the ends in his ears and placed the listening part on Pappy's chest.

Caroline, O'Dell, Dempsey, Wickingson, and Frye, hurrying behind Muse, stopped at the foot of the bed.

"Did he say anything?" Caroline asked O'Dell.

"Just that he and I have to quit meeting in hospitals."

Muse put his fingertips on Pappy's wrist. He counted to himself as he watched the sweep hand on his wristwatch. After Muse had satisfied himself, he turned to the others. "The ticker's a little slow, but his blood pressure's about where it should be. Still we have to watch him, but I think he's going to be all right."

Caroline took hold of Dempsey's hand. She squeezed it as a smile of relief seeped over her face.

Muse stuffed his stethoscope in his pocket. "Look, it's late. I don't know when he's going to wake up again. Why don't you all go home? If anything bad happens, and I don't think it will, I'll call you."

"Can I stay with him?" Caroline asked.

"If you want."

"We'll stay, too," Dempsey said.

"If you boys are going to do that, you park yourselves in the waiting room down the hall. The nurses raise hell whenever they see more than two of us in one of these ICU rooms."

Dempsey looked at Wickingson and Frye. They started from the room, but Dempsey glanced back. "Caroline, you know where we'll be."

She nodded.

O'Dell leaned on the bed's footboard. "How about you, Doc?"

"Long as I'm up here, I might as well look in on some of my other patients. Later I'll put my feet up here for a while. Why don't you go back to Maryville?"

"Well, if you think it'll be all right. You want me to come back, pick you up?"

"Maybe about lunchtime. Digger, by then we're going to know everything there is to know."

"See you then, Doc." O'Dell took Caroline's hands in his and rubbed them. "Girl, that old duster gave me a scare. I thought sure this time I was gonna have him for a customer. He's tough."

"He is, isn't he?"

"Maybe I'll see you when I come back up for Doc."

"You probably will."

O'Dell turned away. He scuffled out of the room, his shoulders hunched, his hands in his pockets.

Muse stood at the foot of the bed, scribbling notes on Pappy's chart. When he finished, he closed the metal cover and slipped the chart into its holder on the bed frame.

Caroline touched his sleeve. "There's something you aren't telling me, isn't there?"

Muse looked up. He gazed long into her eyes. This was not the little girl he knew. There was steel in her bearing. He motioned for her to follow him to the chairs at the side of the room. There they sat.

"Pappy always told me he couldn't fool you long," Muse said.

"What is it?"

"It's his heart, but you already know that. What you don't know is his heart's been fritzing around since fall. It's arrhythmia."

"Yes?"

"Your grandfather needs a pacemaker, and the old fool won't let me put one in. We've been arguing about it for weeks now. You didn't know he was coming to see me, did you?"

"No."

"He didn't want you to know. He didn't want your dad to know. He didn't want anybody to know." Muse pulled the listening end of his stethoscope from his pocket. He played with it as he talked. "When he'd get to hurting, he'd call Walter or Digger to come pick him up at the university library or the bookstore and bring him down to my office."

"So they've known."

"But they're as clam-mouthed as your grandfather."

"And if he doesn't get a pacemaker?"

Muse leaned forward, his elbows on his knees. "Carrie, we doctors talk a good game, but there's just a mountain of stuff we don't know. Pappy could live to be a hundred and ten and see us all in the ground, or his heart could go ballistic tomorrow, though I don't think it will. So, you're going to stay here?"

"Yes."

"Well, I've got a dozen other patients up here. Old Missus Collins, you remember her?" Muse stood, as if to leave.

"She was my third grade teacher."

"She's in Four-sixteen. Broke her hip. Maybe you'd like to see her when you take a break sometime."

"I'd like to do that."

"Well, I'm going to go around and read charts, maybe sit with Missus Collins and the others a little when they wake up. I'll check back on the both of you."

Muse stretched. He scratched at his ribs before he turned the room lights low and shambled out.

Caroline, alone now, watched the monitor and listened to the peep. She looked away, gazing around the room, the white walls gray in the dim light, three less-than-comfortable chairs, the hospital bed, drip bags, the monitor, all kinds of plumbing hooked up to her grandfather. It was a sterile place in need of cheering up. She went down the hall to see Dempsey.

Pappy laid motionless in the bed, except for the rhythmic rising and falling of his chest, his breathing the slow, deep breathing of sleep.

When Caroline returned, she slipped into the chair that O'Dell had abandoned. She took Pappy's hand in hers. "Grandpops," she whispered, "I'm here."

IT WAS NOT YET light outside when Muse returned. He came in without making a sound to find Caroline asleep in her chair, her head on her arms folded at Pappy's side.

He went to the far side of the bed. There he put his fingertips on Pappy's wrist and counted the heartbeats. He flashed a penlight up at the saline drip bag, checked the level. Pleased that all appeared to be all right, that nothing had changed, he snapped his light out.

Muse dragged a chair over. He sat down and parked his feet by Pappy's feet. He gave himself a scalp rub as he settled back. Muse's eyelids, leaden from lack of sleep, closed.

His breathing slowed and deepened.

Beyond the room, the night ICU nurse went off duty.

The day nurse came on. She slipped in on crepe soles, checked the readings on the monitor and noted them on Pappy's chart. She gazed at Muse and Caroline asleep, then went to the window. There she pulled the drapes closed against the morning sun and left as silently as she had come.

The emergency room doctor leaned in the doorway before he left for home and sleep.

The heart specialist also stopped by.

No one disturbed the sleeping trio, no one, that is, until Dempsey, Wickingson, and Frye arrived with arm loads of flowers. Dempsey tripped in the semi-dark of the room. He fell against the bed, startling awake both Muse and Caroline. When she raised her head, she felt the weight of something on her shoulders. Her hand felt for it, her face turning.

"He knows I'm here," she said.

THE TAU UPSILONS came in pairs to sit with Pappy. Don Wright scheduled them for one-hour shifts. They washed his face, shaved him, talked to him even though he could not hear them. Several read chapters to him from his textbooks. One, late, after midnight, read poetry.

Nurses came in and out, Doctor Muse as well. He ordered a glucose drip on one of his stops.

Digger O'Dell took shifts as did Caroline, Dempsey, Wickingson, and Frye, Wickingson and Frye playing chess to pass the time between three and four in the morning. The digital clock in the room never slowed, never stopped.

Twelve hours, twenty-four, thirty, thirty-three.

CAROLINE SAW Pappy at last lift an eyelid. "Good morning, Grandpops, or should I say good midnight?"

Their fingers touched.

"Sweetpea," he whispered.

"Are you going to stay with us?"

"Think so."

"Hungry?"

"Yeah."

"What can I get you?"

"Mmmm, milk shake."

"Pretty tame. I'm going to get the nurses for you."

THE NIGHT NURSE ran all the vitals on Pappy, then sent in two aides who, working together, sponge bathed him. They also changed the sheets on his bed and got him into a fresh hospital gown. As their last act, they propped him up against a mass of pillows.

Muse came in as they left.

He was still there, sitting on Pappy's bed, the two talking when Caroline returned with a Dairy Queen milk shake.

Muse glanced up at her. "Carrie, your grandfather's been yappin' on about the needles in his arm, strangers giving him a bath–women no less–the nurses, me. A couple days of his harping and somebody's going to kill him."

"My sweet little ol' grandpoppy?"

"Sweet? He's sour as a Polish dill pickle."

"Don't you believe him," Pappy said, his voice no longer a whisper but still something shy of normal. "You got my milk shake?"

"I had to plead with the night manager. He wanted to close." Caroline pulled the cap from the cup and stuck a straw in the thick sweetness.

Muse pushed off the bed. "Feed the old crank. I'm going down the hall to visit with some of my patients who appreciate my company."

"They're asleep, Rubble," Pappy called after him.

"I'll wake 'em up."

"To give them their sleeping pill, I know."

"Do you two ever let up on each other?" Caroline asked after Muse had left the room. She sat next to Pappy and held the cup up so he could suck on the straw.

"Gawd, that tastes good."

"Work it down. It's been two days since you've had any real food."

"I know. My stomach's gnawing at my ribs."

Caroline watched him suck and swallow mouthfuls of milk shake until he tired and gave it up.

"There's some left," she said.

"No, you finish it."

"All right." Caroline tipped the cup up. She drained the last swallows, then set the cup aside. "Are you ready for a fight?"

Pappy gave her a perplexed look.

"A fight, Grandpops."

"About what?"

"A pacemaker."

"So the old quack told you."

"Don't you go getting on Doctor Muse."

"He never could keep his mouth shut."

Caroline took Pappy's hands in hers. When he turned away, she leaned across him, to get in his line of vision.

He turned to the other side. Again she moved so he had to look at her. "Why won't you do it?"

"I'm not going to let Rubble or anybody else hack into me."

"You're scared, aren't you?"

"Damn right I am. One slip of the cutter's knife—" Pappy trembled. Again he turned away.

Caroline took hold of Pappy's jaw. She drew his face back. "You look at me when I'm talking to you. What if your heart quits on its own?"

"That'd be God sayin' your time's up, old man. I can accept that."

"I guess you'd have to, because you'd be dead." This time it was Caroline who turned away. Pappy followed her lead. He turned in the opposite direction, toward the window.

She took a yellow rose from a bouquet on the bedside table. She brought it up to her nose and inhaled the rose's spicy perfume. "Grandpops?"

"Yeah?"

"You messed something up, didn't you? And you can't fix it."

"Maybe."

"Has this got something to do with Doctor Berry?"

Pappy did not respond.

Caroline stroked the velvet softness of the petals. "Remember when I was a little kid, and I broke Mom's pearl necklace? She was going to be so mad at me that I ran away from home, and you found me hiding in the back of your truck."

"Yeah."

"I was a crying mess. You made me tell you what I did. You remember what you did?"

Ori-Anna Berry appeared in the doorway in Keds that made no sound when she walked. She wore sweat pants and a UT jacket. Her hair had that slept-on look. Caroline raised a finger when she saw her.

"Remember, Grandpops," she went on, "Mom was away that day, so you went in the house and picked up all those pearls. Some had gone down the register, so you reached in the heating duct. You even opened the furnace to get the last ones out. Then you, with those fat fingers of yours, you strung them all on a fish line—so it will never break again, you told me—you strung them one at a time and in the right order by size. You attached the clasp and put the necklace back on Mom's dresser. You fixed it, Grandpops, because I couldn't. You told me sometimes we need a little help."

Again Pappy did not respond.

Caroline waited. She put the rose back in the bouquet and left the room.

Berry watched her. After Caroline had gone, she came in, to the side of the bed. She put a hand on Pappy's shoulder. "You are obstinate, hard headed, selfish—"

Pappy whipped around. "What the hell are you doing here?"

"I didn't see any sign on the door that said keep out. Caroline called me. So you messed up."

"I sure did."

"Well, not doing what your doctor wants won't fix it. Will, there are people who love you, and they don't want you to leave them just yet."

"Are you one of them?"

"Maybe. I don't know. I know this, you're never going to find out if you don't take care of yourself."

"Gawd, I hate hospitals."

"I know." Berry took a handkerchief from her jacket pocket. She dabbed at her nose. "You believe people die here, but not everybody does. Are you going to do it?"

Muse and Caroline stood listening in the twilight of the hallway, just beyond the door to Pappy's room. He would have seen them had he looked up. Instead, his gaze was on the hand that rested on his hand.

He bobbed his chin.

"It's all right to say it, Will," Berry said.

"I guess," he whispered.

"And one more thing. Grace. Will, she's killing you. You've got to forget her."

Pappy slipped a hand beneath the sheet, crossed his fingers, sure that Berry could not see that action. "Yeah," he said.

Dempsey came pounding up the hall, a radio in his hand. He pushed past Muse and Caroline and dashed into the room, to Pappy.

"Excuse me, Doc," he said to Berry, breathing hard. "Pappy, you've gotta hear this."

He turned his radio on and held it out.

"Good morniiiiiiin', Knoxville! This is WUOT piraaaat radio, rockin' with Johnny Cash and 'Folsom Prison Blues.' Get well, Pappy!"

ABOUT THE AUTHOR

Jerry Peterson, when he was admitted to the University of Tennessee's graduate school two decades ago, told everyone he was the world's oldest graduate student. He probably wasn't, but it made a good conversation starter. He came away from UT with an intimate knowledge of the campus that made this story possible. Peterson also taught high school English and, at the college level, public relations and editing. He also wrote for and edited newspapers. Peterson now lives and writes in his home state of Wisconsin, the land of dairy cows, craft beer, and good books.

UPCOMING TITLES

Coming later this spring, *Capitol Crime*, book 2 in the Wings Over the Mountains series.

Read it here, well, on the next page, chapter 1 of *Capitol Crime* . . .

Capitol Crime

A WINGS OVER THE MOUNTAINS NOVEL

BOOK 2

Chapter 1

The call

"SHERIFF? SHERIFF? It's something awful."

To Quill Rose, the voice on the telephone sounded like it was coming from the far end of the earth. He pressed the receiver tighter to his ear. "Who is this?"

"Oakie Brown, teacher out at Pistol Creek."

"Oakie, you gotta speak up."

"Sheriff, three people out here. They're dead."

Rose spilled his coffee. He motioned to his deputy for a rag to wipe it up. "What did you say, Oakie?"

"Three people, dead I tell ya. At the old Whitlow farm."

"Oakie, where're you calling from? There're no telephones out on Pistol Creek."

"Asa's, in Rockford."

"Why are you calling me instead of the undertaker?"

"'Cause they been kilt."

"Oak, stay where you are. Tommy and me, we're on the way out." Rose snapped the receiver down on the hook of his candlestick telephone. He glanced up in time to snatch a rag that came flying from Tommy Jenks, his chief deputy. Rose went to mopping at the coffee dribbling down the side of his desk into a half-open drawer. "Oakie Brown, do you think he's been drinking again? He's seen some strange things in the past that weren't real."

"Best I know he's still on the wagon. Why?"

"Says he's come on three people dead at the Whitlow place. You better grab your jacket."

Quill Rose had dealt with nine murders in the years he had been sheriff of Blount County, Tennessee, all singles. If this telephone call was right, he was in for his first triple. He headed for the office door. "We'll pick up Doc Stanley. If we've got dead people, we can at least get the paperwork right the first time."

Jenks hustled along. "Taking your gun?"

"You got yours?"

"Yup."

"Then we're fine."

Rose rarely went armed. He preferred wits over weapons.

The lawmen made an odd pair. Rose, tall and lean, with a mustache no one could be proud of, came out of the Tuckaleechee Cove in the high mountains east of Maryville, the county seat. As the only son of parents who had died poor, Rose determined early to get a job at the courthouse so he'd have a steady paycheck. Now he had stood for election six times, the last four unopposed.

Tommy Jenks, wide as a door and weighing the better part of two hundred fifty pounds, was a brawler who had worked for most of the logging crews in the mountains. When Rose got tired of arresting him, he hired him.

Over time, the two had become so close that courthouse regulars said they shared the same toothpick.

JENKS STOPPED the county's new cruiser, a Ford Model B, in front of Hershel's Drugstore. "You want me to come up?"

Rose eased his lank out the passenger door. "We're not going to have to drag him out. This is Doc's shining opportunity to escape from the office. He does love working on dead bodies."

"He's a ghoul."

"Our ghoul and a nice one."

Rose strode off across the sidewalk to the staircase beside the store. He took the steps two at a time. At the top, he banged on an office door.

"Yeah?" a voice called out.

Rose leaned in.

"I'm in the back," the voice said.

Rose peered around Doctor Gallatin Stanley's waiting room. Two women sat at the side, paging through long out-of-date Collier's magazines. Rose gave them a casual wave as he went to an inner door. This he also opened. There before him sat Stanley on a stool, the town's medic prodding at a man's mouth.

Stanley swore. "Wilson, keep your mouth open. I've gotta see back in there."

Rose rapped on the door jamb.

Stanley snatched a quick look over his glasses. "Quill, come here. Look at this."

Rose came around. He leaned down on Stanley's shoulder and gazed where the beam from his flashlight pointed, into the mouth of Everett Wilson.

Stanley maneuvered the beam to spotlight something at the back of the man's throat. "Doesn't that look like tonsils to you, kind of red and swollen?"

"Uh-huh."

"That's what I thought, but old Wils here says another doc yanked his tonsils when he was a kid. Frankly, I think the quack swindled his parents. I'd say they're still in there—Wilson, keep your mouth open—whadaya think, Quill?"

"Sure look like tonsils to me."

"Suppose I shoot 'em off."

The man bit down on Stanley's tongue stick, snapping it in half.

Stanley waved his half in front of his patient's nose. "Dammit, Wilson, now the sheriff's gonna have to arrest you for destroying my property."

"Come on, Doc, I'm not about to do that. You better tell Everett what's really going on."

Stanley glared at Wilson. "You've got a sore throat, that's all. It's a little red back there, but you don't have tonsils. Now get outta here. Go home and gargle with salt water."

Wilson spit his half of the tongue stick into his hand. He opened his mouth, but Stanley jabbed a finger at him before he could speak. "Is your hearing bad, Wils? I said get out of here. You'll get my bill."

Wilson closed his mouth. He got up and shuffled away, the only sound the scuffing of his heels on the pine plank floor.

Rose raked his fingers through his mustache. "Doc, the way you treat your patients, I'm surprised you have any."

"Hell, if I treat 'em nice, they just keep coming back. It interferes with my fishing."

"And your work as a coroner."

Stanley swung around, his eyes dancing. "You've got a dead body for me?"

"I've got three."

"What is it, old age, murder, or did they get run over by one of those damn-fool aluminum haulers?"

"You get to make the call."

"Hot-damn. Quill, let's go." He bolted to a closet for his black bag and coat. His fedora he snatched off the skull of Old Bones, his skeleton standing guard by the inner door. Stanley dashed past the reading women on his way out. "Sorry, Ethel, Min, dead people are calling. You stop back tomorrow, wouldja? And kill the light when you leave."

Rose trotted after Stanley, chuckling. He clattered down the stairs, the coroner well ahead of him. When Rose hit bottom, Stanley was already across the sidewalk, huddled with Jenks, admiring the cruiser. "New, huh?"

Jenks held the backseat door open. "Quill got it last week."

"Red wheels, whitewall tires, my oh my. If I brought this home, my wife'd call it the cat's pajamas. And here I thought the county was broke."

Rose came up. He put his arm around Stanley's shoulders. "Thank our county's moonshiners. They bought it for us. Hop in."

Stanley took the backseat, Rose and Jenks the front, Jenks driving.

Rose motioned ahead. "Take us by way of Rockford—Asa's—so we can pick up Oakie."

Stanley pulled himself forward. "Oakie the one who called this in?"

Rose gave a thumbs up.

"Gawd, he's not drinkin' again, is he?"

"Tommy doesn't think so."

"How about you?"

"Me? I hope he is. If Oakie's just seeing some wild things, we'll have had a nice afternoon in the country and the fresh air that goes with it. I swear the county's got

Satan's helper shoveling coal in the boiler down at the courthouse."

"Hot?"

"Like July."

"My, and in the middle of March. The moonshiners really buy this for you?"

"Yup. We bust up a still, we get to keep the copper and anything else we can sell and then the money when we sell it. The still busting business has been real good to us this winter."

Stanley settled back. He ran his hand over the fabric of the seat. "Sure beats that old T-model the fiscal court judges stuck you with all these year."

"That it does."

Jenks glanced in his side mirror as he swung the cruiser north onto the Knoxville Turnpike. "Doc, help me out here. What's your fascination with dead people?"

"Money, it's as simple as that."

"I don't get it, Doc."

"Look, the county always pays me. With the live ones, I'm never sure I'm gonna get my money. And there's something more."

"What's that?"

"The dead ones, they never complain."

OAKIE BROWN, a tightly built little man with a wild thatch of hair that poked out in all directions from beneath his cap, stood with Rose, Jenks, and Stanley, all gazing down at the body of a dog.

Brown poked the toe of his shoe at the carcass. "This is where it starts."

Stanley knelt. He ran his hand over the dog's side, then riffled the hair back under its jaw. "Cut his throat.

That's what you do when you want to kill the animal's family at your leisure."

Rose rubbed at his elbow. "You're the expert, now?"

"It's what I'd do."

"So, Oakie, what caused you to come by anyway?"

"Simmy. She didn't come to school today. She'd just started on Monday. I was worried."

"They're all in the house?"

"Yeah."

"We'd better go in then."

Rose and Stanley stepped out ahead of Brown and Jenks. They went across the yard toward a one-story that listed to the east, its paint little more than a memory.

Brown stepped up on the porch. "I found the woman in the main room. The man's back in the bedroom."

"And the girl?"

"Simmy? I almost didn't see her until I looked up. Her arm was hanging over the edge of the loft, blood everywhere. Sheriff, all I touched was the door."

Rose, with his elbow, pushed the door open, and the smell of death rolled out. The afternoon light spilled across the body of a woman clothed in a flannel nightgown, crumpled on the floor, one leg twisted back.

Stanley got down on his knees. "Cut her throat." He put a finger on the edge of a blood stain in the middle of the clothing. "There's a gut wound, but I don't think that's all. Can I roll the body over, Quill?"

"Go ahead."

"Give me a hand, Tommy."

Together, Stanley and Jenks rolled the woman onto her stomach.

"Tommy, look at this." Stanley swept his hand along a tear in the back of the nightgown that exposed a gash in the woman's back. It began high on the rib cage and carried almost to her buttocks. "A slash like that, she was running from him. What's this?" He stared at the stump of a right arm, where the woman's hand should have been. "He cut off her hand? Why the hell would he do that?"

Before Stanley could answer his own question, he glanced up, toward the loft, to an arm and the top of a head, and something else. "There's two up there."

Brown twisted away. "Oh, Jesus, not the baby."

Rose also looked up. "There's a baby?"

"Simmy said she had a little brother. Two, maybe three years old."

Rose went to the ladder. He climbed the rungs, stopping when he could see into the loft. "Tommy, the boy's here. He's back in the corner. Doesn't appear to be hurt."

Rose climbed higher, high enough that he could reach the child. He caught him under the arms. "How you doing, little one? Oh phew. Tommy, he's got a load." Rose lifted the boy over the edge and down to Jenks. "Take him and find him some new britches."

Jenks grimaced at the stench. "It's a good thing I love children. Others wouldn't do this job." He hiked off to the kitchen, Oakie Brown with him.

Stanley hefted himself up. He took out a pad and pencil and scratched down some notes. "What's the girl look like?"

Rose lifted her shoulder. "Throat's cut. Slashes on her arms. She's missing a hand, too. What in the world's going on?"

He let the shoulder back down and worked his way down the ladder. "Oakie said the man's in the sleeping room. What's your bet?"

"One hand."

In a side room, from where Rose and Stanley stood in the doorway, they could make out a form in the bed, but couldn't see details because curtains shut out the afternoon sun. Stanley took a small flashlight from his bag. He flicked it on.

They made their way to the bed, one man on either side, Stanley leaning down. "He was asleep, Quill. He never moved. Man cut his throat without ever waking him up."

"Or a woman cut his throat."

"Possible, but I don't think so."

"So you're thinking the wife woke up and ran. Have I got that right?"

"Had to. I know I would have, and as tough as you are, Quill, you would have, too. Only thing that makes sense with her out there and that back wound she's got."

"And the girl?"

Stanley massaged behind his ear. "The woman screamed when she was cut. Wouldn't you if you were being killed?"

"So the girl woke up. She saw what was happening and screamed, too."

"So he had to kill her."

"Then why didn't he kill the boy?"

"I don't know." Stanley twisted on the balls of his feet as he peered around the room barren except for the bed, a caned chair, and a small chest of drawers. "Maybe the boy was under the blanket and God kept him from moving. The man didn't see him."

"Maybe he didn't know there was a baby to look for. You see any toys around? Anything that says baby to you? These people were too poor to have toys for their kids."

"Well, should we look at his arms?"

"I expect we'd better."

Stanley untangled the blanket before he lifted it back. "Lord a mighty, hacked right through the wrist."

"You'd have to have an axe to do that, wouldn't you think?"

"Or a stout knife." Stanley held the stump up, his light on it. "See this? He didn't cut the bone. Just sliced through the tendons and the wrist joint came apart."

Jenks and Brown came back, Jenks carrying the child whose bottom was now swaddled in a diaper made from a flour sack with the Martha White brand on it. "Got him cleaned up, Quill. He's a happy little kid. What're we gonna do with him?"

"What do you think, Doc? We could give him to the nurses at the hospital until we find some relatives."

Brown fidgeted. "Sheriff, open to an idea?"

"Sure."

"Asa's wife would take him, and I could look in on him there for you."

Stanley glanced up from the body. "For God's sake, she's already got six of her own, Oakie."

"But she's always taking in strays."

Rose gazed at the child playing with the flap of Jenks's jacket. "Doc, I gotta admit Addie's a good woman. Tommy, go ahead, take the boy down to the store and see what you can work out. And call Roy. Tell him to get out here with his hearse, that's he's got three bodies to get ready for the ground."

"He's gonna want to know if the county will pay."

"Tell him yes."

Jenks and Brown left with the child while Stanley took up a seat on the edge of the bed. He continued writing notes on the condition of the bodies for his coroner's report.

Rose rummaged through the bedroom, then the kitchen and the main room. He threw up his hands. "Doc, these people have got next to nothing other than their clothes, a couple dishes, and a skillet. That's it."

Frustrated, he took hold of the front door, to close it. "What the hell?"

Stanley peered up.

"Doc, get in here. You gotta see this."

Made in the USA
Middletown, DE
28 October 2024

62949038R00223